INTRIGUE

Seek thrills. Solve crimes. Justice served.

Wetlands Investigation
Carla Cassidy

Murder In The Blue Ridge Mountains
R. Barri Flowers

MILLS & BOON

WETLANDS INVESTIGATION
© 2024 by Carla Bracale
Philippine Copyright 2024
Australian Copyright 2024
New Zealand Copyright 2024

First Published 2024
First Australian Paperback Edition 2024
ISBN 978 1 867 90263 4

MURDER IN THE BLUE RIDGE MOUNTAINS
© 2024 by R. Barri Flowers
Philippine Copyright 2024
Australian Copyright 2024
New Zealand Copyright 2024

First Published 2024
First Australian Paperback Edition 2024
ISBN 978 1 867 90263 4

MIX
Paper | Supporting
responsible forestry
FSC® C001695

Published by
Harlequin Mills & Boon
An imprint of Harlequin Enterprises (Australia) Pty Limited
(ABN 47 001 180 918), a subsidiary of HarperCollins
Publishers Australia Pty Limited
(ABN 36 009 913 517)
Level 19, 201 Elizabeth Street
SYDNEY NSW 2000 AUSTRALIA

Cover art used by arrangement with Harlequin Books S.A.. All rights reserved.

Printed and bound in Australia by McPherson's Printing Group

Wetlands Investigation

Carla Cassidy

MILLS & BOON

Carla Cassidy is an award-winning, *New York Times* bestselling author who has written over 170 books, including 150 for Harlequin. She has won the Centennial Award from Romance Writers of America. Most recently she won the 2019 Write Touch Readers' Award for her Harlequin Intrigue title *Desperate Strangers*. Carla believes the only thing better than curling up with a good book is sitting down at the computer with a good story to write.

Visit the Author Profile page at millsandboon.com.au.

CAST OF CHARACTERS

Nick Cain—Hired to solve the monster murders, he catches himself falling for the officer assigned to work with him.

Sarah Beauregard—Frustrated with her work, she finds Nick a very hot distraction.

Gator Broussard—What exactly does the old man know about the swamp monster?

Ed Martin—Why did the businessman always show up when a victim was found?

James Noman—A mysterious man who lives in the swamp—was he committing the heinous murders?

Deputy Ryan Staub—Is he really a good lawman or a cold-blooded killer?

Chapter One

Private investigator Nick Cain drove slowly down the main street of the small town of Black Bayou, Louisiana. It was his first opportunity getting a look at the place where he'd be living and working for at least the next three months or longer if necessary.

His first impression was that the buildings all looked a bit old and tired. However, in the distance the swamp that nearly surrounded the town appeared to breathe with life and color. And it was in the swamp he believed he would do much of his investigation. At the very thought of going into the marshland, a wave of nervous energy tightened his stomach muscles.

He'd been hired by Chief of Police Thomas Gravois to assist in the investigation of four murdered woman. Apparently, a serial murderer was at play in the small town. He would work as an independent contractor and not as a member of the official law enforcement team.

Before he checked in with Chief Gravois, he needed to find the place he'd rented for his time here. It was Gravois who had turned him on to the room for rent in Irene Tompkin's home. Irene was a widow who rented out rooms in her house for extra money.

Once he turned on to Cypress Street, he looked for the correct address. He found it and pulled into the driveway. The widow Tompkin's home was a nice, large two-story painted beige with brown shutters and trim. An expansive wraparound porch held wicker furniture and a swing that invited a person to sit and enjoy. The neighborhood was nice with well-kept lawns and older homes.

He decided to introduce himself first before pulling out all his luggage so he got out of the car, walked up to the front door and knocked. The early September sun was hot on his back as he waited for somebody to answer.

A diminutive woman with a shock of white hair and bright blue eyes opened the door and her wrinkled face wreathed with a friendly smile. "Even though you're a very handsome young man, I'm sorry but I'm not buying anything today," she said.

"That's good because I'm not selling anything. My name is Nick…"

"Oh, Mr. Cain," she replied before he had even fully introduced himself. "I've been expecting you." She grabbed his hand and tugged him over the threshold. "I'm so glad you're here. It's such an honor for you to stay in my home and the town needs you desperately. Let me show you the room where you'll be staying." She continued to pull him toward the large staircase. "How was your trip here?"

"It was fine," he replied, and gently pulled his hand from hers as he followed her up to the second floor.

"Good…good. I baked some cookies earlier. I thought you might want a little snack before you get to your detective work." They reached the top of the stairs and walked down a short hall, and then she opened a door and gestured him to follow her inside.

The bedroom sported a king-size bed, a dresser and an en suite bathroom. The beige walls complemented the cool mint-green color scheme. There was also a small table with two chairs in front of the large window that looked out on the street and a door that led to an old iron fire escape staircase to the ground.

"Is this okay for your needs?" She turned

to look at him, her blue eyes filled with obvious apprehension.

He smiled at her. "This is absolutely perfect." It was actually far better than he'd expected. His main requirement was that the place be clean, and this space screamed and smelled of cleanliness.

"Oh good, I'm so glad. Well, I'll just leave you to get settled in and then we can have a little chat?"

"Of course," he replied.

She scurried out of the room and he followed after her. At the foot of the stairs, she beelined into another area of the house and he went outside to retrieve his luggage.

Within thirty minutes he was unpacked. He went back downstairs and stood in the entry. "Mrs. Tompkin," he hollered.

She appeared in one of the doorways and offered him another bright smile. "Come," she said. "I've got some cookies for you and we can have a little chitchat about house rules and such."

The kitchen was large and airy with windows across one wall and a wooden table that sat six. She ushered him into one of the chairs. In the center of the table was a platter of what appeared to be chocolate chip cookies.

"Would you like a cup of coffee?" she asked.

"That sounds nice," he replied.

"It's so easy now to make a cup of coffee with this newfangled coffee maker," she said as she popped a pod into the machine. She then reached on her tippy-toes and pulled a saucer from one of the cabinets and carried it over to the table.

"You have a very nice place here," Nick said.

She beamed at him as she placed three cookies on the saucer and then set it before him. "Thank you. Me and my husband, Henry, God rest his soul, were very happy here for a lot of years. He passed five years ago from colon cancer."

"I'm so sorry for your loss," he replied.

"It's okay now. I know he's up in heaven holding a spot for me. And that reminds me, there's no Mrs. Tompkin here. Everyone just calls me Nene."

"Then Nene it will be," he replied.

"I just thought we needed to chat about how things go around here. I have one other boarder. His name is Ralph Summerset. He's a nice man who mostly stays to himself. He's retired from the army and now works part-time at the post office. Cream or sugar?" she asked as she set the cup of coffee in front of him.

"Black is just fine," he replied.

She sat on the chair opposite him and smiled at him once again. Nick would guess her to be in her late seventies or early eighties, but she gave off much younger vibes and energy.

"Anyway, I provide breakfast anytime between six and eight in the mornings and then I cook a nice meal at around five thirty each evening. If you're here, you can eat, but if you aren't here, I don't provide around-the-clock services."

"Understandable," he replied. Even though he wasn't a bit hungry at the moment, he bit into one of the cookies.

"I usually require my guests to be home by ten or so, but I'm making an exception for you." She reached into the pocket of the blue housedress she wore and pulled out a key. "I know with your line of work, your hours are going to be crazy, so take this and then you can come and go as you please. Just make sure when you come in you lock up the door behind you."

"Thank you, I appreciate that." He took the key from her and then finished the cookie and took a sip of his coffee. He was eager to get to the police station and find out just what he was dealing with, but he also knew it was important to build relationships with the locals. And that started here with Nene.

He picked up the second cookie. "These are really delicious," he said, making her beam a smile at him once again.

"I enjoy baking, so I hope you like sweets," she said.

"I definitely have a sweet tooth," he replied. "And I'm sorry, but two cookies are enough for me right now." He took another drink of his coffee.

"I hope you're good at detecting things because these murders that are taking place are frightening and something needs to be done to get the Honey Island Swamp Monster murderer behind bars."

"Honey Island Swamp Monster?" He gazed at her curiously, having not heard the term before.

"That's what everyone is calling the murderer," she replied.

"And who or what is the Honey Island Swamp Monster?"

She leaned forward in her chair, her eyes sparkling like those of a mischievous child. "Legend has it that he was an abandoned child raised by alligators. He's supposed to be over seven feet tall and weighs about four hundred pounds. He has long dirty gray hair and golden eyes, and he stinks to high heaven."

Nick looked at her in disbelief. "Surely nobody really believes that's what killed those women."

Nene leaned back in her chair and released a titter of laughter. "Of course not." The merriment left her face as she frowned at him. "The sad part is now you got town people thinking somebody from the swamp is responsible and the swamp people think somebody from town is responsible and our chief of police seems to be clueless about all of it."

She reached across the table and grabbed one of Nick's hands. "All that really matters is that there's somebody out there killing these poor young women and the rumors are the killings are horribly savage. I really hope you can help us, Mr. Cain." She released his hand.

"Please, make it Nick," he replied as he tried to digest everything she'd just told him. He'd learned over the years not to discount any piece of information he got about a particular crime. Even rumors and gossip had a place in a criminal investigation.

She smiled at him again. "Then Nick it is," she said. "Anyway, Nick, I read a lot of romance books and you look like the handsome stranger who comes to town and not only saves the day but also finds his one true love. Do you have a one true love, Nick? Is there somebody waiting for you back home?"

"No, I'm pretty much married to my job."

"Well, that's a darned shame," she replied. "Now don't make me stop believing in my romances."

"I'm sorry, but I'm definitely no romance hero," he replied. His ex-wife would certainly agree with his assessment of himself. Three years ago, Amy had divorced him because he wasn't her hero. At that time, he'd permanently written love out of his life.

His work was what he could depend on and thinking of that, he rose to his feet and grabbed the house key from the table. "If we're finished here, I really need to get to the police station and get to work."

"Of course, I didn't mean to hold you up as long as I have." She got out of her chair and walked with him to the front door. "I hope to see you for dinner, but I'll understand if you can't make it. I know you have important work to do so I won't delay you any longer."

They said their goodbyes and Nick got back in his car to head to the police station. As he drove toward Main Street, he thought about Nene and the conversation he'd just had with her.

His impression of his landlady was that she was a sweet older woman who was more than a bit lonely. He had a feeling if he would have continued to sit at the table, she would have been perfectly satisfied talking to him for the rest of the afternoon.

With his living space sorted out he could now focus on the reason he was here. When he'd seen the ad in the paper looking for help in solving a series of murders, he had definitely been intrigued.

He'd spent years working as a homicide detective in the New Orleans Police Department. He'd won plenty of accolades and awards for his work and he'd labored hard on putting away as many murderers as possible. However, two years ago he'd decided to quit the department and open his own private investigation business, but that certainly hadn't meant he was done with killers.

When he'd reached out to Thomas Gravois, the man had told him about the four young women from the swamp who had been brutally murdered by the same killer, but he hadn't said anything about fighting between the swamp people and town people. In fact,

Nene had given him more information about the crimes than Gravois had.

Still, that didn't matter. Gravois had hired him over a phone call after seeing all of Nick's credentials. Nick was now more intrigued than ever to get a look at the murder books and see where the investigations had gone so far and what kind of "monster" he was dealing with.

He didn't know if his fresh eyes and skills could solve these murders, but he'd give his all to see that four murdered women got the justice they deserved.

SARAH BEAUREGARD SAT at the dispatch/reception desk in the police office lobby and drummed her fingernails on the top as nervous energy bubbled around in the pit of her tummy.

She'd been working for the police department since she was twenty-one years old and for the past twelve years Chief Gravois had kept her either on desk duty or parked just off Main Street to hand out speeding tickets.

Over those years she'd begged him to allow her to work on any of the cases that had come up, but he'd refused. She had just turned twenty-one when her parents had been killed in a head-on collision with a drunk driver.

She'd been reeling with grief and loss and Gravois, who had been close friends with her father, had taken her under his wing and hired her on as a police officer. However, his protectiveness toward her on the job had long ago begun to feel like shackles meant to hold her back from growing as an officer.

Until now...once again butterflies of excitement flew around inside her. She stared at the front door, waiting for her new partner to walk in.

She frowned as fellow officer Ryan Staub walked up and planted a hip on her desk. "So, the little lady is finally going to get to play at being a real cop," he said.

"First of all, I'm not a 'little lady' and second of all you're just jealous because I got the plum assignment of working with the new guy on the swamp murders."

His blue eyes darkened in hue. "I can't believe Gravois is letting you work on that case. He must have lost his ever-loving mind."

"He's finally allowing me to work up to my potential," she replied firmly. "Besides, you already worked the cases and nothing was solved. And get your butt off my desk."

Ryan chuckled and stood. "Why don't you go out with me for drinks on Friday night?"

She looked up at the tall, handsome blond

man. "How many times do I have to tell you I'm not going out with you? I've told you before, I find you impossibly arrogant and you're a womanizer and you just aren't my type."

He laughed again. "Oh, Sarah, I just love it when you sweet-talk me." He leaned down so he was eye level with her. "Do you want to know what I think? I think you have a secret crush on me and you're just playing hard to get."

Sarah swallowed against a groan of irritation. "Don't you have something better to do than bother me?"

He straightened up. "Yeah, I've got some things I need to get to."

"Feel free to go get to them," Sarah replied tersely. She released a sigh of relief as Ryan headed down the hallway toward the room where all the officers had their desks.

She and Ryan had known each other since they were kids, but it was just in the last month or so that he'd decided she should be his next conquest. And he'd already had plenty of conquests with the women in town.

At thirty-three years old, she had no interest in finding a special man. She'd thought she'd found him once and that romance had gone so wrong. Still, if she was looking,

Ryan would be the very last man on earth she would date.

At that moment the front door whooshed open and a tall, handsome hunk of a man walked in. She knew in an instant that it was *him*…the man Gravois had hired to come in and help investigate the four murders that had taken place.

She'd read his credentials and knew he had been a highly respected homicide detective with the New Orleans Police Department. His black hair was short and neat and his features were well-defined. A black shirt stretched across his broad shoulders and his black slacks hugged his long, lean legs. Definitely a hunk, and her new partner.

He approached her desk and offered a brief smile. Not only were his twilight-gray-colored eyes absolutely beautiful, but he also had thick, long dark lashes. "Hi, I'm Nick Cain, and I'm here to see Chief Gravois."

"Of course, I'll just go let him know you're here." She got up from the desk and headed down the hall to Chief Gravois's office.

It really made no difference to her that Nick Cain was a very handsome man. What she was most eager about was diving into the murder cases and perhaps learning something from the far more experienced detective turned private investigator.

She knocked on the chief's door and heard his reply. She opened the door and peeked inside. "He's here."

Gravois was a tall, fit man with salt-and-pepper hair and sharp blue eyes. "Get Shanks to sit on the desk and you bring him back here so I can talk to both of you at the same time."

Once again, an excited energy swirled around in the pit of her stomach. She opened the door behind which all the officers on duty sat. There were only three men in house at the moment, Ryan and Officers Colby Shanks and Ian Brubaker, who was the deputy police chief. "Colby, Gravois wants you on dispatch right now."

The young officer jumped out of his seat. He was a new hire and very eager to learn about everything. "Sure. Is the new guy here?" he asked as he followed just behind her.

"He is," she replied.

"Cool, I hope he's as good as he sounds."

"Let's hope so," she said.

They returned to the reception area where Nick Cain stood by the desk. "Sorry for the wait, if you'll just follow me, I'll take you to Chief Gravois."

"Thank you," he replied.

As she led him down the hall, she could feel an energy radiating from him. It was an attractive energy, one of confident male.

Suddenly Sarah wondered if her hair looked okay. Was the perfume she'd spritzed on that morning still holding up? She checked these thoughts, which had no place in her mind right now.

While she was working these cases with this man, she was a police officer, not a woman. Besides, one time around in the world of romance had been far more than enough for her.

She gave a quick knock on Gravois's door and then opened it. Nick followed her in and Gravois stood and offered his hand to him.

"Thomas Gravois," he said as they shook hands. "Please, both of you have a seat. It's good to have you here, Nick."

"Thank you, it's good to be here," Nick replied.

"Have you gotten all settled in at Irene's place yet?"

"I have," Nick replied.

"Okay then, first of all I want to introduce you to your new partner, Sarah Beauregard." Gravois pointed at her. "She will work side by side with you while you're here."

Nick nodded at her and Gravois continued. "Right now, you will be the only two working this investigation. If you need additional help then we can talk about that. I've set you two up in a small office that should have all you need. However, if there is something more that you want, please just let me know about it. In fact, I'll take you back there now and show you the setup."

The three of them stood and Gravois led the way down the hall to the office, which was really just an oversize storage area. A table had been set up in the center and a small filing cabinet hugged one of the corners. There was also a large whiteboard on one wall.

"I've put the murder books there in the center of the table, along with extra notepads for you to use. I'm sure you're eager to get started. I'm glad you're here, Nick. We need to get this guy off the streets as soon as possible."

"I hope I can help you with that," Nick replied.

"Later this afternoon I need to have a chat with you to finalize exactly how things are going to work," Gravois said. "I've also got some paperwork for you to sign."

"Whenever you're ready, sir," Nick replied.

"I'll just leave you to it and I'll check in

with you later," Gravois said. He left the room and closed the door behind him.

Instantly the room felt too small. She could now smell the scent of Nick, a spicy intoxicating fragrance that she found very appealing. He gestured her toward a chair at the table and then he sat opposite her.

"Officer Beauregard," he began.

"Please make it Sarah," she said.

"Sarah, how long have you been with the police department?" he asked.

"I've been with the department for the past twelve years," she replied.

"Perhaps you have some insight into the murders?" He looked at her expectantly.

"Uh...to be honest, I haven't been involved in any of the investigations into the murders up to this point," she confessed.

He looked at her for a long moment and then released a heavy sigh. "So, what investigations have you been involved in during the last couple of years? I'm just trying to figure out here what I'm working with."

"You're working with a police officer whose sole desire and interest is to solve these four murders. I'm hardworking and tenacious and I'll have your back like a good partner should," she replied fervently.

His hard gaze on her continued. "I guess time will tell if you're really all that."

It was at that moment Sarah realized her new partner might just be a jerk.

Chapter Two

Nick walked back into Nene's house just before dinnertime. The house smelled of a delicious tomato-based sauce and freshly baked bread. He carried the four murder books up the stairs and placed them on the small table to look at later.

By the time he'd had a brief conversation with his partner, Gravois had called him back into his office for a lengthy discussion about how things would work with Nick hired on as a free agent within the department. There were several documents for him to sign as well.

Once their talk was finally over, Nick made the decision that he'd study the murder books tonight and then first thing in the morning he'd speak with Sarah about where to begin their investigation.

He went into the bathroom to wash up for dinner and as he did, thoughts of his new partner filled his head. She was no bigger than a minute. He would guess her at about five feet tall and no more than one hundred pounds soaking wet.

Her blond hair was short and curly and she could easily be dismissed as a piece of fluff, except for her bright blue eyes, which had shone with a hunger that he had immediately identified with.

He wasn't sure why she'd been partnered with him. The only reason he could think of was Gravois wanted two fresh sets of eyes on the case. And he didn't know why there weren't more officers assigned to the murder cases.

What irritated him as much as anything was the fact that he found his new partner extremely pretty, and the first time she'd smiled at him he'd felt a spark go off deep inside him, something he hadn't felt for a very long time and something he definitely intended to ignore.

He went back downstairs and into the kitchen. "Nick," Nene greeted him with a big smile. "I wasn't sure you'd make it for dinner tonight, but I'm so glad you did. Please, have a seat at the table."

He started to sit, but she quickly stopped him. "Oh, that's Ralph's seat. He's kind of a creature of habit and likes to sit in the same place every night."

"No problem, I'll just sit over here." Nick moved to the other place that was set for dinner. "Something smells really delicious."

"Swiss steak, I hope you like it. We didn't talk about your food likes and dislikes when we spoke earlier. Are there any allergies I need to worry about?" She pulled a large pan from the oven and set it on the countertop where a hot pad awaited it.

"None, and the only thing I really don't eat is brussels sprouts."

"That makes two of us," she replied with a tittering giggle. "To me no matter how you dress them up, they still taste like dirt."

"I totally agree," he replied.

At that moment a tall, fit man entered the room. He had dark brown hair worn in a buzz cut and deep-set brown eyes. Nick rose from his chair and held out his hand. "You must be Ralph," he said. "I'm Nick."

Ralph's grip was firm. "Nice to meet you, Nick," he said as the handshake ended. The two men sat at the table. "I hear you're the man Gravois has brought in to solve these Honey Island Monster murders."

"That's the plan," Nick replied. "Do you have any theories about the murders?"

"Me? Nah, I didn't even know about them until just recently," Ralph replied.

How was that possible? How, in a town this size, did everyone not know about the murders? He could understand the first one not being talked about much, but when the second one had occurred, he would have thought everyone would be talking about them.

The dinner was delicious. The Swiss steak was nice and tender and there were also seasoned green beans, a gelatin salad and homemade rolls. Nene definitely knew how to cook.

Ralph did not attempt to engage Nick in any conversation while they ate; however, Nene filled what might have been awkward silences with chatter about the weather, the town and her plan to bake an apple coffee cake along with biscuits and gravy for breakfast the next morning.

"My biscuits and gravy are a favorite with Ralph, right?" she said as they were ending the meal.

"You know that's right," Ralph replied. "I could eat them every day for breakfast."

"Then I'm definitely eager to try them," Nick replied.

He was grateful that dinner went by quickly, as he was keen to get upstairs and dig into the murder books. When they were all finished eating, he picked up his plate to carry it to the sink.

"Stop right there," Nene said. "I take care of all the cleanup around here."

"And don't even try to argue with her," Ralph said. "She's a very stubborn woman."

"Ha, that I am. Now put that plate down and go on your merry way," Nene replied.

"Then I'll just say thank you and dinner was delicious," Nick replied.

"If you want a little nibble later, I always leave chips and crackers and other snacky stuff on the table overnight for you to help yourself," she said.

"Thanks, Nene, and, Ralph, it was good meeting you." With that said, Nick left the kitchen. He probably should have looked at the murder books with Sarah, but he'd wanted to study the material on his own first.

Once he reached his room, he beelined toward the table. He first grabbed one of the fresh notebooks that Gravois had provided for them. He opened the notebook and made sure he had a pen.

While he read the files, he intended to make his own notes on the cases. He picked up the first murder book, surprised by how thin it was. In fact, he'd been surprised by how thin they all were when he'd picked them up to carry home.

The first thing he saw inside the first book were the crime scene photos. The victim, Babette Pitre, had been found in the back alley behind the post office and town hall. In the photos it appeared her throat had been ripped out and her face held wounds that looked like a wild animal had tried to claw her features off.

The autopsy also indicated that she'd been stabbed three times in the abdomen and it was probably some sort of claw gardening tool that had ripped out her throat and marred her face.

There was also an injection site in her upper arm. The tox screen had come back showing a heavy dose of Xanax in her system. The same was true in all the other victims. It was obviously the way the killer had knocked out his victims.

According to the records the people who had shown up at the crime scene were Gravois, Officers Ryan Staub and Ian Brubaker, the coroner, Douglas Cartwright, and his assistant, and somebody named Ed Martin.

Nick frowned as he set the photos aside and moved on to the actual investigation notes. There were only three interviews that had been conducted at the time, one with a Gator Broussard, another with Babette's mother and finally one with a man named Zeke Maloney. The interviews were short and contained nothing earth-shattering as far as information went.

He was shocked as he checked out the next three murder books and realized it appeared that very little had been done to actually investigate these killings. Why?

Was Gravois that incompetent? Lazy? What about the other officers in the department? Did they really believe enough had been done in an attempt to catch this killer? Nick couldn't believe how lacking the investigations had been.

He leaned back in his chair and stared out the window where darkness had fallen and the streetlights had come on. He hadn't expected this. He hadn't expected the investigations that were done already to be so shoddy...so lacking. He had expected much better police work than this. He released a deep sigh.

Instantly a picture of his new partner filled his head once again. She'd already told him she knew very little about the murders. He also hadn't missed the fact that she hadn't answered him when he'd asked what kind of investigations she'd worked on before.

So, basically, he had crap in the murder files and a partner who he suspected was green as grass. It was a perfect recipe for failure.

However, he now had a vision of the four victims also in his head and they deserved justice, so failure wasn't an option. The way those women had been killed indicated that there really was a monster somewhere in Black Bayou. The length of time between the killings had shortened, so another one could occur any day.

He finally left the table and got ready for bed. He wanted to be sharp and refreshed in the morning. He'd told Sarah to meet him at seven thirty and they definitely had their work cut out for them.

Nick arrived at the police department just after seven the next morning. He was fueled by a good breakfast of the best biscuits and gravy he'd ever tasted and several cups of Nene's strong coffee.

He went directly to the room that had been assigned to them. He set the murder books back on the center of the table and then moved to the whiteboard, where he wrote the names of the four victims at the top.

He was pleasantly surprised when Sarah walked in at seven fifteen. At least she was early rather than being late. "Good morning," she said with a bright smile.

She was definitely very pretty, and once again an electric spark shot off deep inside him. Despite the fact that it was hot and humid outside, she brought in the very pleasant scent of spring flowers. It irritated him that he even noticed her scent.

"Back at you," he said, apparently more gruffly than he intended as her smile instantly disappeared. "Feel free to start reading the murder books. I'll be interested to get your thoughts."

She sat at the table and picked up the first file. He watched her as she read it. To her credit, she flinched only a little bit as she saw the graphic photos of the victims. He also couldn't help but notice that her eyelashes were thick and long. Damn, what in the hell was going on with him?

She flipped through the interviews and then looked up at him with a delicate frown. "Is there more to this?"

"Apparently not, and the other three are just as thin." He joined her at the table.

"Surely there has to be more someplace," she replied with a look of confusion.

"I asked Gravois when I arrived a few minutes ago if there was more information on the murders and he told me what we have is all there is." He attempted to keep all the judgment from his tone, but some of it must have crept in.

Her cheeks turned a dusty pink. "Well, this is embarrassing." She shoved the murder book aside. "This should be an embarrassment to the whole department."

"I'm glad we agree about something. How do you feel about going into the swamp?"

"I don't have a problem with it. I ran in the swamp when I was young. What about you?"

"The same. My mother worked as an attorney in New Orleans and many of the people she represented were from the swamp. It wasn't uncommon for her to take me with her when she went to meet with some of her clients." The back of his throat threatened to close up at the very thought of the swamp. He swallowed hard against his rise of anxiety as he thought about going into the dark bayou.

"So, is that where we begin things? In the swamp?" she asked.

He nodded. "I think we should start by speaking to Lisa Choate's parents." Lisa had been the last woman killed.

"I think that makes sense. That murder is still fairly fresh," she replied.

"But before that, I'd like to take a look at the place where her body was found," he added.

"That was behind the bank. So, are we ready to go?" She gazed at him with big blue eyes that simmered with anticipation.

"Ready," he replied.

She stood. "I'll drive."

"Normally I drive," he said.

"It makes sense for me to since I'm sure I know my way around town better than you do." Her chin lifted as if ready to challenge him. It surprised him, the bit of sass she had in her.

"Okay, then you drive for today," he replied.

They left the room and headed toward the back door of the station, stopping only when another officer was coming their way.

He smiled at Nick. "Investigator Cain, I'm Officer Ryan Staub." He held out a hand and the two shook. "I just want to let you know that if you find Short-Stuff here to be lacking in any way, I'd be available to join your team and help you out."

"Jeez, Ryan, I definitely feel the bus wheels rolling over my back," Sarah replied drily.

"I'll keep that in mind, but I like my partner just fine," Nick said. "So far, I find her extremely intelligent and I know she's going to be a great asset to me going forward."

"Oh…okay," Ryan replied. "Well, let me know if you need more help."

"Will do," Nick replied, and then he and Sarah moved on down the hall and exited into the hot early-September morning.

"Thank you," Sarah said.

"Is he always such a jackass?" Nick asked.

She released a musical laugh that was quite pleasant on the ears. "Only on the days when he's not being a total jerk." She gestured toward a blue sedan parked in a space at the back of the building.

"Do your other officers often mention your…uh…small stature?" He'd been offended by Ryan on so many levels, especially as a fellow officer of hers calling her Short-Stuff.

"No, that's just Ryan," she replied. She unlocked her car doors with her key fob and he got into the passenger seat. The interior of the car smelled like her, that scent of fresh flowers he found so attractive.

What in the hell was wrong with him? It had been years since he'd noticed a woman's scent. Why now? And why his partner?

What he needed was to keep himself in check, solve these murders as quickly as possible and then get back to his life in New Orleans.

SARAH FELT UNACCOUNTABLY nervous as she took off from the parking lot and headed toward the bank. She'd initially written off her new partner as being a jerk, but then he had defended her to Ryan and now she wasn't so sure what to think about him.

He looked as hot today as he had the day before. Clad in black slacks and a short-sleeved gray shirt, and with his shoulder holster and gun in place, he exuded strong male energy.

Not that it mattered as long as they could work together well. More than anything else, Sarah wanted to prove herself to the rest of the department.

She wanted to show them all that she wasn't just a nothing who Gravois gave a job to because he felt sorry for her. She wanted to prove that she wasn't just good for answering the phone or giving out tickets. She was ready to earn her place as a valuable member of the team and this was finally her opportunity to do that. The last thing she wanted was to develop a crush on her partner and lose her focus.

It was a short drive to the bank, where she parked and they got out of the car. "Down this way," she said as she led him down the alley between the bank and Masy's dress shop. "She was found right around here." She pointed to the general area where the body had been discovered.

He stared at the ground and then gazed around the area. "No security cameras back here?"

"None, and there's also no lighting," she replied.

"So, the killer had to know this area well and was able to easily drop the body off and get out of the here fairly quickly without being seen."

"There aren't many people on the streets at two or three in the morning," she replied. "But the killer had to know that this was an ideal place to leave her because of the lack of surveillance and lights."

"You would think the bank would have security cameras all around it."

She smiled at him. "You're thinking like a man from the city. Bank robberies just don't happen in Black Bayou."

He nodded. "Point taken."

He looked around the area for several more minutes and then gazed at her once again. "Let's head to the swamp and at least get a first round of interviews done by the end of the day."

Minutes later they were back in her car and headed to Vincent's, a grocery store located just before the swamp took over the land. One thing the murder book held were directions to Lisa's parents' shanty.

"How was it that you ran the swamp when you were younger?" he asked.

"The house that I grew up in backed up to the swamp," she explained. "My parents worked full time and I was left alone a lot. When I was about eight or nine, I met a few kids who lived in the swamp, so I would go in to visit with them. I found it to be a magical place, but by the time I was a teenager I gave up the swamp for other after-school activities."

"And you were never afraid in the swamp?" he asked curiously.

"Never. My friends taught me a lot about the dangers and I was probably too young and dumb to be afraid," she ended with a small laugh.

"So, what do you think? Is our killer from the swamp? Or is he somebody from town?

Gravois seems to feel certain it's somebody from the swamp."

"I really don't have an opinion about it all right now. I don't have enough information to make an educated call," she replied.

"And that's good police work," he replied. "It's important that we both keep open minds going into all this."

His words warmed her. She hoped he wouldn't realize just how inexperienced she was, that she wouldn't show him what a neophyte she really was in actually working to solve crimes.

"What made you quit the police department and go out on your own as a private investigator?" she asked. "And I'm sorry if I'm being too nosy."

"Not at all," he replied. "In a word, it was burnout. I was working twelve-to fifteen-hour days for years and finally I decided it was time for me to slow down a bit. I now pick and choose the cases I work on."

"Is there somebody waiting for you back home? A wife or a girlfriend?" Sarah instantly wanted to kick herself in the behind for asking the personal question. But she was definitely curious.

"Neither, I've pretty much always been

married to the job. What about you? Do you have a significant other?"

"No, and I'm glad. I want to stay laser focused on these cases without any outside distractions."

"Then we're definitely on the same page," he replied.

She pulled into the parking lot of the small grocery store, where a trail leading into the vast swamp was nearby. A lot of the people who lived in the swamp parked their vehicles here, as the owner of Vincent's was very swamp friendly.

"This is it. According to the directions, Lisa Choate's parents live up this trail and to the right at the second fork," she said.

"Let's go and let's hope Abe and Emily Choate can give us some information about their daughter that will move the investigation along." He led the way as they entered the trail.

It had been years since Sarah had been in the swamp. As she followed behind Nick, she drew in the scents of mysterious flowers and fauna along with the underlying odor of decay. The heat that surrounded them seemed to magnify the scents.

Bugs buzzed around her head as little woodland creatures scurried away on either side of the trail. Spanish moss dripped down from the treetops in beautiful lacy patterns.

Despite the beauty, she was also well aware of the dangers of poisonous snakes and gator-infested pools of water and wild boar that roamed the area.

Thankfully, they encountered none of those things by the time they arrived at the Choates' shanty. Before they could cross the rickety bridge that led up to the front door, a man stepped outside the small, slightly listing home on stilts.

"Who are you?" he asked with obvious suspicion. "What do you want here?"

"Mr. Choate, I'm Sarah Beauregard with the Black Bayou Police Department and this is special agent Nick Cain. We'd like to come in and talk to you and your wife about Lisa."

The tall, shirtless man stood still for a long moment and Sarah wondered if he was willing to speak to them at all. He finally nodded his head. "Come in then."

Nick and Sarah crossed the bridge and Lisa's father ushered them into the small shanty. "They're here to talk about Lisa," he said to the woman who sat on the end of the sofa. She stood as a slash of deep grief filled her features.

"Please, have a seat," she said as she

stepped aside and gestured to the sofa. She twisted her hands before her. "Can I get you something to drink?"

"No thanks," Nick said. "And we're so very sorry for your loss."

He and Sarah sat side by side on the sofa and Emily sat in a chair facing them while Lisa's father remained standing by the door as if ready to kick them out at any moment.

"She was such a good girl," Emily said as her dark eyes filled with tears. "Always happy, always smiling." She swiped at her eyes. "She didn't deserve what was done to her."

"None of the victims deserved it," Sarah replied softly. "And we're going to work very hard to get justice for Lisa."

"Nobody else has been working too hard to catch this killer," Abe said in obvious disgust. "Four dead girls and still no answers."

"We're hoping to change that right now," Nick replied.

Nick took the lead in the questioning and Sarah made notes. For the next hour he asked questions about Lisa and her lifestyle. Her parents insisted that she wouldn't leave the swamp with just anyone, but somebody had led her out of the swamp and to her death.

It would help if they knew where the

women had been killed. The place where their bodies were found had only been the dumping grounds. They had been killed elsewhere, but where?

Her parents didn't know of any town girls who had been friends with their daughter, but she did have a couple of close friends who lived nearby in the swamp. In fact, she had been coming home after having partied a bit with her friends when she had disappeared.

Sarah was impressed by her partner, who asked smart and pointed questions yet displayed a softness and compassion for the two grieving parents.

They finally got up to leave, but Abe stopped them at the door. "You better hope you find this killer afore I do," he said with dark narrowed eyes. "'Cause if I find him, I'll kill him and rip his throat out just like he done my baby girl."

"Understood," Nick replied.

They left the shanty but before heading away, they paused at the bottom of the bridge to talk about what they had just learned. "I didn't see any interviews of Lisa's friends in the file," Nick said.

"That's because there were none there," Sarah replied. Even as inexperienced as she was, she knew this was lousy police work.

There should have been follow-up interviews with all of Lisa's friends.

She was completely embarrassed by the department. She was particularly embarrassed by the man who had given her a job so many years ago. She'd believed Gravois was better than this. She knew there were people in town who believed he was lazy.

Maybe he was or maybe as the chief of police in such a small town he really didn't know how to investigate serious criminal cases like these. Or had he not cared because the victims were from the swamp? All of these thoughts deeply troubled her.

"Shall we interview Hayley Duchamp while we're so close to where she lives?" she asked. Lisa's parents had given them directions to two of Lisa's closest friends' places.

"Sounds like a plan," he replied. "I'm honestly surprised the friends haven't been interviewed before now. They might have some information about Lisa that her parents didn't know." He started up the trail toward Hayley's family shanty.

There was a loud crack. A gunshot! Nick immediately took Sarah to the ground and covered her body with his. At the same time, she heard the path of the bullet as it whizzed through the leaves and slammed into the tree near where they'd been standing.

Chapter Three

Nick's heart pumped sheer adrenaline throughout his body as he quickly pulled his gun. He stared into the direction that the bullet had come from but he saw nobody. He'd already been on the very edge just being in the swamp and now this. What in the hell?

He looked down at Sarah, who was as still as a statue beneath him. "Are you okay?" he asked softly.

"I'm fine," she replied just as quietly, but he could feel the frantic beat of her heart against his and the tenseness of her entire body beneath him.

"Stay here and stay down," he said. He slowly rose up to a crouch and then raced forward, zigzagging among the trees and thicket toward the spot where he thought the shooter might be. He glanced over his shoulder and saw that Sarah had crouched up and had her gun out before her.

No other shots came and it was impossible to specifically locate exactly where the shooter might have been. Nick sensed the danger was over as nothing else happened, but he continued to crouch down as he made his way back to Sarah.

It was only when he reached her that they both finally stood. "What the hell was that all about?" he asked. "Is it possible the people who live around here don't like law enforcement?"

"I guess that's possible, or it's also possible somebody just warned us off our investigation," she replied.

"Did it work? Do you want to be reassigned?"

"Heck no," she replied, her eyes lit with blue fire. "This just makes me more determined than ever to go forward."

He gazed at her for a long moment, looking for any cracks in her composure. That bullet aimed at them would have shaken up the most seasoned professional, but she appeared to have taken it in stride. Either she had a good poker face or she was utterly fearless.

While he could appreciate the first quality, the latter could be deadly. A cop had to function with a healthy amount of fear to stay alive. His partner was still such an unknown commodity to him.

What he did know was beneath her blue uniform and despite her slender frame, she had some definite feminine curves. In the brief moments he'd been on top of her, his traitorous brain had registered that fact.

"Is this something we should call in?" he asked.

"Call in to who?" she asked, and then continued, "It doesn't appear we need backup and we can't even be sure that bullet wasn't from somebody hunting in the area. Now that I really think about it, it's a bit too early for anyone to be that worried about what we're doing."

"The fact that there was only one shot and none following up makes me believe it was just some kind of a random thing. I say we go on to Hayley's place but we proceed with caution," he finally said.

Together they took off with their guns leading the way. They managed to interview not only Hayley, but also Lily Champueau, who was also a friend of Lisa's.

By that time, they decided to head back into the office and not only process what they'd learned that day, but also plan what they intended to do the next day.

Sarah now sat at the table while Nick wrote the names of Lisa's two friends on the whiteboard beneath Lisa's name. When he was finished, he joined her at the table.

"Both women agreed that Lisa had no boyfriends," he said.

"And that she would not just go off with a guy from town," Sarah added dispiritedly. "We didn't really learn anything new that helps us."

"No stone unturned," Nick replied. "Patience is the key here. This case isn't going to be solved overnight. I just really don't understand why more wasn't done on these cases at the time the murders occurred."

Sarah released a deep sigh. "It's probably because they were swamp women," she said. "I'll tell you a dirty little secret about this town. A lot of the people who live in town are very prejudiced against the people who live in the swamp. They believe the men there are all lazy and drunks, and the woman are all worthless sluts." Her cheeks dusted with color. "If it would have been four town women who had been murdered, I think the investigations would have been far more thorough."

"So, what's changed? Why was I brought

in if they don't really care about solving these crimes?"

"Pressure from several influential businessmen who demanded answers about the murders and Gravois's fear of being recalled," she replied. "Things seem to be slowly changing with the newer generation. It's mostly the old guard who are still hanging on to the prejudices."

"Well, it's good if things are changing. If prejudice is what kept these murders from being solved that's a hate crime in and of itself." Nene had hinted at some of this when she'd first spoken to him, but she certainly hadn't laid it out in such stark terms. It ticked him off. All victims, no matter who they were or where they came from, deserved justice.

"I also think it's very possible that the officers involved in the case believe a swamp person is responsible and they've just been waiting for somebody to walk in and either confess to the murders or give up some information about the guilty person."

He frowned. "So instead of actively investigating, everybody has been just hanging around and waiting for the crimes to solve themselves."

"Nick, I swear I didn't know what had been done or not done as far as the investigations were concerned. I was kept away from all this. I'm seeing this all for the first time and it actually disgusts me." She looked so earnest as she held his gaze.

He released a deep sigh. "Okay, so we use what little information there is in the files and we forge ahead. I want to ask you about some of the people in the murder books."

"Okay, ask away," she replied. There was a small piece of green vegetation stuck in her golden strands of hair. He wasn't sure if he wanted to pick it out because it didn't belong there or if he just wanted to touch the hair that looked so silky and soft. Instead, he opened his notebook and tightly grabbed his pen.

"The first person is Ed Martin. According to the murder books, he was at each of the dumping grounds before the bodies were removed."

She frowned. "His father, Gustave, owns most of Main Street. Ed helps his father with his businesses and collects rent from all the store owners. He's married and he and his wife have one son who is around nineteen or twenty. But I can't imagine why he would be anywhere around the bodies or the crime scenes."

"And what about Gator Broussard? He was

interviewed after the first murder, but the notes don't hold much of the conversation."

A small smile curved her lips, igniting that little flutter of something inside him. "Gator is about eighty years old and has lived in the swamp all his life. He is something of a character and he catches gators for a living."

"What would he know about the murders to warrant him being interviewed?" Nick asked.

"Gator knows most everyone who lives in the swamp and he usually has a handle on what's going on there," she replied.

"Definitely sounds like somebody we should reinterview," he said.

"I agree. If anybody knows anything at all about these murders it would be Gator."

"Then let's plan to talk to him in the morning. Finally, do you know Zeke Maloney? He was listed as a potential suspect because he was seen hanging out around Chastain's store the night Marchelle Savoie's body was found in the alley there."

Once again Sarah frowned. "Zeke is in his late thirties or early forties. He lives in one of the rooms at the motel and I think he's a heavy drug user."

"Do you know what kinds of drugs he's into?" he asked.

"No, I'm sorry but I don't," she replied. "But if I was to make a guess, I'd say either cocaine or meth."

Nick leaned back in his chair. "So, tomorrow we'll plan on interviewing those three men... Ed Martin, Gator Broussard and Zeke Maloney. At some point later I want to talk to Gravois about the fact that we were shot at. Whether it was a stray bullet from a hunter or something else, he should be made aware of that fact."

"I agree," she replied. "Do you want me to go with you when you speak to him?"

"I don't think that's necessary." He closed his notebook and looked at his watch. It was just a few minutes after five. "Why don't we go ahead and call it a day and we can pick up fresh in the morning. I'm sure we are going to have some late nights going forward."

They both got up from the table. "Then I'll see you in the morning," she said. Once she left the room, he sank back down at the table.

He hoped like hell that she hadn't noticed how absolutely terrified he'd been the minute he'd stepped foot in the swamp. The swamp had haunted his nightmares for years, so going into the dark, mysterious marsh today

had been a real challenge. It had been a ter-
rifying journey for him.

He hoped his partner had seen none of his
internal battle between duty and fear. The
last thing he would want was to appear weak
in anyone's eyes, but especially to his new
partner.

He still didn't know what kind of a partner
Sarah was going to be, but already he found
her damned distracting. Her beautiful smile
felt like a gift each time she flashed it at him.
Her eyes were the vivid color of sapphires and
shone just as brilliantly.

She wore her uniform well. The light blue
shirt emphasized the blue of her eyes and the
navy slacks fit her like they'd been tailored to
showcase her nice butt and slender legs. Her
lips looked so soft and kissable.

Why didn't she have a boyfriend or a significant other? She was bright and pretty and
he couldn't believe nobody in town would be
interested in her.

And why in the hell was he sitting here
speculating about her? He'd had many female
partners through the years, but with none of
them had he wanted to know anything about
them outside of the job.

Something about Sarah was different and
she had him more than a little bit out of his

comfort zone. Starting tomorrow he had to get his head on straight where she was concerned.

SARAH JERKED AWAKE with her heart racing and adrenaline flooding through her veins. Frantically she looked around the room as she slowly came out of the nightmare that had awakened her in the first place.

She turned over and checked the time. Just a little past five. Instead of going back to sleep for another hour or so, she decided to go ahead and get up. She turned on the bedside lamp and got out of bed. She then went into the kitchen and fixed herself a cup of coffee.

As she sipped the hot brew, she thought about the nightmare that had jerked her awake. She'd been back in the swamp, tangled in the vines that held her captive while shadow people had been shooting at her. It was easy to figure out why she'd had the dream.

Being shot at the day before had scared the living hell out of her. She hoped her partner hadn't seen her abject fear and she'd played it off okay. The last thing she wanted to do was give him the impression she wasn't up to the job.

She stared out the nearby window where the morning sun was just beginning to peek over the horizon. She had bought this house four years ago after having lived in an apartment since her parents' deaths. It was a nice three-bedroom with a fenced-in yard.

She'd had such high hopes for a happy life at that time. She'd been engaged to Brent Williamson, a man she'd believed was her soulmate, and she was busy planning her wedding. That, along with all of her confidence as a woman, had been destroyed by a single image on his phone.

Instead of dwelling on thoughts of her past heartbreak, she finished her coffee and then headed for the shower. A half an hour later she was dressed, but it was still too early to go into the police station.

She made herself another cup of coffee and carried it into her living room and sank down on the sofa. While her bedroom was decorated in pink and white, this room was done in blacks and grays with bright yellow accents.

She also had a guest bedroom done in shades of blue and a room with a desk set aside as an office which she hoped to actually use now that she was officially investigating crimes.

As she sipped on her second cup, she couldn't help but think about Nick. She could usually figure out people fairly well, but she couldn't get a good read on him. She'd found him supportive yet standoffish. His gaze had alternated between a warm gray and a distant deep steel, all in the course of a single day.

He was a hot, handsome man who could become a total distraction if she allowed him to be. But she couldn't let that happen. All she wanted to do was prove herself to be a hardworking officer who could get the job done, somebody who had the respect of her coworkers.

And thinking about that, she realized it was time to go. Hopefully today they could find out something that would lead them closer to catching the killer.

The intense heat and humidity of the summer months had finally broken and today was supposed to be a more pleasant temperature in the low eighties.

Knowing they would be driving several places, today she parked in front of the police station and entered through the front door.

"Good morning," she said to Ian Brubaker, who sat at the reception/dispatcher desk.

"Morning, Sarah," he replied. "Your partner is already here."

"Thanks, then I'll just head on back. Have a good day, Ian." Her stomach knotted up a bit with anxious energy as she walked down the hallway and anticipated seeing her partner again.

"Her partner," that's how she had to think about him in her mind. She didn't want to think about him being Nick, because Nick was a man she was very attracted to.

She hadn't really dated much in the last couple of years and it ticked her off a little that the first man she found appealing on all levels was strictly off-limits.

She opened the door to their little office and walked in. Nick was seated at the table. "I'm just going over the people I think we need to talk to today," he said as a greeting. He gestured her toward the chair opposite him.

Instantly she smelled the scent of him, a mixture of soap and shaving cream and the spicy cologne. This morning he wore a gray polo that perfectly matched the color of his eyes, and his usual black slacks.

However, his eyes appeared distant, bordering on cold as he read off the list of people for questioning and then looked at her. "Anyone you want to add for today?"

"No, your list sounds good to me," she replied.

"Then let's get moving," he said, and stood.

She quickly got to her feet and followed him out of the office and down the hallway. "I'll drive today," he said once they were outside. "You can navigate from the passenger seat."

She wasn't about to argue with him, not in the mood he appeared to be in. He led her to a black sedan and after he unlocked the doors with his key fob, she slid into the passenger seat.

The interior smelled like him, a scent that instantly stirred her. She watched as he walked around the front of the car to get to the driver door.

Why couldn't he have a paunchy stomach and sloped shoulders? Why couldn't he smell like menthol rub and mothballs? That would have made it so much better, so much easier for her.

"I figured we'd start with Ed Martin this morning. I'm assuming he works out of an office?" He started his car.

"He does. His office is down a few blocks on Main Street," she replied.

"Any self-respecting businessman should

be in his office by this time of the morning, right?"

"You would think so." She fastened her seat belt and they took off.

"Is there anything I should know about Mr. Martin before we go in to talk to him?"

"To be honest, I really don't know much about him other than what I already told you," she replied.

She couldn't help but notice that Nick's voice seemed brusquer today and she also couldn't help but wonder if she'd done something to somehow offend him. Or maybe he was just a moody person.

Just like she couldn't know whether the killer was from the swamp or from town because she didn't have enough information, the same was true about Nick. She just didn't have enough information about him to even hazard a guess as to what kind of a personality he might really have.

It took only minutes for them to pull up in front of Ed's office. The writing on the large window in the front announced the business to be Martin's Enterprises.

There was a small sign on the door that indicated the office was open. They got out of the car and Nick opened the door and ushered

Sarah inside. A small bell tinkled overhead to announce their arrival.

There were several chairs in front of the window and Ed sat at a large desk. He rose as they walked in. He was a small man with jet-black hair. He had a neatly trimmed mustache and was dressed in a suit that was probably worth Sarah's salary for a month.

"Good morning," he said in greeting. He nodded at Sarah and then turned his attention to Nick. "Sir," he said as he held out his hand. "I don't believe we've met."

"Nick Cain," Nick replied, and the two men shook hands. "And I assume you know Officer Beauregard."

"Yes," Ed said with a nod to her. "Please, have a seat," Ed said, and gestured to the chairs right in front of his desk.

Sarah and Nick sat and Ed returned to his seat. "Now, what can I do for the two of you this morning?" Ed asked.

"We're in the process of investigating the murders of four women. In going over the files we noticed that you were present at each of the scenes where the bodies were found. Why were you there, Mr. Martin?" Nick asked bluntly.

Sarah would have sworn that Ed's face momentarily paled. He cleared his throat and leaned forward in his chair. "Mr. Cain, my father has invested heavily in the town of Black Bayou. He's now an elderly man who has health and mobility issues, and so I'm his ears and eyes out here on the streets. I told Chief Gravois that I wanted to be notified of anything that was happening in town."

"You realize your presence there was highly unusual," Nick replied. "You probably contaminated a crime scene just by being there."

"I stayed outside of the perimeter and was only there as an observer," Ed replied.

"It's still highly unusual and definitely not a good idea," Nick replied. "What's your son's name, Mr. Martin?" he asked.

Ed straightened in his chair. "Why? He has nothing to do with any of this. I know he has alibis for all the nights of all the murders."

"All I asked for was his name," Nick replied.

Even Sarah, as much as she was a beginner in all this, recognized that Ed's response had been strange and made her wonder about Ed's son.

"Gus...his name is Gus," Ed said reluctantly.

"Thank you," Nick replied. "We're just trying to keep our records clear. You'll be available should we need to speak with you again?"

"Of course," Ed said.

"We appreciate your time, Mr. Martin." Nick stood and Sarah did the same.

"I think he should be the first name on our suspect list," Sarah said the minute they got back in the car.

"He and his son," Nick replied as he started the engine.

"He definitely protested too much when you simply asked for his son's name. Is Daddy showing up at the scenes to make sure there is no evidence that might point to sonny boy's guilt?"

"Makes you wonder, right?" he replied. "Gus Martin is definitely somebody we need to speak to, and not with his father present. If he's over the age of eighteen then we can interview him without Daddy. Now, let's head on over to the motel and see what we can learn from Zeke Maloney. I know where the motel is. I passed it on the way into town."

"Okay, then navigation is officially off," she replied lightly.

They drove in silence for a couple of minutes. "Is there a big drug problem around here?" he asked, breaking the silence.

"Are there some people using here, yes.

Is there a big drug problem here, definitely not," she replied.

"Have you ever wanted to try anything?" There was genuine curiosity in his question.

"Never." She hesitated a moment and then continued, "If I was ever going to use, it would have been in the weeks after my parents were killed. I was so grief-stricken in that time I could understand the need...the utter desire to numb the excruciating pain, but even then, I wanted nothing to do with drugs."

"How and when were your parents killed?"

"I had just turned twenty-one when they were killed in a head-on crash by a drunk driver," she replied. She was vaguely surprised that even after all this time, thoughts of her parents still brought up an edge of deep grief in her.

"I'm so sorry for your loss," he replied with a kindness in his tone that made her believe him.

"What about you? Have you ever used?"

"No, never had the desire to screw up my career, although there were several people on the force who I knew used."

It was as if the ice had been broken between them and any brusqueness that had been in his voice earlier was now gone.

"Were you close to your parents?" he asked.

"Very close. They were my best friends," she replied. "I still miss them very much." Sarah wanted to keep the conversation going, but at that time he pulled into the motel parking lot.

"Zeke lives in unit three," she told Nick.

The motel was a place of hopelessness and despair. The outside of the eight-unit structure was a dismal gray, made only worse by the intense weathering of heat and humidity.

There was a lot of history here. Years ago, in unit seven a young prostitute had been murdered in a crime that had shocked the town, especially when it was revealed that a highly respectable businessman had been responsible for the crime after an innocent man from the swamp had spent years in prison for the murder.

Beau Boudreau had returned to Black Bayou after his years in prison and had hooked up with his old girlfriend, Peyton La-Croix. Peyton was a criminal defense lawyer and together they had solved the crime and cleared Beau's name. Peyton was still working as a lawyer and Beau was making a name for himself in home construction and repair. They had rediscovered their love for each other and were now a happy couple.

Nick pulled up in front of unit three and parked. They got out of the car and Nick knocked on the door. "Yo...yeah...coming," a voice yelled out. A moment after that the door flew open to reveal Zeke.

He looked at both of them, then frowned. "Oh...uh... I was expecting somebody else."

Zeke might have been a good-looking man at one time, but now his cheeks were hollow and his teeth were rotten and an air of unhealthiness clung to his slender frame.

"Hi, Zeke, my name is Nick Cain, and this is Officer Beauregard. We were wondering if we could come in and ask you a few questions."

"Questions about what?" Zeke reached up and worried a scab on the side of his face. He dropped his hand to his side and shot a glance over his shoulder.

"We have a few questions about the murders that have occurred. We aren't interested in anything more than that," Nick replied pointedly. Sarah knew he was assuring Zeke that they weren't interested in his drug use... at least not for today.

Zeke stared at Nick for a long moment and then released a deep sigh and opened his door fully. Nick stepped in and Sarah followed right behind him.

The room was steeped in squalor. The blankets and sheets had been torn off the bed, displaying a dirty gray mattress. Used fast-food containers littered the floor and the top of the dresser. Flies sat on the old food wrappers, as if too full to fly.

"I'd invite you to sit, but there's really no place for you to do that," Zeke said. He bounced from one foot to the other. "I don't know what kinds of questions you want to ask because I don't know anything about the murders."

"What were you doing out on the streets on the night of June 23 around two in the morning?" Nick asked.

Zeke frowned and began to pick at his face once again. "I don't really remember that night in particular, but there are lots of nights when I just feel like getting out of this room. I like to wait to go at a time when there aren't any people around to look at me and judge me. So I often walk in the middle of the night, but I had nothing to do with those poor women."

"When you're out walking, do you ever see anyone else out and around?" Sarah asked. She did not intend to be a silent partner, and it was time she assert herself just a little bit.

Once again Zeke frowned. "I've seen Ed

Martin a couple of times and Officer Ryan Staub and Chief Gravois out and about once or twice. I've also met up with Dwayne Carter a few times. He's a friend and we just hang out together."

"Is there a reason you hang out with your friend that late at night?" Nick asked. Sarah knew the reason. Dwayne Carter was the local drug dealer.

"Uh…we're just both night owls, I guess."

"Did you see or hear anything that particular night that might have looked or sounded suspicious?" Sarah asked.

"No, not that I remember."

"Then you had no idea that Marchelle Savoie was dead in the alley next to where you and your friend were hanging out," Nick said.

"God no," Zeke replied. "I didn't find out about her murder until the next day. Look, I'll admit I'm a dope addict. I shoot and snort a lot of stuff, but I'm not a killer." He shook his head. "No way, nohow could I ever kill anyone."

"I think he's a dead end," Nick said minutes later when they were in his car and headed toward the swamp.

"I agree." She cast him a quick glance. "I

hope I didn't irritate you by jumping in with some questions."

"Not at all. I want you to feel free to do that with anyone we interview. We're partners, right?" He cast her what appeared to be a genuine, warm smile.

"We are," she agreed. As he focused back on the road, she stared out her side window and again fought the wonderful warmth his smile had evoked inside her.

Nick seemed to have a split personality where she was concerned. One minute he was cool and distant and the next warm and engaged.

When he was warm and engaged, she found herself wanting to be his partner...his best friend and lover. She sat up straighter in her seat as the word...the very thought of *lover* whispered through her head. She hadn't been with anyone since Brent, hadn't even thought about a lover until now.

Nick had been nothing if not professional with her and she had absolutely no reason to believe he was into her in any kind of a sexual way. Still, she swore there was something between them, some snap in the air...a momentary absence of breath and a palpable energy she found very hard to ignore as it enticed and excited her.

She'd be a fool to allow these thoughts any more oxygen in her brain. Nick was here to do a job and not to play cozy with his partner, and it was in Sarah's best interest to remember that.

Chapter Four

Nick tried to keep his attention off Sarah as they drove to Vincent's, where he parked the car. "Do you know where this Gator lives?" he asked once they were out of the car.

"Not specifically, but from what I've been told he's most always around and all we really have to do is go in a little ways and holler for him," she replied.

He looked at her in open amusement. "If we go in there and yell Gator, I hope that isn't a wake-up call to all the alligators in the area."

She laughed, those same musical tones that he found so attractive. He'd tried to keep cool and aloof from her. He was sorry to learn about the tragedy of her parents' deaths. He hadn't wanted to know anything about her personal life. But now he did and despite any notion to the contrary, he found himself wanting to know more about her.

Surely it wouldn't hurt if they became friends as they worked together, he told himself. It was the thought of friends with benefits he didn't want...couldn't entertain.

They walked into the mouth of the marsh with their guns drawn as a precaution. As it had yesterday, his heart beat faster than normal as a wealth of anxiety knotted in his stomach and tightened his chest.

You'll be fine, he told himself. *You're an adult and you have a gun. The swamp can't hurt you.* He said the words over and over again like a mantra. It was his effort to still the irrational fear that pressed so tight against his chest.

They hadn't gone far when they came upon a large dead fallen tree trunk. They stopped there. "Gator Broussard," Sarah yelled in a surprisingly strong voice that sent birds flying from the tops of several nearby trees. They stood still and waited. After several moments had passed, she yelled for him again.

"I'm here, what's the damn fuss all about?" The old man seemed to magically appear from the thicket to their left.

Gator was clad in a pair of jeans held up at his slender waist by a piece of rope. A gray T-shirt stretched across his narrow shoulders. His hair was nearly white and his tanned face was weathered with wrinkles. He also leaned on a cane. But his eyes shone with not only a deep intelligence, but also a sparkling humor.

"Mr. Broussard, I'm Nick Cain." He held out his hand to the old man.

Gator gave it a firm shake. "Well, ain't you the fancy one shaking my hand and all." Gator looked at Sarah. "And look who it is… little Sarah Beauregard all grown up."

"Hi, Gator," Sarah said with a smile.

"Mr. Broussard, we'd like to ask you some questions," Nick said.

"Gator, son. Make it Gator, and what do you want to talk to me about?"

"Is it possible we could go to your house so we can discuss some things with you in private?" Nick asked.

He wanted to go to Gator's place because they were still hunting for the killing grounds. While there was no way he believed a man as old and as thin as Gator had killed those women and transported them into town, they would at least be able to positively exclude his place.

"I suppose I could take you home with me, but I gotta warn you, it ain't company-ready," Gator replied. Without saying another word, he turned and headed up the narrow trail.

Nick gestured for Sarah to go before him,

and so she fell in just behind the old man and Nick brought up the rear. Despite the use of the cane, Gator scampered fairly nimbly through the thicket.

As they went deeper in, pools of dark water lined their way and the trail narrowed. Bugs buzzed around Nick's head and a slight edge of claustrophobia and apprehension tightened all the muscles in his entire body. The tree limbs pressed so tight into the trail and the thick underbrush seemed to be reaching out for him.

Suddenly he was five years old again and he was hopelessly lost in the dark and scary swamp. The waters were filled with huge gators that gnashed their jaws in the anticipation of eating him. The Spanish moss clung to his head and tried to blind and suffocate him. He wanted out. God, he needed to get out.

Thank God at that moment a small shanty appeared and snapped him out of his dark memories. He wasn't a little kid anymore and he had important work to do.

A rickety narrow bridge led up to the front door. Gator raced across it and threw open the door and the two officers followed him inside.

It was a small structure with another single door that Nick assumed was his bathroom. A single cot obviously served as his bed and sofa and a potbellied stove looked dirty with use. There was only one other chair in the room, an old, broken recliner.

"I warned you it wasn't company-ready," Gator said. "Go ahead and have a seat." He gestured them toward the cot and then he sat in the recliner. "I suppose you're here about the murders."

"We are," Nick replied.

"What makes you think I know anything about them?"

"Gator, you know most all of the people who live here in the swamp. You know where they go and what they do. You would know if any of the men here are capable of committing such horrid crimes," Sarah said.

"I told Gravois when he first came around asking questions after the first murder that I didn't think a man from the swamp was the killer and nothing since then has changed my mind. My gut instinct tells me this is the work of somebody from town and my gut instinct rarely steers me wrong." His eyes darkened.

"What?" Nick asked. There seemed to be more that Gator wanted to say. "Gator, is there something else on your mind? Something you want to say?"

Gator frowned. "There is one man here in the swamp…name is James Noman. He lives in a shanty deep in and nobody knows much about him. Word is he's a bit touched in the head and folks steer clear of him."

"Sounds like somebody we should talk to," Nick replied. "Can you tell us how to find his shanty?"

"I don't think I can tell you, but I suppose I could show you," Gator said with a bit of reluctance in his tone.

"Can you show us now?" Sarah asked.

"We would really appreciate it if you could," Nick added.

Gator rose to his feet and she and Nick did the same. Could it be this easy? Was it possible this James Noman was the person they sought?

They left Gator's place and headed down a trail. Once again Gator moved quickly as they navigated over tubers and under branches. More water appeared on either side of them as the trail narrowed.

Nick lost track of time as he focused solely on staying on the trail, which had now nearly disappeared, and the direction that they were going in. The sunlight that had shone through the branches overhead earlier had faded. It was no longer feasible to see through the heavy canopy of leaves.

The air grew much cooler and a cacophony of sound filled his head. Fish jumped and slapped in the waters and strange birdcalls came from the trees.

He had never been this far into the swamp before and there was an air of deep mystery here that had him on edge. This was sheer torture for him. He had to keep reminding himself that he wasn't that lost little kid anymore. He was now an adult...with a gun and a desperate need to solve these murders.

Finally, Gator came to an abrupt stop. He pointed straight ahead where a shanty was almost hidden by the tupelo and cypress trees that surrounded it.

"That's Noman's place." Gator turned to look at them. "And this is as far as I go." Nick could have sworn there was a touch of fear in the old man's eyes.

"Thanks, Gator. We'll take it from here," Nick said with forced confidence.

Gator stepped aside so she and Nick could go ahead of him. "If you get lost on the way out, just holler for me." He quickly turned and headed back the way they had come. Nick took the lead, with his gun held tight in his hand as they slowly approached the small shanty.

From the outside, the place appeared completely abandoned. There was nothing on the porch and one of the side windows was broken out. The bridge that led to the place was narrow and missing several of its old boards.

"Mr. Noman," Nick yelled when they reached the foot of the bridge. They waited and listened for a response. After several seconds had ticked by, Nick hollered again, but there was still no answer.

"He must not be home," Sarah said. Nick thought he heard a touch of trepidation in her voice. He felt more than a little uneasy as well.

They had no idea what they were getting into here. Gator had mentioned that Noman was touched in the head. What exactly did that mean? Dealing with somebody who had mental issues was always concerning and sometimes dangerous.

"Maybe we should go up and knock on his door," Nick said. And maybe they could get a peek in his windows and see what might be inside.

"Okay," Sarah replied.

He tucked his gun back into his holster to navigate the narrow, hazardous bridge. Once he was on the other side, he pulled his gun once again and watched as Sarah slowly came across.

Once she was by his side, he turned and

knocked on the door. "Hello?" he called out. "Is anybody here? Mr. Noman? Are you there?"

There was a thick scent of decay around the small structure that instantly raised the hackles on the back of Nick's neck. It wasn't the smell of vegetation decay, but rather it was the odor of animal or human rot.

"Do you smell that?" Sarah asked softly.

"I do," Nick replied.

He walked up to the door and knocked. All of his muscles tensed. He had no idea what to expect, but the smell alone raised all his red flags.

As a homicide detective, he'd smelled this offensive odor far too many times in the past. So, what was going on around here? What was Noman doing in this isolated shanty?

He knocked once again on the door and still there was no response. "He's either not here or he's not answering." More than anything he wanted to just open up the door, but there were rules about things like that and working with a cop as his partner, he had to abide by the rules. Besides, if this was their killer, he didn't want to do anything that would mess up a prosecution.

Thankfully, at the moment his abject fear

of the swamp was usurped by the desire to get some answers.

"So, what do we do now?" Sarah asked.

"I want to get a peek in the windows," Nick replied. He walked around on the narrow porch and reached the broken window. One glance inside showed him nobody was in the place.

There was a cot half-covered in a raggedy, torn quilt and a potbellied stove. Nick stared in shock at the walls, which were covered in bones. Large bones and smaller ones, Nick was unable to identify what kind of bones they were. Were any of them human?

His gaze caught and held on one corner of the room. Blood. Old blood and fresh blood, it spattered the walls and pooled on the floor.

Was this the killing place they'd been looking for?

SARAH AUDIBLY GASPED as she saw the bones and the blood inside the shanty. Without thinking, she tightly grabbed hold of Nick's forearm. "Is…is it possible this is the place where the women were all killed?"

"Anything is possible at this point," he replied. "I'd like to get inside and get a closer look at those bones and the blood."

She withdrew her hand from his arm, deep

inside registering the warmth of his skin and the play of taut muscle beneath. "What now?" she asked.

"We head back and see if we can get a search warrant for this place." Frustration was rife in his tone. She had a feeling if she wasn't with him, he would have gone on inside. But that would screw up the prosecution who would want a clean, by-the-book investigation.

They each crossed back over the bridge. "Do you know how to go back or do we need to yell for Gator?" she asked. She certainly had no idea how to get them out of here. She'd been too focused on not falling off the narrow trail and into the gator-infested waters.

"I can get us back," Nick replied. "I paid special attention as to where we were going so I could get us back without Gator's help."

"Thank God," Sarah replied.

There was a sudden loud rustle coming out of the brush next to them. Sarah caught the flash of a slender, bare-chested man darting down the trail in front of them.

"James Noman," she yelled, and took off after him. He jumped over a pool of water and plunged into the thicket on the other side. She hesitated only a moment before leaping over the water, grateful to land on soggy marsh. "James, stop. We just want to talk to you."

She desperately wanted to catch him for questioning. She also desperately wanted to prove herself to Nick. Tree limbs tore at her as she ran by them as fast as she could to keep up with him. She was vaguely aware of Nick following close behind her.

Her heart pounded and her breaths came in deep gasps as she struggled to keep up with the man she knew was James Noman. He zigged and zagged through the brush and Sarah remained on is heels.

"James, please," she gasped out. "We just want to talk to you."

Like a gazelle, he leaped over another large pool of water.

This time she didn't hesitate and jumped after him. She didn't make it to the other side and instead plunged into the shoulder-deep water. She instantly tossed her gun to the trail and then gasped and flailed, momentarily shocked by the unexpected plunge.

Her heart exploded in fear as she thought of all the alligators that might be close to her. She tried to calm herself and then struggled to get out.

It wasn't until Nick offered her a helping

hand that she was finally able to get her footing again and get out of the water.

By that time Noman had disappeared. "Damn," she exploded in sheer frustration. She wasn't mad only that they'd lost their suspect, but also by the fact that she now stood before Nick like a drowned rat. So much for impressing him with her prowess.

"We'll try to get him tomorrow," he said. "Let's get you back to the car. I have a towel in my trunk."

"Thanks," she replied, grateful that he took the lead so she could do her walk of utter shame behind him.

She shivered several times from being soaked in swamp water. Damn, why hadn't she judged the jump better? She felt like a total fool in front of the man she had most wanted to impress.

It seemed to take forever for them to finally get back to Nick's car in Vincent's parking lot. He opened his trunk and inside was not only a towel but there were also bottles of water, a box of energy bars and a kit for collecting evidence.

"You look like you're prepared for everything," she said.

"I'd like to tell you I was a Boy Scout in my youth, but the truth is I just like to try to make sure I have what I need to survive should I get stranded somewhere." He handed her the towel.

"Thanks." She ran the fluffy towel over her body, trying to get as dry as possible, and then placed the towel on the passenger seat and got into the car.

He closed the trunk and slid behind the steering wheel. "If you give me directions to your place, I'll take you there so you can change clothes."

"I appreciate it, and I'm really sorry, Nick." She felt so miserable about this. She should have judged the jump before leaping. Now they were having to take time out of their busy day for her stupid mistake.

"Don't beat yourself up about it," he replied. "I appreciate the effort you gave it."

"I'm just glad a gator didn't get me."

"Trust me, I wouldn't have let that happen. I've never lost a partner yet and I don't intend to start with you." He shot her a surprisingly warm smile. "So you're stuck with me."

"I'm surprised you want to be stuck with me," she replied. She released a deep and miserable sigh. "In case you haven't noticed yet, I'm totally inexperienced when it comes to investigations like this. I've been stuck on desk duty and handing out speeding tickets for the last twelve years of my career."

"To be honest, I kind of guessed as much," he said.

"I'll understand if you prefer to ask for another partner. Ryan has certainly indicated he'd like to work with you and Ryan is far more experienced than I am." She half held her breath for his reply.

"Nah, I'm good with you. On a positive note, I think you have really good instincts and besides, this way I can teach you how to conduct a murder investigation the proper way."

She released a dry laugh. "Then that will make me the only person in the department who can investigate properly. Turn left at the next street," she instructed him.

"Got it," he replied.

"All I can smell right now is nasty swamp." She plucked at her wet shirt. "At least I managed to keep my gun out of the water, but I hope your car doesn't smell bad once I get out of it."

He laughed. "That's the last thing I'm worried about."

A shiver raced up her spine. This time it wasn't from her damp clothes but rather because of the deep, delicious sound of his laughter.

"Make a right here," she said. For the second time, she felt like the ice had truly been broken between them. If all it took for him to share a laugh with her was for her to jump in the swamp, then she'd do it every day.

"My house is the fourth one on the left," she said.

He pulled up in her driveway. "Nice place," he observed.

She looked at the house that sported gray paint and black trim. The lawn was neatly trimmed and two wicker chairs sat on her front porch with bright red cushions. "Thanks. Are you waiting for me? My car is at the station."

"Sure, I'll wait," he agreed.

She turned in her seat to look at him. "Please, Nick, come on inside. I don't want you having to sit out here in the car when my sofa is pretty comfortable." She opened the car door, relieved when he opened his as well.

Together they approached the front door. She unlocked it and then gestured him inside. Nick was the first man to be in her house since her breakup with her fiancé. But he wasn't here for a visit, she reminded herself.

He was here because of her own stupidity. God, she felt so dumb.

"Please, make yourself at home and I'll be out as quick as I can," she said, and then headed for her bedroom. Once there she stripped off her wet clothes and started the shower.

Within minutes she stood beneath the warm spray and washed all the swamp off her, chasing the nasty smell away with her fresh-scented soap.

She was still confused about her feelings toward Nick. The more they spent time together, the stronger her physical attraction to him grew. Even when he'd grabbed her hand to pull her out of the water, an electric current of pleasure had raced through her at his touch.

Still, it was thoughts of Nick waiting for her that made her not dawdle. She got out of the shower, dressed in a clean uniform and then took a couple of minutes to blow-dry her hair. She spritzed on her favorite perfume and then left her bathroom.

When she returned to the living room Nick stood in front of her wall of photographs. There were pictures of her with her parents and her with Gravois. She also had photos of herself with two of her girlfriends, girlfriends she'd neglected for the past couple of weeks.

He turned when she came in the room and offered her a smile. "I'm assuming these are your parents," he said, and pointed to a picture that had been taken when she was twelve years old.

"You'd be assuming correctly," she replied. She stepped up next to him. "Are your parents still alive?"

"They are," he replied. "When I'm back home my mother insists I have dinner with them at least once a week."

"That's nice. And what about siblings? Do you have any?"

"I have a sister who is two years older than me and a brother who is two years younger," he replied.

"And are you all close?"

"We are," he replied. "What about you? Any siblings?"

"No, I've got no family." A hunger filled her, the hunger that had been with her for a long time. It was the desire to have somebody in her life in a family kind of way. But at this point in her life, she wasn't really looking for anybody.

She'd thought she had found that with Brent, but that had ended up being nothing but a heartache and now she was reluctant to ever try romance again.

"There are days I'd gladly share my brother with you," Nick said with a touch of humor in his tone. "He teases me unmercifully and is a real pain."

She laughed. "I'd like to see that. Shall we go?"

"Yeah, I just realized it's almost six, which means I'm too late for dinner at Nene's place. I was wondering if you'd like to go to the café for a quick dinner. We can talk about things while we eat."

"Yeah, okay," she replied. She hadn't realized how late it had become and she was definitely surprised by his offer. It was nothing more than a business dinner, she told herself as she followed him back out to the car.

So why did she wish that it was something different? Why did she wish it was a real date?

Chapter Five

Once again Nick found himself fighting off a simmering desire for his partner. It had begun again the moment he had pulled her out of the water. Her wet uniform had clung to her body and shown off all her curves.

It wasn't just that. It had also been how quickly she'd responded to seeing the man on the trail and her bravery in taking the leap that had landed her in the water.

It had also broken his heart more than a little bit for her when he'd heard the haunting loneliness in her voice when she'd spoken of having no family at all. At that moment all he'd wanted to do was draw her into his arms and hold her tight.

Now in the small confines of his car, it was her scent that drove him half-dizzy with the desire to pull her close to him and taste the sweetness of her lips.

Jeez, what in the hell was wrong with him?

He hadn't felt drawn to a woman in the last three years. Why now and for God's sake why her? Somehow, he was definitely going to have to try to keep himself in check.

"Have you eaten at the café before?" she asked.

"No, not yet. Is the food good there?"

"I think it's excellent," she replied. "How is Nene's food?"

"Very good. She'd an amazing cook. Do you cook or do you eat out a lot?" he asked.

"I rarely eat out. I like to cook, although there are nights when I'm too tired and I just throw something in the microwave. What about you?"

"Other than eating with my family one night a week, I cook for myself. My mom made sure all of us kids knew how to cook when we were teenagers."

"Smart woman," she replied.

"She told us it was a life skill that we all needed to know to survive on our own."

By that time, he had pulled into the parking space behind the café. He cut the engine and then the two of them got out of the car.

"Nice evening," he observed as they walked around to the front door of the place. The temperature was pleasant and the skies were clear with the sun slowly drifting down in the sky.

"It's beautiful out," she agreed.

He opened the front door and ushered her in before him. Once inside he looked around with interest. It was the usual setup for a café with booths along the two outer walls and a row of tables down the middle.

The walls were painted yellow, but two of them held what appeared to be really nice hand-painted murals. One was of Main Street and the other was of cypress trees dripping with Spanish moss.

The scents inside were positively wonderful. They were of simmering meats and savory sauces. There was also a sweetness in the air that made him think the desserts here might be terrific.

He was vaguely surprised by how many people were dining on a Thursday night, definitely a testament to how good the food must be. He spied an empty booth near the back and guided her there.

"Is this okay with you?" he asked.

"It's fine with me," she replied, and slid into the seat. He slid in across from her and picked up one of the menus that were propped up between the tall salt and pepper shakers.

It didn't take long for a waitress wearing

the name tag of Heidi to come to wait on them. "Can I start you two off with something to drink?" she asked.

"I'll take a sweet tea," Sarah said.

"Make that two," he added.

"Are we ready to order some food? Or do we need more time?" Heidi asked.

"I'm ready to order. I'll have the bacon burger with fries," Sarah said as she placed the menu back in place.

"And I'll have the shrimp platter," he said.

"Okay, let me get those orders into the kitchen and I'll be back with your drinks."

As she moved away from their booth, he put his menu back in place and then leaned back in the seat. "Let's talk about today," he said. He needed this to be a business dinner, otherwise it would feel too much like a date and the last thing he wanted to do was to date his partner.

"Where do you want to start?" Sarah leaned forward, her beautiful blue eyes filled with that hunger to learn, a look he found incredibly sexy.

"Let's start with Zeke. Even though it's obvious the man has a bad drug issue, that's one reason why I'm reluctant to pull him off the suspect list," he said.

"Who knows what kind of drug-induced

delusions he might suffer and what might he do when in those delusions?"

"Exactly," he replied. He liked that she always seemed to know what was in his mind. "In my gut do I believe he's our guy? No, but I think we need to keep him on our suspect list until we interview him another time."

"I totally agree," she replied.

The conversation paused for a moment as Heidi delivered both their drinks and their food. His shrimp platter included both scampi style and fried shrimp. It also had slaw and garlic bread and it all looked and smelled delicious.

"Now let's talk about the elephant in the room," he continued.

"When you drop me off back at the office, I'll type up the paper requesting the search warrant for Noman's place. Hopefully we'll have it by sometime tomorrow afternoon."

"Good. I can't wait to get in there and check out both the bones and the blood. Have there been any missing women reported in the past?" he asked. If any of those bones belonged to women, then those women had to have come from somewhere.

"Not that I've heard about." She took a big bite of her burger. He appreciated the fact that she could eat while they talked about blood and bones. That was another mark of a good cop.

She chewed and then swallowed. "However, that doesn't mean girls haven't disappeared from the swamp and it just hasn't been reported."

He frowned. "I guess I don't have to ask why it wouldn't be reported."

"I'm sure the people from the swamp have lost all belief in the police department," she replied. "They have to recognize that little to nothing was done to investigate the murders of those young women."

For the next two hours they ate and talked about not only these particular crimes, but also some of the cases he had worked on in the past as a homicide detective.

She was an apt listener, stopping him only to ask questions. It was a new experience for him to talk with somebody who was actually interested in what he was saying. Amy had never wanted to hear about his work.

"I'll share with you one more story and then I'll shut up," he said as he realized he'd monopolized much of the conversation.

"Please, keep sharing," she replied. "I'm enjoying this and I'm learning so much."

"Let's order some dessert and coffee," he replied. Once he got Heidi's attention, he ordered a piece of caramel apple pie and Sarah got a piece of chocolate cream pie. They both got coffee and then he continued with the last story he intended to share with her.

"When I was a rookie cop, I got involved in a foot chase. We were after a guy who had committed the armed robbery of a convenience store. He'd already tossed his gun away so I knew he was unarmed. I really wanted to be the one to catch him, to prove myself worthy to the rest of the more seasoned officers that were with me."

"I know that feeling well," she replied with a rueful smile. God, she had a beautiful smile.

He took a drink of his coffee and then continued. "Anyway, I was running as fast as I could and he eventually darted into a clothing shop that had an open-air doorway. At least I thought it was completely open-air until I ran face-first into a pane of glass."

"Oh no," she gasped, her eyes wide.

He laughed. "Oh yes. I not only shattered the glass but I also broke my nose and my pride."

She laughed, that beautiful sound that reached in and somehow touched his soul. "I'm so sorry, I don't mean to laugh."

He grinned at her. "It's perfectly okay to laugh."

To his surprise she reached across the table and touched the back of his hand, shooting a rivulet of warmth through him. "Thank you so much for sharing that with me."

She pulled her hand back from his and picked up her fork and he immediately missed the warmth of her touch. As they ate their desserts, they talked about their plans for the next day.

"First thing in the morning we'll go back to the swamp and try to make contact with Noman again," he said.

"And after that?" she asked.

"I'd like to talk to Zeke once again and ask him about alibis for the nights of the murders. I'd like to see if we can either exclude him for sure from the suspect pool or keep him on."

"And maybe we need to catch up with Ed Martin's son and see if he has any alibis for the murders," she added.

"Absolutely," he agreed. "I find Ed Martin's reason for being at the crime scenes very sketchy. If he wants to stay up on what's happening in town, a simple phone call to or from Gravois would have sufficed. He didn't need to be at the scenes."

"I completely agree."

By that time, they had finished their desserts and coffee. "I guess we should get out of here," he said with a bit of reluctance. He'd enjoyed the food, but what he'd really enjoyed was the conversation and just looking at her across the table.

He motioned to Heidi for their bill. Sarah insisted she pay her own way and although he would have been perfectly fine to pay for them both, they wound up splitting the tab.

Night had completely fallen and the moon was nearly full in the sky. Now that they were out of the restaurant, he could smell the sweet flowering scent of her again. It tightened the muscles in his stomach, pulling forth a desire he desperately fought against.

She smiled up at him. "I hate to say this, but talking about murder sure gave me a big appetite."

He laughed. "That just means you're a good cop."

Her smile faltered as she held his gaze intently. "I'm not a good cop yet, but I'm definitely determined to become one."

They got into his car and he headed toward the police station where hers was parked. "I'm going to sleep good tonight," she said. "My tummy is so full, it's the end of the day and I'll definitely sleep well."

"That makes two of us," he agreed.

"My car is in the back parking lot," she said as he approached the station.

He pulled around back and her car was one of three in the dark lot. "I'm just going to head inside and get that paperwork done for our search warrant," she said as she unbuckled her seat belt.

"Do you need any help with that?" he asked.

"No, I think I've got it." She got out of the car and he did as well.

"I'll walk you to the door," he said, unsure what motivated him to do so.

"Okay," she agreed. "So, what time do we start in the morning?"

"Why don't we keep it at seven thirty," he said.

They reached the back door and she turned to face him. The moonlight caressed her pretty features. As she smiled up at him all he could think about was kissing her. Her lush lips seemed to call to his and he leaned forward.

It was only when he saw her eyes widen slightly that he snapped back in place, horrified by what he had been about to do. "Good night, partner. I'll see you in the morning." He turned quickly on his heels and walked back to his car.

SARAH WENT THROUGH the back door, her heart beating wildly in her chest. Had he been about to kiss her? She could swear she saw a flicker of desire in his eyes as he'd leaned toward her.

In that brief moment in time, she'd so wanted him to kiss her. She'd wanted to feel his lips against her own. She'd wanted him to pull her against his body and hold her tightly against him.

She headed to their workroom where her computer sat at the desk waiting for her. She had decided that morning to start bringing her computer with her each day, anticipating the time when something like a search warrant would come up. She'd also been keeping notes on it about the investigation.

She logged into her official account and searched to find the appropriate form. Once she found it, she began the process of filling it out.

Thankfully, about a year ago the department had paid to get things streamlined and online for the officers. Normally a search warrant would not be considered by a judge if it was without a senior officer on the application. However, she added Nick's name to the request and hoped Judge Harry Epstein would grant it.

She emailed the form to the judge and then closed down her computer and packed it up to carry home. Hopefully, they would hear something back on the warrant by tomorrow afternoon.

Minutes later as she walked back to her car, she thought about the evening that had just passed. There had been moments when it hadn't felt like a business dinner at all, but rather like a date.

She had loved hearing about his past cases and it had been especially kind of him to share the story of him running into the door and breaking his nose. She knew he'd told it to her in an effort to make her feel better about landing in the swamp waters.

She definitely was developing a mad crush on her partner and she couldn't stop thinking about that single breathless moment when she'd believed he was going to kiss her.

Did he feel it, too? That snap of electricity? That surge of warmth in the room whenever they were together? Had the desire she thought she'd seen in his eyes tonight just been a trick of the moonlight or had it been real? Only time would tell.

She got home, changed into her nightgown and immediately got into bed. She was utterly exhausted and almost instantly she fell asleep.

Her phone woke her, playing the rousing music of a popular song. She fumbled on her nightstand to find it and when she did, she saw that it was Nick calling her.

"What's up?" she asked, noticing that it was just after two. A knot formed in her chest. This could only be bad.

"We've got another one," he said curtly.

"Where?"

"She's in the alley behind Madeline's Hair and Nail Spa."

"I'll be right there," she replied. She hung up the phone and shot into action. She dressed quickly and ran a fast brush through her hair, then grabbed her car keys and headed out.

Damn, she'd hoped there wouldn't be another victim, that she and Nick would be able to capture the killer before a fifth woman was murdered.

The only thing she could hope for at this time was with Nick on the job he would find some clues that had been lacking in all the other murders. They needed something to go on, some clue they could run with.

Night still clung to the skies. At least the moon overhead shot down a silvery light that cut through the darkness.

The streets were deserted until she reached the beauty shop. Parked out front was Nick's car, Gravois's vehicle, another patrol car and several other cars she didn't recognize.

She pulled in next to Nick's car and parked, her heart racing with adrenaline. She walked down the side of the shop and turned into the alley.

Several bright lights had been set up and shone on the body and the surrounding area. She nodded to both Nick and Gravois and then gazed down at the victim. Seeing the women in crime scene photos was much different from seeing one of the victims in person.

Her stomach clenched and she fought against nausea as she saw the poor victim. Even though she wore jeans and a bright yellow blouse, it was obvious she'd been stabbed several times in the stomach, but it was her throat and face that sickened Sarah.

The victim's throat was ripped out and her face was shredded beyond recognition. It was gruesome and horrifying to think that another human being could be responsible for this kind of monstrosity.

"We're just waiting for the coroner," Nick said.

She nodded. They couldn't begin their work until after the coroner arrived and examined the body and the conditions. They all turned at the sound of footsteps approaching. Ed Martin came around the corner.

"Gentlemen... Sarah," he said in greeting.

"I thought you understood it was inappropriate for you to be at a crime scene," Nick said, his anger rife in his tone.

"Gravois called me to let me know another murder had occurred and as a businessman in this town I..."

"I don't give a damn who you are, and what I think is it's damned suspicious of you to show up here," Nick replied.

"Suspicious? Do you really think I have something to do with these murders?" Ed asked incredulously.

"Gentlemen, please stop," Gravois said firmly. "Now isn't the time for any arguments."

"Who called this in?" Sarah asked, hoping to further diffuse the situation.

"Zeke did. Apparently, he and his dopehead friend Dwayne Carter decided to come back here and party, but they found her instead," Gravois said. "I've got Zeke locked up in the back of my car and Dwayne is locked up in the back of Brubaker's car. I'm holding them both for questioning."

"Do we know who she is?" Sarah asked.

"Not yet. Hopefully somebody will come forward to help us with an identification," Gravois replied. "We'll take her fingerprints but if she isn't in the system then that won't help us." Gravois then began to take the crime scene photos.

He had just finished up when the coroner, Dr. Douglas Cartwright, arrived with his assistant, Jimmy Leyton. They all remained silent and let Old Man Cartwright do his work.

Cartwright had been the coroner for as long as Sarah remembered. He had to be in his late seventies or early eighties by now, but she'd never heard of him being interested in retiring.

He immediately took the body's temperature and then bagged her hands. Hopefully she'd fought back and gotten some skin from the attacker beneath her fingernails. They could only get so lucky.

She glanced at Nick, who appeared laser-focused on what was going on. Since this was the first murder scene she'd ever been at, she also watched everything that was being done with apt interest.

She so hoped that with this one they could get a good, solid clue as to who the Honey Island Swamp Monster murderer was. So far, their investigation had been just flying by the seat of their pants. Although James Noman was very high on the suspect list, if the blood and bones in his place turned out to be animal, then they would be back to square one. At least if this woman had to die then Sarah hoped her death yielded the clue that broke the case wide open.

Cartwright finally finished and stood up straight. "Jimmy, go get the gurney," he said to his assistant. "Needless to say, I'm ruling this as a homicide," he said. "Manner of death appears to be knife wounds to the stomach. I'd say she's been dead no longer than two hours. I'll know more after conducting the autopsy."

"Can Officer Beauregard and I be at the autopsy?" Nick asked.

"Of course. However, I don't like to put things off so as soon as you are finished up here, come on to the morgue and we'll immediately do the autopsy," Cartwright replied.

Minutes later the body had been taken away and that was when the real police work began. Ryan Staub was called in by Gravois and when he arrived, he went to interview Zeke and Wayne while the other three of them began processing the scene.

They gathered up anything and everything that had been beneath and around the body. Nick walked between the buildings, hoping to find something on the path the body had been carried in. However, to Sarah's eyes, nothing they collected had anything to do with the murder or murderer. It was mostly just trash.

Almost three hours later they pulled into the morgue's parking lot. The morgue was housed in a small building next to the Black Bayou hospital.

As Sarah got out of her car, a nervous anxiety played in the pit of her stomach. It had been difficult enough to see the Jane Doe dead in person. The autopsy would test her emotional strength in a way she knew it had never been tested before.

Nick joined her at the front of the car. "Are you ready for this?"

"I'm not sure," she replied honestly. "The last time I was here it was to identify the bodies of my parents."

"Oh, Sarah. I'm so sorry," he said. He took a step closer to her and for a brief moment she thought he was going to wrap his arms around her, but he stopped just short of her. "If you want to skip out on this, then I wouldn't have a problem with it."

She smiled up at him. "Thanks, Nick. But I need to do this. I need the experience and I need to hear what her body might tell us."

"Autopsies are pretty brutal. If you need to bow out at any time while it's going on, don't feel bad about it."

She offered him another smile. "I'll keep that in mind."

Together they entered the building where there was a small reception area with a half a dozen chairs.

A woman Sarah didn't recognize greeted them from behind the window. "Dr. Cartwright is waiting for you. Head straight down the hallway and he's in the last room on the right." She buzzed open the door and Nick and Sarah walked through.

The air was much cooler inside. Sarah fought against a shiver, and she didn't know if it was due to the temperature change or for what was to come. She was definitely dreading this.

They passed two doorways and then came to the last one. Nick knocked on the closed door and Cartwright opened the door to allow them inside. This room also had a small reception room with several chairs, a viewing window and an inner door she knew led into the actual autopsy area.

He handed each of them a plastic suit, a hairnet, and booties and gloves to put on. Once they were all suited up, they went into the room where their Jane Doe was on a steel table. She was covered in a sheet with only her ravaged face showing.

"I would estimate our victim to be between twenty and twenty-five years in age. She weighs one hundred and twenty-seven pounds and is five feet three inches tall," he said.

He took off the sheet that had covered the body, which was now naked. "And now we'll begin."

It was a difficult thing to watch, from the first cut to the last. The room filled with the smell of death and several times Sarah was tempted to bow out.

But she didn't. Cartwright talked into a recorder as he worked, memorializing the surgical process. He finished up with the body, finding a total of four stab wounds in the stomach and an injection site in her arm.

"Her last meal consisted of fish," he said.

"Which she probably ate at home or with friends in the swamp," Nick said.

Dr. Cartwright finally moved to her mouth where he discovered a small piece of blue fabric caught in her bottom teeth. He shut off the recorder as he removed the item and placed it on a sterile table next to him.

"Ladies and gentlemen, we have our first solid clue. It appears she tore this from her attacker's clothes," he said.

Nick moved closer to the table and stared

down at the small piece of fabric and then gazed up at her. "We'll have to get it tested, but at first look, it appears that it might have come off a police officer's uniform shirt."

A chill raced up her spine. Was it possible one of the men she worked with, a man who had taken an oath to protect and serve the people of Black Bayou, was the Honey Island Swamp Monster murderer?

Chapter Six

"I bet the tox screen will come back the same as the others with a high dose of Xanax in her system," Nick said.

"I would hazard a guess that you're right. It's obvious that's how the killer is knocking them out and then carrying them out of the swamp and to the place where he kills them," Cartwright replied.

"Still, I'm really pleased about that little piece of material. At least she got a bite out of him," Nick said. "And we got a nice clue to follow up on."

"Too bad she didn't get any of his skin along with the material," Sarah said.

Nick looked at his partner. He'd seen the play of emotions on her face during the autopsy and there had been several times when he'd thought she was on the verge of dipping out. But she'd hung in there and he was proud of her for it. Autopsies were definitely rough.

He knew some seasoned cops who couldn't make it through one.

"Let me put this beneath my microscope and I can give you a pretty good idea of the blend." Cartwright picked up the small piece of material with his tweezers and placed it beneath a high-powered microscope. "It looks to be about thirty to thirty-five percent cotton and sixty or sixty-five percent polyester." He looked up at them. "That's just my educated guess. I'll send it off to the lab to get it confirmed."

"Then I guess we're finished here," Nick said.

"I uploaded her fingerprints so you can run them through the system and see if you get a hit for an identification."

"Thanks, Dr. Cartwright," Nick replied. He and Sarah took off their protective clothing. As they stepped out of the building, the sun was rising in the sky and painted everything with a soft gold glow.

He heard Sarah's audible sigh of relief. "Are you okay?" he asked.

She flashed that brilliant smile of hers. "I'm fine now that it's over."

"Can I ask you a favor?"

"Sure," she replied.

"Do you mind if I take a look at your shirt label?"

"I don't mind at all." She stepped in front of him, so close he could feel her body heat. The sunlight sparked in her hair and that wonderful floral scent surrounded him.

He was going to have to touch the back of her neck. This was part of the investigation, he told himself. Still, he was reluctant to do this because there was a part of him that wanted to see if her skin was as soft as it looked.

"Nick?"

He realized he'd been standing behind her and doing nothing for too long a time. "Yeah, I'm here," he said and then gently pulled her collar out toward him. He couldn't help that his fingers brushed the skin of her neck.

He quickly looked at the label and then tucked it back in. She turned to gaze at him and her cheeks appeared slightly flushed. "What is it? I've never paid any attention to it before."

He stepped back from her. "It's sixty-five percent polyester and thirty-five percent cotton." Was it really possible a cop was responsible for the murders? Nick wasn't sure what to believe at this point. Noman was still at the top of the suspect list, but this little blue piece of material presented a whole new suspect pool to think about.

"How are you feeling?" he asked. It had already been a long night.

"Energized. Once we get an identification, we'll have a lot more people to interview and hopefully soon we'll have that search warrant in hand." She hesitated a moment and then looked at him somberly. "Nick, surely other people besides police officers wear shirts with the same material makeup."

"Sure," he agreed. "Why don't we head back to the office and see where we need to go from here."

She got into her car and he did the same. There was a sense of urgency inside him, but without an identification of the victim, he couldn't interview her parents or friends.

He was definitely intrigued by the tiny blue piece of fabric that had been found in her teeth. He'd told Sarah that the material could have come from anyone, but he thought it was very possible it had come from an officer's shirt.

How dicey was this going to be? And how dicey was it that he felt such an incredible draw toward his partner? He pulled into the parking lot behind the police station and Sarah parked next to him.

Together they got out of their cars and headed to the door. "I suggest we both get a tall cup of coffee to fuel us for what's probably going to be a very long day," he said.

"At least at this time of the morning the coffee might be decent," she replied.

They went inside and directly to the small break room. Inside the room was a vending machine holding sodas and snacks, a round table, and a small table holding a coffee maker. Thankfully the coffee carafe was nearly full and the brew smelled nice and fresh.

They each grabbed one of the foam cups provided and once they had their drinks they headed to their little room. As Sarah took a seat, he set his coffee down and then went to the whiteboard, where he added Jane Doe to their list of victims.

"We need to get Staub's and Brubaker's interviews of Zeke and Dwayne," he said.

"Their reports should be done now and they should be at their desks." She got up. "I'll go get them."

She stepped out of the room and he drew a deep breath and stared at the whiteboard. So much carnage done by a man…no, it was definitely a monster. It would take a monster to do what had been done to those women.

How did he move so well under the radar? How could he commit these murders and not leave anything of himself behind? Most serial killers began to make mistakes, but not this guy. Five dead and the killer didn't appear to be getting sloppy or disorganized. He had to be incredibly intelligent.

But somehow the latest victim had gotten a bite of a shirt. He hoped like hell that little blue piece of material led them to the killer.

"Sorry it took so long," Sarah said as she came back through the door a few minutes later. "Ryan was still typing up his notes, but I've got them both now."

She laid the papers on the table and he sat to go over them. She moved her chair closer to him so she could review them with him.

The interview was much like the one they had conducted with Zeke, and Dwayne's mirrored Zeke's. The two had just been hanging around and had accidentally stumbled on the body.

Nick looked at Sarah in frustration. "I just find it a huge coincidence that these two men have somehow bumbled their way into being around two of the bodies."

"Do you think maybe our killer is two people?" she asked.

Nick considered the question thoughtfully.

"No, I believe we're looking for one man. And to be honest, I can't imagine Zeke and Dwayne carrying out these kinds of murders while drugged up or sober. I just don't think they're smart or organized enough."

"I just wonder what they might have seen or heard while they were out on the streets, something that they haven't told us, something they don't even know is important," she replied.

"Who knows," he replied. "All I know for sure is our killer is definitely organized and smart. He's managed to commit these murders without leaving anything behind...no foot or fingerprints...nothing."

"But now we have a little piece of material," she said with obvious hope in her tone.

"She must have fought hard for her life, and now we need to fight just as hard to find this killer for her."

Sarah was silent for several minutes and then released a deep sigh. She looked toward the room's closed door and then leaned closer to him, so close he could see tiny shards of silver in the depths of her bright blue eyes.

"I keep wondering, who would make those girls feel safe enough to walk out of the swamp with him? And who would have the knowledge to pull off a crime like this and leave absolutely no forensic evidence behind?" Her voice was just a mere whisper.

"A cop," he replied, his voice also a whisper.

"Bingo." She sat back in her chair and her eyes grew dark. "Although I find it very hard to believe that a man I've worked with for years, a man I might have been friends with for years, could be our monster."

"At this point, all we can do is follow the evidence," he replied.

A knock sounded on the door and then it opened. It was Ryan. "Hey, we got a hit on her fingerprints," he said. "Her name is Kristen Ladouix. She was arrested twice for having drug paraphernalia on a public street. I pulled her rap sheet and all the information available on her and printed it off for you." He handed Nick the sheets of paper.

"Thanks, man," Nick replied. Ryan left the room and Nick got up to change the Jane Doe on the whiteboard to Kristen Ladouix.

He returned to his chair and looked at what Ryan had brought him. "She was twenty-four years old and it looks like her parents live here in town. Grab your coffee and let's go."

They stepped back outside where the sun was bright and warm. "Your car or mine?" she asked.

"Mine," he replied.

They took off and headed toward the address given for Kristen's parents. For the next four hours they interviewed not only Kristen's parents but also several of her friends.

They learned that Kristen drifted from house to house in the swamp. She had no boyfriend and she was battling her drug addiction, which meant both Zeke and Dwayne probably knew her.

It was just after five o'clock when they finally called it quits for the day. Given the fact that their day had started at two in the morning, Nick was exhausted and he knew Sarah was, too.

"We'll regroup in the morning," he said as she closed down her computer. "Same place...same time."

"I'll be here," she replied. She smiled at him but her smile wasn't quite as big as usual.

"It's been a long day," he said as they walked out together. He was impressed that she hadn't complained once throughout the day.

"It's been a hell of a long day," she replied. "But at least we're making progress. I'm just sorry we didn't hear anything on our search warrant. I hope Judge Epstein isn't out of town."

"Hopefully we'll hear something on it tomorrow." He walked with her to her car door.

Why was it that every time he told her goodbye, he fought the need to pull her into his arms and kiss her? And why was it she looked at him as if she wanted his kiss? Or was he only imagining that?

There was an awkward silence between them for several moments. "I'll just see you in the morning," she finally said, and quickly slid into her car.

He watched as she drove away and then he got into his car. God, he was exhausted, but that didn't explain his growing feelings for Sarah.

He liked her. He liked her a lot. She was bright and had a sharp sense of humor that matched his own. Even though they were working together, he enjoyed his time spent with her. When they were just resting for a moment their conversations about other things came easily.

Still, he was afraid to make any kind of a move on her because if it all went wrong it could potentially make their working relationship very difficult, and that's the last thing he wanted to happen.

He was so tired he decided to skip dinner and just head straight up to bed. Even then it took him a while to fall asleep as his brain churned with visions of the murder victims, the interviews they had conducted that day and the possibility that the little piece of blue fabric had come from a police officer's uniform.

He must have finally drifted off to sleep, for he awakened suddenly with fight-or-flight adrenaline flooding through his veins. He bolted upright, grabbed his gun from his nightstand and then quickly turned on the lamp.

It illuminated the room in a soft glow. Nothing. There was nobody. There was absolutely nothing in the room to warrant his explosive reaction. He drew in a couple of deep breaths and slowly relaxed. It must have been a dream that had jerked him out of his sleep.

He placed his gun back on his nightstand, turned off the lamp and settled back in. Then he heard it…a strange rattling noise coming from under his bed. In fact, there was more than one rattling sound.

What the hell?

He turned the lamp on once again and then grabbed his phone and turned on the flashlight feature. He bent over and looked beneath his bed. He froze as his blood ran cold.

Snakes...rattlesnakes. They coiled and churned together in a mass of deadliness.

SARAH'S PHONE AWAKENED HER. It was just after two in the morning and as she grabbed the phone, she stifled a groan. Surely there couldn't be another body already.

The caller ID read Brubaker. She frowned. Why would Ian be calling her at this time of the night? "Ian?" she answered.

"Hey, Sarah, I thought you might want to know that I just took a call from your partner. Apparently, he's trapped in his room at Irene's because there's a bunch of rattlesnakes under his bed."

"What?" She bolted upright. Rattlesnakes under his bed? Icy chills rushed through her body. Was she having some sort of a nightmare? How could this even be real?

"Uh... Sarah, are you there?"

"Yeah, thanks, Ian," she replied.

She disconnected quickly and dressed as fast as she could in a pair of jeans and a T-shirt that had a Black Bayou Police Department logo on the front. She buckled on her holster, grabbed her gun and then flew out of her house.

Rattlesnakes under his bed? How on earth had something like that even happened? Had he been bitten? God, if he didn't get the anti-venin in time, he could potentially die. What paramedic would be willing to get him out of a room full of poisonous snakes?

Her head spun with all kinds of bad scenarios as fear tightened her chest and made it difficult to breathe. The back of her throat closed off after she released a gasp of fear.

She couldn't lose Nick. The whole town needed him. She needed him. Oh God, who could have done such a heinous thing as to put snakes in his room? How had something like that even been accomplished?

The streets were dark until she turned down the street where Irene Tompkin's house was located. There she saw the swirling red and blue lights of Gravois's vehicle and another patrol car. She pulled up along the curb, as Nick's car and another one was in the driveway.

She jumped out of her car and ran toward the front door, her heart banging an anxious rhythm in her chest. The first person she saw in the entryway was Nick.

He was clad only in a pair of black boxers. Seeing him alive and seemingly okay caused a burst of deep emotion to explode inside her. She ran to him and leaped into his arms, sobs of relief coursing through her.

"Sarah, it's okay," he said softly. "I'm all right."

She looked up at him. "Oh, Nick, I was so scared for you."

She barely got the words out of her mouth when his lips suddenly took hers. It was a fiery kiss that instantly sliced through her fear with steaming desire.

It was as quick as it was hot. He instantly drew back from her. "I'm sorry, Sarah… that…that shouldn't have happened."

"I… I've wanted it to happen," she replied.

At that moment heavy footsteps came down the staircase. Gravois came into view as he walked down to where they stood. He was followed by Colby Shanks. Gravois looked both tired and angry. "Gator bagged five so far and he's got a couple more left to get."

"How did this even happen? H-how on earth did they get in Nick's room?" Sarah asked. This was only one of the many questions she had among others. Gravois looked pointedly at Nick.

She glanced at Nick and tried to focus on what he might say instead of how very hot he looked clad just in his underwear. His body was amazing. His shoulders were so broad and his hips were slim. His arms were well-muscled, as were his long legs. She hadn't even had the time to process the very quick, very good kiss they had just shared.

"I made a very big mistake when I moved into the room," Nick said and a muscle ticked in his jaw. "I didn't check to see if the back door was locked or not. It was a stupid mistake that could have been a deadly error."

He raked a hand through his dark hair. "I didn't think that old fire escape would actually hold anyone, but it must because somebody must have sneaked up those stairs while I was sleeping and put those snakes in my room." His eyes were darker than she'd ever seen them. "Thank God I heard their rattles before I stepped a foot out of bed."

"As soon as I got the call, I sent Officer Lynons to the swamp to get hold of Gator, who is up there now getting all the snakes into a bag," Gravois said. Officer Judd Lynons was a thirty-five-year-old man who had spent the first ten years or so of his life in the swamp.

"Once Gator has all of them wrangled, we'll go in and fingerprint the door and the fire escape. Hopefully we can lift a couple of prints that will give us the identity of who is responsible for this," Gravois said.

"This was attempted murder," Sarah said, once again fighting a chill that tried to race up her spine.

"That's what it appears to be and we'll investigate it as such," Gravois replied. "It was definitely a devious way to try to hurt Nick."

"Where is Nene?" Sarah asked, suddenly thinking about the older woman. She must have been terrified to wake up to the news that there were rattlesnakes in her home.

"She's in the kitchen with Ralph, her other boarder," Nick explained.

"Is she okay?"

"She's surprisingly fine," Nick replied. "She seems to be taking it all very well."

"She's a strong woman," Gravois said.

Gator came down the stairs with Judd following behind him. Gator carried over his shoulder a large burlap bag that writhed with movement. He also had a pair of jeans and a T-shirt which he tossed to Nick. "Thought you might need these," he said.

"Thanks," Nick replied. "So, what was the grand total?" He gestured to the bag.

"Eight big ones," Gator replied. "I'd say somebody doesn't like you too much, Mr. Nick."

"Yeah, I got the message loud and clear," Nick replied. "If you all will excuse me for just a minute, I'll just get dressed."

He walked over to a doorway that she assumed led to a guest bathroom and closed the door behind him. It was a shame for him to cover up his hunky body. And that kiss, it had momentarily taken her breath away. She was just disappointed it hadn't lasted longer. She had a feeling they would definitely need to talk about it later.

"We checked out the entire upstairs, but the snakes were confined to Nick's room," Judd said.

"If Mr. Judd would take me back home now, I'll release these snakes back into the wild," Gator said.

Nick came back into the room, now clad in the jeans and a gray T-shirt. Gravois said, "Judd, go ahead and take Gator home. Shanks and I will go back up there and start processing the scene. Nick, as the victim in all this, you realize you can't be part of the investigation. This is going to take us a while."

"Nick, you want to come to my place to hang out until this is all squared away?" Sarah asked, hoping her invitation sounded casual.

"That's a good idea, Nick. We're still going to be a couple of hours here," Gravois said.

Nick looked at Sarah. "Are you sure you don't mind? You could just go home now and go back to bed."

"I'm far too wired up to go back to sleep

and no, I don't mind at all, otherwise I wouldn't have offered," she replied.

Nick frowned. "My car keys are upstairs."

"That's okay. I'll drive you," Sarah replied. She turned to Gravois. "Is there anything else you need from him?"

"Not at this moment, but I'll need to get an official statement from you, Nick," Gravois replied. "But that's something we can get to later. You're free to go now. I'll just check in with both of you sometime tomorrow."

Nick and Sarah left the house. "What in the hell, Nick," she said once they were in her car.

"Imagine my surprise when I heard the rattling beneath the bed and then saw those snakes," he replied.

"I can't imagine any of it. Just thinking about it sends shivers up and down my spine," she said. "I can't imagine who would do something so vile, so cunning as that." Despite the fact that it was the middle of the night, she still smelled the faint scent of his cologne wafting from him.

"My first question to you would be who have you fought with or had a bad time with in town? Who might hold a grudge against you? But I know you haven't had much of a chance to interact with anyone other than in the investigation," she said.

"You've got that right," he replied. "The only thing I can think of off the top of my head is that we've now somehow officially threatened somebody with our investigation."

She pulled into her driveway and parked and then they both got out of the car. They were silent as she unlocked the door and they went inside. "How about a drink?" she asked. "I've got whiskey and rum. I can't think of a better reason to have one than snakes under your bed."

He released a small, tight laugh. "You're right, and I'd love a whiskey and cola." He sank down on the sofa.

"Coming right up." She went into the kitchen and made the drink for him and then one for herself. She carried them both into the living room, set them on the coffee table and then she collapsed onto the sofa next to him.

"So, what do you think has threatened who?" she asked. She definitely wanted to discuss this, but at some point before she took him home, she intended to talk about the explosive kiss they had shared for far too brief a time.

"Really the only thing I can think of is that little piece of blue material threatened somebody."

"But who would know about that except

for us?" She watched as he took a drink before replying.

"Gravois would have known," he replied.

"Surely you don't believe he's our monster," she replied in protest. "There's no way I believe he has anything to do with those murders. I know Gravois and there's absolutely no way."

"But he probably told somebody in the department about the evidence we got and I would guess by noon today almost all of the officers in the department knew about it."

It was her turn to take a big gulp of her drink. "Then you really believe one of the officers is our main suspect." Even the warm burn of the whiskey couldn't take away the chill of thinking that one of her workmates was the monster they sought.

"At this point in time I believe it's more possible than not. Got any idea who might like to wrangle snakes in their spare time?"

"I wouldn't have a clue," she replied. "Although Judd Lynons has a little experience in the swamp, I think it has to be somebody who is well acquainted with it." She took another drink and then placed her hand on Nick's knee.

"Oh, Nick, when I think of what might have happened if you'd been unaware and had stepped out of your bed for anything, it makes me sick to my stomach. You could have been bitten dozens of times. You could have died or at the very least become very, very sick."

His hand covered hers. "Trust me, I'm well aware of that."

"How did you manage to get off the bed with the snakes still in the room?" She tried to fight against the delicious warmth that flooded through her at his touch.

A dry laugh escaped him. "Very carefully. Actually, Gator distracted the creatures under my bed while I made my escape into the hallway. By the way, how did you even know about all this?"

"Ian called me after getting the call from you," she explained. "He thought I might want to know what was happening to my partner."

As they continued to discuss the night's events and the potential suspect pool, they imbibed in another drink and she found herself seated closer to him on the sofa.

She wasn't sure who leaned in first, but suddenly his lips were on hers in a tender kiss that deepened as he dipped his tongue in to taste hers.

The kiss grew less tender and more hungry. His arms pulled her tighter against him.

She wrapped hers around his neck, wanting to get closer...closer still to him. She felt as if she'd wanted his kiss for months...for years and now she couldn't get enough of him.

Their tongues battled together and the kiss continued until she was utterly breathless. His lips left hers and instead trailed nipping kisses down the length of her throat.

His hands moved to cup her breasts and she moaned with pleasure. However, her moan seemed to snap whatever had gripped him. He pulled his hands away from her and then he stopped kissing her.

He stared at her with dark eyes that still held a hunger that fired through her blood. "Sarah, I'm so sorry." He swiped a hand through his hair and released a deep sigh. "I... I can't seem to help myself around you."

"Please don't apologize," she replied, her heart still thundering an accelerated beat in her chest.

"It's obvious I have a very strong physical attraction to you..."

"As I have for you," she interjected.

"But, Sarah, we can't do this. We need to maintain a professional relationship."

"Why can't we have both?" She leaned closer to him. "I'm not looking for forever, Nick. I'm aware that once we solve this crime you'll go back to New Orleans. I just want you, Nick, and it won't change the way we work together."

"Sarah, you're killing me here," he whispered softly.

She got to her feet, her heart still beating a chaotic rhythm as warmth suffused her body. "Instead of me taking you home, why don't you let me take you to my bedroom."

She had never been so forward in her entire life, but she had never felt this kind of desire for a man before. It was raw and rich and surely if they made love just once it would get it out of their systems. She held her hand out to him.

Chapter Seven

Nick felt as if he'd been drugged by his desire for her. At some place in the very back of his mind, he knew this was all a bad idea, but kissing Sarah had flooded his veins with the desire for more, for so very much more. Her hand beckoned him to have more and he couldn't deny his own hunger for her.

He slid his hand over hers and stood and allowed her to lead him down the hallway. He followed her past a bedroom that appeared to be a guest room and on the other side was an office. She turned to the left and into her bedroom.

The room smelled of her, the evocative scent that further dizzied his head. The king-size bed was rumpled, with a spread in bright pink and white yanked back to expose pale pink sheets. A silver lamp created a pool of soft light.

It was obvious she had jumped out of bed

and run when she'd heard about the snakes in his room. He was sorry she'd been so frightened for him, but right now all he could think about was how much he wanted her.

He immediately drew her back into his arms and captured her lush lips once again with his. She tasted of a little bit of whiskey and a whole lot of hot passion.

He pulled her closer and she molded her small body to his. He loved how she fit so neatly against him...like their bodies had specifically been made for each other.

The kiss continued until they were both breathless. She finally stepped back from him and swept her T-shirt over her head. She wore a plain white bra and he'd never seen anything that looked sexier. Until she took off the bra.

Her breasts were fairly small and absolute perfection. Her nipples were erect and he wanted nothing more than to taste them. His knees weakened and threatened to buckle with the sweet, hot desire that shot through him.

"Are you sure about this, Sarah?" he asked, wanting to give her an out if she needed one. "I want you to be very sure about this."

"I'm completely sure. I want you, Nick,"

she replied, her voice husky. "I... I feel like I've wanted you for a very long time."

He yanked his shirt over his head, all caution thrown to the wind. They were two intelligent adults. Surely they could enjoy this night together without letting it interfere with their day-to-day working relationship.

This thought erased the last of his worries and instead unleashed the desire he'd had for Sarah since the first day she'd smiled at him.

They finished undressing until she was just in her panties and he was in his boxers. Together they got into the bed and he pulled her back into his arms.

Her bare breasts against his chest felt warm and right as his mouth plied hers with all the fire that burned inside him. She answered him with a fire of her own as her tongue brushed against his and her hands clutched at his back.

As he began to trail kisses down her throat, he slowly rolled her over on her back. His mouth continued down until he captured one of her nipples.

He licked and sucked, loving the sound of her sweet moans. He licked at the first one and then the other. His blood surged inside him and he was fully aroused.

However, he wasn't ready to take her yet.

He wanted to pleasure her as much as possible before that happened. His hand slid from her breast down the flat of her stomach and then back and forth across the top of her panties. She arched her hips and moaned in obvious frustration.

Then he slid his fingers over the top of her panties to the place where she wanted him most. She gasped and moved her hips against him and then stopped and wiggled her panties down to her feet. She kicked them off and then he caressed her again.

This time he felt her damp warmth and the rising tension inside her. He teased her at first, dancing his fingers against her in a light flutter, and then he moved his fingers faster and faster. He felt her release as she shuddered against him and cried out his name. Her climax shot his desire for her even higher.

He kicked his boxers off, his need for her now all-consuming. But before he could take her, her hand encircled him. "Ah, Sarah," he groaned as her hand slid up and down the turgid length of him.

He allowed it for only a moment or two and then pushed her hand away and moved between her legs. He hovered above her for only a moment and then moaned with sheer pleasure as he entered her. She wrapped her legs around his back, pulling him deeper inside her.

He locked gazes with her as he began to pump his hips. Her eyes shone with a wild desire. Slowly at first, he slid in and out of her. Her eyes closed as she hissed a soft "yes" and her hands clung to either side of his hips.

His pace increased as the pressure inside him built. Faster and faster, he moved. She had another orgasm and at the same time he climaxed as well.

He finally rolled over to the side of her, his breaths coming in deep gasps that mirrored hers. They remained that way for several long minutes, until their breathing had returned to some semblance of normal.

She placed her hand on his chest and rose up a bit and smiled at him. "That was way better than I'd imagined."

He grinned. "Have you been imagining this for a long time?"

"Only since the very first day you walked into the office," she replied.

"I started imagining this the first time you smiled at me," he confessed. "But you realize this wasn't the right thing for us to do."

"How could something that felt so right be

so wrong?" she replied. "Nick, this doesn't have to interfere at all with our working together. We are two rational adults and we can handle this, right?"

Her blue eyes were so appealing and she was so earnest. "I hope so," he finally replied.

"Now, since it's so late, why don't you just spend the rest of your night here."

It felt ridiculous for him to insist she take him home. It was just after four in the morning and neither of them would be any good unless they got some sleep.

"Okay. Why don't we sleep until about noon and then head into the office."

"Sounds good to me. I'll be right back," she replied as she got out of the bed. "Feel free to use the guest bathroom in the hallway before we go to sleep."

As she disappeared into her bathroom and closed the door, he got up and grabbed his boxers from the floor. He went into the bathroom across the hall, cleaned up and put his boxers back on.

He stared at his reflection in the mirror above the sink. Damn, everything had happened so fast there hadn't been a single thought about birth control. It had been over three years since he'd last had sex. Was that what had made making love to Sarah so amazing? Because it had been utterly amazing.

He sluiced cold water over his face, suddenly exhausted. There was a lot to process... snakes in his room and the possibility that a cop was their killer, but he couldn't think about all that tonight. He definitely couldn't think about the fact that he'd just made love to his partner.

After some sleep he would better be able to handle all the new developments and emotions. He left the bathroom and returned to the bedroom where she was back in the bed and clad in a bright pink spaghetti-strap nightgown. She looked positively charming with the pink of the gown and her hair tousled in disarray.

He slid into the bed and she immediately moved to his side, obviously wanting to cuddle as they fell asleep. He'd almost forgotten that he'd once been a snuggler, too, so he had no problem with her filling his arms.

"Good night, Nick," she said softly, her voice already drowsy with impending sleep.

"Night, Sarah," he replied. The lamp on the nightstand was still on, but it didn't deter either of them from finding sleep.

Nick awakened first. The sun shone bright

through the blinds at the bedroom windows, letting him know it was probably time for them both to wake up.

However, he was reluctant to move out of the bed. His body was spooned around hers and she fit neatly against him. She felt small and fragile and he realized even though he hadn't known her for very long, he had developed real, deep feelings for her, feelings that went far beyond their partnership in crime.

But their relationship couldn't go anywhere. He had nothing to offer her for any kind of future. His ex-wife had told him he was a terrible husband, and so he would never try to be a husband again. Why make another woman miserable?

The fact that he was even thinking these thoughts after only one night with Sarah disturbed him. It was definitely time to get up and get to work.

He rolled away from her and she immediately woke. She stretched like a kitten waking up from a nap and offered him a groggy smile. "Good morning...or is it afternoon?"

"It's eleven thirty," he replied as he pulled his T-shirt over his head and then reached for his jeans. At the same time, she slid out of the bed.

"Give me about twenty minutes and I'll be

ready to go." She walked over to her closet and grabbed a uniform and then headed to the bathroom.

"I'll be in the living room," he replied. He left her bedroom and sank down on the sofa to wait for her. His head whirled with myriad thoughts that would take time to sort out.

True to her word, about twenty minutes later she walked into the living room, looking and smelling fresh from her shower.

"When we get to my place you can just drop me off and I'll meet you at the station within a half an hour or so," he said as they got in her car.

"Aren't you afraid to go back into that room?" she asked.

"Nah, I have faith that Gator got all the snakes out. Now all we have to do is try to figure out is what snake put them all in my room," he replied darkly.

SARAH SAT IN the small room in the station and stared at the whiteboard. She should be thinking about all the criminal activity that had taken place recently, but all she could think about at the moment was the night she'd shared with Nick.

Making love with him had been magical. He'd been both tender and masterful, taking her to heights of pleasure she'd never known before.

Almost as magical had been falling asleep in his arms. She'd felt so safe in his embrace as she'd drifted off to sleep. His arms had felt big and strong as they'd enfolded her and his familiar scent had enveloped her.

She knew she shouldn't be developing any real feelings for him, but she couldn't rein in her heart. The truth was she was more than half crazy about him.

She admired his professionalism. He challenged her to think deeper, to analyze everything. More than that, he made her feel like a breathless teenager when she was around him. She didn't remember feeling this way about her ex-fiancé and at the time she'd believed she had loved him with all her heart. But things felt different with Nick.

And who had tried to kill him last night? It had been a particularly cunning way to try to commit murder. One step off his bed and he could have been bitten dozens of times.

Again, chills raced up and down her spine at the very thought. Thank God he'd heard the rattles before he'd made a move. Who could have gotten those snakes from the swamp, carried them up that old fire escape and then released them into Nick's room?

She jerked around as the door flew open. She stifled a groan as Ryan walked in. "Good morning, Short-Stuff," he said as he threw himself into the chair next to her.

"What do you want, Ryan?" she asked, unable to keep her irritation out of her voice.

He gave her a hurt expression. "Gee, I never get a chance to talk to you anymore. You and Mr. Hot Stuff are always together."

"We're working," she replied pointedly.

"I think you're doing more than that together. I see the way you look at him. You've got the hots for him."

"Don't be ridiculous. I look at him like he's my partner and my friend." The last thing she would want was for her and Nick to become the subject of office gossip. The last thing she wanted was for anything to undermine her professionalism to her coworkers. Nobody had to know what was going on between her and Nick. It was their private, personal business.

"What have you two come up with so far? You have a suspect in mind?"

"We don't have anyone in particular, but we're definitely narrowing it down," she said, careful to not give anything away.

"I heard you got a nice piece of evidence from the last victim," he replied.

"I guess news travels fast around here," she replied.

"But it's a big deal," he said. "We got nothing from all the other victims. At least you now have something to work with," he said.

"Yeah, we'll just have to see where the evidence takes us," she replied.

Before she could say anything else, the door opened and Nick walked in. Ryan immediately jumped up out of the chair and smiled at Nick. "Hey, man, I was just visiting a little bit with Sarah."

"No problem," Nick replied.

"I just haven't had a chance to talk to her lately. But I'll just get out of here now and let you two do your thing."

He didn't wait for Nick to say anything, as he quickly left the room. Nick sat in the chair opposite her and grinned with amusement. "Anything important come up in your conversation with him?"

She smiled. "There's never anything important in my conversations with him, although he did ask about where we were at in the investigation. I didn't tell him anything other than we were narrowing down on suspects."

As usual, Nick smelled fresh and clean and of the spicy cologne she found so attractive. He was clad in navy slacks and a light blue shirt and as always, her heart beat a little faster at the mere sight of him.

"Uh…before we get down to work, I think we need to talk for a minute about last night."

Her heart seemed to stop beating as she stared at him. "Please don't take it back. Nick, please don't tell me you regret it," she replied softly.

He smiled, that soft smile of his that warmed her heart like a fiery furnace. "How could I take back something that was so wonderful?"

She continued to breathe again. "It was wonderful. So what do we need to talk about?"

"I wanted you to know that it has been years since I've been with anyone, but things happened so fast last night I didn't think about birth control."

"It's also been years for me," she admitted. "And I'm on the pill, so we're safe." It was a slightly awkward conversation and she felt the faint blush that warned her cheeks. She supposed these kinds of conversations happened a lot in the dating world today, although she had to remind herself that they were definitely not dating.

All they'd shared was a very hot night together, one that she'd be eager to repeat again and again. However, the ball was in his court on that issue.

"So, let's talk about last night and what happened in my room," he said. "Let's talk about the fact that I was a damned fool not to check to make sure the back door in my room wasn't locked." He grimaced. "I only looked at it once on the day that I moved in and I guess in my mind once I saw the terrible condition of the fire escape, I dismissed the idea of anyone coming in that way. It was a very stupid mistake on my part."

"Don't beat yourself up, Nick. Who would have guessed somebody would use those stairs to dump nearly a dozen snakes in your room?" she replied.

"I spoke to Gravois on my way in. They didn't get any prints off the door or the railing," he said. "I didn't think they would. Whoever did this was smart...smart enough not to leave any prints behind."

A tight pressure built up in her chest. "Do you think it was our killer?"

"I believe it was definitely somebody who wanted to take me out of the investigation," he replied, his eyes the color of stormy skies. "So yeah, I think it was our killer."

"Why didn't he just burst in and try to kill you?"

"Probably he didn't because he knew I'd have a gun within my reach," he replied.

She opened up her computer and turned it on. "If we believe a cop is behind this, then maybe I should pull up the schedules for this week, especially for the night of this last murder. At least it will show us who was on duty both that night and last night and we can eliminate them from our suspect pool," she said.

"It's a good place to start," he agreed.

"Wait...there's a notification that I have a message waiting." She clicked on the message and then looked up at him in excitement. "We just got our search warrant for James Noman's place."

"There's a lot of blood in that shanty, and I imagine living in the swamp he would be quite adept at snake-handling, so let's go."

She printed the search warrant off using the printer in the little office area down the hall and then together they took off in Nick's car.

She didn't know how the fabric caught in Jane Doe's teeth might relate to James Noman, but Nick was definitely right about the blood in his shanty and the fact that the man probably knew all about snakes.

Even though solving these murders would mean the end of Nick's time here, more than anything she wanted this vicious killer off the streets and behind bars.

ADRENALINE PUMPED THROUGH Nick as he parked in Vincent's lot. At the moment James Noman was as much a suspect as anyone. He would have access to the women who lived in the swamp, although he had no idea if the man had a vehicle or not to transport the bodies into town.

However, James could probably move like a shadow on the streets, getting in and out of the dump of the women without being seen by anyone, and there was no question in Nick's mind that the man was capable of catching snakes.

In the back of his mind, Nick still held the possibility of the killer being a cop, but right now he had Noman in his sights and he couldn't wait to explore that shanty in greater detail.

He had to stay focused on solving this crime as soon as possible. He needed to get away from Sarah as quickly as possible, before things between them got too deep. He'd already developed feelings for her he'd never expected to happen. The last thing he wanted to do was hurt her in any way.

As always, as they entered the swamp, his heart beat faster and he fought against the dark memories of his childhood trauma that sometimes haunted his dreams in the form of nightmares.

He thought it would get easier, but each time he had to enter the marshlands, his anxiety went through the ceiling. His throat threatened to close off and his mouth became unusually dry. The last thing he wanted was for Sarah to see his anxiousness. He didn't want her to realize that the big, bad homicide cop was nothing more than a ball of nervous angst.

Even now he was acutely aware of her as they moved through the swamp. Despite the pungent odors surrounding him, he could still smell the scent of her perfume. He imagined he could feel her body heat even though she trailed behind him by several feet.

He clutched his evidence kit harder in an attempt to stay focused on the matter at hand. He intended to take samples of the blood and take photos of all the bones on the walls. He was hoping Dr. Cartwright would be able to give them some quick answers without him having to send it all to a lab where it would take weeks or even months to get results back.

If the blood came back as human, then a lot more would have to be done to process what all was there and he would probably need to call in more officers to help.

As the trail narrowed, he turned around to face his partner. "Are you okay?" She nodded in response.

He turned back around and continued walking, trying to make as little noise was possible as they got closer to Noman's shanty. He'd definitely like to find the man at home and be able to question him.

They finally reached the bridge that led to Noman's shanty. He paused at the foot of it and looked all around. Like last time they'd been here, the place appeared deserted from the outside.

His heart raced fast in his chest. They had no idea if Noman had a gun or not. There was no way to even know if he was inside the structure.

"Mr. Noman," he yelled, and waited for a reply. When there was none, he shouted one more time and then carefully maneuvered over the rickety bridge. Once he was on the other side, he drew his gun and watched as Sarah came across.

When they were together on the porch, he immediately went to the broken window and looked inside. There was nobody there. He holstered his gun and went to the front door. It easily opened and the two of them stepped inside.

The stench inside was horrendous and the place looked just like it had before. He glanced at the old quilt on the cot. It was multicolored and had shades of blue in it. Was that where the blue fabric that had been in Jane Doe's mouth had come from? Perhaps he had wrapped the victim up in the quilt before he'd killed her or as he'd carried her out of the swamp.

"Why don't you take the photos of the bones and I'll get busy taking some blood samples," he said.

"Sounds like a plan," she agreed. "The sooner we get out of here the better as far as I'm concerned. This place definitely creeps me out."

It creeped him out as well. As she began snapping photos, he got busy scraping off blood samples from various places in the large pool of dried blood and storing them in his evidence kit.

They were just about finished when the door flew open and James Noman came inside. "Who are you people and why are you in my home?" he asked, with anger flaring his nostrils and a definite edge in his deep tone.

Nick slowly rose from where he'd been crouched down and Sarah inched closer to his side. James Noman was rail thin with dark hair that spilled down past his shoulders. He wore only a pair of nasty-looking gray shorts and his eyes were dark and wild.

He also brought with him a sick energy that instantly put Nick on edge. "Mr. Noman, I'm Nick Cain and this is my partner, Sarah Beauregard," he replied in a soft, hopefully calming voice. "We're here with a search warrant to take some samples of this blood. We're almost finished here and then we'll leave." Nick attempted to hand him the search warrant, but James waved it away.

"Mr. Noman, can I ask you a few questions?" Sarah asked, and gave him her brightest smile.

He stared at her for a long moment. "You're real pretty. I never get any pretty girls here."

"Thank you, so can I ask you a few things?" Sarah kept her tone light and easy.

He slowly nodded. "Okay. Only you, not him." He pointed to Nick with a frown.

"Is James Noman your real name?" she asked.

He frowned. "I don't know my real name. I picked James and then decided to call myself Noman because I am no man to anyone. I've been alone here for as long as I can remember."

"What happened to your parents?" she asked curiously.

"I don't know. I don't remember them," he replied.

"I'm sorry to hear that, James. So, you've always been alone here?" Her voice held a touch of sympathy. While she continued to ask him questions, Nick returned to collecting the last of the blood samples.

"Why are you here? Why is he doing that?" James asked, a thick tension back in his voice as he divided his gaze between her and Nick.

"Have you heard about the swamp women who have been murdered?" she asked.

He frowned. "No, but nobody ever talks to me. People don't much like me and I don't much like people. I talk to the trees and the plants and the animals and that's all I need."

"What are all these bones?" she asked.

"They're the bones of the animals that I've eaten. I put them on the wall to honor them because they gave their lives for me. Sometimes they talk to me, 'specially in the middle of the night."

"And what do they say to you?" she asked.

A smile curved his lips. It wasn't a pleasant smile. "Nothing you need to know." The smile snapped off his face. "So, why are you here? It's not against the law to kill animals for food."

Nick joined Sarah's side, having gotten what he needed of the blood samples and feeling a definite shift in James's demeanor and energy. "We're finished in here, Mr. Noman, so we'll just leave now."

"Don't come back. Do you hear me? Don't come back here. It ain't right. It ain't right at all to just walk into a man's home and do stuff," he said, suddenly angrily. "You had no right to come in here."

Nick took Sarah's arm to guide her out the door as James's temper seemed to be growing with each minute that passed. Once they were outside, he had her go over the bridge first and then he quickly followed her.

James stood on his porch, watching them

go with narrowed eyes and bunched shoulders. Thank God apparently the man didn't own a gun because Nick wasn't convinced James wouldn't have shot to kill them.

Chapter Eight

The next three days flew by. They continued to interview as many people as possible from any and all the murders. They interviewed family members and friends, all pretty much with the same results.

They'd dropped the blood samples and photos off to Dr. Cartwright, but there had been a deadly car accident on the same day with four dead, so he'd been too busy to get back to them with any results.

It was about seven o'clock in the evening of the third night and they were seated at the table, after having updated their notes.

He leaned back in his chair and released a tired sigh. "You know what I'm thinking about right now?"

She looked up from her computer and smiled at him. As usual that smile of hers tightened all the muscles in his stomach and caused a wave of warmth to sweep over him. "What?" she asked.

"A nice juicy steak and a good, stiff drink."

"Sounds good to me," she replied.

"So, where do two tired cops go to get those things in this town?" he asked.

"The café has a decent steak, but if you want a really good steak and a nice stiff drink, then the place to go is Tremont's."

"Are you up for it?" he asked, and stood.

She immediately jumped up from her chair. "Your car or mine?"

He laughed. "Now that's a woman I don't have to ask twice."

Minutes later they were in his car and headed to the high-end restaurant. "So, are you hungry?" he asked and glanced at her. Even after a ten-hour day, she still looked fresh and pretty.

"I'm starving," she replied.

He focused back on the road, as always fighting his desire for her. Since the last time they'd made love, all he'd been able to think about was being in bed with her once again.

However, he kept telling himself he had to remain strong and not go there again. At least they were spending the rest of this evening out in public because if they were in a private place, he wasn't so sure he could remain so strong.

He pulled up to the sleek-looking restaurant where he had to go around the building to park in the back as the places in front were all full.

He fought the impulse to grab her hand in his as they walked around to the front door. Only then did he touch her and that was by placing his hand on the small of her back as he ushered her inside.

They were greeted by a hostess who led them past a long bar filled with well-dressed drinking men and to a booth toward the back of the busy place. They slid in on either side of the seats with red upholstered bench backs and then the hostess handed each of them a large glossy menu.

"Your server should be with you shortly," she said with a friendly smile and then left their booth.

Both of them immediately began to peruse the menus. "Have you eaten in here often?" he asked.

"Not too often, but occasionally. I can tell you I've never had a bad meal here." She closed the menu and grinned at him. "You made me hungry for a nice, juicy steak."

"Ah, the power of suggestion," he replied

with a small laugh. He sobered then. "Before the waitress gets here, let's get one thing straight... I'm paying and I don't want any arguments from you."

"That doesn't mean you aren't going to get one from me." She leaned forward, her eyes sparkling brightly. "We're partners and that means we each pay our own way," she protested.

"But I have an expense account and can ultimately write this off as a business dinner. Besides, Sarah, I really want to pay for your meal tonight. Please let me do that."

She held his gaze for a long moment. "Okay," she finally relented.

"Good, now that we have that settled, we can move on to other topics of conversation." At that moment their waitress appeared at their booth.

There were two sizes of the ribeye steak. He got the big one with mashed potatoes and corn and she ordered the smaller size with a baked potato and corn. He ordered a whiskey and Coke and she got an iced tea.

Once their orders were taken and the waitress had scurried away, Nick leaned back in his seat and gazed at Sarah. "Tell me why a pretty, intelligent and charming woman like you isn't married or have a boyfriend?"

She blushed and averted her gaze from his. "I came really close to getting married about three years ago."

"So, what happened? Did you get cold feet?"

She looked back at him and released a small, dry laugh. "No. I was all in on it. I was engaged to a man who I adored and we were getting married in three months' time. I was spending all my time planning the wedding. I got us a venue and we went cake-tasting together and I thought he was all in as well."

She let go of a deep sigh. "One night we partied with some friends and he got pretty smashed. I put him to bed and as I took his phone out of his pocket, something told me to look at it. I really didn't expect to find anything bad." Her eyes deepened in hue.

"But you did." He fought the desire to reach out and take her hand in his, if nothing else for support as she spoke of what was an obviously hurtful time.

"Oh, I definitely did. I found a recording he'd made of him and one of my best friends having sex and the date stamp on it was for the night before we'd gone to order flowers for the wedding."

Her eyes suddenly snapped with a fiery anger. "The creep was carrying on a full-blown affair with her while planning to marry me. I wasn't sure who I was angrier with, him or the woman who was supposed to be my friend. Anyway, I kicked them both to the curb. Since then, I haven't really been looking for a man to add to my life."

"I'm so sorry that happened to you," he replied. "You deserved so much better than that."

"Thanks, Nick," she replied.

At that moment the waitress arrived with both their drinks and their food. "What about you?" she asked once they had been served and were alone again. "I could certainly ask the same of you. Why isn't a good-looking, intelligent and charming man like you not married or with a girlfriend?"

"Actually, I was married for four years. It's funny, it was about three years ago that like yours, my life fell apart," he said. "My wife sat me down one night and told me I was a lousy husband. I thought everything was fine and that we were trying to start a family and that night she told me she would never have kids with a worthless man like me."

She held his gaze for a long moment. "I can't imagine this, but were you really a lousy husband?" she asked.

"I didn't think I was, but I know through

our four-year marriage I was working a lot of hours. According to what she told me, I guess I didn't see her needs. I wasn't available to her the way I should have been so I guess ultimately, I probably was a lousy husband. That's made me realize I should probably never marry again."

"Have you ever considered that maybe she wasn't as patient with you as she should have been? Did she communicate her needs to you? Did she tell you she was unhappy before that night?"

He appreciated that Sarah seemed to be trying to rehabilitate him, but he knew the truth and the truth was he hadn't been and wasn't now great husband material. "No, she really didn't tell me anything until the day she walked out on me."

In fact, she'd never asked him about his work. When he'd tried to talk with her about it, she'd made it clear she wasn't interested in what he did for a living. When he'd ask her how her day had gone, she'd just say okay and that was it.

"Did she work or was she a stay-at-home housewife?" Sarah reached for the bottle of steak sauce on the table.

"Are you really going to do that?" he asked.

"Do what?" she asked.

"Are you really going to smother the goodness of that steak with that stuff?" he asked teasingly.

She laughed. "Yes, I am. I'm a saucy kind of woman." She shook the sauce out in a large pool next to her steak and then put the bottle back where it belonged. "And you never answered my question about your ex."

"She worked as a teller at a bank."

"You realize there's really nobody outside this business that understands the long hours and the dedication it takes in getting bad guys off the streets," Sarah said.

He cut into his steak and nodded in agreement with her. "So your next boyfriend should be another cop. Ryan seems to have a definite thing for you." He'd noticed Staub sniffing around Sarah whenever he got a chance.

"Bite your tongue. That man would be the last one on earth that I would ever want to date," she replied.

Nick was ridiculously happy to hear that even though he shouldn't be. As they ate, they talked about how difficult it was to maintain a relationship with a cop.

"In a perfect world, people in law enforcement should just marry each other," she said. "Except there's nobody in my cop world that I'd want to marry."

"I don't have a cop world anymore," he replied.

"Do you miss being on the police force?" she asked.

"Sure, from time to time I miss it. I mostly miss the companionship of my cop friends. I've tried to stay in touch with them but it's been difficult. Right now, as I told you before, I can work as little or as much as I want. I pick and choose the cases that I work and I don't have to worry about red tape," he replied.

"Don't you eventually want children?" she asked.

"When I married Amy, I wanted two, hopefully a boy and a girl, but now I just don't think about it. What about you? Do you want children?" he asked.

"In a perfect world, if I was happily married, then yes, I'd like to have two kids," she replied. He heard a slightly wistful tone in her voice.

As they continued to eat, they talked about his work and about where she saw herself once this case was solved.

"I'm hoping to gain some respect once this is all over. We have had some crime problems in the past that I would have loved to work and hopefully now Gravois will let me do more than sitting on a corner giving tickets or working the dispatch desk," she said.

"You're too good a cop to be wasted that way," he replied.

Her eyes sparkled as she smiled at him. "Thanks, that means a lot coming from you."

"Well, I mean it," he replied. She had the intelligence and the natural instincts to be a really good cop. All she needed was a chance to show those traits.

"Tell me this, did anything in your entire life scare you more than realizing there were snakes under your bed?" she asked as they continued to eat.

He felt so comfortable with her now. In fact, he felt far closer with her than he had ever felt with his ex-wife. "Actually, that wasn't the scariest time of my life," he slowly admitted. "I told you before that my mother would often take me with her into the swamp. I guess I was about five or six when she took me with her to a client's shanty."

She leaned forward, her gaze intent on his. There were times when he felt as if when they locked gazes it was as powerful a connection as them making love. Her beautiful eyes drew him in so deeply.

"The adult conversation quickly bored me," he continued. "And all I wanted to do was go outside to play, so when nobody was paying any attention to me, I slipped outside and went exploring. It wasn't long before I was completely lost and absolutely terrified."

He released a dry, humorless laugh and looked away from her. "Suddenly the trees looked like tall monsters and I thought the Spanish moss was trying to eat me. I believed there were gators all around me just waiting to grab me with their big jaws and I was absolutely scared to death."

"Ah, poor baby." She reached across the table and took his hand in hers. He looked at her once again and her eyes widened slightly and she squeezed his hand harder. He was sure she could feel the clamminess that had taken over his skin as he'd confessed this fear.

"Oh, Nick, I'm so sorry you had that experience." She finally released his hand but held his gaze intently. "So how hard was it for you to go back into the swamp for this case?"

Feeling her unwavering support, he decided to be completely truthful. "To be perfectly honest, it's been very difficult every time we've had to go in." He laughed. "So much for the big, bad macho homicide cop, right?"

"You're human, Nick, and you had a bad experience as a child. Those kinds of experiences sometimes shape our adult life. But you should have told me about this before now," she replied.

"Why? So you could hold my hand in the swamp?"

"I would hold your hand anytime you needed me to." Her gaze was so soft and so accepting it squeezed his heart tight with a depth of emotion.

"We'd better eat up now before our food gets too cold," he finally said, and swallowed hard against the emotions she evoked in him.

They small-talked for the remainder of the meal. The steak was great and the sides were just as good. As always, their conversation flowed easily and he found himself wondering what it would be like to be married to her.

It was easy for him to imagine coming home from work to her. She would ask him questions about the job he'd done that day. She'd want to know what case he was working on and he'd want to know all about her day and she'd share it all with him.

It was crazy how easily he could imagine it with Sarah and how difficult it had been with Amy. Would it be so different with somebody who shared his same passion? Who loved what he did for a living?

He checked himself. What in the hell was

he doing even thinking about being married to Sarah? They were just partners and that was it. He'd be leaving here as soon as the case was solved and he'd go back to his solitary...slightly lonely life in New Orleans.

"Coffee and dessert?" he asked.

"Coffee for sure. I'm not sure about dessert, I'm pretty full," she replied.

"At least look at the dessert menu," he urged her.

"Chocolate lava cake with ice cream and a river of chocolate syrup," she read aloud. "I'm not only tempted, but I'm going for it and you are a very bad influence on my girlish figure."

He laughed. "Stick with me, woman, and I'll lead you down the path of decadent desserts. And trust me, there is absolutely nothing wrong with your figure."

"Thank you, sir," she replied, and a soft pink filled her cheeks.

He waved for the waitress and ordered the lava cake for her and for himself he got something called the caramel dream, which involved a special spice cake with caramel syrup and butterscotch chips. He got coffee for them both.

Minutes later they had the desserts in front of them. "Hmm, you've got to taste this," he said after taking his first bite. He got a spoonful and held it out toward her.

She leaned forward and took it into her mouth. Just that quickly his desire for her roared back to life. He remembered exactly how her mouth had felt against his and he wanted to taste her again. But the closest he got was when she offered him a spoonful of her lava cake.

An attractive couple appeared by their booth. The man was handsome and well-dressed and the woman with him was absolutely beautiful. "Sarah," he said in greeting.

"Hi, Jackson, hi, Josie," she replied. "Jackson, this is Nick Cain and, Nick, this is Jackson Fortier and his wife, Josie."

The two men shook hands. "We don't intend to interrupt you for long. I just wanted to meet you, Nick, and let you know you have a lot of people supporting your efforts here."

"Thank you, I appreciate that," Nick replied.

"If you find yourself needing anything at all that you can't get through the department, then feel free to call me and I might be able to help out," Jackson said.

"Again, I appreciate that," Nick said.

"And now we'll just move along and let you enjoy your desserts," Jackson said, and then he and Josie followed the hostess on to their table.

"Jackson is one of the wealthiest men in town and he's a major reason why you are here," Sarah said once the couple was out of ear reach. She then explained to him how Jackson and several of his fellow business-men had confronted Gravois and demanded he bring in help to solve the murders.

She also shared with him how Jackson, a man from town, had met the lovely Josie from the swamp and the danger Josie had been in when one of Jackson's friends had tried to kill her. Thankfully there had been a happy ending and the bad guy had been arrested.

They were just finishing up their coffee when Nick's phone rang. With a frown he dug it out of his pocket. "It's Dr. Cartwright," he said to Sarah, and then answered the call.

He listened to what the coroner had to tell him, thanked him and then hung up. He gazed at Sarah for a long moment and then released a deep sigh. "All the blood samples from Noman's place came back as animal. There was no human blood and he was able to identify the bones as animal as well."

She frowned as she held his gaze. "So where does that leave us now?"

"With a small piece of blue fabric that is our only clue," he replied.

Her eyes darkened. "And that means our pool of suspects has now narrowed down to the members of the police department."

THE NEXT MORNING Sara arrived early for work. It was a few minutes before seven when she got a cup of coffee and then went to their little workroom.

She set up her computer and then sipped on her coffee. She'd tossed and turned all night as she considered the possibility that one of the men she worked with could be their Honey Island Swamp Monster murderer.

If that wasn't enough it was thoughts of Nick that had kept her from sleep. Even knowing there was no future with him, she found herself falling hard for him.

She'd seen the depth of emotion inside him as he'd talked about being a lousy husband. No matter what had gone down in his marriage, she suspected he'd been hurt deeply.

Even though she hadn't been married to Brent, they'd dated for three years before he'd betrayed her so badly. She'd not only written Brent out of her life, but also her girlfriend Casey, who had decided it was okay to sleep with Sarah's fiancé. But once her anger had left her, the pain of their betrayal had remained with her. So, just like Nick, she'd been hurt by love before.

Then there was his confession about getting lost in the swamp when he was a little boy and the residual effect it had on his adult life.

She'd wanted to find that lost little boy and comfort him. She'd wanted to gather him into her arms and hold him tightly until he was no longer afraid.

She admired him so much for being able to push through his fear and go into the very heart of the swamp to find a killer. However, it sounded like the next leg of their investigation wouldn't take place in the swamp.

She and Nick had both been through the fires of loss and knowing that had only made her feel closer to him. She had a feeling heartache and betrayal were in her near future. Nick was going to break her heart and if it was true that one of her brothers in the police department was the killer, then she would feel utterly betrayed by that.

She turned as the door opened and was surprised to see Nick, who was also early. "Morning, partner," she said.

He gave her a smile that made her stomach

swirl with warmth. "You're an early bird," he said as he set his cup of coffee on the table.

"I had trouble sleeping last night," she replied.

"Yeah, that makes two of us." He sat across from her. "I imagine we both had the same thoughts keeping us awake."

She seriously doubted he'd lost sleep over her. "The few clues we have point to somebody in the department." She kept her voice low.

"We have the fabric and we also have the fact that all of those women would have trusted a cop who approached them in the swamp." His voice was equally low. "How many officers are there in total?"

"Fourteen, plus Gravois."

He nodded. "First of all, from here on out we write nothing down on the whiteboard. We don't need anyone to walk in here and see what kind of internal investigation we're about to start doing."

"Agreed," she replied.

"We'll document everything on your computer and make sure you take your computer home with you every night."

"Again, agreed," she replied. "So, where do we start?" She dreaded this whole process, but was determined to follow through with it.

If the monster was hiding in the department, then he needed to be found.

"We need to pull up the schedules for every officer for as long as they go back."

"That's going to take up most of the day," she replied.

"Then let's go ahead and get started."

For the next four hours or so, Sarah printed off the schedules for all the officers in the past two months, which was all that was available to her online. As she finished with each one, Nick stapled them together and began making a chart of who was where during the nights of the last two murders.

It took them two days to narrow down what they could but there was no way they could know what the officers did on their nights off.

She told him everything she knew about her fellow officers, their personalities and temperaments. They both knew their monster was intelligent and still highly organized. He'd made no mistakes until the last victim, who had gotten that piece of material from someplace on him.

She also told Nick about their living spaces. They were still looking for a killing ground, so they needed to know not only where the officers lived but also if they owned any other property in or just out of town.

On the afternoon of the second day, they went into city hall to research who owned what. By the end of that day, they had more lists to go through and check out.

One of the things Sarah had learned while working with Nick was that a murder investigation wasn't just about chasing a suspect through the swamp or anywhere else. Good police work was also long hours of research and desk time.

So far, they had managed to keep their investigation close to their chests. However, sooner rather than later they were going to have to start interrogating the cops in the department, and that was going to open up a whole new can of worms.

It was just after seven when they knocked off for the day. She packed up her computer, along with all the paperwork that had been generated.

"Tired?" Nick asked as they walked out of the building together.

"Yeah, I am. I'm ready to zap something in the microwave, eat and then drop into bed," she admitted.

"Looks like we could get a downpour," he said. The night was dark and overcast with storm clouds as he walked her to her car. The forecast was for thunderstorms overnight.

"I just hope whatever storms we get don't keep me awake," she replied.

They reached her car and she put her computer and their paperwork in the passenger seat and then straightened back up and turned to him.

There was a simmering tension between them that had only grown with each day that passed. She felt it and she knew he did, too. There were moments when their gazes would lock and she saw his desire for her in the depths of his beautiful gray eyes.

She saw it now, shining with a hunger that burned in her blood, into her very soul. "Nick..." she whispered softly.

"Ah, Sarah, what are you doing to me?" He gathered her into his arms and kissed her.

She molded her body close against his as she wrapped her arms around his neck. Their tongues danced together in a fiery kiss that drove all other thoughts out of her mind.

The kiss went on for several long, wonderful moments and then he stepped away from her. The hunger was still there in his eyes as he pulled her back against his chest.

"Woman, you drive me crazy," he finally said as he stroked his fingers through her hair.

"You drive me just as crazy," she replied softly.

"You know we can't go there again," he finally said, and released his hold on her.

She didn't know that, but she wasn't going to throw herself at him. He was trying to be as professional as possible and she didn't want to take that away from him. But this was so miserably hard because she wanted him again so badly.

It was a few minutes later when she was driving home that she realized she was in love with Nick. The knowledge filled her heart with joy and happiness. After Brent she hadn't thought she would ever love again. She hadn't believed she would ever be capable of falling in love again.

Nick was not only the man she loved, but he had also become her best friend. She felt as if she could talk to him about anything and everything and in fact, they had shared both serious conversation and silly ones that had made them both laugh.

However, her happiness at realizing she was in love with Nick was short-lived. She had no idea how he felt about her. Oh, she knew he was into her sexually, but how did he feel about her aside from their terrific sexual chemistry?

She released a tired sigh as she pulled into her garage. She parked and then grabbed her things from the passenger seat and got out. She entered the house and put her computer and the paperwork at one end of her kitchen table and then she headed directly to the freezer to see what was for supper.

She grabbed a fried chicken dinner and got it working in the microwave. While it cooked, she grabbed a soda and popped it open. She took off her holster and gun and then sank down at the table.

God, she was so exhausted. The late nights were definitely starting to catch up to her. Hopefully a good night's sleep tonight would remedy that.

The microwave dinged, announcing that her dinner was ready. She ate in record time and then headed for the shower. It was only when she was under the spray of warm water that she thought about Nick once again.

She had a feeling that they were getting very close to catching the killer and then Nick would be gone. He'd already told her he had no intention of becoming a husband again. What more did she need to know to realize her relationship with him was doomed?

By the time she got into bed she was too exhausted to think about anything anymore. She allowed her soft mattress to envelop her and almost immediately she was asleep.

She jerked awake and bolted to a sitting position, her heart pounding a million beats a minute. A flash of lightning was followed by another boom of thunder that rent the silence of the night. The thunder must have been what had awakened her. She relaxed and drew in several deep breaths to calm the rapid beat of her heart.

As the lightning shot off again, her heart suddenly stopped beating as she let out a small gasp. She could swear that a dark figure just darted past her doorway. Had it only been a figment of her imagination, a trick of the light, or was somebody really in her house?

Her heart resumed a frantic rhythm as she slowly slid out of bed. What should she do? Damn, her gun was in the kitchen on top of the table. Should she call for help? Was there really somebody in her house? Who and why?

For a long moment she stood next to the bed, frozen by fear and yet needing to know if she wasn't alone. She grabbed her cell phone and held it tightly in her hand.

Was it possible she was being robbed? She really didn't have anything worth stealing other than her television. She supposed somebody could pawn that for a little bit of extra money.

She didn't care about her television, what she did care about was that somebody was in her home...in her sanctuary. Was the person dangerous? Oh God, what should she do? The last thing she wanted to do was call for help when she didn't need it.

With a deep breath she stepped into the hallway and turned on the light. Another rumble of thunder sounded, adding to her frantic anxiety. There was nobody in the hallway and she also heard nothing.

Maybe it really had been a figment of her imagination. Maybe there had been no dark figure at all. Maybe it had just been a trick of the lightning. She continued down the hallway, looking carefully in each room she passed and turning on all the lights.

Surely if she were being robbed, the lights would scare the person away. She finally stepped into the living room and gasped as a man in dark clothes and a ski mask rushed toward her from the kitchen.

He shoved her so hard she fell back on the floor, crying out with pain as the back of her head and her body made contact with the carpeting.

Before she could get up, the person flew out her front door and disappeared into the night.

She finally got to her feet, her head pounding as she sobbed and closed and locked the door.

Who was the man? Oh God, what had just happened? Who was he and why had he been in her house? She'd scarcely gotten a look at him but with the ski mask on there had been no way for her to identify him.

She still didn't feel safe. With tears falling down her cheeks, she hurried into the kitchen to get her gun.

As she flipped on the kitchen light, she gasped once again. Her gun was still on the table, but her computer and the paperwork were gone.

Chapter Nine

Nick stood next to Sarah and fought the need to pull her into his arms. She looked so small and so vulnerable as she watched Gravois and Officers Judd Lynons and Jason Richards check out the broken window in the bedroom that served as her office.

Apparently, that had been how the thief had gotten into the house. The idea of her being in the house all alone while somebody had come in half terrified Nick for her.

It could have all gone so terribly wrong. It was bad enough that the man had shoved her to the floor. Thank God he hadn't shot her, or fought with her. What would have happened if she'd gotten to her feet and had really confronted him?

"I'm not managing to lift any prints from anywhere on the window," Lynons said in frustration after having tried for several minutes.

"I'm sure he was probably wearing gloves," Nick replied.

"Let's move into the kitchen and see if we can get something pulled off the table," Gravois said.

They all congregated in the kitchen and Lynons got to work fingerprinting the table. Once again Nick wanted to draw Sarah into his arms. What chilled him to the bone was he had a feeling that tonight she had shared her house with the Honey Island Swamp Monster murderer.

The killer had obviously decided that their investigation was hitting too close to home and so he'd stolen the very work notes and the computer that might have pointed to him.

It was the only thing that made sense. And whoever the killer was, he must have a deep enough bond with Sarah that he hadn't wanted to really harm her.

There was no question that the loss of the paperwork and the computer would set the investigation back a bit, but at the moment he was more worried about Sarah's well-being.

She was clad in her pink nightgown and a short white robe. Her face was unusually pale and her entire body appeared to tremble. When she'd called him and told him her house had been broken into, he couldn't get to her fast enough. He'd heard the fear in her voice and all he'd wanted to do was get to her as quickly as possible.

Lynons managed to lift a bunch of fingerprints off the table but they all appeared the same and everyone was sure they probably belonged to Sarah. Her fingerprints were on file with the department so it would be easy to check for certain.

The storm overhead had passed and it was after two thirty when everyone finally left. The moment they all stepped out the front door, Nick closed and locked it and then went to Sarah, who stood still as a statue by the coffee table.

He immediately pulled her into his arms, holding her tight as she trembled against his chest. She began to cry softly. "It's okay," he whispered to her. "You're okay now."

She continued to cry for several more minutes and then with a deep sigh she stepped back from him. She sank down on the sofa and he sat next to her.

"When I realized somebody was in the house with me, I got so scared," she said, her voice trembling a bit. "And then when I saw him and he pushed me, I was in shock. Then I saw the computer and everything was gone and I realized the man who had come into my house was probably the killer."

"Thank God you weren't seriously hurt," he said as he took one of her hands in his. "Thank God, you didn't jump up and run after him." The idea of her being killed shot an iciness through him.

"Now that it's all over I'm also so damned mad." She gazed at him with sad eyes. "He got all of our work product...everything."

"We can generate all that again," he replied.

"Who is this person? And why steal all our things now?"

"The killer was desperate to see exactly what we were doing," he replied. "I think our killer must have seen that you downloaded all the schedules and that scared him. It let him know that all the cops in the department were suspects."

He squeezed her hand. "He wanted our work notes to see if we had narrowed down anything. If it's any consolation at all, he must have a friendship with you and that's what kept you alive tonight."

"That is no consolation at all," she replied, some of the fire back in her eyes. "I want this bastard behind bars and I don't give a damn if I have a friendship with him or not. He's sick and perverted. The way he kills these women make him a monstrosity."

"I've been trying to work up a psychological profile of the killer and why he would want to basically erase his victim's faces," he said.

"He obviously hates women," she replied.

"True, but the psychology goes much deeper than that. Maybe he's trying to replace somebody and when he gets them to his kill place, he's angry that they don't look like what he wants…what he needs."

"Mommy issues?" she suggested.

"Maybe," he replied. "Now, do you have something I can use to board up that broken window in your office?" He released his hold on her hand and stood.

"There are some old pieces of plywood in the garage. They were there when I bought the house." She also got up from the sofa. "I'll get you a hammer and some nails."

Thirty minutes later the window was boarded up, but he was still reluctant to leave her and he could tell she didn't want him to go.

"Do you want me to stay for the rest of the night with you?" he asked.

"Would you mind?" Her gaze was soft and faintly needy. She'd been through a frightening ordeal and he could understand her not wanting to be alone right now.

"Of course I wouldn't mind," he replied, and smiled at her. "When my partner needs me, I'm there."

"Thank you, Nick."

Fifteen minutes later they were in bed and she snuggled into his arms. As always, the desire she stoked in him rose to the surface but he fought against it. Thankfully, it didn't take her long to fall asleep and he soon followed.

He awoke at some point later. The room was still dark, and even though he was still half-asleep, Sarah's body moved against his and he was fully aroused.

Clothes disappeared and warm limbs wound around each other. Her small gasps of pleasure whispered in the room. It was as if he were in a dream as they slowly made love. It was a wonderful dream. He felt as if he belonged here with her and then he was sleeping once again.

When he awakened again it was a few minutes after seven. He was spooned around Sarah and they both were naked, letting him know that what he'd thought was a wonderful dream had really been a reality. They had made love once again.

Damn, his body was a traitorous thing.

Apparently even in sleep he wanted her and she wanted him. He slowly moved back from her warm sweetness and slid out of the bed. She stirred, but didn't awaken, which he was grateful for. She needed to sleep.

He stood next to the bed for several moments and simply gazed at her in the golden morning light that flowed in through the window.

The illumination shone in her tousled hair, turning it into a soft halo around her head. Her lips were slightly parted, as if just awaiting his kiss. She was so beautiful even in slumber.

He loved her wide-eyed wonder when he taught her something new and he adored her when she laughed over something funny. He loved talking to her about anything and nothing.

With a frown he grabbed his jeans and T-shirt off the floor and left the room. He dressed quickly in the bathroom and then quietly left the house.

As he drove to Nene's place, he realized with a jolt that he was in love with his partner. He didn't know when he'd fallen for her. He didn't know if it had been when she'd landed in the swamp while enthusiastically chasing James Noman, or if it had been when she'd held his hand after he'd shared his childhood trauma with her.

He didn't know when it had happened, but it had. He was crazy in love with Sarah. The thought brought him no happiness. There was still no future for the two of them. He had no intention of seeking a relationship with her once these murders were solved.

What he'd done last night by making love with her once again was give her hope. He had a feeling she was totally into him. The signs had been there with her...the way she looked at him and how she touched him when it wasn't necessary. Yeah, he knew she had deep feelings for him.

However, the worst thing he could do was plan a life with her. He knew what he was and he would never want Sarah to suffer his flaws. She definitely deserved so much better than him.

When he reached Nene's, the older woman met him at the door. "Is Sarah okay?" she immediately asked, her eyes filled with a wealth of concern.

"She's fine," he replied. "News definitely flies fast in this town."

"The gossips were busy this morning. A break-in must be a frightening thing," Nene said. "Poor Sarah, I'm sure she was scared to death."

"She was definitely frightened, but thank God she was unharmed physically," he replied.

"Thank God for that. Snakes in your bedroom and then a break-in…you've really shaken somebody up." She shook her head.

"I guess we have," he agreed.

She looked at him slyly. "At least Sarah has you by her side, just like in a good romance novel."

"Unfortunately, this isn't a romance novel," he replied.

She released a deep sigh. "Well, I won't keep you any longer. I know how busy you must be but I just wanted to make sure Sarah was okay. She's a lovely woman and has always been very kind to me."

He smiled at her. "Yeah, I'm just on my way upstairs for a quick shower and then I need to head back into the office again."

"I certainly hope you catch this man," she said.

"We will, Nene," he replied firmly.

"There are some blueberry muffins in the kitchen if you want to grab one to take with you," she said. "In fact, take two and give one to Sarah."

"Thanks, I just might want to do that." He headed for the staircase and she went into the kitchen. It took him only minutes to shower and then dress in a clean pair of navy slacks and a navy polo.

On his way out he detoured into the kitchen where Nene wrapped up two of the huge muffins for him to take and then he was on his way back to the office.

He had no idea when to expect Sarah. He hoped she slept as long as she needed, long enough to feel refreshed and ready to go again. They'd both been working long hours with plenty of nighttime interruptions. He was used to this kind of a schedule when working a case, but he knew she wasn't.

Once he reached the station he went into their little office, grabbed a fresh notepad from the filing cabinet and then sank down at the table.

Whoever the thief was that had stolen the computer and paperwork must have believed that it would stymie the investigation for weeks to come. But they hadn't stolen Nick's mind and his memory.

The notes that had been on the computer were still fairly fresh in his mind. He began to make a list of the men on the force that they hadn't been able to alibi with work for the nights of the murders. As he worked, he ate one of the muffins, which was delicious.

He'd written down several names when the door opened and Sarah came in.

"Sorry I'm late, partner," she said, and took the seat opposite him with her usual beautiful smile.

"You aren't late," he replied. "How are you feeling?"

"Rested and ready to get back to work."

He was relieved that apparently they weren't going to talk about their lovemaking in the middle of the night. What was there to say about it? It had happened and it had been wonderful, but it had also been another mistake. He had a feeling she wouldn't want to hear that.

"I've just been sitting here writing down all the names of the officers who we couldn't find an alibi for on the nights of the murders," he explained. "Thankfully a lot of our work is still fresh in my mind."

"Let me see who you have so far." She moved into the chair next to his and pulled it closer to him. With his love for her burning hot in his chest, everything about her nearness right now was sheer torture.

The soft curve of her cheek…the plump lusciousness of her lips and the scent that belonged to her alone...he had a feeling they would all...that she would haunt him for a very long time to come after he left this little town.

She added a few more names to the list he'd made and then pushed the remaining muffin before her. "A gift for you from Nene," he said.

"That was nice of her, but where's yours?"

"Gee, I don't know what happened to it," he said.

She grinned at him. "That story would be much easier to believe if you didn't wear the evidence in the form of muffin crumbles on your chin."

"Busted." He laughed and quickly brushed off his chin.

Their levity didn't last long as he leaned back in his chair. "You know we can't keep this investigation a secret any longer," he said as she ate her muffin.

"I know," she replied solemnly.

"It's time for us to start interrogating some of these officers."

"I'm not looking forward to it. I still can't believe one of the officers I've worked with here is a suspect," she replied, and shoved the last of the muffin away.

He looked at her equally solemnly. "I truly

believe in my gut that a cop is not only our suspect, but one of them is definitely the Honey Island Swamp Monster murderer," he replied.

"I THINK BEFORE we go any further, we need to let Gravois know where our investigation has led us," Nick said.

"Should we go to speak to him now?" Sarah asked. She was torn between the dread of finding out who among them was the monster and wanting to get the monster behind bars as soon as possible.

That wasn't the only thing she was torn about since awakening that morning. She and Nick had made love again last night. It had been slow and sleepy and beyond wonderful.

He had to love her just a little bit. He didn't strike her as the kind of guy who would have sex with absolutely no feelings behind it. In one of their many talks he had told her he had been completely faithful in his marriage and she believed that of him.

He was the man she wanted for the rest of her life. She was drawn to so many qualities about him and she could easily imagine marrying him and living happily ever after. They would share their love of crime stories and she would give him babies. It would be perfect...except it wasn't.

"Yeah, let's head down to Gravois's office now," he replied.

As she followed him down the hallway, she knew there would come a time when she would tell him exactly how she felt about him. She couldn't let him leave Black Bayou without him knowing the depths of her love for him. But before that could happen, they had a killer to catch...a killer that at this very moment might be in the building with them.

Nick rapped on Gravois's door and after Gravois called enter, they both did. "We need to speak with you," Nick said somberly.

"Then come in." Gravois gestured them into the chairs in front of his desk. "What's going on? Is there a break in the case?"

"We're getting very close. We believe that the killer is a cop here in the department," Nick said.

Gravois reeled back in his chair with obvious stunned surprise. His features paled and then filled with a ruddy color. He leaned forward and frowned. "Are you absolutely sure about that?"

"As sure as we can be," Sarah replied grimly.

"A cop would easily be able to get those

women to come with him out of the swamp. He would also know the best areas in town to dump the bodies, and he'd know about forensics," Nick said.

"And then we have that piece of material which is the same makeup as the officers' shirts," Sarah added.

"All of our other suspects had been cleared, leaving us to believe one of your officers is our killer," Nick said.

"I'll be a son of a bitch," Gravois said. "Do you have a specific suspect in mind?"

"No, not yet," Nick replied.

"So, what do you need from me?" Gravois asked.

"We have a list of officers we'd like to start interrogating," Nick explained. "I'm trained in interrogation and hopefully I'll get a tell from the guilty party along with some evidence."

"We certainly don't expect anyone to confess, but we need to find out who has solid alibis for the nights of the murders and who doesn't," Sarah said.

"I'll make sure all the officers know they are to fully cooperate with you," Gravois replied.

"We appreciate that, but we'd like to start

the interviews immediately with the men who are on duty today," Nick replied.

Gravois nodded. "That's fine with me, but please keep me in the loop. If you get a solid suspect, then dammit, I want to know."

"By all means, we'll definitely keep you in the loop," Nick said as he rose to his feet. Sarah stood as well and minutes later she and Nick were back in their little room.

The first officer they pulled in for an interrogation was Judd Lynons. He hadn't been working on the nights of the murders but he was working today.

Sarah went into the officers' room where Judd sat at a desk eating a candy bar from the vending machine. "Hey, Judd."

"Hey, Sarah." He smiled at her. Judd was in his mid-thirties and was physically fit with broad shoulders and big arms. He was big and strong enough to carry a victim.

"Could you come with me into our office for a few minutes?"

His smile faded into a look of curiosity. "Uh...sure." He took the last bite of his candy bar, crinkled up the wrapper and threw it away and then got up from the desk and followed her down the hallway.

Nick stood as they entered the room and then he gestured Judd into a chair at the table.

"What's going on here?" Judd asked in confusion. "Why do you need to talk to me?"

"We're in the process of narrowing down our pool of suspects," Nick said.

Judd looked at Sarah and then at Nick in astonishment. "Am I a suspect?"

"We're going to be talking to all the officers over the next couple of days," Nick said.

Judd's eyes widened. "You think a cop did those murders? Man, that's messed up." He shook his head and settled back in the chair. "If you have questions for me, then ask away. I don't have anything to hide."

"We understand that you grew up for the first ten years of your life in the swamp," Nick said.

And so, the first interrogation began. Judd appeared to be open and honest and provided an alibi for the night of the fourth murder that they could easily check out. According to him, he'd been in Shreveport for a buddy's wedding and he had the hotel records to prove that fact.

If his alibi checked out, then he wasn't their killer. They knew without a doubt that the same man had killed all the women, so if somebody had a solid alibi for one of the murders that exonerated them from being the person they sought.

"If you get a chance later today or tomorrow, please bring us the receipts you have," Nick said to Judd.

"And the names and phone numbers of some of the people who were with you in Shreveport," Sarah added.

"I definitely will," Judd replied. "Does that mean you're finished with me?"

"For now," Nick replied.

A moment later Judd was gone. Sarah frowned as she saw who they next needed to talk to. "Ryan and I grew up together. I can't imagine him doing something like this. He might be a total jerk, but I can't imagine him being our killer."

Nick reached across the table and covered her hand with his. "You knew this was going to be difficult. I'm so sorry, Sarah, that one of these men you've viewed as your friend and coworker is probably a serial killer." He squeezed her hand and then released it. "But at this point in the investigation, it's important to keep an open mind."

She definitely appreciated the gesture and his support. "So, now I'll go get Ryan." She got out of her chair, left their little space and then went back to the officers' workroom.

Apparently, Judd hadn't returned to the workroom. He might be in the break room or he might have been called out for something. Whatever the case, Ryan was alone reading something on his phone when she went in to get him.

"Hey, Ryan, you want to come with me to speak with Nick?"

"Speak to him about what?" he asked.

"You'll find out when you get there," she replied.

He shrugged his shoulders and turned off his phone. He then rose from the table and grinned at her. "You know I'll follow you anywhere, Short-Stuff."

Sarah sighed, but was grateful he followed her back down the hallway silently. Ryan had worked several of the murders, but they needed to know what he'd done in the hours before the bodies had been found. It would have been easy for him to kill a woman and then show up a couple of hours later on duty. There were two murders that he hadn't been on duty for and hadn't been called in for.

"Hey, man," Ryan said in greeting to Nick.

"Officer Staub…please have a seat. We have some questions to ask you," Nick said.

"And I'm sure I have some answers for you," Ryan said flippantly.

"Where were you in the hours before you

showed up to work the Soulange murder?"
Nick asked.

Ryan looked first at Nick and then at Sarah
in surprise. He then leaned back in his chair
and laughed. "Is this some kind of a joke?"
he finally asked.

"It's absolutely no joke," Sarah replied.

"You really think I'm the big, bad killer
you're looking for?" He turned his gaze once
again on Sarah. "Short-Stuff, you should
know better than this."

"Her name is Sarah or Officer Beauregard." Nick's eyes were the color of dark
storms. "If I hear you diminish her name or
stature again within this department, I'll file
a lawsuit on her behalf."

Ryan stopped laughing and met Nick's
gaze. "Oh, give it a rest, tough guy. You aren't
going to do that."

"Try me. You'll find out that I don't play,"
Nick said with a deadly calm.

"Sarah doesn't mind if I tease her," Ryan
said with a little less assurance in his voice.

"Actually, Ryan, I do mind," she said.

"Duly noted," he replied to her. "I'm sorry
if I've hurt you." His mouth said the words,
but his blue eyes were a dark shade that she'd
never seen there before. He didn't look sorry.
He looked angry.

Was it really possible the man who had been asking her out for the past couple of months was the Honey Island Swamp Monster murderer?

Chapter Ten

Ryan was unable to provide a solid alibi for any of the nights of the murders. He thought he was on a date before one of the murders and then he said he was home alone and in bed. He needed to check his planner to see where he might have been and who he might have been with. He'd have to get back with them.

When he left their room, Sarah released a deep sigh. "God, he sounded guilty as hell," she said.

"Maybe…maybe not," Nick said. "A lot of innocent people when put on the spot can't name what they were doing on any particular night."

"But on several of those nights he investigated heinous murders, you would think his activities for those nights would be burned in his brain," she protested.

"We'll see what kind of alibis he can provide once he checks his planner," Nick replied.

"Planner, my butt," she retorted.

Nick laughed. "You don't believe he has a daily planner?"

"He has a daily planner like I have a flying blue dog," she replied, making Nick laugh again.

"We'll see if he can provide us something tomorrow," he said.

Sarah appeared utterly miserable and again Nick recognized how difficult this all must be for her. These were men she'd worked with, fellow officers she'd considered friends.

"I keep going over and over it again in my mind," she said with obvious frustration. "If one of the officers really is our killer then why didn't I get a sense of that kind of darkness in him? Why didn't I feel something off about him?"

"Sarah, honey, hiding in plain sight, that's what these kind of people…that's what these kinds of killers are good at. He's a cool customer and he definitely believes he's much smarter than us."

"Is he? I mean, is it possible we won't ever be able to identify him?" Her eyes simmered with a wealth of worry.

Nick took her hand in his. "We're going

to get him, Sarah. He doesn't realize he's up against a partnership better than Batman and Robin, smarter than Sherlock and Dr. Watson and more tenacious than Scooby-Doo and Shaggy."

She immediately laughed at his silliness, which was exactly what he wanted. He loved the sound of her laughter and the fact that the darkness that had been in her eyes was momentarily gone. He squeezed her hand and then released it. "You can't give up now, Sarah. We're so close and when we do get him, think of all the young lives we'll be saving."

She sighed once again. "I only wish you would have been brought in earlier," she replied. "Then maybe he would have been taken off the streets much sooner and some of these women would still be alive."

"Unfortunately, we can't go back in time, but we're here now and we're getting closer and closer. Now, who should we talk to next?"

He still saw how troubled she was, but he couldn't do anything to make this process easier on her. He wished he could, but the truth was he couldn't. Still, the torment in her eyes hurt him for her.

They did one more interview and then stopped for a quick lunch of burgers from a drive-through called Big Larry's. After eating they interviewed two more officers.

There were no other officers in house to speak with and so for the rest of the afternoon they made phone calls and scheduled interviews for the next day with some of the men who worked nights.

It was just after six when he sent Sarah home. They would have a full day the next day as they tried to get to as many officers as possible.

Once Sarah was gone, the scent of her lingered in the room. She had to know he was more than a little crazy about her. Surely she'd seen his emotions for her shining from his eyes when he gazed at her. Surely she felt it whenever he touched her even in the simplest way.

However, sometimes love just wasn't enough. He had loved Amy when he'd married her, but his love hadn't been enough to keep his marriage intact. When it came to relationships, he was a total loser and Sarah deserved far more than a loser in her life.

His mind shifted to the interviews they had conducted so far that day. He'd been trained in interrogation techniques and how to read body language. So far today none of the men had given him the tells that they were lying in any way.

Ryan had come closest as he'd deflected a lot during the questioning and his body language had been closed off and defensive. Nick was eager to see what kind of receipts Ryan brought the next day as alibis for any of the nights of the murders.

Unbeknownst to Sarah, Nick had another suspect in mind, one that she'd already firmly rejected as a possibility. Gravois. The name now thundered in his brain.

Was it possible Gravois hadn't worked too hard in solving these murders because he didn't want them solved? As much as Nick had seen a lot of growth in Sarah, why would Gravois partner him with the least experienced officer in the department? Somebody who hadn't worked on any of the previous murder investigations?

Gravois was physically strong enough to carry the women out of the swamp and to a kill place. He would then be strong enough to take them to the places where their bodies had been found. The women would willingly interact with the head lawman without protest.

Still, Nick didn't intend to jump to any conclusions where Gravois was concerned. He would continue to exclude all the other men in the department and only then would he come at Gravois.

He didn't know how long he sat there lost in his thoughts, but he finally got up from the table and headed for the building's back door.

It was another gray evening with dark clouds hiding the sunlight and gloomy shadows taking over the landscape. He had just reached the driver side of his car when a gunshot fired off. He automatically hit the ground, aware that the bullet slammed into the driver door of his car.

He grabbed his gun as adrenaline fired through his entire body. Two cars over he saw some movement. He didn't return fire... at least not yet. Right now, he realized he was a sitting duck where he was and he needed to move around his car for more cover.

He started to rise to a crouch, but another bullet flew mere inches by his head to hit his car door once again. He dropped down and slithered like a snake on the ground to get around his car bumper and only then did he return fire by shooting twice in the direction where he'd seen the movement.

What the hell? Who was shooting at him? He waited, his heart beating frantically. He shot a quick glance around the bumper but saw no more movement.

The shadows were deepening by the minute. Was the shooter still there? Just waiting for him to leave his cover? Had the person moved to a different location where he could get off another shot?

He looked to his left and then his right, unsure where danger might come from next. He tightened his grip on his gun, ready to fire again if necessary.

Seconds turned into long minutes and nothing more happened. There were no more gunshots but still, Nick was reluctant to move from his cover.

At that moment the back door of the building flew open and Officer Colby Shanks stepped out. He was nothing but a kid and the last thing Nick wanted was for him to somehow get hurt.

"Get back inside, Shanks. There's an active shooter in the parking lot," Nick yelled.

Instead of going back inside, the kid dropped into a crouching position and pulled his gun. "Where is he?" He pointed his weapon first to the left and then to the right.

By that time Nick had a feeling the danger had passed. Slowly he rose to his feet. Somebody had just tried to kill him. There was no doubt in his mind that the Honey Island Swamp Monster murderer was or had been in this parking lot with him and wanted him dead. That was a sure way to stop the investigation.

SARAH HAD USED her evening to try to de-stress. She'd taken a long, hot lilac-scented bath and then had baked a seasoned chicken breast and had added steamed broccoli for dinner.

She'd then sunk down on the sofa and had turned her television to a comedy show she occasionally watched. The show had just begun when Nick called.

Oh God, please not another body, she thought as she hit Pause on the remote and then answered. "Hey, partner, what's up?"

Nick never called her unless something had happened.

"Not much, I just decided to give you a call and make sure you were doing okay," he replied.

She frowned. Something had happened. She felt it in her bones. The phone call was completely out of character for him. "Okay, Nick...what's really going on? You've never called me before just to check on my well-being."

There was a long pause and then she heard him sigh. "I played a part in the gunfight at OK Corral tonight, only it happened in the station parking lot as I got to my car."

"What?" She tightened her fingers around her phone. "Are you okay?"

"Yeah, I'm fine. Thankfully whoever it was wasn't a terrific shot. He fired on me twice and missed and by that time I'd managed to move to some cover. Then Shanks came out of the back door and the shooter disappeared."

"Do you have any idea who it was?" she asked.

"Yeah, it was our killer. Am I certain who he is? No. I didn't get a look at him."

"Did you go in and report it to Gravois?"

"I attempted to, but he'd already left for the day. Ryan was also gone."

Even though his voice held no judgment, the pit of her stomach burned with anxiety. There was still no way she believed Gravois had anything to do with the murders, but she couldn't say that for sure about Ryan.

"Anyway," he continued, "I just wanted to call and make sure you were okay."

"Let's be honest, Nick. The killer wants the investigation to stop and he obviously doesn't see me as any kind of a threat. I'm just Officer Beauregard, who passes out speeding tickets and sits on the desk."

"The biggest mistake the killer can make is to underestimate you," he replied. "But you need to make me a promise, Sarah."

"What?"

"You need to promise me that if anything happens to me, you'll go on fighting to find this killer," he said.

"Nothing is going to happen to you, Nick," she protested. She didn't even want to think about him being hurt or killed. Her heart wouldn't be able to stand it.

"Just promise me, Sarah," he replied pleadingly.

"Okay, okay… I promise," she replied. "Maybe I should be your bodyguard as well as your partner," she said more than half-seriously. "I could pick you up in the mornings and drive you home in the evenings. With the two of us together, it would be far more difficult for somebody to attack you. Please, Nick…let's do that."

"I don't want to place you in any risk," he protested.

"We'll protect each other. So, it's settled, I'll pick you up in the morning at around seven."

His low laughter filled the line. "You are one stubborn woman."

"Yes, I am, when something matters to me, and you matter," she replied. "So I'll see you in the morning at Nene's and in the meantime, stay safe, Nick," she said, fighting against the words she really wanted to say.

She wanted to tell him that she loved him with all her heart and soul and that she couldn't imagine her life without him. But she also knew in her heart and soul that now wasn't the time for him to hear those words from her. He'd just been attacked by the killer, involved in a gunfight. The mood definitely wasn't right now for a romantic confession.

"Okay, partner, I'll see you in the morning," he replied, and with that they hung up.

The relaxation she'd found earlier in the evening was now gone, destroyed by the fact that somebody had tried to kill Nick in the parking lot.

Had it been Ryan? Or had it been another officer, one they had yet to interview? She didn't have the answer. All she knew was somebody had lain in wait for Nick and tried to kill him.

Chills raced down her spine. The stakes had been high to begin with in this case, but with the killer trying to take out Nick, the stakes had now shot through the ceiling.

The next morning, she pulled into Nene's driveway at ten after seven. Nick immediately walked out the front door, letting her know he'd been watching for her.

He got into the passenger side and grinned at her. "I have to say, you're one of the prettiest bodyguards I've ever seen."

She laughed. "Don't let all this prettiness fool you. I'm a mean bitch when it comes to protecting those I love." Realizing what she'd just said, she quickly pulled out of the driveway.

"We're going to have a long day," he said as she turned onto Main Street. "We've got a lot of interviews lined up for today but the good news is we'll only have four left to do tomorrow."

"And then we check out all the alibis and see where we're at," she replied.

"Exactly," he agreed. "I'd say within the next week we'll be able to name our killer."

"I hope so, and I hope there isn't another murder in the meantime," she replied.

If the case ended in a week, then it would be time for him to leave. What she wanted to tell him was how badly she'd miss him. She'd miss their deep conversations and their shared laughter. She would miss his touch and his warm smiles. God, she would miss everything about him.

However, she said none of that. But she was determined that before he left Black Bayou, he would know how much she loved him, how deeply she was in love with him.

They made one stop on the way in at a small bakery where they got tall cups of coffee for themselves and two dozen doughnuts. "We'll offer the officers a doughnut and while they enjoy the sweet, we'll dig deep into their heads," Nick said.

By the time they got to the office, the first officer on their list of interviews had arrived. Bart Kurby worked nights and Sarah didn't know him very well. On the nights of the murders, he'd been off work.

He was a tall, middle-aged man, physically fit and with dark, hooded eyes. He sat at their table and didn't accept their offer of a doughnut.

He appeared tired and impatient as it was past time for him to go home and get some sleep after being on duty all night long. "We'd like to talk to you about the nights of the murders," Nick said.

"Yeah, I heard you were talking to everyone in the department," Bart replied. "I can't believe you two really think one of us is the Honey Island Swamp Monster."

"We're just following where the evidence takes us," Sarah said.

He shot her a quick glance and then looked back at Nick. "So, what do you want to know from me?"

Sarah frowned. The man had dismissed her with that single look and it definitely irritated her. Apparently, Nick had caught it, too, for he looked at her and gave an imperceptible nod of his head.

"Bart, we have seen from scheduling that you weren't working on the nights of the murders. We need to know what you were doing on those nights between the hours of about six and one in the morning," Sarah said with as much authority as she could muster.

Bart looked at her once again, this time with a little more interest. "I think on most of the nights, I would have been in bed by about nine in the evening."

"Anybody in bed with you?" she asked. She did know that Bart wasn't married.

He raised a dark eyebrow. "I'm really not the type to kiss and tell."

"Better to kiss and tell than wind up in prison for murders you didn't commit," she replied.

He hesitated a long moment. "Fine, on the night of the last murder I was with Paula Kincaid. We were together all evening and she spent the night at my place."

"Speaking of places, we know you live in an apartment here in town, but you also own a property just outside of town. What is that?" she asked.

"That's my parents' old place. I've been working on it and plan to move in there within the next couple of months," he said.

"Okay, I think that's all we need from you right now," she said, and stood to dismiss the man.

"Good work, partner," Nick said as soon as Bart left.

"He definitely ticked me off by dismissing me. Thanks for letting me do the interview," she replied.

"No problem, you did a good job."

"Thanks. You know what's really interesting? Paula Kincaid is supposedly happily married to George Kincaid, who travels for business. I wonder if push comes to shove, she'll substantiate Bart's alibi."

"Time will tell, and speaking of time, our next officer should be ready to be interviewed," Nick replied.

And so, the day passed. It was half past

six by the time they were finished. There were two doughnuts left in the box and Sarah's head was filled with all the information they'd garnered that day.

"How about dinner at the café," Nick suggested as they packed up their notes to leave.

"Sounds good to me," she agreed. Together they left the station and got into her car.

"While we eat, we can talk about everything we learned today," he said once they were headed to the café.

"Good, because my brain feels like it's about to explode with all the new information," she replied. "I'm hoping you can help me make sense of it all."

"I'll do my best, but I was hoping you could help me make sense of it all," he replied with a small laugh.

Fifteen minutes later they were seated at the café and had ordered their dinner. He reached across the table and took her hand in his. She loved when he held her hand, and he did it often.

"I'm so proud of you, Sarah," he said. His beautiful gray eyes held her gaze intently as his thumb rubbed back and forth on her hand. "You've come a long way since you took that bath in the swamp."

She laughed. "There was really no other

way than up at that point." Warm shivers stole up her spine as he continued to make love to her hand with his.

"Seriously, you've become a formidable officer and I hope that when all this is over, you aren't handing out tickets or stuck on the dispatch desk. You deserve to be working on criminal cases."

He released her hand only when their food arrived. They had both ordered burgers and fries and for the next hour and a half they ate and talked about the suspects they had interviewed that day.

"What I find so interesting about today is that Ryan didn't bring us any alibis," he said.

Sarah dragged a fry through the pool of ketchup on her plate. "Maybe he lost his day planner," she replied drily.

Nick laughed but sobered quickly. "If he doesn't bring us anything tomorrow, then we need to pull him in for a less friendly interview."

"Sounds like a plan," she agreed. "I want this killer caught and if it's Ryan, then he deserves to go to prison."

"Whoever it is, he's going to be spending the rest of his life in prison. You look tired," he said as they finished up the meal.

"I am," she admitted. "I just need a good

night's sleep and then I'll be ready to go hard in the morning."

Minutes later they left the café and as they walked to her car, his hand once again sought hers. He had to love her, she thought. He had to love her more than a little bit. He reached to touch her far too often for this relationship to be strictly partners in crime solving.

None of that mattered as they reached her car and he got into the passenger side while she got behind the wheel. "What about you? Are you tired?" she asked.

"Yeah, I am, but like you all I need is a good night's sleep and I'll be ready to go again."

They were quiet on the ride to Nene's and within minutes he was gone, leaving only the scent of his cologne behind. She had no idea where they would go after the investigation was over and the killer was behind bars.

He'd already told her he never wanted to be a husband again and Sarah was at a place in her life where she didn't want to settle for less. She wanted a husband and children. She wanted a family. Ever since her parents had died, she'd had a desire to build her own family.

She couldn't think about all this right now. They had a killer to catch and then she'd see what happened with Nick. Still, no matter how she twisted things in her head where he was concerned, she just didn't see a happy ending.

Chapter Eleven

Sarah's head now was filled with alibis and questions concerning all the men they'd spoken to that day. Even talking to Nick over dinner hadn't managed to quiet the chaos in her head.

She got home and pulled into her garage, then entered her house. She dropped her car keys on the table but carried her gun back to the bedroom. She didn't intend to make the mistake of being without her gun at night ever again.

After a quick shower, she got into her nightgown and crawled into bed. As always, her mattress embraced her and within minutes, she was sound asleep.

Her phone woke her. She fumbled for it on the nightstand and noted that it was one o'clock. The call could only be bad news.

She was surprised that the caller identification showed that it was Gravois calling her. She answered. "Gravois?"

"Sarah, I just got a hot tip that the killer is going to act tonight, probably within the next hour or so."

"A hot tip?" She frowned. "A hot tip from who?"

"I'll explain everything when you get here," he said.

"Get where?" She sat up and gripped her phone tighter.

"To the swamp," he said with an urgency in his voice. "You know where the old fallen tree trunk is?"

"Yes, I do."

"Meet me there as quickly as possible. I've already called Nick so there's no reason for you to speak to him. Don't waste any time, Sarah. We're going to get the bastard tonight."

"I'll be there as quickly as possible," she replied.

The minute the call ended she flew into action. As she dressed, she wondered what kind of a tip Gravois had gotten and who was the tipster?

Would they really be able to catch the killer tonight? Oh God, she hoped so. It was past time to get him behind bars, especially before another woman died. She was ready to go within ten minutes and then she got into her car and headed to Vincent's.

The night was unusually dark with a heavy layer of clouds hiding the moon and stars. The streets were deserted so she was able to push the speed limit and arrive at Vincent's in record time.

She didn't see Gravois's or Nick's car in the lot, but she knew where to go and hopefully the two men would show up quickly.

She decided to shoot a quick text to Nick. Gravois called me and I'm here just waiting for you and him to show up. Tonight, we get him! She sent the text and then got out of her car.

She hesitated before entering the darkness of the swamp. On the one hand she wanted… no, needed to turn on the flashlight on her phone, but on the other hand she didn't want a killer to see her or know she was out here.

With it being so dark, she finally decided to turn on the flashlight and point it directly toward the ground. She didn't want to trip and hurt herself. She wanted to be an active participant in taking down the killer. She'd worked so hard for this.

A tipster. Obviously, somebody knew something about the killer and had decided to contact Gravois with this important information. Hopefully no other woman would die after tonight.

She kept the light shining on the ground and hoped nobody would see her. It didn't take her long to find the fallen tree trunk. Once there, she sat on the trunk and shut off her light.

She tried to listen for the sounds of the two men approaching but the swamp was filled with noises of its own. Bugs buzzed around her head and someplace in the distance, a fish slapped the water. Wind blew through the tops of the trees and little creatures rustled in the brush nearby.

She nearly screamed out when a hand clamped down on her shoulder. She whirled around to see Gravois. "Jeez, you scared me half to death," she whispered.

"Sorry," he replied. His flashlight was on and he shone it on himself.

"What's going on? Are you going to tell me who your tipster is?" she asked, her voice still in a whisper.

"Not right now. According to what he told me, we don't have much time," he replied, also whispering.

"I wonder where Nick is?" she asked.

"I don't know, but we can't wait for him. We need to get in position."

"Is the killer coming in this way?" she asked, a faint chill trying to walk up her spine.

"That's what I was told," he replied. "We need to crouch behind this trunk and hide and wait to see who shows up. I definitely think it's going to be one of the officers."

"Your tipster didn't tell you specifically who it was?" she asked.

"No. I was lucky to get as much information as I did out of him," Gravois replied. "Now, we need to get into position."

Who would it be? Who was going to come into the swamp with another heinous murder on his mind? She stood to move behind the trunk, but before she could take a step, Gravois slapped her phone out of her hand and then crushed it with his heel.

She stared at him in stunned surprise. "Gravois...wha-what are you doing?"

As she stared at his face, she suddenly realized his eyes were narrowed and his features were tensed in a mask of evil she'd never seen there before. A daze of shock held her in place as her mind grappled to make sense of what was happening.

Danger. Danger. It flashed in her head that she was in trouble. Gravois...it had been him all along. Oh God, he was the Honey Island Swamp Monster murderer.

"Sarah..." he said softly, and then reached out for her. It was then she saw it...a hypodermic needle in his hand. The daze of shock and surprise snapped and she ran. Blindly she raced into the swamp with Gravois on her heels.

She ran for her life. Frantically she sped into the darkness, knowing that if he caught her, she would be the next victim of the monster.

NICK'S NOTIFICATION DING awoke him, indicating he had a text. Who on earth would be texting him at this time of the night?

He grabbed his phone and read the message from Sarah. Gravois called me and I'm here just waiting for you and him to show up. Tonight, we get him!

He read the message twice and then, with his heart pounding, he jumped out of bed and got dressed. Gravois. The name thundered over and over again in Nick's head.

He immediately tried to call her, but it rang and rang and then went to voice mail. He quickly dressed and then strapped on his holster and gun. If Gravois had hurt a hair on Sarah's head Nick would kill the man. Sarah had said she was there and waiting for him, but she hadn't told him where she was.

All he knew for sure was that he believed Sarah was in trouble. Her message had implied that Gravois had contacted him, but that hadn't happened. Yes, Sarah was definitely in danger. If what he believed was right then she was alone with the man who might be the killer.

The swamp. That was the only place that made some sort of insane sense. She had to be there. He jumped into his car and headed out. He continued to try to call her, but all his calls continued to go to her voice mail.

Thank God at a few minutes after one in the morning the streets were deserted, allowing him to get to Vincent's in just a few minutes. And thank God he'd guessed right in coming here as Sarah's car was in the parking lot.

He got out of his car and as he gazed into the dark entrance of the marsh the back of his throat closed up and the familiar high anxiety tightened his chest.

Dammit, he wasn't a frightened little boy anymore. He was a grown man and he needed to go into the swamp and find the woman he loved…a woman he feared was in terrible danger.

With that thought in mind, he swallowed against his fear, turned on the flashlight feature on his phone and headed in. The anxiety he now felt wasn't due to him being in the swamp; rather it was because he needed to find Sarah.

It didn't take him long to reach the old fallen tree trunk and as his flashlight swept the area, it landed on a phone... Sarah's phone. The blood seemed to rush out of his body, leaving him light-headed.

If he needed a physical reason to believe Sarah was in danger this was it. He reached down and picked up the broken phone. He pressed the power button, but nothing happened. He slid the phone into his pocket.

This was why she hadn't answered his phone calls. Who had done this? Who was out here with her? Was it Gravois? That seemed to be the only answer given her text message to Nick.

"Sarah!" He yelled her name as loud as he could. His heart ached as all kinds of possibilities raced through his head. Where could she be?

"Sarah," he yelled once again.

"Nick... Nick, help me." Her voice came from someplace deeper in the swamp.

He released a deep gasp of relief. She was

alive! But she was definitely in danger. He raced toward the sound of her voice, desperate to get to her.

"Sarah, I'm coming...keep yelling to me," he shouted.

"Nick...hurry." Her voice was filled with a terror that torched a like emotion inside him. He had to get to her. Oh God, he needed to save her from whoever was after her.

He ran as fast as possible, batting back tree limbs and jumping over pools of water. Any fear he'd had about being in the swamp was gone, replaced by his need to find the woman he loved.

He stopped for a brief moment, panting for air, and then he called her name again. There was no response. "Sarah," he cried, needing to hear her to find her in the vast vegetation.

She screamed, a blood-curdling sound that shot icy chills through him. "Sarah," he cried desperately. There was no reply. "Sarah?" he called her name over and over again as he hurried forward.

Oh God, why wasn't she answering? And what had made her scream like that? Frantically he ran. His biggest fear was that she was now in the clutches of the Honey Island Swamp Monster murderer.

He didn't know how long he continued

to search, but without her calling to him it was futile. Was she still here in the swamp? Maybe. He just didn't know what to believe.

Gravois called me and I'm here just waiting for you and him to show up. Tonight, we get him!

He read her text again. Gravois. He had to be the killer and he'd lured Sarah here to make her his next victim. It didn't matter that she didn't fit his usual profile. The proof was in the text she'd sent to him. Gravois had called her and lured her out here.

Gravois. The man's name pounded over and over again in Nick's head. He needed to find the lawman as quickly as possible.

With this thought in mind, Nick ran to exit the swamp. There was nothing more he could do here by himself. The marshland was simply too big for him to find her by himself.

He finally reached Vincent's parking lot where Sarah's vehicle was still parked. He got into his car and leaned his forehead against the steering wheel, for a moment overwhelmed with emotion. Tears burned hot at his eyes and his chest tightened as a deep sob escaped him.

His love for Sarah ached inside him. He needed his partner. Was it already too late?

No, he refused to believe that. It couldn't be too late. With this thought in mind, he swiped the tears out of his eyes, put the car into drive and tore out of the parking lot.

Hell, he didn't even know where Gravois lived. He'd have to go to the station and see if somebody there knew. He drove as fast as possible, aware that time was of the essence.

He pulled to a halt in front of the police station and went in the front door where Judd Lynons was on the front desk. "Hey, man, do you know Gravois's address?" Nick asked.

"Why? What's going on?" Judd asked curiously.

"I just need his address. It's important," Nick replied. He didn't want to waste time by explaining everything.

"I don't know his exact address, but I know he lives on Tupelo Lane. Tupelo Lane is off Main Street by Mike's Grocery store. His house is in the middle of the block. It's a blue two-story and..."

Nick didn't wait to hear anything more. He turned on his heels and then raced back outside to his car. He tore away from the curb and headed down Main Street where he knew the grocery store was located.

He gripped the steering wheel tightly as tears once again blurred his vision. *Please let her still be alive. Please let her still be alive.* The words repeated over and over again in his head. It was a mantra...a prayer that went around and around in his brain.

He reached the grocery store and saw Tupelo Lane. He made the left onto the street. Tall trees encroached on the narrow street as Nick drove slowly, checking the houses on either side of the road.

The neighborhood was old, but the houses appeared well-kept. And then he saw it. The house was a slate blue with a wraparound porch, and Gravois's official car was in the driveway.

He parked along the curb and his heart thundered as he got out of the car and raced to the front door. He knocked. There was no response. He knocked again, this time loud enough to wake the entire neighborhood.

"Hang on," Gravois's voice drifted out. After only a moment he opened the door. The man was without a shirt and was clad only in a pair of sleep pants. His hair was disheveled as if he'd just been pulled from his bed.

"Nick, what in the hell is going on?" he asked.

Nick stared at the man in confusion. This was not the Gravois that he'd expected to find. "Sarah is missing," he said.

Gravois frowned. "Missing? What do you mean she's missing? Isn't she at home? It's the middle of the night."

"No, she isn't home. She said you called her and told her to go to the swamp?"

Gravois's frown deepened and he stepped out of his door onto the porch with Nick. "I didn't call Sarah. The last time I spoke to her was this morning at the station. So what's going on here?"

"I don't know, but this is what I do know. Sarah was in the swamp." Nick went on to explain as quickly as possible everything that had happened when he'd arrived at the swamp.

"Dammit, if somebody has harmed Sarah, there will be hell to pay," Gravois said angrily. "I'll meet you at the station in fifteen minutes. I'll call in all the men and we'll search the swamp until we find her."

"I'll be at the station waiting for you," Nick replied, and then he got back into his car. As he headed back to the station his brain whirled. Did he believe Gravois? Yeah, he tended to believe him. He'd certainly reacted in a way that made Nick want to believe him. If he didn't believe Gravois was responsible, then who was?

Who had called Sarah and impersonated

Gravois? Had she been too sleepy when she'd answered the phone to know that it wasn't Gravois? Was the call so short that somebody had fooled her? He supposed that was certainly a possibility.

So, who was it? Who had lured Sarah to the swamp? He believed it was the Honey Island Swamp Monster murderer. Sarah had believed she was too unimportant in the investigation for anyone to come after her, but somebody had definitely seen her as a threat.

By the time he reached the station, he was once again overwhelmed by a wealth of emotion. He went back into the little room he and Sarah had shared and sank down at the table to wait for Gravois to arrive.

Her scent was everywhere, that fresh floral fragrance that he found so attractive. He thought of her bright smile, the one that always made him feel like the sunshine was in his chest. She couldn't be dead. She had to be still alive. He needed her.

He jumped up out of the chair when he heard Gravois's voice booming down the hallway. He met the lawman in the hall. "I've called in all the men. The only one I couldn't get hold of was Ryan, but I left him a message to meet us at the swamp and that's where all the other men will meet us, so we need to head out."

"I'm right behind you," Nick replied, a new urgency filling his soul.

Twenty minutes later the men were all at Vincent's. All of them carried high-powered flashlights. It was impossible to do a normal grid search so Gravois appointed the men areas to go. Right now, it was a search-and-rescue operation. He hoped like hell it didn't change to become a recover maneuver.

He hurried to the place where he'd last heard her voice. Right now, the swamp was alive with the sounds of all the officers calling out her name.

Her name resonated in his heart, deep in his very soul. They had to find her and they had to find her alive. He continued to crash through the marsh, looking everywhere for her.

"Mr. Nick." Gator stepped out of the brush, nearly scaring Nick half to death. "What's going on here?"

"Gator, Sarah has gone missing and I last heard from her here in the swamp." Nick quickly explained what had happened. "Did you hear anything out here tonight? Did you see anything?"

"Most nights I'm out and about, but tonight

I slept until I heard all the commotion, so the answer is no. I'm sorry, but I didn't see or hear anything. I'll help the search now."

"Thanks, Gator," Nick replied.

The old man nodded at him and then disappeared back into the brush and Nick continued moving forward. One more person searching could only help.

They searched until dawn when Gravois called things off because the men needed a break. They all agreed to reconvene at the station in a half an hour for more instructions.

Nick remained in Vincent's parking lot after the others had left. The morning sun was sparking on the trees, turning it all a rich golden color.

She wasn't there. His gut instinct told him she was no longer in the swamp. The search had been far-reaching, but the swamp was vast. But he now believed she'd been taken away from the swamp.

Had she been taken to the killing grounds? Where was that? How long did the killer keep his victims there before killing them? Maybe minutes…hopefully hours.

Once again, a wealth of emotion tightened his chest and tears blurred his vision. Where was Sarah? If what he believed was true, then one of the cops who had helped search for her was the same person who had taken her.

And where was Ryan? He hadn't shown up for the search. Suddenly it was imperative that he find Ryan.

Chapter Twelve

Sarah regained consciousness slowly. The first thing she noticed was the huge headache that stretched painfully across her forehead. She tried to open her eyes, but she was still too groggy and it felt as if her eyelids weighed a thousand pounds.

She remained still and simply breathed, but there was a noxious smell surrounding her. It was horrible and it reminded her of the stench in James Noman's shanty. Oh God, is that where she was?

No…that wasn't right. Her brain began to slowly clear. She'd gotten a call from Gravois and she'd gone to the swamp. Her smashed phone and the race through the swamp…all the events of the night suddenly flashed in her head.

Gravois. Dear God, it had been him all along. He was the Honey Island Swamp Monster killer. She'd run so hard and so fast last night to escape him and the hypodermic needle he'd held in his hand.

When she'd heard Nick, she'd hoped...she'd prayed he would get to her before Gravois did, but that hadn't happened. If she hadn't tripped over a big tuber, she might have escaped him. But the moment she hit the ground he was on her.

. She screamed and fought with him, but ultimately, he'd managed to get the needle in her arm. She'd continued to fight for several more moments before darkness had gripped her and she knew no more.

So where was she now? She finally managed to open her eyes. She was tied to a straight-backed chair and appeared to be in a basement. Even though there were few basements in the area, there were some. This wasn't just any basement; she knew she was in the killing ground.

Oh God. Dried blood stained the floor all around her chair. The stench was so horrendous and she knew it came from what was left of the poor victims. This was where Gravois not only stabbed the women, but also where he ripped out their throats and tore off their faces.

She had to get out. She struggled against the ropes that held her arms behind her as gasping cries escaped her. She twisted and turned her wrists. If she could just get one hand out of the ropes, she would be able to untie herself and escape.

There were no sounds from the upstairs and she sensed she was alone in whatever place she was at. Was the basement in Gravois's house? It had been years since she'd been inside his home.

She continued to fight to get free, but there was no give in the ropes. She fought until she was out of breath and gasping with pain and sheer terror. How long would it be before Gravois would come back here?

She finally leaned her head back and sobbed. Nobody would know that the chief of police was the monster. Except Nick. If he got her text then he should know.

So why wasn't he here? Did her text not go through? You couldn't always depend on technology. If for some reason he hadn't gotten her text then nobody would know she was here. Nobody would ever suspect the chief of police. She'd even assured Nick that there was no way she'd believe that Gravois was responsible for the murders. She'd been wrong...so very wrong.

Right now, she was on her own. Somehow, someway, she had to get out of here. She drew in several deep breaths and then began working her hands once again, twisting and turning them until she was once again crying and her wrists felt raw enough to be bleeding.

It took several minutes for her to calm herself. She had to stay calm so she could think rationally. She did not want to become another victim of the Honey Island Swamp Monster murderer.

For the first time she began to look around the room. In front of her was a small wooden workbench with two deep drawers, but there was nothing on top of it. However hanging above it was a gardening claw. The tool looked dirty with rust-colored stains she believed to be blood.

Was that what he used to tear out his victim's throats? To rake their faces off? She swallowed hard against the new wave of emotions that rose up inside her. It wasn't just terror; it was also abject horror that filled her.

This felt like a scene from a horrible horror film, one of those sick, bloody films that she had always refused to watch. And now she was living it.

To her left was a staircase leading up and to her right...dear heavens...there was an old red recliner chair and in the chair was an intact human skeleton.

Gravois's missing wife. The one who had supposedly left him years ago. Yvette. She hadn't left at all. She'd been murdered and her body had been here all along.

For the first time since she'd opened her eyes, Sarah screamed.

THANKFULLY GRAVOIS WAS at the station when Nick arrived. Nick immediately went into his office. "We need to check out Ryan. He didn't show up for the search and he could be our man."

"You're right. With all the commotion going on, I didn't miss him being there, but it's very suspicious that he didn't show up at all."

"Where does he live?"

"He has a little house just outside the city limits. I'll gather up a couple of men and we'll head there right now." Gravois got up from his desk and twenty minutes later Nick was following behind his car to Ryan's place.

The man had brought them no alibis for the nights of the murders and he'd been no place to be found when Sarah had disappeared. Nick also hadn't realized the man lived in a house just out of the city limits. A house that might hold the killing grounds. A man who possibly had Sarah right now.

The tiredness from the all-night search disappeared as a new burst of adrenaline filled Nick. This had to be it, and he prayed that they weren't already too late. The last thing he wanted to do was find Sarah's body, her throat torn out and her beautiful face ravaged, behind some random building in town.

At least Gravois drove fast as if filled with the same anxious energy Nick felt. Behind Nick were two more patrol cars, each carrying two officers.

They finally pulled up in Ryan's long driveway. The house was small, probably a two-bedroom. There was also a detached garage. Ryan's vehicle was in the drive, indicating that he was home.

Gravois took the lead, marching up to the front door and knocking. He waited a moment and then knocked again more forcefully.

"Officer Staub," he yelled.

"Yeah…yeah, I'm coming," Ryan yelled. A moment later he opened his door. The man looked like hell. He was clad in a pair of sleep pants and a gray T-shirt. His face was unusually pale and he looked at them all in confusion.

"What's going on? I'm sorry I missed the search but I'm sick as a dog," he said. "I've got a temperature of 102 and I've been throwing up my guts for most of the night and day, so why are you all here?"

"We're still looking for Sarah," Nick said. "Mind if we come in?"

Ryan looked at him in surprise. "You think Sarah is in here? You really think I'm the killer?" He opened his door wide to allow them entry. "It's not me, man. You're all wasting your time here."

"Check out the garage," Gravois said to the other men and then he and Nick stepped into the house.

There was a blue sheet on the sofa and a box of tissues and a bottle of cold medicine on the coffee table. There was no nasty scent to indicate anything nefarious had happened in here.

"Feel free to look around," Ryan said as he sank back down on the sofa. "I can't even believe you all think I'd have anything to do with the murders or whatever happened to Sarah. I would never, ever hurt that woman."

They did look around. Gravois went into the kitchen while Nick looked in each of the two bedrooms. There was nothing suspicious anywhere in the house. The other officers returned from outside and shook their heads, indicating there was nothing in the garage.

Bitter disappointment shot through Nick.

She wasn't here, so where was she? They all agreed to meet back at the station in a half an hour or so. Once there, they would try to figure out where to go from here.

Nick returned to the station and sat in their little room, a sickness filling his soul. So much time had passed since he'd heard her cries in the swamp. If she was still alive, he knew time was running out for her.

Frantically, he went over all the notes they'd made that day, looking for something that would jump out at him.

He was so afraid. His childhood trauma, snakes beneath the bed and the gunfire in the parking lot...none of that had prepared him for the kind of fear that torched through him now.

He'd made her promise to carry on if anything happened to him, but he'd never seen the danger that was coming after her. Why in the hell hadn't he realized that she was at risk?

His job had been to come in and solve this case. He'd told her he'd never lost a partner before but she was so much more than his partner.

Now he didn't know where she was and his heart was slowly dying.

SARAH HAD FOUGHT against the ropes for what felt like hours...days, and she still found no give in them. She'd fought as hard as she could and had wept all her tears she had inside her.

She now leaned her head forward and began to feel a weary acceptance. She was going to die at the hands of the man she'd believed had loved her as a daughter. She was going to die here in this chamber of horrors.

Why, in all the years she'd known him, hadn't she seen the darkness that must be in his soul? Why had she never seen the utter evil that resided inside him?

Thank God, she hadn't burdened Nick by telling him how much she loved him. Hopefully he would go on with the investigation and he'd eventually get Gravois behind bars.

That didn't stop her from mourning what might have been. Even if things hadn't worked out with Nick, she'd still wanted to be somebody's wife. She'd wanted babies to fill her arms and to build a real family with some special man. She hadn't realized how badly she'd wanted that, and she had wanted that with Nick. Now she would never get any of those opportunities.

At least with her death she would be reunited with her parents in heaven. She'd once again be with the two people who had loved her unconditionally and had been her best friends.

A vision of Nick filled her head. His handsome features were ingrained in her brain, along with the sound of his deep, wonderful laughter. She loved the way his forehead wrinkled when he was deep in concentration and the way his smile warmed her throughout. She loved everything about him and she just wished she would have had an opportunity to tell him goodbye.

She straightened up as she heard the sound of a door opening and then closing from upstairs. It had to be Gravois and he was probably here for one reason...to stab her and then rip out her throat and tear off her face.

Once again, she began struggling against the ropes, sheer panic coursing through her. The door at the top of the stairs opened and she began to cry.

Gravois's heavy footsteps coming down the stairs sounded like the rhythm of death coming for her. Then he stood before her.

"Ah, Sarah, I'm so sorry it's come to this," he said with pity in his voice. "Unfortunately, your boyfriend seems to have angel wings of protection around him. The snakes didn't kill him nor was I able to shoot him to death. But

I'm sure your death will mess with his mind so much he'll have to quit the investigation."

"He'll never stop. He's going to throw you in jail, Gravois," she said angrily. "You'll suffer for the rest of your life in prison. I can't believe you killed all those young women. I can't believe you're such a monster. And... and is that Yvette?"

"It is my lovely Yvette." His features softened as he gazed at the skeleton in the chair. "It's been years now, but we had a fight and I pushed her. She fell over and hit her head on the edge of the coffee table. Unfortunately, it was a fatal blow. My beautiful, loving wife died."

"Why didn't you go to the authorities? If it was an accident then you wouldn't have been in any trouble," she replied. She needed to keep him talking, on the off chance somebody would find her...that somebody could save her.

"For God's sake, Gravois, why not at least give her a proper burial?" she asked.

"I didn't want anyone taking her away from me," he replied, his voice raised and his eyes slightly wild. "I love her more than anyone on the face of the planet and I needed her here with me. I needed to keep her here with me. I'll love her until the day I die."

"So, why kill all the women from the swamp?" Sarah asked softly, trying to calm him.

"Yvette looked like a lot of the women from the swamp. She had the same beautiful features as the swamp women. I just needed to find the right face. If I found the right one, then I would be able to give Yvette a face back."

Sarah stared at him in true revulsion. This was something out of the worst horror movie. "Gravois, you need help." He was obviously horribly mentally ill. To think that he was hunting for a face to give to his dead wife... the thought shuddered inside her.

"I don't need help," he yelled, his face turning red. "I just need to find the right damn face. So far, they've been all wrong. When I got them back here, I realized their faces were all wrong, so I erased them."

He stalked over to the workbench and opened one of the drawers. He withdrew a sharp-looking knife and then turned back to face her.

"Gravois, you don't want to do this," she cried frantically. "Please, you don't have to kill me. Let me go and I won't tell anyone about this. I'll make sure I screw up the investigation so nobody will ever come after you."

"Ah, sweet Sarah, you're just lying to me now."

"I'm not... I'm not lying to you," she replied fervently. She would say anything to him just to get him to let her go unharmed. "Gravois, please, you can trust me."

He shook his head. "I would never trust you. You've become a good cop, Sarah, and good cops want to get the bad guys off the streets. You're definitely a threat to what I'm trying to accomplish here."

"But I have loyalty toward you. You helped me so much after my parents died. You were there for me, Gravois, and I haven't forgotten that. Now I want to be here for you."

He laughed, but there was no humor in the laughter. Instead, it was a sick, twisted sound. "You're good, Sarah. You're very good. But nothing you say is going to stop what's about to happen."

He jabbed the knife forward. "I'm sorry that the first couple of stabs are going to hurt you, but hopefully you won't be conscious when I rip out your throat and tear your face off."

He stabbed the knife into her stomach and she screamed as excruciating pain ripped through her and she realized she was definitely the next victim of the Honey Island Swamp Monster murderer.

NICK SAT IN the room and went over all their notes and picked apart everything that had happened. Somewhere in the minutiae of it all, he had made a mistake or overlooked something important. He thought about everything that had happened since the moment he'd received the notification from Sarah on his phone.

The notification had said that Gravois had called her yet the man had denied that had happened. When Nick had gone to Gravois's house, the man had looked disheveled and as if he'd just climbed out of bed. But how easy would it have been for him to tousle his hair and change into a pair of sleep pants?

He'd stepped outside his house to talk to Nick. Why hadn't he invited Nick inside? A headache pounded in Nick's head. Gravois, the name once again thundered in his head.

Why had he not investigated the cases better? Why had he partnered Nick with somebody who knew nothing about the cases? Where had Gravois been on the nights of the murders? And where was Gravois now? Why would he call for a half an hour break in the search efforts?

God, Nick had been such a fool. He jumped up from the table and ran down the hallway to Gravois's office. He knocked once and then threw open the door. Gravois wasn't there.

A wild panic rose up in him. Gravois, it was the only thing that made sense. Dammit, Nick had suspected the man and now it was imperative that Nick get to his home and see if Sarah was there.

Colby Shanks and Ian Brubaker were standing by the dispatch desk. "Can you two come with me?" he asked urgently.

"Where?" they asked in unison.

"To Gravois's place. I think Sarah is there and I need you two to back me up."

"You think Gravois is the killer?" Shanks asked in shocked surprise.

"I do and I think Sarah is there and in danger. Will you come with me?"

The two officers looked at each other. "I'll go," Shanks said, and looked back at Nick.

"I definitely need to go, too," Brubaker agreed.

"Then let's go." Nick ran outside to his car, got in and tore out of the parking lot. All his nerves were electrified, shooting a fierce alarm through him. A glance in his rearview mirror showed him that the two officers were behind him.

Was it already too late? Oh God, how much of a lead did Gravois have on him? Had the man had enough time to go home and kill Sarah?

Tears of fear and frustration filled Nick's eyes. It couldn't be too late. She couldn't be gone already. His heart beat so fast he felt as if it might explode right out of his chest.

He reached Tupelo Lane and turned left, cutting off another driver who honked at him and gave him the finger. Nick didn't care, he had to get to Gravois's place as quickly as possible.

He pulled into Gravois's driveway behind the lawman's car. He parked and flew out of the car. It was only when he reached the front door that a wave of doubts overcame him.

Was he jumping to conclusions? Was this just all a big mistake? No, it couldn't be. His gut instinct told him that this was right. Shanks and Brubaker joined him on the porch. Nick knocked hard on the door and it creaked open.

He immediately drew his gun. The minute he stepped into the house he knew for certain he was right. The faint odor of human blood and decay filled his nose.

The two officers followed right behind him. "Check the bedrooms," he said to them.

While they disappeared down the hallway, Nick checked the living room and kitchen, but found nothing incriminating.

Where was the man? He had to be home. His car was outside. Brubaker and Shanks walked into the living room. "Nothing," Shanks said.

"Gravois," Nick yelled.

"Nick! We're down here," Sarah called.

He nearly fell to his knees at the sound of her voice. She was alive! Down here? There must be a basement. He opened one door and found a closet.

He ran to the kitchen where there were two doors. He'd already checked them once. The first one was a pantry. The second appeared to be a broom closet, but now on closer inspection, Nick saw that it had a false back. He pulled it away and a staircase was revealed.

"Gravois," he shouted. "It's over, man. Don't hurt her." Nick took two steps down and bent over to see the situation. The stench down here was horrendous and as he perused the area, his blood ran cold.

She was tied in a chair and Gravois stood before her with a bloody knife in his hand. "Put the knife down," he yelled. "Put the knife down right now." He raced down the rest of the stairs and pointed his gun at Gravois. "If you don't put it down right now, I'm going to shoot you."

Gravois looked at him and in the man's eyes radiated the evil that was inside him. "Can you really shoot me before I stab her?" he taunted.

Nick fired. The bullet hit Gravois in the thigh and with a scream of pain the lawman went down to the ground. Nick kicked the knife out of his hand and across the floor. "Call for an ambulance and put him in cuffs," Nick said to the others.

He ran to Sarah's side. "It's okay, baby. You're safe now," he said. He left her only to look in the workbench drawer for something he could use to cut the ropes that held her. He found another knife there and hurried back to her side.

She was quietly crying as he worked the knife back and forth against the thick rope. As he labored, he gazed around the kill chamber, horrified by the skeleton that sat nearby in a chair.

He didn't know who the skeleton belonged to but eventually he would find out. It appeared it was another murder Gravois would be charged with. He continued to talk soothingly to Sarah as Gravois yelled his rage.

"Why didn't you just shoot me in the heart?" Gravois screamed.

"Because I want you alive to face all the disgust from your officers. I want you alive to waste away in prison," Nick said tersely.

"Damn you," Gravois yelled as Brubaker and Shanks got him in handcuffs.

"Nick..." Sarah said with a gasping breath.

"It's okay, honey. You're almost free now," he replied. He cut through the last of the rope and it fell not only from her hands but from her waist as well.

It was only then he saw it...the blood that covered her stomach. "Sarah, oh God." He pulled up her shirt and saw the two gaping, bloody wounds in her belly.

"Nick," she whispered. Her eyes fluttered several times and then she fell unconscious.

"Get an ambulance here now," Nick cried. Had he been too late after all? Had Gravois mortally wounded Sarah? His heart cried out with anguish.

Chapter Thirteen

Nick sat in the waiting room in the emergency area of the hospital. The ambulance had finally arrived and Sarah was now in emergency surgery. She'd never regained consciousness while she'd been with Nick.

Once again, an abject fear coursed through him. He had no idea how badly she'd been hurt, how deep the stab wounds had been. But he couldn't help but remember the other victims had died from their stab wounds.

He'd been waiting for about an hour now to hear something, anything about her condition but so far nobody had come out to speak with him.

He knew Gravois was also here in the hospital getting surgery for his gunshot wound. He was also being guarded by Officers Kurby and Shanks.

Brubaker was the deputy police chief and he would be taking over the mess that Gravois had left behind until a special election could be held to appoint a new chief.

Brubaker would also be in charge of the crime scene and collecting the evidence that would send Gravois away for the rest of his life. There was no question in Nick's mind that the blood of all the victims was in that basement.

He couldn't believe what a hellhole Sarah had been held in. He couldn't begin to imagine what kind of horror she must have felt when she saw that skeleton sitting in the chair. God, she must have been so afraid.

She had to be all right. Please, she had to survive this. She was a fighter, but could she fight for her life despite those knife wounds?

He leaned forward and dropped his head in his hands. *Please let her survive.* He couldn't imagine a world without her in it. The world needed that beautiful smile of hers.

The outer door whooshed open and he was surprised to see Ryan walk in. He looked better than he had earlier that morning. "My fever broke and I heard the news about Sarah," he said. He sank down two chairs away from Nick. "Have you heard anything?"

"Nothing," Nick replied.

"I can't believe it was Gravois all along," Ryan said.

"He's not only a serious danger, but he's also a disgrace to law enforcement," Nick said with disgust.

"This is certainly going to shake up this entire town," Ryan replied. "I wouldn't be surprised if this doesn't make national news, a police chief who is a serial killer. So, does this mean you'll be leaving soon?"

"Not for a week or so. I want to make sure we get all the evidence we need for the case. Don't worry, I'll be out of your hair soon and then the path will be clear for you with Sarah." Even saying those words shot an arrow of pain through Nick.

Ryan released a dry laugh. "There's no path forward for me with Sarah. In case you haven't noticed, she's totally in love with you."

Nick didn't reply. Ryan's words only made Nick's heart hurt more. "I appreciate you coming here," he finally said.

"Despite what it's looked like, I care about Sarah as a friend and coworker. I would never want this for her."

"You should see Gravois's basement," Nick replied, and then described the utter madness to Ryan.

"I can't imagine how Sarah felt trapped there," Ryan replied.

"I just wonder what's taking so long? Why hasn't the doctor come out to talk to me yet?" Nick said in frustration.

Was it a good sign or a bad sign that it was taking so long? Was she still in surgery or had she succumbed to her wounds?

Fifteen minutes later a tall, dark-haired man came into the room. Both Nick and Ryan jumped to their feet. "Mr. Cain, I'm Dr. Etienne Richards," he said.

"How's Sarah?" Nick asked as his heart pounded with an unsteady rhythm.

"Given no complications, she should be fine. Unfortunately, one of the knife wounds caught her gallbladder so I had to remove it and I also had to do some muscle repair. Her wrists are raw but right now she's in stable condition."

"Can I see her?" Nick asked.

The doctor shook his head negatively. "She's sleeping now and I intend to keep her comfortable with pain medicine for the rest of the day. It would be better to come back and visit with her tomorrow."

Nick was disappointed but wasn't about to argue. "Thank you, Dr. Richards," he said. The doctor nodded at both of them and then went back through the door.

"At least we know she's going to be okay,"

Ryan said. "And now I'm dragging myself back to my sofa. See you later, Nick." Ryan left the waiting room.

Nick left as well. It was time to work the crime scene. He got in his car and headed back to Gravois's house. As he drove his heart was filled with wild relief. She had survived her time with a serial killer. Thank God, she was going to be okay.

Now he needed to do his job to ensure that all the evidence was photographed and collected. Everything had to be done by the book so there was no way Gravois would be freed on a technicality.

When he pulled up out front of the blue house on Tupelo Lane there were three patrol cars there plus a hearse, which indicated the coroner was also there.

As Nick reached the front door, Officer Ken Mayfield and the coroner's assistant carried up a stretcher with the skeleton on top. Dr. Cartwright followed after them.

"Hell of a day," he said to Nick. "Is Sarah okay?"

"She had to go through surgery, but at the moment she's stable," Nick replied.

"Good, at least she's better than that poor woman," he said, and pointed to the skeleton that was being carried to the hearse. "Who knew that Gravois was so sick. He had to have been sick to keep that and to kill all those young women." He shook his head. "Hell of a day," he repeated. "I'll talk to you later." He headed toward the hearse.

Nick went into the house and down the stairs where Brubaker appeared to have a good handle on things. There were three other officers with him and two of them were collecting blood samples around the chair while the other officer was standing by.

"Hey, Nick, what's the word on Sarah?" Brubaker asked.

Nick told him the same thing he'd told Dr. Cartwright. "How can I help?"

"I think we've got it covered right now. We've already taken the crime scene photos and collected both the knife and a claw gardening tool. We'll probably be here for the rest of the day collecting the evidence that hopefully will tie him to all the Swamp Monster murders."

Brubaker shook his head. "I can't believe he was responsible for all the carnage. He was a man I looked up to, the man I worked closely with. Damn, but I'm so disgusted right now, both with him and with myself for not seeing the evil in him."

Nick clapped Brubaker on the shoulder.

"Don't beat yourself up. Nobody saw him for what he was. A lot of responsibility just fell on your shoulders. I have confidence that when I leave here the department will be in good hands."

"Thanks. I really appreciate that coming from you."

"If you don't mind, I'll just hang out here awhile and if you need me just tell me what to do," Nick replied.

"That would be great," Brubaker replied. "The problem is this is a relatively small space so not many people can work it. Right now, those two are getting what we need." He gestured to the two officers taking blood samples.

Nick took a seat on the stairs and he remained there until dinnertime. He missed Sarah. While he wouldn't want her down here in the stench and the memories of being tied up, he wished she was here by his side.

He missed the scent of her perfume surrounding him, her leaning over to whisper something in his ear. At least he could see her tomorrow, although he didn't know how long she'd be in the hospital.

As much as he missed her today, it wouldn't be long before he would leave Black Bayou and Sarah behind. He'd leave his heart here with her and it would take a very long time to get over her.

But he had to leave her. The worst thing he could do was allow her to continue loving him. She would eventually want marriage and he knew what kind of a husband he was.

She deserved a terrific husband in her life and so the kindest thing he could do was let her go.

SARAH AWOKE AND for a moment didn't know where she was. She started to jerk up but then pain tore through her stomach. She looked around and realized she was in the hospital. Evening light cast in through the window and she was alone in the room.

She relaxed back and tried to process how she had gotten here. The last thing she remembered was being tied up in Gravois's basement as he stabbed her. She reached down and touched her stomach, which had bandages across it.

Then she remembered Nick coming down the stairs. Nick. He'd found her. He'd shot Gravois and saved her very life. Her love for him blossomed in her chest, filling it with a delicious warmth.

Somehow, she'd been brought here and whatever the doctor had done for her, it had obviously saved her life as well. She needed to know what had been done to her. Would she still be able to have children, or had Gravois taken that away from her with his knife wounds?

She looked around until she found a call button and then she pushed it, hoping whoever answered would be able to give her some information.

Moments later a nurse came in and introduced herself as Kelly. "I know Dr. Richards has been waiting for you to wake up. I'll just go get him now."

"Thank you," Sarah replied, and raised the head of her bed.

"How's my patient?" Dr. Richards asked as he came into the room a few minutes later.

"I'm having some pain, but what I want right now is some information."

As she listened to what the doctor had done, a wave of relief rushed through her. Who needed a gallbladder anyway? At least there had been no other real damage to her.

"Before you go, Dr. Richards, have you seen my partner, Nick?"

"He was here earlier and wanted to see you, but I told him it would be better if he came back tomorrow to visit with you."

"Okay, thank you," she replied.

"I'll see that the nurse gets you some more pain meds and I'll see you in the morning as well." Dr. Richards left and the nurse came in and administered the pain medication.

It wasn't long before Sarah drifted back off to sleep. She awakened with the morning sun streaming brightness into the room. Her stomach was sore but she knew it was going to take some time for her to heal.

She raised the head of her bed and wondered when Nick would be in to see her. The crime was now solved and so there was nothing more keeping him here. He would be leaving her any day now.

Unless...unless her words of love for him would keep him with her. She was running out of time. She had to talk to him today and tell him how much she loved him. Along with the ache in her stomach, her nerves formed a wave of anxiety as she anticipated laying her heart out on the line to him.

She hadn't been awake long when breakfast arrived. Breakfast consisted of coffee, broth and gelatin. She immediately took off the lid to the coffee and sipped on it. She hoped when they dismissed her, she would be armed with information about diet after gallbladder removal. Hopefully it wouldn't be broth and gelatin for the rest of her life.

She wound up drinking all the broth and eating the gelatin, then continued to sip on her coffee as thoughts of Nick swirled around in her head.

Her breakfast tray had just been removed when Dr. Richards came into the room. "Sarah, how are you doing this morning?"

"Better than last time I spoke with you," she replied.

"That's always what a doctor wants to hear."

"I do have more questions for you this morning."

"Hopefully I have answers for you," he replied.

She asked him about recovery time, surprised when he told her six to eight weeks. Then she questioned him about diet and finally she asked when she could be released from the hospital. Without any complications, she could go home in two to three days.

Once the doctor left, she turned on her television to pass the time. She was halfway through a game show when he walked in. As always, Nick looked handsome clad in black slacks and a gray polo that perfectly matched his eyes. His familiar scent smelled like safety...like home.

"Sarah," he said softly as he sat in the chair next to her and reached for her hand.

All the trauma she'd been through suddenly rose up inside her and she began to cry. "Oh, honey…don't do that. It will only make you hurt more."

"Oh, Nick, it…it was so horrible," she choked out amid her tears. "Being in—in that basement wi-with so much death surrounding me. And—and then Gravois there with a knife. I—I was so sure I was going to die down there."

"But you didn't," he replied gently.

"Thanks to you." She managed to get her crying under control as she squeezed his hand tightly. "How did you know it was Gravois?"

She listened as he told her everything that had happened after she'd disappeared from the swamp. "Thank God, you sent me that text, but Gravois was a crafty one and initially fooled me."

They continued to talk about the case for the next half an hour or so. "You look tired," she observed. His features were slightly drawn with what looked like exhaustion.

"I was up most of the night helping the men collect all the evidence at Gravois's house," he replied.

"He needs mental help. He told me the

skeleton was his wife and he was taking the swamp women hoping he could somehow take their face to put on her. But each time he got them to his basement he realized their faces were all wrong. He's definitely mentally ill."

"I doubt he'll get much help in prison, and that's where he belongs," Nick replied. "The good thing is it's finally over. The bad guy is behind bars and according to what the doctor told me you're going to be just fine."

"I'm not going to be fine, Nick. I'm so deeply in love with you. I won't be fine without you," she said. She watched him closely and felt the press of tears once again burning in her eyes as his turned a cold dark, slate gray.

"I want to marry you and give you babies. I want to spend the rest of my life with you. Please, Nick. I know you love me, too," she babbled. Why were his eyes so emotionless while she felt herself falling completely apart?

"Sarah." He pulled his hand from hers. "You knew going into this that eventually I'd go home. I never promised you anything. I even told you I'm not husband material."

"But you are," she protested. "Maybe you and your ex-wife weren't right for each other, but we are, Nick. Look into my eyes, Nick, and tell me you don't love me." She held his gaze, looking for a softening, and she gasped with relief as she saw it.

"That doesn't matter, Sarah. Even if I do love you, I don't intend to do anything about it. I'm sorry, Sarah, but in a couple of days I'll be going home and hopefully in time you'll find the perfect man for you here in Black Bayou."

She stared at him as he stood. How could he not see they were perfect for each other? "Have you ever considered that your ex-wife was wrong about you? You couldn't have been a lousy husband, Nick, because you're not a lousy man. You're the man I choose. I don't want anyone else but you."

"I'm so sorry, Sarah. It was never my intention to hurt you. I'll check in with you before I leave town and now, I'll just let you rest." With that, he left her room.

Rest? Her heart had just been ripped out of her very body. A rush of tears overwhelmed her and she began to cry in earnest. She'd been so hopeful, so sure that he loved her as much as she did him.

She'd been filled with such dreams of the two of them together. She'd been so sure they would have a life together and now all those dreams had been destroyed.

She didn't know how long she wept. By the time she pulled herself together Ryan and Judd Lynons walked in carrying a large vase of flowers.

For the rest of the afternoon officers came in carrying flowers and plants and good wishes. There was definitely a new respect in the way they interacted with her. At least she'd gained that, but nothing could warm her heart with the loss of Nick so fresh.

By the end of the day her room looked like a floral shop and all the officers had been in to visit with her. She directed the nurse to disperse some of the flowers to other hospital rooms.

As the darkness of night fell, so did more tears. She wept until she could weep no more. She'd been so excited to tell Nick how she felt and in her heart of hearts, she'd thought he'd sweep her up in his arms and tell her how much he loved her, how much he wanted to spend the rest of his life with her. Now she just felt empty, so achingly empty.

Over the next three days the emptiness was filled with heartache as she continued to mourn the loss of her dreams…the loss of Nick. She kept hoping he would come back in and tell her he couldn't live without her after all, and that he wanted a life with her. But that hadn't happened.

She was finally released from the hospital and Ryan drove her home. She'd been settled in at home for two days when a knock fell on her door. She went to answer and found Nick on her doorstep.

She hadn't heard from or seen him since he'd walked out of her hospital room and taken her heart with him. She opened her door and gestured him in. As he swept past her, she smelled that familiar scent of him, a scent that now only brought her more pain.

"Hi, Sarah." He stopped just inside the door. "I told you I'd stop by on my way out of town."

"So, you're leaving," she replied. Her heart began a new dull ache of loss.

"I am. I'll probably have to come back a couple of times as it relates to the prosecution of Gravois, but for right now I guess this is goodbye." He oozed discomfort as he gazed at her.

She wasn't going to let him off the hook so easily. "You were an excellent partner. You taught me so much and I loved the time we spent together."

"We were good partners," he agreed.

"We could still be good partners in life,"

she said softly. "Oh, Nick, if you'd just look deep within your heart, I know you'll find the kind of love for me that will last us a lifetime. All you have to do is take a chance on me, take a chance on us."

His eyes darkened. "I'm sorry that I can't give you what you want, Sarah," he replied with regret rife in his tone.

"I hate your ex-wife," she replied suddenly. He looked at her in surprise. "I hate her because I think she made you believe things about yourself that aren't true, things that have destroyed your ability to believe in yourself, to know what kind of a good man you are. Trust me, Nick. Don't trust her."

"Sarah, I just came by to tell you goodbye." He edged back toward the door.

"I love you, Nick," she said one last time, knowing once he walked out of the door, she would never see him again.

He hesitated for a long moment and in that moment, she held her breath, hoping...praying that she'd finally reached him. "Goodbye, Sarah," he finally said, and then walked out the door.

She wanted to run after him and throw her arms around him. She wanted to beg him to reconsider, but she did have a little bit of pride left. She sank down on her sofa, her heart pain too deep for even tears at this moment.

What would be the point of chasing after him? He knew how she felt and he'd rejected her anyway. Twice he'd rejected her. There was no more she could say to him. Now she had to figure out how to live without him.

Three weeks passed and physically she was feeling pretty much back to normal. But there wasn't a minute that went by that she didn't miss Nick. She had so many memories of him burned deep in her heart and she couldn't forget them.

She had been off work on sick leave and the house echoed around her with emptiness. Her loneliness was intense but she knew nobody else would assuage it except the man who had been her partner.

Hopefully, when she did return to work Brubaker would assign her to some serious case or another so she could immerse herself in something other than missing Nick. Hopefully Brubaker would see her for the good police officer she'd become.

It was right after noon on the twenty-third day since she'd last seen Nick and she'd just made herself a sandwich for lunch when there was a knock on her door.

She left her lunch and went to the door. She gasped in stunned surprise as she saw Nick.

What was he doing back here? Did he need something as far as the case was concerned? Weeks ago, she had given Brubaker her official statement about her time with Gravois. What could Nick need from her?

For a moment she wished she were dressed in something other than a slightly faded pink T-shirt and a pair of gray jogging pants. He looked amazing in a pair of jeans and a white long-sleeved dress shirt.

She put up all her defenses as she opened the door. "Hi, Sarah, can I come in?" he asked.

Silently she ushered him in. He went directly into her living room and sank down on the sofa.

"What are you doing here, Nick?" she asked as her heart beat an unsteady rhythm. She didn't sit, but rather remained standing. She didn't want to be close enough to him to smell his cologne or allow him to touch her in any way.

"How are you feeling?" he asked.

"As good as new," she replied. Did he have any idea what his presence here was doing to her? As much as she wanted to be strong and unaffected by him, her love for him still burned deep inside her heart and soul. "Why are you here? I'm sure you didn't travel here just to ask me how I'm doing."

"Actually, I was hoping you could help me solve a case."

She frowned at him. "What kind of case?" Had he lost his mind? Why would he be back here in Black Bay asking her about a case?

"It's about a missing woman. I've realized over the past three weeks that I need her in my life. She's a woman I want to desperately find because she fulfills me in a way I never expected." He stood, his gaze soft and warm on her. "Oh, Sarah, I've been such a fool."

She took a step toward him, her heart thundering in her chest. Was this for real? Was he really here for her? She was so afraid to believe it.

"But there's more," he said, stopping her in her tracks. "The woman has to be willing to relocate for me. The bad news is she'll need to leave everything here behind, but the good news is the New Orleans Police Department is always looking for good officers and if that's what she wants she'll easily be able to get a job."

He took a step toward her, his gaze so soft...so loving. "Sarah, I love you so much and I can't imagine you not being in my life.

The last three weeks without you have been absolute hell. Marry me, Sarah, and I promise I will try to be the very best husband you would ever want. Marry me and make me the happiest man in the world."

"Are you sure, Nick?" she asked, her heart on the verge of exploding with happiness.

"I've never been so sure in my entire life," he replied.

She could stand it no longer. She flew into his arms where he wrapped his arms around her and kissed her long and deep. When the kiss ended, he stared down at her intently.

"Are you sure you're willing to relocate? I mean, you have a house here and ties to your friends," he said.

"I can sell my house and honestly, Nick, this has never really felt like home. I found home with you and yes, I'm more than willing to relocate," she replied.

He laughed. "I guess Nene was right about me after all," he said.

She looked up at him curiously. "Why? What did she say about you?"

"On the first day I arrived here she told me that I was like one of the heroes in the romance books she read. I was the handsome stranger who had come to save the day and, in the process, would find my own true love."

He grinned down at her. "Funny how right she was."

"Funny how right you were to come and get me. You are my hero, Nick, and I will always love you," she replied.

"And I will always, always love you," he replied.

He took her lips once again in a kiss that whispered of passion but screamed of love. Even though she hadn't been looking for love, Nick had come into her life and everything had changed for her. She was truly home with him and she knew their partnership was going to last a lifetime.

* * * * *

Murder In The Blue Ridge Moutains

R. Barri Flowers

MILLS & BOON

R. Barri Flowers is an award-winning author of crime, thriller, mystery and romance fiction featuring three-dimensional protagonists, riveting plots, unexpected twists and turns, and heart-pounding climaxes. With an expertise in true crime, serial killers and characterizing dangerous offenders, he is perfectly suited for the Harlequin Intrigue line. Chemistry and conflict between the hero and heroine, attention to detail and incorporating the very latest advances in criminal investigations are the cornerstones of his romantic suspense fiction. Discover more on popular social networks and Wikipedia.

Visit the Author Profile page at millsandboon.com.au.

DEDICATION

To H. Loraine, the love of my life and best friend, whose support has been unwavering through the many wonderful years together. To my dear mother, Marjah Aljean, who gave me the tools to pursue my passions in life, including writing fiction for publication; and for my loving sister, Jacquelyn, who helped me become the person I am today, along the way. To the loyal fans of my romance, mystery, suspense and thriller fiction published over the years. Lastly, a nod goes out to my wonderful editors, Allison Lyons and Denise Zaza, for the great opportunity to lend my literary voice and creative spirit to the successful Intrigue line.

CAST OF CHARACTERS

Madison Lynley—A law enforcement ranger who goes after a serial killer on the Blue Ridge Parkway, while having to work with a former boyfriend assigned to the case. Can they put aside their differences to solve crime and rediscover each other?

Garrett Sneed—A national park service special agent who finds the death of young women eerily similar to his mother's murder in the Blue Ridge Mountains thirty years ago. Could there be a connection? And, with the help of the woman he mistakenly walked away from, can the Cherokee investigator uncover it?

Nicole Wallenberg—A park ranger involved in the investigation and trying to avoid becoming a victim.

Ward Wilcox—A park maintenance ranger who seems to be caught in the middle of the case. Does he have something to hide?

Ray Pottenger—A deputy sheriff assisting in the serial killer investigation and equally determined to solve it.

Blue Ridge Parkway Killer—The unsub is stabbing women on the Parkway to death and has set his sights on a certain pretty law enforcement ranger... Can he be stopped?

Prologue

Jessica Sneed was a proud member of the Eastern Band of Cherokee Indians, a tribe based in North Carolina. But she was even prouder of being the mother to a rambunctious little dark-haired boy named Garrett. Being a single parent at age twenty-five was anything but easy. Had it been up to her, she would be happily wed with a strong marriage foundation and Garrett would have both parents to dote on him. That wasn't the case, though, as his father, Andrew Crowe, wasn't much interested in being a husband. Much less a dad. Besieged with alcohol-related issues and a self-centered attitude, he'd left the state two years ago, abandoning her, forcing Jessica to go it alone in taking care of her then three-year-old son. Well, maybe not entirely alone, as her parents, Trevor and Dinah Sneed, did their best to help out whenever they could.

Shamelessly, Jessica took full advantage of

the precious little time she had to herself, such as this sunny afternoon when she got to hike in the Blue Ridge Mountains. She loved being in touch with nature and giving back to the land her forefathers had once roamed freely, through retracing their footsteps in paying her respects. She made sure that Garrett, whom she'd given her family surname, was aware of his rich heritage as well. They spent some time in the mountains and forest together when he wasn't in school.

But today, it's just me, Jessica told herself as she ran a hand down the length of her waist-long black hair, worn in a bouffant ponytail. She was wearing tennis shoes along with a T-shirt and cuffed denim shorts on the warm August day as she trekked across the hiking trail on the Blue Ridge Parkway, the hundreds-of-miles-long scenic roadway that meandered through the mountains. She stopped for a moment to enjoy some shade beneath the Raven Rocks Overlook and took a bottle of water from her backpack.

After opening it, Jessica drank half the bottle and returned it to the backpack. She was about to get on her way when she heard a sound. She wondered if it might be coming from wildlife, such as a chipmunk or red squirrel. She had even noticed wild turkey and white-tailed deer roaming around. Humans had to adapt more than the other way around. Some did. Others chose not to.

She heard another noise coming from the woods, this one heavier. Suddenly feeling concerned that it could mean danger, Jessica headed back in the direction from which she'd come.

But the sounds grew louder, echoing all around her, and seemed to be getting closer and closer. Was it a wild animal that had targeted her? Perhaps rabid and ravenous? Should she make a run for it? Or stay still and pray that the threat would leave her alone? As she grappled with these thoughts, Jessica dared to glance over her shoulder at the potential menace. It was not an animal predator. But a human one. It was a man. He was dark haired, with ominous even-darker eyes and a scowl on his face. In one large hand was a long-bladed knife.

Her heart racing like crazy, Jessica turned away from him to run but pivoted so quickly that she lost her balance and the backpack slipped from her shoulders. She fell flat onto the dirt pathway, hitting her head hard against it. Seeing stars, she tried to clear her brain and, at the same time, get up. Before she could, she felt the knife plunge deep into her back. The pain was excruciating. But it got much worse as he stabbed her again and again, till the pain seemed to leave her body, along with the will to live. What hurt even more was not getting to say goodbye to her son. She silently asked Garrett for forgiveness in not being around for him before complete darkness and a strange peace hit Jessica all at once.

HE TOOK A moment to study the lifeless body on the ground before him. Killing her had been even more gratifying than he had imagined in his wildest dreams. He recalled his mother once telling him as a child that he was messed up in the head. The memory made him want to laugh. Yes, she'd been right. He had to agree that he wasn't all there where it concerned being good and bad, much more preferring the latter over the former. His sorry excuse of a mother had found out firsthand that getting on his bad side came with dire consequences. Too bad for her that he'd put her out of her misery and made sure no one ever caught on that he'd been responsible for her untimely death.

His eyes gazed upon the corpse again. How lucky for him that she'd happened upon his sight at just the right place and time when the desire to kill had struck his fancy. It had been almost too perfect. A pretty lamb had come to him for her slaughter. He wondered what had been going through her head as she'd lain dying, a knife wedged deep inside her back. Maybe it had only been his imagination, but there had almost seemed to be a ray of light in her big brown eyes before they'd shut for good, as though she'd been seeing something or someone out of his reach.

He grabbed the knife with his gloved hand and flung it into the flowering shrubs. There were plenty more where that had come from. And he intended to make good use of them. Too bad for the next one to feel the sting of his sharp blade. But that wasn't his concern. A man had to do what a man had to do. And nothing and no one would stop him.

He grinned crookedly and walked away from the dead woman, soon disappearing into the woods, where he would slip back into his normal life. Before the time came for a repeat performance.

Chapter One

Thirty years later, Law Enforcement Ranger Madison Lynley drove her Chevrolet Tahoe Special Service Vehicle along the Blue Ridge Parkway in the Pisgah Ranger District of Pisgah National Forest, where she was stationed in North Carolina. It was a gorgeous span of nearly five hundred miles of scenery that ran through the Blue Ridge Mountains.

She had been employed as a law enforcement ranger with the National Park Service for the past eight years, or since she'd been twenty-seven, after completing four months of basic training. Along with receiving her bachelor's degree in natural resource ecology and management and a master's degree in environmental science from Oklahoma State University. In the process, she had chosen to go in a different direction than her brothers, Scott and Russell, who were both FBI special agents, as well as their adopted younger sister, Annette, who was a sheriff's department detective. All of them had followed in the footsteps of their parents, Taylor and Caroline Lynley, with long careers in law enforcement. Their father had been a chief of police with the Oklahoma City Police Department, while her mother had once been an Oklahoma County District Court criminal judge.

The fact that both were now deceased pained Madison, as they'd been the rocks of the family, leaving it to their children to carry on without them. All seemed more than committed to doing just that, remaining fairly close, in spite of each going their separate ways in adulthood as they navigated their lives, careers and other interests.

In full uniform on a slender five-eight frame, Madison continued to drive. She admired the forest—rich in chestnut oak, birch and buckeye trees—on this late summer day. As one of only a relatively small number of rangers patrolling the more than eighty thousand acres of land along the parkway, she never tired of this, loving the freedom and appreciation of nature and wildlife the job provided. Beyond patrolling the park in her vehicle, she had also ridden on bicycles, snowmobiles, ATVs, boats and even horses in the course of the job. She had participated in search-and-rescue missions, dealt with car accidents, wildfires and dangerous or wounded animals, you name it.

Then there was the criminal activity, such as illicit drug use, drug dealing and occasional crimes of violence that forced Madison into the law enforcement part of being a ranger. She was equipped with a Sig Sauer P320 semiautomatic pistol in her duty holster, should she need it when having to deal with hostile and dangerous park visitors.

Thank goodness I've never had to shoot anyone yet, she thought, while knowing there was always a first time for everything.

Madison's mind turned to her love life. Or lack thereof. She was now thirty-five years old, nearly thirty-six, and still very much single. She couldn't even remember the last time she had gone out on a real date. Actually, she could. It was two years ago when she'd been dating Garrett Sneed, a handsome Cherokee special agent with the National Park Service Investigative Services Branch. For a few months there, they'd been hot and heavy and had appeared headed for bigger and better things. And then, just like that, it had been over, as though it had never begun.

She couldn't really put a finger on why they'd broken up. Only that neither had seemed ready to make a real commitment to each other and

the opportunity to fix things that had gone un-
said or undone had slipped through the cracks.
Before she could even think about trying to get
back together, Garrett had gotten a transfer to
another region, as though he couldn't leave soon
enough. They'd lost touch from that point on,
leaving Madison to wonder about what might
have been if they had tried harder.

When she got a call over the radio, Madison
snapped out of the reverie and responded. It was
her boss, Tom Hutchison.

"Hey," he spoke in a tense voice, "we just got
a report of a dead woman discovered by a hiker
along the Blue Ridge Parkway."

"Hmm…not a great way to start the day,"
Madison muttered, never wanting to hear that a
life had been lost, whatever the circumstances.
"Are we talking about an accident, suicide, animal attack or…?"

"Could be any of the above." Hutchison was
vague. "Check it out and make your own assessment. We'll go from there."

"I'm on my way," she said tersely, after being
given the location.

As was the case any time she had to deal with
a death, all types of things went through Madison's head. Who was the victim, and why had
the person been at the park? Was this something that could have been prevented, such as

the taking of one's own life? Or was it the result of actions beyond the control of the deceased, such as an encounter with a black bear? Or a human predator.

Bad news no matter what, Madison told herself frankly. She would soon get some clarity, as she parked her car and was met by an anxious-looking African American woman in her fifties, with curly black crochet braids and hiking attire.

"I'm Ranger Lynley," Madison said. "And you are?"

"Loretta Redmond."

"You found a body?"

"Yeah. While I was hiking, though I nearly missed seeing her where the body was located. I could tell she was dead." Loretta took a deep breath and shook her head in dismay. "I still can't believe it."

Madison understood, as seeing a corpse outside of a funeral setting was something that was hard to forget for most people. "Can you take me to her?"

She followed Loretta through a wooded area and down a steep embankment, asking, "Did you see anyone else coming or going?"

"No one," Loretta replied without hesitation.

"Okay." Madison was thoughtful as they reached a spot off a trail that was overgrown, where there lay the body of a tall and slim female. She was lying flat on her stomach, wearing a purple-colored sports bra, printed blue running shorts, and white tennis shoes. Blood spilled onto the dirt from several gashes in her back, neck and elsewhere that Madison speculated had come from a long knife. She glanced at the thirtysomething victim's short red hair in a pixie cut with tapering sideburns.

Only then did a sense of familiarity hit Madison like a hard smack in the face. Upon closer inspection of the person's discolored round face that was turned awkwardly to one side, her lids shut, Madison realized with shock that she was looking at her friend and neighbor Olivia Forlani, a brown-eyed attorney from the nearby town of Kiki's Ridge. Both loved to jog and just yesterday had met up on Madison's day off for a run on the popular trail at Pisgah National Forest.

As though sensing her troubled expression, Loretta said, "You look like you've seen a ghost."

Madison swallowed thickly in turning away from Olivia's body. "Worse than that," she remarked, maudlin. "There's nothing supernatural about what's happened here. It's very real. Someone killed her."

Which left Madison wondering who would

have done such a horrible thing to her friend. It would be left largely up to the NPS Investigative Services Branch to figure that out. She would need to phone this in and have them get a criminal investigator out there right away, while wondering who would do the honors with Garrett now working on the other side of the country.

All things considered, she believed that was probably for the best as neither of them needed distractions, and her friend's death as a near certain victim of homicide would be the top priority of the ISB agent sent.

"A WOMAN HAS reportedly been stabbed to death on the Blue Ridge Parkway," Carly Tafoya, the recently appointed director of the South Atlantic-Gulf Region of the National Park Service Investigative Services Branch, said glumly.

ISB Special Agent Garrett Sneed cocked a thick brow as the shocking news registered while they stood in his midsize, sparsely furnished office in Region 2, in Atlanta, Georgia, where he was stationed. His sable eyes gazed at the petite green-eyed director who was ten years older than his age of thirty-six but looked younger. She had short brunette hair in an A-line cut and wore a brown pantsuit with black pumps.

"That's terrible," he uttered candidly.

"Tell me about it." She rolled her eyes. "This isn't the way we want to greet visitors to the park. Not by a long shot."

Garrett couldn't have agreed more, as he towered over her at six feet, two and a half inches on a muscular frame. "Who called it in?" he wondered, knowing this was ranger territory.

"Law Enforcement Ranger Madison Lynley," the director replied.

Garrett reacted to this revelation, though having guessed that his ex-girlfriend would be at the center of the investigation, whether he wanted it or not, with the strained history between them. Some things in life simply couldn't be helped.

"Ranger Lynley," he said equably. "We worked together when I was with the region previously."

"Makes sense." Carly nodded. "Apparently a hiker spotted the victim and reported it."

Garrett pinched his nose. "What about the perpetrator?"

"Still on the loose, unfortunately." She frowned. "I'm assigning you this case, Sneed," she told him without preface. "Should be right up your alley. Especially after you recently cracked the Melissa Lafferty case."

He thought briefly about the missing person investigation at the Grand Canyon National

Park in northern Arizona. Turned out that the missing twenty-two-year-old Lafferty had been abducted by an ex-boyfriend who'd held her prisoner for weeks in a room at his Phoenix house before she'd been rescued and the kidnapper arrested and charged with multiple offenses. Garrett was happy that though Melissa Lafferty had been put through the ringer, she'd survived, knowing that wasn't always the end result, with the current Blue Ridge Parkway case a sad but true example.

He winced while running a hand through his hair. Eyeing the director squarely, Garrett said painfully, "My mother was murdered in the Blue Ridge Mountains while hiking."

"What? That's awful. I'm sorry to hear that." Carly wrinkled her nose, thoughtful for a beat. "If this hits too close to home, Garrett, I can assign the case to another special agent."

"I've got this," he told her flatly. "It happened a long time ago." Moreover, Garrett knew that with fewer than forty ISB special agents in the entire country under the authority of the NPS, none had the luxury of picking and choosing assignments based on their history or personal circumstances. It was no different with him, even if he had more than one reason for not being enthusiastic to return to North Carolina. "I can be there in three hours," he told her, taking into account normal traffic and speed limits along the way.

"Good." Carly gave him a soft smile. "The sooner you can wrap this up, the sooner we can ease the legitimate concerns of park-goers."

"I agree." In Garrett's mind, it also meant the sooner he could get out of North Carolina and the bad memories he'd left behind, which did not include his prior involvement with Madison. It was perhaps the one bright spot, even if things had ended between them prematurely. At least it seemed that way to him, looking back.

Garrett drove his department-issued silver Chevrolet Tahoe Special Service Vehicle back to his two-bedroom, nicely furnished, nearly a-century-old condominium on Peachtree Street in downtown Atlanta. There, he packed a bag, placed his loaded Glock 23 40 S&W caliber semiautomatic pistol in a shoulder holster, and was out the door.

Soon, he was on I-85 North en route to the Blue Ridge Parkway. Garrett pursed his lips as he thought about the stabbing death of his mother, Jessica Sneed, who'd been part of the Eastern Band of Cherokee Indians, a federally recognized sovereign nation in Western North Carolina. He'd been just five years old at the time, when someone had taken her life that hot summer day thirty years ago. The case had never been solved, and Garrett was forced to live with that haunting reality, blaming himself for not accompanying his mother that day to protect her from a killer. Of course, he'd been too young to have been able to do much to thwart the brutal attack, but he only wished the opportunity had been there to try his hardest to make a difference. After her death, he had been taken in by his maternal grandparents, Trevor and Dinah Sneed, who lived in the Qualla Boundary, land owned by the EBCI and kept in trust by the US government.

When he'd reached adulthood, Garrett had left the Qualla, still stung by the memory of his mother's death. Having never known his father, it had been Garrett's grandparents who'd taught him how to be a proud Cherokee and to fend for himself. He'd attended North Carolina Central University, where he'd gotten his bachelor's degree in criminal justice, before becoming a park ranger and working his way to being an NPS ISB special agent.

Garrett's musings turned to Madison Lynley, an attractive ranger he had fallen hard for. He was pretty sure she'd been equally into him, the few short months they'd been an item. But somehow, the timing had seemed off and they'd broken up. Though it had been mutual and he believed they'd parted on good terms, if that were possible, rather than put pressure on either of them while working in the same space, he'd put in for a transfer to the National Park Service Investigative Services Branch Southwest Region and had been assigned to the Grand Canyon National Park field office. But three months ago, Garrett had been reassigned again to the South Atlantic-Gulf Region, opting to stay in Atlanta and not make things uncomfortable for Madison.

Now he wondered if that had been a mistake. Two years had gone by since he'd last seen her. No texts, emails, phone calls or video chats. Nothing. Had she truly forgotten everything that had existed between them? What about keeping in touch as they had pledged to do? Was he any less guilty of breaking that promise than she was? For his part, if honest about it, Garrett knew that not a day had passed when he hadn't thought about Madison on some level, wondering how she was getting on and if she had moved on with someone else. He had not. Some relationships were hard to substitute, even if they'd failed to progress into something truly meaningful and lasting.

When he arrived at the Blue Ridge Parkway a few hours later, Garrett was admittedly as nervous about seeing Madison again as he was determined to solve the homicide on the parkway.

I'll just have to suck it up and treat this like any other investigation, he told himself, getting out of the vehicle and approaching a group of law enforcement and personnel from the medical examiner's office. But from the moment he laid eyes on Madison, looking as gorgeous as ever, even in her law enforcement ranger uniform that hid that hot body and with her long and luscious blond hair tucked away in a bun, Garrett knew he had to throw that game plan right out the proverbial window. This would definitely be anything but "any other investigation" as long as she was part of it.

She separated herself from the others and met him halfway, those big pretty blue-green eyes widening quizzically beneath choppy bangs and above a petite nose and full lips on a heart-shaped face.

"I wasn't expecting the ISB special agent I requested to be you," Madison spoke in clear shock. He hadn't decided if it was a good or bad shock on her part.

Garrett grinned awkwardly. "Surprise." He thought about giving her a quick hug, if only for old times' sake. Being able to make body contact wouldn't be bad either. But he sensed it would be an inappropriate gesture at this time.

A hand rested on a hip of her slender frame

as she questioned, "So, how long have you been back in this region?"

Uh-oh, he told himself. Was there any right way to answer her?

"Not long." Garrett took a middle of the road approach. "I was planning to call you," he lied. Though perhaps he would have gotten around to it sooner or later. Or was that just a convenient rationalization for not knowing whether or not it was smart to go there?

"Right." Her curly lashes fluttered cynically. "Anyway, this isn't about us," she stressed, with which he concurred. "Someone I know has been murdered, and we need to work together to solve the crime."

Garrett was caught off guard on the notion that she'd been acquainted with the dead woman, giving him even more incentive to complete the investigation as soon as possible—hopefully leading to an arrest or otherwise preventing the unsub from harming anyone else.

"Sorry to hear that you were connected to the victim, Madison," he voiced sincerely. "Why don't you take me to the body and fill me in on any details you have thus far, and we'll proceed from there."

"Fine," she told him tersely. "Olivia deserves no less than to have whoever did this to her off the streets and behind bars."

Garrett thought back to his mother and her untimely demise. He only wished she had gotten the justice she'd deserved. Maybe this time around it would be a different outcome. "We're in total agreement."

Chapter Two

I almost wish he wasn't still so handsome, Madison thought as she assessed Garrett Sneed, her ex-boyfriend. Had that been the case, it might not be as bad to see him walk back into her life after two years apart. But as it was, if anything, the ISB special agent was actually even more striking than she'd remembered. He had dark eyes, a Nubian nose, prominent cheekbones reflecting his Cherokee heritage and a square jawline on an oval face, with a light stubble beard. The thick dark hair, she realized, was different. Instead of the hipster style he'd worn before, it was now in a mid-fade haircut that suited him. Tall and well-built, he was wearing a short-sleeved green shirt, tan slacks, and a vest that had Police Federal Agent on the back, along with comfortable plain toe Oxfords.

Madison blushed when he caught her studying him, though she had noticed him doing the same in seeing how she'd been holding up since the last time they'd met. Knowing her food-and-exercise regimen, she was confident that she'd passed the test just fine. Assuming he was grading her.

"Follow me," she told him, trying to keep this professional.

"Lead the way," he said evenly.

She introduced him to sheriff's deputies from Transylvania, Buncombe and Watauga Counties and staff from the medical examiner's office before they headed down a well-worn path toward the crime scene.

"This is really hard," Madison commented. "Not exactly the way I expected to meet again."

"I know." Garrett followed close behind her through the grove of trees. "Losing anyone you're connected to is a hard pill to swallow. Not what I was expecting, either, in seeing you again, but duty called for it."

Along with the fact that you just happened to have returned to this region, which made such an unlikely reunion even possible, she thought, feeling his breath as it fell on her skin. She wondered just how long he had been in her neck of the woods and never bothered to get in touch, if only for old times' sake. Or was that really necessary, considering that things had ended for them and there was no going back?

She came upon the area that had been cordoned off with yellow tape and had crime scene investigators searching for and collecting evidence. Weaving her way through with Garrett, who flashed his identification as the lead investigator but unfamiliar to some at work, they headed down the steep embankment to where the decedent was located beneath dense brush.

Madison gulped. "There she is." It pained her to see what was once a living, breathing, healthy human being now a murder victim. On hand was Deputy Chief Medical Examiner Dawn Dominguez. The fortysomething doctor was small boned and had brunette hair in a stacked pixie.

"Long time no see, Special Agent Sneed," Dawn remarked as she planted brown eyes upon Garrett.

"It's been a minute, Doc," he allowed.

"Sorry you had to be brought back in under these circumstances."

"So am I. But it comes with the territory." Garrett favored Madison with an even look and returned to eyeing the victim. "What can you tell us?"

Dawn, who was wearing nitrile gloves while conducting a preliminary examination of the body, responded, "Well, my initial read is that the decedent was the victim of a multiple-stabbing attack, resulting in her death."

His brow furrowed. "Any defensive wounds?"

"None that I can see thus far. It appears as though the assailant caught her by surprise and from behind before going on the attack."

Madison anguished over the thought of her friend's painful victimization and agonizing end to her life. "What was the estimated time of death?"

Dawn took a moment or two to contemplate and answered, "I have to say she's probably been dead for anywhere from four to six hours. I'll know more when the autopsy is completed."

"Any indication of a sexual assault?" she had to ask, even if Olivia was fully clothed.

"Doesn't appear to be the case. Again, I can be more definitive after the autopsy."

"The sooner I can get that report, the better," Garrett stressed.

"Understood," the medical examiner said. "We all want to get to the bottom of this."

Madison nodded in concurrence, while hopeful that Olivia hadn't suffered the further indignity of a sexual victimization in the course of losing her life.

After the decedent was put in a body bag, placed onto a gurney and wheeled to the medical examiner's van, Garrett asked Madison, "Any sign of the murder weapon?"

"Our initial search has turned up nothing,"

she told him, wishing that weren't the case. "Hopefully, the CSIs will find the knife used in the attack." But truthfully, she wasn't holding her breath on that one. These days, any killer who watched true-crime documentaries, or even scripted procedurals, would likely leave with the murder weapon to avoid being tracked down through DNA or fingerprints tying them to the crime. There were always exceptions, of course, with those who were overconfident or not privy to modern-day police work.

Garrett scratched his chin. "What about the victim's personal belongings?"

"The key to her car was still in her pocket and collected as evidence," Madison pointed out. "But Olivia's cell phone, along with her driver's license, is apparently missing. As for other belongings, given that she appeared to be on the parkway for a run, she probably kept her wallet or handbag hidden in her car. That isn't to say Olivia didn't have cash on her when she started out. If so, it's missing now."

He seemed to make a mental note before saying, "We can assume that the unsub may have taken the cell phone and anything else of immediate value."

Madison lifted a brow. "You think this was a robbery gone horribly wrong?"

"Quite the contrary. The apparent viciousness of the attack tells me that it was personal. Or something to that effect. Taking her possessions, if any, was strictly after the fact."

This made sense to her, though Madison was unaware of any clear-cut enemies Olivia had. Though she had recently ended a relationship, it had appeared as though it had been mutual and without malice either way.

Much like how we parted ways, Madison thought.

"We'll be reaching out to the public for any photographs or videos that may have been taken this morning in and around the area," she said, "to assist in our investigation. Or if anything or anyone suspicious was seen during the livestream of the Blue Ridge Parkway's webcams."

"Good." Garrett nodded. "Let's see what comes up."

Madison sighed. "Whoever did this was brazen and is obviously very dangerous while still on the loose."

"Tell me about it."

He frowned, closing his eyes for a moment, and she sensed that Garrett might have been thinking about the stabbing death of his own mother on this very parkway some thirty years ago in what had turned out to be an unsolved homicide. Madison knew he had a chip on his shoulder because of it. Even going so far as to believe that, at five years of age, he might have been able to thwart the deadly attack had he only been present. Would these painful reminiscences hamper his ability to conduct this investigation?

"Do you know if the victim has any relatives in the area?" he asked, bringing Madison back to the present.

"Her dad lives in Kiki's Ridge," she said. "Not far from where Olivia stayed."

"I need to go see him." Garrett's voice was equable. "Apart from notifying the next of kin and you identifying the victim, we still need a family member for formal identification of her."

"I know." Madison understood how things worked from both her own experience as a law enforcement ranger and her siblings in the business who were also called upon to be the bearer of bad news from time to time. "I'd like to be there when you tell her dad, Steven Forlani. I owe Olivia that much as her friend and neighbor."

"Of course." He gazed at her. "This is your case as much as it is mine. We'll do this together."

"Thank you." She welcomed his cooperation and understanding. Moreover, she liked the notion of them working together on a case. Even if they had failed at working things out romantically.

Madison received word on her radio that a vehicle registered to Olivia Forlani had been located in a Blue Ridge Parkway Visitor Center parking lot. "We're on our way," she told dispatch.

"Maybe the car can tell us something," Garrett speculated.

"Maybe," she agreed, but she suspected that the attacker had not followed Olivia from her vehicle. Instead, it seemed more likely that the unsub had either been lying in wait for her off the trail or had come upon Olivia randomly, while still targeting her for the kill.

When they reached the parking lot, Madison recognized her friend's white Toyota Camry.

"It was undisturbed and all by its lonesome," Nicole Wallenberg, a park ranger, reported.

Madison examined the vehicle. There were no indications that something was amiss. It was locked, and nothing seemed unusual inside at first glance. She spotted an item of clothing on the back seat that appeared to be concealing something beneath it, such as Olivia's handbag.

She gazed at the twentysomething ranger, with a tousled dark bob parted on the side and blue eyes, and asked her to be sure, "You saw no one checking out the vehicle?"

"Nope."

Another park ranger, Leonard Martin, joined them. African American, tall, solid in build and in his thirties, with curly dark hair beneath his campaign hat and wearing shades, he backed Nicole up. "I took a look around and didn't see anyone who was acting suspicious."

"Why don't you see if the ranger in the visitor center can tell us if Ms. Forlani ever went inside," Garrett told them. "And if she had company or there was anyone who may have followed her."

Leonard nodded and Nicole said, "We'll check it out," before they walked off.

Madison took out her cell phone. "I'll try calling Olivia and make sure she didn't leave her phone inside the vehicle."

"Good idea," he said and looked in the car window. "Go ahead."

She made the call, and it rang through her end. Neither of them heard Olivia's phone coming from the car or otherwise gave any indication that it was in the car.

"It's not there," Madison surmised, which told her that, short of the phone being located by investigators, there was a good chance that it was in the possession of the unsub.

"We'll ping her number and see if we can pinpoint the cell phone's location."

She nodded. "Let's hope it's being used or was left on."

"In the meantime, Forensics can see if they can come up with anything material to the investigation when they go through the car," Garrett said.

"Given that her car key wasn't taken, I'm thinking that the unsub never had any interest in stealing the vehicle," she said.

"I think you're right." He studied the vehicle again. "Whoever murdered your friend, he or she had another agenda than auto theft."

Madison squirmed at the thought of who might have wanted Olivia dead. "We need to know exactly what that was."

He nodded. "First, the victim's next of kin needs to know what happened to her."

"Right." She gulped, dreading what had to be done.

GARRETT WAS ADMITTEDLY finding it hard to keep his concentration on the road as he drove down Highway 18 South with Madison alongside. He vividly remembered when they'd been all over each other before everything had fallen apart. Now they were simply supposed to forget their history and focus on what, the present investigation and nothing else?

"So, how have you been?" he asked, hoping

it didn't come across as awkward as it sounded to him.

"I've been good," she responded coolly, without looking directly at him. "How about you?"

"Same. Just work and more work." He wondered if she was seeing anyone. Though he had gone on a date every now and then, the truth was she was a hard act to follow for any other woman.

Madison batted her eyes wryly. "Not even a little play?"

Garrett chuckled. Was this a test to see if he was sleeping around? "Only when I forced myself to step away from the demands of the job," he told her. "Maybe a little hiking, working out or whatever distractions came my way." *Did I just give her the wrong message?* he asked himself, though not exactly sure what that was.

"I see," she muttered thoughtfully. "Thank goodness for those distractions that life can offer."

"It's not what you think," he spoke defensively.

"Not thinking anything," Madison insisted. "What you do and who you do it with these days is your own business."

"True enough." He couldn't argue with the philosophy of her tart statement. Which was just as true in reverse. Their relationship had ended before he'd left. They weren't dating any longer. Therefore they didn't owe the other any explanations on their love lives. Or lack thereof. So why did he feel the need to clarify where things stood with him in that department? While also wondering what lucky guy, if any, had taken his place in her life.

"I am curious, though, about how you ended up back in the South Atlantic-Gulf Region," she said. "What, did they kick you out of the Southwest Region? Or maybe you grew homesick?"

Garrett was struck by the bluntness of her inquiries. Sounded like she'd missed him. Or was that more wishful thinking? "Well, I was actually making a real impact with the field office in the Grand Canyon," he responded confidently. Never mind the fact that maybe he had been a bit hasty in his departure from North Carolina. If he could backtrack, things might have gone a different way between them.

"So, what happened?" Her voice crooned with impatience.

"What happened is that Special Agent Robin Grayson unexpectedly retired and, since they were already short on qualified agents with my experience, I was brought back to this region to take her place." He wrinkled his brow. "Not like I had much of a choice."

"And if you had?" Madison regarded him challengingly.

Sensing it was a backed-into-a-corner-type question, Garrett gave an answer that maybe even surprised himself a little. "I think it would have been the same result." Not sure how he wanted her to read that, he lightened the response by saying, "It gets too damned hot in Arizona, and the wasps and bees were a pain in the neck, no pun intended."

She laughed. "I'll bet."

Garrett liked the sound of her chuckle. She hadn't done it enough the first time around. Now seemed like it might be a wise time to change the subject again. "So, how's your family?"

"Everyone's doing great." She paused. "We got together earlier this summer for my sister's wedding and had lots of fun."

"Nice. Congrats to the newlyweds." A twinge of envy and regret rolled through him. It would have been nice to have tagged along. Even if their own romance had fizzled.

Garrett gazed at the road. If truthful about it, when they'd been together, he had found himself slightly intimidated by Madison's family members, all in law enforcement professions. It had been almost as though he'd needed to prove himself. On the other hand, he felt more than up to the task of doing just that. Maybe the opportunity would present itself again.

"So, how long have you been friends with Olivia?"

She considered this. "Probably seven or eight months. Why?"

"Just wondering if there was anyone in her life who may have wanted her dead."

"She never said anything to me about being afraid of someone." Madison drew a breath. "Not that she would have necessarily, as not everyone is as comfortable talking about such things, sometimes believing it was something manageable. Till proven otherwise."

"What about a boyfriend?"

"Olivia had been seeing someone till about a month ago," Madison informed him. "A bank manager named Allen Webster. They supposedly ended things amicably, and I never heard her say anything about him being a problem after the fact."

"Hmm…" Garrett's voice was low, thoughtful. He understood that not all things were as they seemed. Especially when it came to dating and domestic violence and the ability of many to keep up appearances, for one reason or another. Was that the case here? "Do you know if she started seeing anyone else?"

"Olivia went out on dates every now and

then, but she never indicated that anyone was stalking her."

"We'll see about that," he said, "assuming the investigation doesn't point in a different direction."

They reached Kiki's Ridge, and shortly thereafter he pulled up to a ranch style home on Ferris Lane. Parked in the driveway was a silver Ford Escape. "Someone's home."

"That's Steven Forlani's car," Madison noted.

Garrett took a breath. "Better deliver the bad news."

She nodded, and he could see that this would be difficult for her but knew she would handle it as a pro. Just as he would in having to deal with this part of their occupations.

THEY HEADED UP to the house and heard a dog barking inside. The door opened just as they stepped onto the porch. Olivia's father was in his midsixties and kept his head shaved bald. Madison could see the French bulldog in the backdrop, itching to come out but trained enough not to do so.

"Hi, Steven," she said, ill at ease.

"Madison," he acknowledged tentatively, turning his gray eyes upon Garrett.

"This is National Park Service Special Agent Sneed," she introduced.

Steven nodded at him. "Agent Sneed." He turned back to her.

"We need to talk to you about Olivia."

"What's happened?" he asked nervously.

"Can we talk inside?" Garrett spoke up.

Steven allowed them in and peered at Madison. "What's going on?"

She glanced at the dog, who was studying her with curiosity as he sat beside a leather recliner, and then at Garrett, before eyeing Olivia's father steadily. "I'm afraid I have bad news," she began. "There's no easy way to say this. Olivia's dead."

Steven's knees buckled. "What? How?"

"She was killed on the Blue Ridge Parkway."

"By who?" he demanded.

"That's still under investigation," Garrett told him. "I'm sorry for your loss."

Steven ran a hand across his mouth. "Why would someone do this?"

"We're trying to figure that out." Madison looked at him compassionately.

Garrett said, "Sir, we need you to come to the morgue to positively identify the body."

Olivia's father lowered his chin in agreement, and Madison knew that his pain would get worse before it got better, as was the case for all secondary victims dealing with homicides.

While they waited for him outside, she told

Garrett, "You know, his only true peace will come when we catch the unsub. And even then…"

Nodding, he said thoughtfully, "Sometimes that peace never comes." He sighed, and she mused about the grief that was obviously still in his heart over his mother's tragic death. Something that Madison could relate to on a different level in losing her own parents in a car accident. "But we can't let that stop us from giving it our best shot, right?"

"Right." Madison knew that while the victimization of Garrett's mother had moved into the cold-case category that might never be resolved, Olivia's case was still very much open and solvable as they moved forward in the investigation.

Chapter Three

After her shift ended, Madison drove her duty car down the Blue Ridge Parkway and onto Highway 21 North before soon reaching the area where she lived in Kiki's Ridge. Nestled in the Blue Ridge Mountains, the quaint town had fewer than two thousand residents—most of whom knew or had heard of each other and would therefore be affected to some extent once the news spread about the murder of Olivia Forlani.

Turning onto Laurelyn Lane, Madison came upon her two-story, two-bedroom mountain chalet. She had purchased it three years ago and loved everything about it, including the creek out back, a great deck and easy access to walking trails and the river. The only thing missing was someone to share it with.

Having grown up in a large family, she was anything but a loner. But the one person she'd thought there might be a future with had just upped and left, putting that fantasy to bed. Now he was back, reminding Madison of what they'd once had, even when she fully expected Garrett to return to Atlanta when the current case was over.

Parking and going inside, she took in the place with its open concept, a floor-to-ceiling window wall with amazing views of the landscape, midcentury furnishings and hickory hardwood flooring. She headed up the winder stairs, removed her clothing and hopped into the shower of her en suite bathroom. Afterward, she wrapped her long hair in a towel and slipped into a more comfortable cotton camp shirt and jeans before heading back downstairs barefoot.

Madison went into the rustic kitchen, took a beer out of the stainless-steel fridge and went into the living room, where she grabbed her cell phone. Sitting on a retro button-tufted armchair, she called her sister, Annette, for a video chat to catch up.

After she accepted the request, Annette's attractive face came onto the screen. Biracial and a few years younger than Madison, her wavy brunette hair was long and parted in the middle with bangs that were chin length. Annette's brown-green eyes twinkled as she said, "Hey."

"Hey." She smiled back, while feeling envious that her sister had recently tied the knot with her dream guy and was experiencing the marital bliss that Madison could only dream of at this point.

"What's happening in the Blue Ridge Mountains these days?" Annette asked her.

"Since you asked, some bad and still-yet-to-be-determined things."

"Hmm… Why don't you start with the bad," her sister prompted.

"All right." Madison sat back. "A friend of mine was murdered today on the parkway."

"Oh, that's awful." Annette made a face. "I'm so sorry."

"Me too. Olivia was so full of life, and now that's been taken away from her."

"Do you have the killer in custody?"

"Not yet." Madison furrowed her brow. "It's still under investigation, but as long as the killer remains on the loose, it's not a good look for the National Park Service and park visitors in general, who want to feel it's a safe place to hang out."

"I'll bet. I'm sure you'll solve the case soon."

"Hope so."

Annette paused. "So, what's the still-yet-to-be-determined news?"

Madison took a sip of the beer and responded ambiguously, "You'll never guess who showed up from the NPS as the lead investigator in the case."

Her sister cocked a brow. "Garrett…?"

"Yeah." Madison was not at all surprised at her quick powers of deduction, given that Annette had held her proverbial hand when things had gone south between her and Garrett. "He was reassigned to this region and handed the case."

"How do you feel about that?"

"Truthfully, I'm still processing it," she answered.

"Maybe he is too," Annette threw out. "Have you had a chance to talk?"

"Not really, other than about the investigation and generalities."

"Well, my advice to you is just wait and see how things play out," Annette told her. "You never know, you two just might be meant for each other after all, bumps in the road notwithstanding."

Madison chuckled. "I wouldn't get too carried away with this," she said. "Things between us ended for a reason. There is no magic wand that will change that. We both have a job to do and will do it. No expectations. No pressures."

"Whatever you say." Annette smiled. "Just know that I have your back, wherever life takes you."

"Thanks, sis. I have yours too."

After ending the conversation, Madison heated up some leftover chicken casserole to go with a freshly made tossed salad, ate and thought about losing a friend and possibly regaining a friendship all in the same day.

THE NEXT MORNING, Madison drove to the headquarters of the Pisgah Ranger District on Highway 276 to update her supervisor, Law Enforcement Ranger Tom Hutchinson, on the investigation into Olivia's death. It was hardly an everyday occurrence on the Pisgah Region of the Blue Ridge Mountains but was something that needed to be dealt with in as expeditious a manner as possible.

When she arrived, Madison went directly into Tom's small office, cluttered with computer equipment and papers. He was sitting at a wooden desk, talking on his cell phone. In his late forties, thickset, with thinning brown hair in a short, brushed back style and blue eyes, he was in uniform. Only a few months on the job, he had replaced the previous district ranger, Johnny Torres, who had been fired after getting arrested for soliciting an undercover cop whom he'd believed to be a sex worker.

Cutting his call short, Tom said, "Hey."

Madison said the same and then, "I wanted

to drop by and talk about what happened on the parkway."

"Sit." He motioned toward a well-worn guest chair, which she took. "I'm sorry about your friend," he said sincerely. "There are no words to express how shocked I am."

"I feel the same," she told him, but she wanted to express her feelings anyway. "Olivia loved running in the park. That someone would go after her is unconscionable."

"I agree." Tom sat back in his ergonomic office chair. "The fact this happened on my watch, and yours, makes it a priority that we work hand in hand with the special agent assigned to the case."

"I know." Madison gazed across the desk. "His name is Garrett Sneed. We've worked together before." She saw no reason to mention their prior romantic involvement, as that had ended two years ago and had no bearing on the current homicide investigation.

"That's good," Tom said. "Should make it easier to coordinate your efforts, along with other law enforcement, to solve this case."

"True." She had no problem working with Garrett, as he was obviously very good at his job, having been brought back to this region because of that. "I'll be sure to keep you updated on any developments along the way."

"Thanks, Madison." He smiled. "Let me know if there's anything you or Agent Sneed need in bringing this case to a close."

"I will."

After leaving the office, Madison drove to the Blue Ridge Parkway, wondering what Garrett was up to this morning. She pictured him starting the day with a workout of some sort before getting down to business. Apart from wanting to do his job successfully, she suspected that losing his mother in a similar manner had given Garrett even more motivation to solve Olivia's murder.

Madison's daydreaming was interrupted when she received a call over the radio from Nicole, who said, "I've got a potential witness regarding the murder who you may want to talk to."

Madison was attentive. "Who?"

"Maintenance Ranger Ward Wilcox."

After Nicole gave her the location, Madison said hurriedly, "I'm on my way." Before she passed this along to Garrett, she needed to see if the information was credible.

Upon going through a tunnel and farther into the Blue Ridge Mountains, driving alongside mountain ridges, she reached her destination. She parked and headed into a wooded area, not far from where Olivia's body had been found.

Nicole and Leonard were standing there with Ward Wilcox.

Madison recognized him, having seen him around and spoken to him on occasion as a park employee. In his midsixties, Ward was tall and seemed in reasonably good shape for a man his age. He had dark eyes with heavy bags underneath on a weathered square face and wavy, gray locks in a shoulder-length bob. He wore a maintenance uniform and sturdy work shoes.

"Hey," Nicole said, wearing a campaign hat with her uniform.

"Hey." Madison glanced at the other ranger.

"Ward has something interesting to say," Leonard told her.

Madison gazed at the man. "Ward."

"Tell her what you told me," Nicole urged him.

"Okay." Ward sighed. "Yesterday, I saw a guy who was acting strange and holding on to a cell phone as if it contained the secrets to the universe. When I tried to talk to him, he ran off and disappeared into the woods."

"When was this?" Madison asked.

"I'd say around eight in the morning or so. Hadn't really given it much thought till I heard later about the young woman found dead on the parkway and started to put two and two together." Ward ran a hand through his hair.

"Maybe it was nothing at all. Maybe it was something. Thought you needed to know, one way or the other."

"Glad you reported this," she told him, well aware that any possibilities in a murder case were worth pursuing, even if they led nowhere. She was curious, in particular, about the cell phone the man had been carrying. Olivia's phone was still missing and was believed to have been taken by the unsub. "Do you remember the color of the cell phone the man was holding?"

"Yeah," Ward said without prelude. "It was red."

Olivia's phone case was red, Madison told herself. Coincidence? The timeline for when Olivia might have been murdered fit too.

"You said this man was acting strange. How so?"

Ward scratched his chin. "I don't know. Just seemed like he was agitated. Something was definitely off about him."

"Can you describe him?" she asked intently.

"Yeah, I think so."

Madison listened as he gave the description of a slender, lanky, sandy-haired man with a scruffy beard in his early to midtwenties and wearing dirty jeans, a T-shirt that may have had something resembling blood on it and dark tennis shoes.

"What do you think?" Nicole pursed her lips in looking at Madison. "Could this be the killer?"

"Seems to fit," Leonard contended.

Though unwilling to take that leap, it was more than enough for Madison to look into the possibility seriously. "I think we need to find him and have a talk with him...and soon."

GARRETT WAS UP early in the two-bedroom log mountain cabin he had rented, located just off the Blue Ridge Parkway. It had contemporary furnishings, a full kitchen, Wi-Fi, white-oak hardwood floors, a private deck and enough space for him to operate. He had turned one of the bedrooms into his temporary office, using the oak table within as his desk. Admittedly, he hadn't slept very well, as Madison had been as much on his mind as the death of her friend. It was unfortunate that a homicide should bring them back together. At least in an investigative capacity. Though he wasn't necessarily opposed to rekindling what they'd had two years ago, Garrett doubted that Madison had much interest in going down memory lane. Could he blame her? What was done was done. No going back. Was there?

Having had a quick run on the property's hiking trail, he now sat in the small accent chair in front of his laptop, sipping on a mug of coffee, while reading the autopsy report on Olivia Forlani. According to the medical examiner, the victim had been stabbed eleven times in something akin to a horror movie, with deep stab wounds to the back, neck, shoulders and buttocks. Based on the injuries and patterns thereof, the still-missing murder weapon was described as likely a survival knife with a smooth eight-inch, single-edged blade. The cause of death was ruled a homicide, resulting from acute multiple sharp-force trauma inflicted upon the victim.

Garrett sucked in a deep breath, closing his eyes at the thought of the horrible death. He couldn't help but reminisce once again about the similar way that his mother's life had ended. Though he seriously doubted one had anything to do with the other, the two stabbing deaths still struck an eerie chord. Olivia Forlani's murder wouldn't go unpunished if he had any say in the matter.

His cell phone rang, and Garrett answered, "Sneed."

"Agent Sneed, this is Deputy Sheriff Pottenger."

Garrett recalled meeting Ray Pottenger of the

Transylvania County Sheriff's Department yesterday when arriving at the Blue Ridge Parkway to take over the investigation. "Deputy," he said.

"Wanted to let you know that we pinged Olivia Forlani's cell phone and have tracked it to a campground not far from the parkway."

This told him that the unsub had turned on the phone and was likely using it. "Send me the info, and I'll get the ball rolling on a search warrant and meet you there."

"You've got it," Pottenger said.

After setting the wheels in motion for what he hoped would lead to Olivia's killer, Garrett phoned Madison to let her know what was going on. She answered after two rings. Before he could speak, she said, "There's a person of interest in Olivia's murder that you need to know about."

"Oh..." Garrett was all ears. "Go on."

"A maintenance ranger named Ward Wilcox reported seeing a man acting weird on the parkway yesterday at around the time Olivia may have been killed," Madison told him. "He was holding a cell phone that looked an awful lot like the one she owned. There may also have been blood on his T-shirt."

"Actually, I was calling you on that very subject," Garrett informed her, piqued by the news. "Deputy Sheriff Pottenger from the Transylvania County Sheriff's Department just phoned to say that Olivia's cell phone has been tracked to the Sparrow Campground on Bogue Lane."

"Really?" He could hear her voice perk up.

"Yeah. I'm on my way over there right now."

"I'll meet you there," she said eagerly.

"Okay." Garrett hoped they weren't in for a disappointment, knowing that this was personal for Madison. And if the truth be told, it was for him too. Her friend's death had managed to dredge up memories he would just as soon have kept buried. He was on his feet and got out the Glock 23 handgun he kept in a pistol case when not in use. Putting it in his shoulder holster, he headed out the door.

MADISON'S HEART WAS racing as she and the others approached the campsite. Her pistol was out and ready to use, if needed. She wanted to get a look at the unsub and possibly Olivia's killer. The fact that Ward Wilcox had seen what might have been her cell phone, coupled with it pinging in this location, seemed too much of a coincidence. When Garrett ordered the suspect out of the A-frame tent and there was no reply, deputies opened it. There was some clothing and other items for outdoor living haphazardly spread about. But no unsub.

Wearing latex gloves, Garrett went through

the things in search of the cell phone. He came up empty but did pull out a T-shirt that appeared to have dried blood on it as well as what looked to be a hunting knife. "We need to get these analyzed and see if either has Olivia Forlani's DNA."

Deputy Sheriff Ray Pottenger, who was six-five and in his thirties with a dark crew cut beneath his campaign hat, gazed at him and said, "I'll get them straight over to the lab."

Madison took a peek inside the tent, and something caught her eye. "Looks like methamphetamine in the unsub's lair," she stated knowingly, "along with drug paraphernalia."

"I saw that," Garrett acknowledged. "Another reason to find out who this tent belongs to."

Putting away her gun, Madison got out her cell phone. "I'll try calling Olivia's number." She hoped that whoever had the phone and apparently cut it off before they could locate it had turned it back on.

To her surprise, she heard the phone ring. It was coming from the woods. She spotted a tall, slender man holding the phone. He promptly dropped it like it was a red-hot coal and bolted.

"Stop that man!" Madison's voice rose an octave. "He had Olivia's phone."

"We'll get him," Garrett promised, and they went after the unsub.

Following in pursuit, Madison took her gun back out while trying to keep pace. It didn't take long before they had the suspect cornered behind a beige Winnebago Revel RV. He was taken into custody without incident on suspicion of murder in the death of Olivia Forlani.

Chapter Four

The suspect was identified as Drew Mitchell. He was a twenty-six-year-old unemployed army vet, who'd served in Afghanistan before being discharged for misconduct. Garrett sat across from him in a wooden chair in an interrogation room at the Transylvania County Sheriff's Office in the city of Brevard on Public Safety Way. He gazed at the person of interest in Olivia Forlani's violent murder, while awaiting results from the DNA testing. Mitchell was around six feet tall, slender and blue eyed with dirty-blond hair in a long undercut and a messy beard. Apart from his current predicament, there was an outstanding warrant for Mitchell's arrest in South Carolina for burglary and drug possession.

"Why don't we just get right down to business," Garrett told him in no uncertain terms. "You're in a heap of trouble, Mr. Mitchell. But I'm sure you already know that."

"Okay, you got me." Mitchell's nostrils flared.

"Yeah, busted for being an addict and stealing drugs. That's what happens when you run out of options."

"We're talking about more than drug addiction and possession." Garrett peered at him as he slid the cell phone that was inside an evidence bag across the table. "Care to tell me about this?" The suspect remained mute. "It belongs to a woman named Olivia Forlani. She was stabbed to death yesterday. Have anything to say about that?"

Mitchell squirmed. "I didn't kill anyone," he spat defiantly. "I swear."

Garrett rolled his eyes doubtingly. "You want to explain how you were caught with the victim's cell phone?"

"I found it." His voice thickened. "The phone was lying near some bushes. I needed a cell phone, so I took it. I had no idea the person the phone belonged to was dead."

"Is that why you ran when we came looking for you in your tent?" Garrett wasn't sure he was buying this. "Or why you took off when the maintenance ranger confronted you yesterday while you were in possession of the phone?"

"I ran when you guys showed up because I knew there was a warrant for my arrest. I freaked out." The suspect sucked in a deep breath. "I ran away when the maintenance dude came up to me because I thought he might try to take away the cell phone. I didn't want to give it up. So I fled."

Garrett remained less than convinced he was on the level and glanced up at the camera, knowing that Madison and other law enforcement were watching the live video. "Why was there blood on the T-shirt you wore yesterday?" he asked pointedly.

"I cut myself," Mitchell said tersely.

"What were you doing with a hunting knife inside the tent?" Garrett pressed the suspect. "Did you use it to cut someone?" Even in asking, in his mind, it didn't appear to be the same knife described in the autopsy report as the murder weapon in Olivia Forlani's death.

"I only used the knife for gutting an animal and have it for defending myself," Mitchell insisted. "I never cut anyone with it!"

Garrett went back and forth with him for a few more minutes, in which the suspect stuck to his story of innocence in the murder of Madison's friend. When they were interrupted by Deputy Pottenger, Garrett stood and walked over to the door.

"What do you have for me?" he asked him.

Pottenger sighed. "The tests on the T-shirt and knife have come back. It's Mitchell's blood on the T-shirt," the deputy said. "Blood found on the hunting knife came from an animal."

Garrett frowned. "So, no DNA found belonging to the victim?"

"Not as yet." Pottenger glanced at the suspect. "I think he's telling the truth about finding the cell phone."

Even though he wanted to believe otherwise, Garrett was inclined to side with the deputy. Drew Mitchell was going down on drug and theft charges—but apparently was not the killer of Olivia Forlani.

WITH DREW MITCHELL seemingly no longer the lead suspect in Olivia's death, it seemed logical to Madison that they go back to square one in the investigation. That meant interviewing the last known person Olivia had been involved with—Allen Webster. Though there were no obvious red flags to believe he'd had anything to do with her death, he needed to be checked out. Between her own years in law enforcement and stories she'd heard from her siblings and parents, Madison knew that a high percentage of female victims of homicides were killed by current or former significant others. Could that have happened in this instance?

I'll withhold judgment till we speak to Allen, Madison told herself as she drove with Garrett to Kiki's Ridge Bank on Vadon Street, where Allen Webster was the manager.

"Mitchell could have still killed Olivia and gotten rid of the murder weapon," Garrett suggested, behind the steering wheel.

Madison turned to his profile. "You really think so?"

"It's possible, though unlikely." He pulled into the bank's parking lot. "We have to keep all suspects on the table, so to speak. But as for now, Mitchell seems too messed up and sloppy to have pulled this off without a hitch."

"You're probably right," she agreed musingly. "We'll see what Olivia's ex has to say."

"Yeah." Garrett turned to her. "You okay?"

She met his eyes. "I'm fine. Like you, I just want answers, you know?"

"I do." He touched her hand, and she got a surprising jolt, as if struck by lightning. "We'll find them, wherever we need to look."

Madison nodded, feeling reassured somehow by his strength in words and conviction, along with the gentleness of his touch. They left the car and headed inside the bank. After Garrett flashed his identification to a burly and bald security guard, they made their way to Allen Webster's office. Sitting at a U-shaped desk, Madison recognized the man from a time she'd gone out for drinks with Olivia and him. In his late thirties and wearing a navy suit, Allen was muscular and gray-eyed with dark hair in a short fade.

"National Park Service Special Agent Sneed," Garrett told him.

"Agent Sneed." Allen shifted his gaze and said, "Madison...er, Ranger Lynley... I guess you're here to talk to me about Olivia?"

"That's correct." Garrett eyed him. "We need to ask you a few questions."

"Of course. Please sit." He proffered a long arm at the designer guest chairs in front of his desk, which they took. "I'm still trying to wrap my head around what happened to Olivia. Not sure how I can be of any help, but I'll do my best."

"Thank you," Madison said politely. "We're just covering the bases as we try to find out who killed her."

"I understand," he said evenly. "Olivia and I stopped seeing each other a few weeks ago. I have no knowledge about who might have murdered her. If there was something else you needed—"

"You can start off by telling us where you were yesterday between, say, seven and ten in the morning," Garrett said.

"Right here." Allen quickly lifted his cell phone and studied it. "Just wanted to take a look at my schedule to pinpoint exactly what was going on then." He paused. "Had a staff meeting to start the morning and then made a few phone calls and did some work on my laptop. All of this can be easily verified."

Madison had no reason to doubt that he was telling the truth, though they would check out his alibi. Still, she asked, "So why did you and Olivia break up anyway?"

Allen sat back with a frown on his face. "We stopped clicking, to put it bluntly. It just seemed like we were spinning our wheels trying to make it work, till deciding mutually that we were better off as friends. I certainly never wanted anything like this to happen to her."

Neither did I, Madison thought sadly, while also relating to the reality that some lovers were better off as friends. She wondered if that was true with her and Garrett. "Do you know if there was anyone who might have wanted to harm Olivia?" she asked Allen.

He chewed on this for a moment, then responded, "Not really. But if you asked me if there was anyone who might benefit from her death, I'd have to say the person who was Olivia's chief competitor at the law firm where she worked—Pauline Vasquez. They had both been trying to make partner, and someone would be left out in the cold, so to speak. I'm not suggesting in any way that Pauline would have gone so far as to kill for the job. That's for you to determine."

"We'll look into it," Garrett said.

"Hope you solve this case." Allen took a breath. "Our differences aside, Olivia was really a good person and she deserves some justice."

"I agree." Madison met his eyes. "We'll do our best to see that she gets it."

They stood, along with Allen, who walked with them and introduced them to other employees, who verified his presence the previous morning, seemingly eliminating him as a suspect.

"WHAT ARE YOUR thoughts on the so-called rivalry between Olivia and Pauline Vasquez?" Garrett asked as he drove away from the bank.

"I'd heard Olivia mention it from time to time but saw it as a spirited but friendly competition, more or less, to make partner at the firm," Madison admitted. "But who's to say it didn't go much further than that? Women are just as capable of committing acts of violence as men, even if there's a lower incidence of it in society. It wouldn't be the first time that jealousy and fierce competition led to murder."

"True. Or the last. The law firm's not far from

here," he pointed out. "We might as well swing by and see how Vasquez reacts."

"We should." She was in total agreement. "All possibilities remain open at this point, right?"

"Right. I have to say, though, that after reading the autopsy report, the viciousness of the attack has me believing the culprit is more likely than not a male."

"We'll see about that," she said, glancing at him.

Garrett kept an open mind. The fact that the case against Drew Mitchell fell through meant that the hunt for Olivia's killer was wide open and the potential suspects were not gender specific.

They reached the Kiki Place Office Building on Twelfth Street and Bentmoore. After parking in an underground garage, they took the elevator up to the third-floor law offices of Eugenio, Debicki and Vasquez.

"Why don't you interview Ms. Vasquez," Garrett told Madison as they stepped inside the lobby. "I'll check out the rest of the firm and see if anyone might have had it in for Olivia."

"All right," she agreed, and they approached a reception desk.

MADISON ENTERED THE carpeted office of Pauline Vasquez, the newest partner in the law firm. *She didn't waste any time*, Madison thought as she was greeted by Olivia's former colleague. In her thirties, Pauline was small and attractive with long brunette feathered hair and green eyes. She wore a brown skirt suit and high heels.

"Law Enforcement Ranger Madison Lynley," she introduced herself.

"Pauline Vasquez." She offered her hand, and Madison shook it. "All of us here have taken Olivia's death very hard. She was a valued employee."

"And one you no longer have to worry about beating you out for partner," Madison said in pulling no punches.

Pauline expressed disapproval. "If you're suggesting that I had something to do with Olivia's death…"

"Did you?" Madison questioned sharply to see if this shook her up any. "You apparently had the most to gain by her death."

"I had nothing to do with that," she insisted, running a hand liberally through her hair. "Yes, we were both battling to make partner, however, I was actually given the news that I'd been the one chosen several days ago, but was told to keep it under wraps till the official announcement, which coincided with Olivia's tragedy." Pauline sighed. "In any event, I would not have resorted to murdering my rival for the privilege. I achieved this on my own merits as a hard worker. Nothing more."

Madison held her gaze. "In that case, I'm sure you have a rock-solid alibi for where you were yesterday morning between seven and eleven?"

Pauline sighed exaggeratedly. "As a matter of fact, I do. I was in Raleigh, doing work for the firm. I arrived the night before and returned to Kiki's Ridge last night after eight o'clock. You can check the flights, the hotel I stayed at, two restaurants I went to and, of course, the meetings I attended."

"I'll do that." Madison took down her information to that effect. As it was, she sensed that they were climbing up the wrong beanstalk with Pauline as Olivia's killer. Should it be proven that she had hired someone else to do her dirty work, that would come out sooner or later.

She forced a smile at the attorney. "Thanks for your time. I'll show myself out."

GARRETT STOOD BY a floor-to-ceiling window in the office of Henry Eugenio, the fiftysomething CEO of the law firm. Henry, who was slender and wearing a designer suit, with wavy gray hair in a side-swept style, expressed remorse about the murder of Olivia Forlani. This seemed genuine enough to Garrett. As did the support for Pauline Vasquez, whom he insisted had been chosen to make partner before Olivia's untimely death and, as such, would not have had any reason to harm her.

This only fed into Garrett's belief that the unsub was a male perpetrator. "Did Olivia ever have any trouble with men in the firm?" he asked him.

Henry pushed the silver glasses up his long nose and blinked blue eyes. "Not that I knew of. Everyone got along great with her."

No one gets along perfectly with everyone, Garrett thought. "So, you never heard anything about unwanted advances or anything like that?"

Pausing, Henry gazed out the window and back. "I was once told that one of our newer junior associates made a pass at Olivia," he said. "But as we strongly discourage office romances, that was put to rest pretty quickly. Olivia never indicated it went any further than that."

But what if it had and escalated into something more ominous than nonviolent sexual harassment? Garrett asked himself. "I'd like to question this junior associate, if I can."

"No problem," Henry responded. "I'll buzz him to come in."

"Actually, if it's all the same to you, I'd rather speak with him alone," Garrett said, not wanting the suspect to be unnerved by an interrogation in front of his boss, perhaps causing him to lie.

"Whatever you say, Agent Sneed."

"What's his name?"

"Alex Halstead."

"Just point me in the right direction, and I'll find him," Garrett said after Henry had walked him out of the office.

"All right," he agreed, touching his glasses. "I'm sure you'll find that Alex was not involved in Olivia's death."

Garrett knew there was a tendency to see the best in people. Till proven otherwise. "Hope you're right about that."

A few doors down, he saw the nameplate and went into the office. In his late twenties, tall and fit, Alex was blue-eyed and had dark hair in a French crop style. He was standing and approached Garrett.

"Alex Halstead?"

"Yeah?" He tilted his face. "Did we have a meeting scheduled?"

"No," Garrett responded, realizing the man had him by two inches. "I'm Special Agent Sneed from the Investigative Services Branch of the National Park Service. I'm investigating the murder of Olivia Forlani."

Alex wrinkled his nose. "Sorry to hear about

Olivia," he claimed. "She was a great lawyer." He paused. "What do you need from me?"

"I understand that you hit on her," Garrett said, peering suspiciously.

"Yeah. It was a mistake."

"Some people don't know how to take no for an answer," Garrett stated.

"Not me," Alex insisted. "I apologized and never went there again."

"Can you account for your whereabouts yesterday morning?"

"I was at my apartment, sleeping through a hangover after getting wasted the night before," he responded quickly. "Didn't get up till noon. It was my day off."

Garrett eyed him. "Can anyone verify this?"

Alex cocked a brow. "If you're asking if I was with someone, the answer is no." He frowned. "If you're implying that I went after Olivia on the parkway because she didn't go out with me, you're way off base. I may not be perfect, but I'm definitely not a killer."

Aware that not all alibis included witnesses, Garrett was left to give him the benefit of the doubt, in the absence of evidence to the contrary. "I'll take your word for that."

"Thanks," he said smugly.

"By the way, you don't happen to own a survival knife, do you?" Garrett thought he would throw that out there, considering that the murder weapon was still unaccounted for.

Alex narrowed his eyes. "I'm not a hunter, outdoorsman, survivalist or anything like that," he contended. "So that would be no."

"Then I guess that will be all for now," Garrett told him. "If anything else comes up, I know where to find you."

He left the office, believing that Alex Halstead had not killed Olivia Forlani.

Chapter Five

"Do you want to grab a bite to eat?" Madison asked Garrett during the drive, after they had compared notes on Pauline Vasquez and Alex Halstead. Neither seemed likely as Olivia's killer, joining Drew Mitchell as former suspects as things stood. That meant they still had their work cut out for them if they were to catch the perpetrator before the case could start to run cold.

"I'm down with that," Garrett told her. "Actually, I'm starved."

For some reason, Madison felt relieved, as though she'd feared he would decline the dinner invite, which she'd only made because she too was hungry. Since they were still out, it seemed like a good idea, with no expectations beyond a good meal.

"I thought we could go to Janner's Steakhouse," she suggested, given that it was just around the corner. Never mind the fact that it had been a favorite place for them to dine when they'd been dating.

He smiled. "Sounds good."

Soon they were seated at a table by the window, where Madison ordered a boneless ribeye steak and heirloom tomato salad, then watched as Garrett went with familiar lamb chops and au gratin potatoes. *Apparently some things never change*, she thought, amused. They both chose a glass of Cabernet Sauvignon wine to sip on.

"So, what's next in the search for a killer?" Madison asked as a relatively comfortable conversation starter while she tasted the wine.

Garrett considered this. "Well, we need to go back over everything we have and don't have, including going through Olivia's belongings with the cooperation of her father, and see what we can gauge from this in deciphering possible clues on the unsub."

"I get that, but what do you think drove the perp into attacking Olivia in particular?" she posed to him curiously as the chief investigator. "Since it doesn't appear as yet that she was being stalked."

"That's the thing," he said, sitting back. "We don't know that is the case. Yes, it could well have been a random attack. But if Olivia was a regular jogger on the parkway, the unsub may have been aware of this pattern and waited for just the right time to strike."

Madison cringed. "Olivia and I liked to jog together sometimes on trails in the Pisgah Region," she noted. "Not to mention my own solo runs. Her killer could have been spying on me as well."

"That's always a possibility." Garrett furrowed his brow. "Did you ever see anyone who aroused your suspicions?"

"I honestly can't say that was the case," she replied contemplatively. "On the other hand, I always try to be on guard for any human or wildlife threats, but it's quite possible that an unassuming predator could have escaped my notice."

"Well, do me a favor—let's not have any more solo runs for the time being until we catch this person. I'd hate for you to be faced with the threat of a knife-wielding killer."

"All right." She felt that his concern for her safety was as much for what they'd had as his being a special agent. Not that she would have expected anything less, as his safety on and off the job was important to her too. "I won't make myself an easy target." Carrying her firearm when off duty, even for a run, was never a guarantee of safety these days. Especially if an assailant was armed too.

"Good." Garrett tasted his wine. "Of course, if you need a temporary running mate, I'm happy to volunteer for the job. Just let me know."

"I will." Madison had not forgotten that he ran too and that they had enjoyed jogging and hiking together. She wondered if doing so would be so simple, if he had no intention of sticking around just as she started to grow comfortable with him again.

GARRETT FELT QUEASY at the thought that Olivia's killer could have had Madison in his sights. As a male assailant was the most likely unsub at this moment in time, Garrett was going on that assumption in their search for the culprit. Though there was no reason to believe as yet that Madison was being targeted, he was glad to know she would not make herself an easy mark for anyone. Of course, as an active member of law enforcement for the NPS and with family in this line of work, he had no doubt she could handle herself in almost any situation. But that didn't stop him from being concerned for her safety. Especially as long as he was around to help keep an eye on her, and her seeming willingness to allow him to do so.

When the food arrived and they began eating, Garrett felt the urge to see where things stood in Madison's love life at the moment. He studied her as she ate, finding himself turned on even with this normal act. She was once again in uniform as a ranger and still kept that hair in a bun. Neither stopped him from appreciating what was right in front of him. "So, are you seeing anyone these days?"

Madison looked up as though startled by what seemed to him a reasonable question. She stopped eating and responded succinctly, "No, I'm not."

He tried to read into that. Was this because she had just broken up with someone? Had she been single since their own relationship ended? Or was she not interested in dating anyone right now? "Any decent prospects?"

She laughed. "No—not even any indecent ones."

He grinned crookedly while slicing into a lamb chop. "Has there been anyone in your life since we broke up? Or is that none of my business?"

"No, and yes," she told him. She forked a piece of steak. "To be honest, I haven't been asked out by anyone who captured my fancy enough. But that could change." Madison rested her gaze upon him. "As for it being your business, you gave up that right when you moved across the country."

"Fair enough," he conceded, even when it had

seemed best at the time. "Sorry for getting into your business. My bad."

"What about you?" Madison asked. "My turn to be bad. Who are you dating right now?"

"Not a soul." Garrett held her gaze. "Tried dating once in a while but, truthfully, it's been hard to get you out of my system. Not to say I've ever wanted to, even if we went our separate ways."

"Why did we anyway?" she posed in a casual manner.

"Excuse me?" He wasn't sure what she was getting at.

"Why did we go our separate ways?" Madison squared her shoulders. "I mean, it seemed like we had a good thing going. Then, just like that, it all went away." She sighed. "Or you did."

Garrett set down his scoop of au gratin potatoes. "As I recall, we both decided it was best that we end things between us. Or am I living in an alternate reality or something?" He regarded her questioningly, wondering if he somehow had it all wrong.

She took a deep breath. "You're not. It was what we both wanted. At least I thought so at the time. But we never really talked about this the way we probably should have. It was like burying our heads in the sand was easier than seeing if what we had was worth holding on to."

"I agree." He drank some water and grabbed his fork again reflectively. "It just seemed like neither of us was ready for a commitment, for whatever reasons. Maybe we were just trying to shield ourselves from being hurt. Or maybe the maturity or confidence level wasn't there to take that step in our relationship."

"We should have tried harder to see if there was more there." Madison pouted, while playing with her food. "I mean, didn't we owe ourselves that much? Or is it only me who can see that?"

"It's not just you." Garrett wasn't going to shy away from being equally culpable for their breakup. "I regret that we didn't hash through things more. Whatever we were running away from, we should have stopped and laid it all out and let the chips fall where they may. For better or worse."

Her mouth hung open. "You think?"

"Yeah," he admitted. "In hindsight, I wish I had stayed and worked harder to see where we went wrong. Or steered off course. But given the state of things, I thought that if I had stayed, it might be too weird being around each other and trying not to step on the other's toes while doing our jobs."

"You're right," she told him. "Probably would've been weird. Even if I wish we had done things differently."

"Me too." Garrett sat back, wondering where they went from here. Was there any chance at all for a redo? Was she open to this? Was he? "I never wanted us to stop being friends," he spoke truthfully. "But when I never heard from you again via text message, calls or whatever, I just assumed you had moved on and wanted no part of me in your life anymore."

Madison arched a thin brow. "I never meant for us to lose communication," she said in a heartfelt tone. "I wanted us to stay connected in some way. But after you left, I wasn't sure you felt the same way and didn't want to press it."

He nodded understandingly. "I did feel the same way," he promised her. "And didn't reach out to you more for the same reasons."

She smiled. "Looks like our communication skills really suck."

Garrett chuckled. "Yeah, probably could use some work."

"So, now that you're back in this region, can we at least be friends again?" Madison put forth hopefully. "We probably owe ourselves that much, regardless of how things ended between us."

In his mind, the *at least* part implied she might've been open to going beyond the friendship level. He felt that way too. Or at least exploring the possibilities. "Yes, I would like that," he told her.

She flashed him a toothy grin. "Cool."

He smiled back, already believing they had turned a corner and that the door was wide open for whatever might come next, over and beyond the investigation into Olivia Forlani's murder.

WHEN SHE GOT home that night, Madison was still thinking about the unexpected "airing things out" with Garrett. *It was overdue*, she told herself. She was unsure exactly what it meant in terms of going forward. Both had admitted to mistakes in the way they'd handled the situation two years ago. She wished they could go back and make things right. But there was no such thing as time travel, except in sci-fi, so they could only take what was handed to them and see what they wanted to do with it. They had agreed that a renewed friendship was a great place to start. Would it really be that simple though? Could either of them forget about what they'd once had and not want to have it again once the comfort level had kicked in?

Madison showered, brushed her teeth and went to bed. It was a country-style bed, like the other furnishings in the spacious room, and reminded her that it was where she and Garrett had first made love. A flicker of desire caused her temperature to rise before she brought it back down. She realized that in spite of the sexual chemistry that still existed between them, any attempts at recreating the passions they'd shared might do more harm than good. Even if he planned to stick around once the investigation had run its course, Atlanta, where Garrett lived, was still hours away. Did it really make sense to want to jump into what amounted to a long-distance relationship that could just as easily fizzle like the last time around?

Before an answer could pop into her head, Madison fell asleep. In her dreams, thoughts shifted to Olivia and the terrible way she died, along with needing to bring the killer to justice. No matter what it took.

OLIVIA FORLANI'S KILLER walked deep in the forest, surrounded by hemlock, hickory, birch and white pine trees. He was pensive as he approached Julian Price Lake along the Blue Ridge Parkway. The moon was starting to set beyond Grandfather Mountain, reflecting on the water's surface. He listened to the hoot of an eastern screech owl, then heard the crunch of his own cap-toe ankle boots on the dirt path. He was tempted to stop and take in his surroundings while breathing in the night air. But he forged on instead, eager to return to his campsite.

He thought about the one he had stabbed to death two days ago. It was something he had been thinking about for a long time, and when the opportunity had come his way, he hadn't hesitated to take it. Well, maybe he had paused for consideration, knowing that once he'd moved ahead, there would be no turning back. But the urge in him had been much too great to have second thoughts. Not when he had contemplated this moment in his head time and time again. But something had held him back, as if a voice from the grave was warning him against proceeding.

He'd suddenly become deaf to this as another voice had prodded him to continue what he had started long ago. This mighty call to kill had overtaken him the way illicitly manufactured fentanyl might get an addict in its grip.

So when Olivia Forlani had gone for her predictable run, he'd lain in wait to strike. And he had, over and over again. Till her blood-curdling screams had been no more, silenced by death. Making his getaway had been tricky, as others on the parkway could have spotted him and notified the authorities. But he was too smart to be caught, blending in as he had learned to do so well in his life. He had succeeded in taking away a life and rejuvenating his own in the process.

As he reached the campsite and the tent he called home these days, he could only crack a smile at the thought of his hiding from pursuers in plain view. Just as rewarding were the dark musings in his head that told him that the adrenaline rush he experienced in his homicidal urges was bound to come back again. Sooner than later. When that happened, he would find another to take the place of Olivia Forlani, in feeling the cold steel of his knife as he plunged it inside of her till death came mercifully.

He laughed in admitting that he was showing no mercy in his acts of violence. But then, none had been shown to him when he'd needed it most. Life worked out that way sometimes. He accepted this and wanted no sympathy. Nor would he give any.

Another wicked laugh escaped his lips, even as another call of an owl rang out, letting him know he was in preferable company as he retired for the night.

Chapter Six

The outdoor funeral service for Olivia Forlani was held at the Kiki's Ridge Cemetery. Garrett stood beside Madison to pay his respects to her friend. The fact that they had yet to make an arrest in her death bothered him. Someone was still out there, perhaps overconfident in the ability to avoid detection and apprehension. As he glanced at Olivia's father, Garrett couldn't help but think about his own mother and how the five-year-old version of himself had been overwrought at the notion that he would never see her again. Now Steven Forlani was in the same boat, more or less. The fact that he had gotten to see his daughter reach adulthood and achieve some of her professional objectives didn't make the pain of losing her prematurely to senseless violence any less.

Garrett gazed at Madison, remembering that she, too, had known such loss with the tragic death of her parents. No matter the manner of death, it was still a shock to the system and was something that would always be with you, whatever your lot in life.

"You okay?" he whispered to her.

Madison nodded. "Olivia's in a better place," she surmised.

"Yeah." Garrett wanted to believe this too for her friend, their parents and everyone who had moved on from this world.

He scanned the other mourners, seeing Olivia's colleagues huddled together. They seemed genuinely moved, and he wanted to believe none of them had anything to do with her death. Garrett eyed others in attendance, while wondering if Olivia's killer could be among them. As sick as it was, he was aware that some killers liked to come to funerals to gloat about their kills under the cloak of grievers. Was that the case here?

Garrett pondered this as he listened to the pastor sing the praises for Olivia, even as the perpetrator remained at large and the Blue Ridge Parkway a danger zone as a consequence. Till an unsub was made to answer for the homicide.

TWO DAYS LATER, Madison was on duty, patrolling the parkway. Garrett was still investigating Olivia's death, but no arrests had been made thus far. Madison was certain that it was only a matter of time before the unsub was behind bars. As she well knew, these type cases were not always cut and dried. The perp could have gone after Olivia for any number of reasons and now be as far away as Timbuktu in an effort to escape justice.

Well, you can run, but you can't hide, she thought. At least not forever.

Her musings turned to Garrett. They had resumed a friendship, which she liked, while also seemingly gone out of their way to smother any flames that could erupt into something more, as though a bad thing. Was it really? Or should they let it happen and deal with whatever came after?

Madison snapped out of the thoughts as she received a report over the radio that a black bear had been spotted on the parkway. And, worse, that it was threatening a young couple. Or was it the other way around? Black bears were, in fact, omnivores. They took up residence along the Blue Ridge Parkway and weren't afraid to venture out of their habitat in search of food. But sometimes curiosity and fascination got the better of visitors, who got too close to a bear, placing themselves in danger. Was that the situation here?

Either way, Madison was duty bound to come

to their assistance. "I'm on my way," she told the dispatcher.

Shortly, she turned off US 221 at Milepost 294 and entered the parkway near Moses H. Cone Memorial Park and Bass Lake. Passing by a grassy hill, Madison spotted Leonard and Ward in a parking area. They were flagging her down, as though she couldn't see them.

When she pulled up to and exited her vehicle, Leonard said ill at ease, "The feisty black bear went after a couple just trying to enjoy their lunch."

"Where's the couple now?" Madison was concerned. "Were they harmed by the bear?"

"They're holed up in a Jeep Grand Cherokee Laredo over there," Ward said. "Apparently when the bear got aggressive, they were able to fend it off long enough to get into the SUV, with only a few scratches."

"Well, that's good anyhow," she told them. "Any sign of the bear?"

"As a matter of fact, it looks like we've got its attention." Leonard's voice shook. He angled his eyes toward the woods. "And it's scaring the hell out of me."

Madison saw that the black bear had re-emerged and sized them up as potential prey, while snorting, popping its jaws and stomping its feet. With her heart skipping a beat, and not particularly interested in being the bear's meal, she raced back to her Tahoe and pulled out a 12-gauge shotgun. It was loaded with cracker shells which, when fired, would emit a loud booming sound in hopes of scaring off the animal.

As what looked to be a three-hundred-pound male took the measure of them while bellowing and standing on its hind legs, Madison ordered the two rangers to get behind her vehicle. Just as she was about to take cover too, the bear suddenly began to charge across the parking lot toward her. Tempted to panic but refusing to do so, she screamed at it and, remaining steady, placed the gun barrel at a forty-five-degree angle, firing the projectile in the bear's direction. It traveled some four hundred feet downrange before there was a flash and huge bang.

Repeating this seemed to do the trick as, spooked, the bear abruptly stopped in its tracks, pivoted and ran back off into the woods. Only then did Madison lower the shotgun and let out a deep breath. "Is everyone all right?" she asked, to be sure.

Leonard and Ward came out from behind the Tahoe. "We are now," Ward said. "Glad you showed up when you did, Ranger Lynley."

"Good shooting," Leonard quipped.

"You do what you have to do," she told them

modestly, thankful things hadn't gotten out of control for her or the bear.

"You can come out now," Ward shouted to the young couple, still huddled inside their SUV. "I think the danger has passed."

Madison wasn't sure that the bear might not come back, when regaining his courage and desire for something to chow down on. She interviewed the couple, visiting from Hawaii, and could see that they were still shaken up from their ordeal. But otherwise not the worse for wear. Still, given the fact that the bear had attacked humans at all meant that rangers and wildlife biologists would need to locate it and act in accordance with the protocols of the North Carolina Wildlife Resources Commission.

With the present threat contained, Madison thought she might check out the woods close to the grassy area where the couple had been picnicking. She wanted to be sure that the black bear hadn't first gone after some other vacationers, who might be in trouble. The last thing she wanted was to see someone's dream turn into a nightmare, with no one the wiser till too late. Hopefully that bear had not caused more havoc to deal with.

Having walked along the trail and through the tall trees, with the sounds of nature all around her, Madison felt a sense of calm. She decided maybe all was well and she could get back in her patrol car. Later, she imagined that Garrett would probably tease her about the black-bear encounter. When something caught her periphery, Madison jerked her head in that direction. There was something lying between trees. Or someone.

Putting a hand to her mouth, she realized that it was Ranger Nicole Wallenberg who was lying flat on her back. At first glance, Madison thought that the black bear might have attacked her before going after the couple. But homing in on her fellow ranger, she believed otherwise.

Blood oozed from cuts through Nicole's uniform that appeared to have come from a knife. Her blue eyes were wide open but gave no signs of life.

Madison gulped. *It wasn't a bear attack*, she told herself. This wasn't the work of an animal but a homicide perpetrated by a human being. Much like that of Olivia. Someone was targeting women on the parkway.

GARRETT HELD MADISON as she rested her head on his shoulder. She wept a little over the murder of their colleague. Coming on the heels of Olivia's death, and apparently in the same manner, had undoubtedly shaken Madison. It grated on his nerves as well, as this told Garrett that they were likely looking at a serial killer who had chosen the Blue Ridge Parkway as the killing grounds.

Madison pulled away from him and uttered diffidently, "Sorry about that." She wiped her nose with the back of her hand. "Just kind of overwhelming that this would happen again."

"I know. And you don't have to apologize." Indeed, it felt quite natural to be comforting her, and he would happily do so anytime she needed this. "You have every right to feel unsettled with what happened."

"We both do," she pointed out. "Nicole was one of our own. Now she's dead."

"Yeah." Garrett turned to look at the dead ranger, lying just as Madison had found her. She had clearly been put through an ordeal before someone had taken her life. Who? Why had someone gone after the ranger? Did she have any connection with Olivia Forlani? Or were both women victims of opportunity?

The immediate area had been cordoned off, and the crime scene technicians and sheriff's deputies were processing it for evidence. Garrett contemplated the scenario: Madison had staved off a black-bear attack, preventing herself and others from being a good bear meal. This had been, in and of itself, an act of bravery on her part, even though it was part of the job description. Then a routine and necessary check of the perimeter and she'd come upon Nicole. Could Madison have scared the killer off? Or was this act of violence a pattern of behavior that had been well planned and executed before the unsub had made a getaway?

"So, you didn't see anyone?" Garrett asked evenly.

"No," Madison replied. "But I'd just left two rangers, and another ranger joined us. Haven't had the chance to question them as to whether or not anyone saw anything."

"Okay." He gazed at the dead ranger's body. "What about the couple who said they were attacked by the black bear?"

"They apparently left the parkway afterward, upset by the incident."

"Did either ranger actually witness their encounter with the bear?"

"I believe the rangers arrived after the fact." She looked up at him. "You think they might have something to do with Nicole's murder?"

"Probably not," Garrett answered, rubbing his jaw. "On the other hand, if they had, the bear roaming around would have been a convenient diversion. Then there is the timeline. Assuming Nicole was victimized around the same time, this would have given the couple a perfect means for distraction and escape. At the very least, they may have seen something while on the grassy hill. Or someone."

"Between webcams along the Blue Ridge Parkway and a good description of the vehicle driven by the couple," Madison said, "I'm pretty sure we can track them down."

"Good." Garrett turned to see that Dawn Dominguez had arrived to take over from here. "Dr. Dominguez," he acknowledged.

"Special Agent Sneed." Dawn looked to Madison. "Ranger Lynley."

Madison nodded. "The latest victim is a member of the National Park Service," she voiced sadly.

Dawn frowned. "So sorry about that." She glanced at Nicole. "I'll do my best to expedite matters in giving you what I can for your investigation."

"Thank you."

Garrett added, "We need to know how she died, signs of a struggle and approximately how long ago we're talking about when the incident occurred."

"Got it." Dawn met his eyes and slipped on nitrile gloves before immediately giving the decedent a preliminary examination.

After a few minutes, she told them, "From the looks of it, the victim was stabbed at least six times, maybe more. There does appear to be some defensive wounds, but no evidence thus far that she was able to get DNA from her attacker. No initial signs that this was a sexual assault."

"What about the time of death?" Garrett asked.

Dawn touched the decedent. "I'd say she was killed in the last hour or two."

Or in the same time span that the couple claimed they were attacked by a black bear, he thought. Looking at Madison, it was clear that she was thinking the same thing. They needed to find the pair, if only to eliminate them as suspects.

THIS WAS MADISON'S second time speaking on the phone with Tom since learning of Nicole Wallenberg's murder. Only this time it was on video chat and was no more of an easier pill to swallow than the first time. "The deputy medical examiner has more or less confirmed that Nicole was stabbed to death."

Tom's brow furrowed, and he muttered an expletive. "She had big dreams with the NPS," he said sourly. "They probably would have all come true."

"I think so too." Though Madison hadn't been that close to Nicole, they'd had the chance to speak on occasion outside of work. And the ranger had been enthusiastic in her job and where it might take her over a long career. Now any such plans had been put to rest.

"Where are things in the investigation?" Tom asked fixedly.

"We're interviewing anyone who may have information," she responded, knowing they had yet to locate the young couple who had been supposedly in fear of their lives from an aggressive black bear. Though she could attest to that much herself, Madison still had to consider them persons of interest in Nicole's death. Till they were ruled out.

"Do you and Special Agent Sneed believe this is related to the murder of Olivia Forlani?"

"It looks that way, at this point." Madison almost wished that weren't the case, hating to think that a serial killer was in their midst. But the similarities between the homicides couldn't be ignored. Including the fact that the murder weapon was yet to be found in either case.

Tom wrinkled his nose. "If true, we need to get to the bottom of it as soon as possible," he stressed. "We can't have a killer running amok on the parkway or anywhere in the Pisgah Ranger District."

"I understand," she told him. "We're utilizing all the resources at our disposal to come up with answers."

"Keep me posted."

"I will."

After disconnecting, Madison got out of her vehicle when she saw Law Enforcement Ranger Richard Edison drive up. He had been working on the parkway since transferring from the Commonwealth of Virginia, where he'd been a ranger at Shenandoah National Park, four months ago. Single and her age, he was flirtatious and wasn't bad looking but still not her type. He exited his car and approached her, tall and well built in his uniform. Beneath his campaign hat was a bleached-blond Caesar haircut. Sunglasses covered his blue eyes.

"Hey," he said in a level tone.

"Hey." She forced a smile.

"You okay?"

"No, not really," she confessed. "Our colleague was just murdered."

"Yeah, it sucks." His voice dropped an octave. "Nicole was a great ranger."

Madison smiled at the thought. "Yes, she was."

He paused. "You wanted to see me?"

She nodded, eyeing him. "Weren't you with Nicole earlier?"

"Yeah," he said readily. "We rode together for a bit, and then I let her out for foot patrol."

"Did you see anyone else hanging around at the time?"

"Yeah, lots of visitors and workers." Richard adjusted his glasses. "If you're asking if I saw anything unusual going on, the answer is no."

"Did Nicole indicate she was planning to meet with someone?" Madison asked.

"Not that I can recall." He leaned on one long leg. "I think she may have been dating someone, but I'm not sure."

Madison regarded him. "Did you ever go out with her?"

Richard's mouth creased. "No way. We were friends, but she was too young for me to date."

I'll have to take your word on that for now, Madison thought. "If you think of anything that might help in the investigation, let me know."

"I will." He jutted his chin. "I want whoever did this to Nicole to be brought to justice just as much as you do."

"Okay." Madison had no reason to believe this wasn't true. "See you later."

Next, she met up with Leonard at Julian Price Memorial Park, neighboring Moses H. Cone Memorial Park, at Milepost 297. He had been out questioning parkway visitors, with nearby road closures during the investigation given there was a killer at large.

"Hey," she said. "Get anything?"

"Nothing suspicious as yet," he reported. "Other than some sightings of the black bear, most people I spoke to apparently didn't hear or see anything that got their attention."

"Hmm…" Madison figured that Nicole would have screamed or made other sounds while being attacked. Could the perp have knocked her out first to prevent this? "Did Nicole ever say anything to you about being stalked by someone?"

"No." Leonard tilted his campaign hat. "We were cool but never talked about issues outside of working for the NPS and in the Blue Ridge Mountains."

"All right." She wondered if Nicole had known her attacker. Or if he'd known her. "Maybe someone will come forward with information."

"I'll let you know," he said.

As she headed back to her vehicle, Madison received a call from Ray Pottenger. "We've located the couple who first reported spotting the black bear," he informed her.

"That's great news," she told him.

"I'm sending you and Special Agent Sneed the address where you can find them."

"Okay." Madison reached her vehicle. Inside, she texted Garrett to let him know she was ready to follow up with the couple if he wanted her to interview them. Whatever it took to get the jump on Nicole's and, apparently, Olivia's killer.

Chapter Seven

Garrett drove to Linville Falls, in the Blue Ridge Mountains, at Milepost 316, where he located Maintenance Rangers Ward Wilcox and Ronnie Mantegna. They were picking up trash in the picnic area. Garrett hoped one or the other might have some useful information regarding the fatal attack on the parkway.

After bringing the men together, Garrett flashed his ID and said, "I'm investigating the murder of Park Ranger Nicole Wallenberg." He peered at Ronnie, who was in his midfifties, solid in build and had brownish-gray hair in a buzz cut and raven eyes. "When did you last see Ranger Wallenberg?"

"I saw her this morning," he responded. "She was with Ranger Edison, alive and well. Never saw either of them afterward."

Garrett took note of this. He turned to the other maintenance ranger. "What about you?"

Ward wiped sweat from his brow with the

back of a work glove. "I saw Ranger Wallenberg on foot near where the black bear was located. She was alone. By the time Ranger Lynley arrived on the scene, Ranger Wallenberg had moved farther into the woods, away from the area." He paused. "That must have been when she was attacked."

Garrett recalled that he had run into Drew Mitchell on the parkway, who'd been in possession of Olivia Forlani's cell phone, before fleeing. "Did you see anyone else in the vicinity of Ranger Wallenberg?"

"Yeah, as a matter of fact," Ward answered surely. "The couple who reported being confronted by the black bear had been hanging around that area earlier."

Garrett nodded and then handed both men his card. "If either of you see or hear about anything else pertinent to this investigation, give me a call."

"We will," Ronnie said, stuffing the card into the pocket of his shirt.

"Yeah, count on it," Ward seconded.

Garrett was already back in his car when he listened to the voice mail from Ray Pottenger, informing him that they had found the persons of interest in the death of Nicole. He texted their address. Garrett saw the text as well from Madison. He called her and, when she answered, said, "Hey. Got the text. We should check out the couple together and see where it leads."

"Sounds good to me," she told him. "Where are you?"

Garrett told her, and they arranged a place to meet. He welcomed any opportunity to spend time with Madison, on and off the job. And if it could help them crack what was becoming a more and more unsettling case, all the better.

THEY DROVE TO the Rolling Hills Bed and Breakfast on Danner Road, where Madison immediately recognized Stan and Constance Franco. They were standing outside the two-story Victorian. According to Deputy Pottenger, they were visiting from Honolulu. It was hard for Madison to imagine that they had decided in the middle of a vacation to the mainland to become killers along the way. But stranger things had happened.

"That's them," she told Garrett.

"Okay," he said. "Let's do this."

They exited the car and approached the couple. Both were in their late twenties, fit and good looking. Stan was tall, tanned, with slicked-back long hair in a man bun and brown eyes. Constance was nearly as tall and had big green eyes and fine blond hair in a short blunt cut, parted in the middle.

"Hi again," Madison said, after having spoken with them following the bear attack.

Constance smiled at her. "Hi."

"Ranger Lynley, right?" Stan said, eyeing her questioningly.

"Yes, and this is Special Agent Sneed," she told them. "We need to ask you a few questions."

"About the black bear?"

"Actually it's about a murder that took place on the Blue Ridge Parkway," Garrett said.

"Murder?" Constance grimaced. "Who?"

"A park ranger named Nicole Wallenberg," Madison informed them.

Garrett narrowed his eyes. "Someone stabbed Ranger Wallenberg to death during the time you were on the parkway."

Stan pursed his lips. "I'm sorry to hear that," he said. "But you don't think we had anything to do with it, do you?"

"We're questioning everyone who was there or may have seen something," Madison answered evenly. She didn't want to frighten them unnecessarily. But there was never an easy way to confront potential suspects in crimes. "Ranger Wallenberg was killed not too far from the grassy area where you said you had a picnic. Did you hear or see anything?"

Constance's eyes darted to her husband's and

back before responding, "Actually, around the time we spotted the black bear, there was what sounded like a woman crying out. But then the bear began making noises, and we thought that was what we heard."

Garrett regarded Stan keenly. "That true?"

"Yeah, it is," he insisted and turned to Madison. "When you showed up, along with the other rangers, to scare the bear off and nothing seemed to come of the other sounds, we assumed it was either our imagination or too much wine. Or the bear."

To Madison this seemed somewhat plausible, if convenient. "Did you see anyone leaving the area?" she asked, eyeing Constance.

"Yes." Her voice rose. "I saw a man running off in the woods."

"What did he look like?" Garrett asked.

She batted her lashes nervously. "I only noticed him at a glance, so I can't really tell you much about him. Honestly, I never gave it much thought one way or the other at the time. Sorry."

Madison turned to Stan. "Did you get a look at him?"

"Just the back of him as he was running into the forest," he told her. "I couldn't tell you anything else about him because he was too far away. And, to be honest, I don't know if he was trying to escape or just out for a jog."

"Neither do we," Garrett told him candidly. "But he's certainly someone we'd like to talk to."

"Afraid we can't help you there," he said.

Garrett looked at him. "How long will you be in town?"

"Till the end of the week."

"And you've been here for how long?"

"We arrived yesterday afternoon," Constance responded.

Stan frowned. "Why do you ask?"

"No reason in particular," Garrett answered, though Madison knew it was to establish an alibi for their whereabouts when Olivia had been killed. If this was true, it would eliminate them as suspects, making it less likely they could have been involved with Nicole's death. "In case we have any more questions, we'd like to get your contact information."

"Sure, no problem," he agreed.

Madison gazed at Constance and said smilingly, "Hope the ordeal with the black bear hasn't scared you off."

"Honestly, I'm still a bit shaken from it," she said. "But it's even scarier to think that a murderer is apparently on the loose."

"Yeah," her husband grumbled. "Not exactly what we bargained for when deciding to vacation in North Carolina."

"None of us bargained for this—trust me," Garrett told him with an edge to his tone. "Unfortunately, things happen. Our job is to try to solve the case."

"Thanks for your time." Madison grinned at Stan. "We'll get out of your hair."

He nodded, and Constance said, "Thanks for coming to our rescue when the black bear didn't seem to want to leave us alone."

"Just doing my job," she said, diffident in accepting gratitude in this instance.

When they left, Garrett said, "What do you think?"

"I think they're innocent." Madison adjusted in the passenger seat. "Their alibi is easy enough to check out, if needed."

"True." He drove off. "If this man they saw running off is the real deal, then there's a good chance he was running away rather than toward something."

"Exactly." She faced him. "So, we really are looking at a likely serial killer?"

Garrett paused. "We'll see what the autopsy reveals on the cause and method of death," he voiced. "And what Forensics comes up with. But as of now, it seems like a distinct possibility."

"At least we have a solid lead to work with in trying to track down the perp," she pointed out.

"Yep. We just need a better description of the unsub in narrowing down the search."

Madison concurred. "Whoever he is, the unsub apparently knows his way around the Blue Ridge Parkway, if not the entire Pisgah National Forest," she speculated, what with his ability to avoid detection.

"I had that thought too." Garrett clutched the steering wheel. "Which makes him all the more dangerous."

Madison angled her face. "Are you thinking the unsub could be someone who works for the National Park Service?"

"Not necessarily. Apart from the many people employed by the NPS, there are plenty of regular visitors who are outdoorsmen, adventurers, hunters, survivalists, you name it, who choose to interact with nature in their life and times. Any one of them could have decided to become a killer along the way."

"Chilling," she uttered.

"Yeah." He drew a breath. "But we'll do whatever we have to in order to stop this from escalating," he told her.

Madison thought about her siblings investigating serial killers. She wondered how they managed to cope with the multiple lives lost at the hands of one or more killers. If they were suddenly dealing with this in her neck of the woods, she only hoped the unsub could be stopped in his tracks sooner rather than later. Having Garrett as lead investigator made her believe that this was a battle they would definitely win, no matter the obstacles before them.

When he pulled up behind her car, Garrett waited a beat, then turned toward Madison and leaned into her for a short kiss on the mouth. She felt her lips tingle, welcoming the kiss, but was still confused. "What was that for?"

"I just felt like kissing you," he responded point-blank. "Your lips are still as soft as I remember."

"Oh." She blushed but tried not to show it.

"Did I overstep?"

"No," she told him, realizing it was something that almost seemed inevitable, in spite of their attempts to place limitations on the nature of their relationship. But now was not the time to test those limits further. "I'll catch you later."

Garrett lowered his chin. "All right."

Madison exited his vehicle, sensing him watching until she had gotten into hers. He followed her briefly, till veering off in a different direction.

Though it had been quick and sweet, Garrett still had heart palpitations from kissing Madison when he walked inside his rented log cabin.

He probably shouldn't have kissed her, aware that it could only lead them down a path they had mutually rejected before. But he didn't regret it. On the contrary, kissing her was maybe the best move he'd made since returning to Kiki's Ridge. He believed that Madison was amenable to it as well and that it was a step in the right direction toward reestablishing what had existed between them before. Even if he had no idea where they might be headed, one thing was clear to him: he didn't want to let fear of failure be his guide. What was meant to be would happen, one way or the other. He preferred to control his own destiny, while hoping it could align with hers.

After grabbing a beer from the refrigerator, Garrett broke away from thoughts about his personal life in favor of the criminal investigation that had shifted in a different direction somewhat with the discovery of a second murder victim, Nicole Wallenberg. She had been isolated just long enough for a killer to come after her. This was a similar pattern to the stabbing murder of Olivia Forlani. Why had the unsub targeted them? Or could they be separate incidences with two different killers?

Either way he looked at it, Garrett knew that public confidence was bound to be eroded in the comfort level and security surrounding the

Blue Ridge Parkway for as long as safety was an issue. It was up to him as the main investigator in this region to solve these unsettling homicides. Or save the day. While hardly a superhero, this was his forte as an ISB special agent, and he didn't intend to let down those who depended on him. That included Madison, who had known one victim and discovered another in the course of her own duties as a law enforcement ranger. She needed to feel safe in her own workspace without having to constantly look over her shoulder for fear that a killer might be lying in wait.

IN THE MORNING, Garrett stuck with his routine of a jog and a workout to get the blood flowing. He hoped to get to do this with Madison soon, knowing that he had asked her to refrain from going out alone on the parkway trails as long as one or more killers were at large. He couldn't help but think about the ultimate workout they could have together in bed. Madison was a great lover, and it was one of the things he missed most about being with her. Would they get to experience the pleasure of one another's intimate company again? Or had that opportunity passed, in spite of a new understanding between them?

By the time he had gotten back to the cabin,

showered and changed clothes, Dawn Dominguez had sent Garrett the autopsy report on Nicole Wallenberg. He read it on his laptop. The medical examiner confirmed that Nicole had been the victim of a vicious stabbing attack. She'd been stabbed ten times, including in the chest, stomach, back and arms, resulting in death as a homicide. He took note that, similar to Olivia's death, the undiscovered murder weapon was an eight-inch, single-edged blade knife characteristic of a survival knife.

I have to assume these homicides were perpetrated by the same offender, Garrett told himself while he drank his coffee. They were indeed facing a serial killer on the parkway. And the unsub had no qualms about stabbing his victims in a brazen daytime attack. This evoked thoughts once again to Garrett about his mother's murder in the same Blue Ridge Mountains thirty years ago. Who had gone after her and gotten away with it? He didn't want to think about history repeating itself with a new killer in the forest and mountains. Handpicking or having stalked his victims and never having to answer for it.

On his laptop, Garrett contacted his boss, Carly Tafoya, for a video chat to update her about the investigation. When she came on, he got right to the point. "There's been new developments to the case."

"Tell me," Carly voiced anxiously.

Having phoned her yesterday about the sad news of Nicole's murder and the speculation of its link to the murder of Olivia Forlani, Garrett said firmly, "We do think we have a serial killer on our hands. The autopsy report indicated that Nicole was stabbed to death in a way that mirrors Forlani's death, by and large. The murder weapon in both homicides is believed to be a survival knife."

Carly muttered an expletive while making a face. "That's not good."

"Not at all." Garrett frowned. "There's more. Witnesses reported seeing a man who may have been running from the scene of Nicole's murder. Though we haven't nailed down a solid description as yet, it fits with the strong suspicions on my part that the killer of Nicole and Olivia is male."

Carly sighed. "Use everything you have at your disposal, Sneed, to stop this man."

"I intend to," Garrett assured her.

"Whatever support you need, just ask."

"I will." As of now, what he needed most was to alert local and other federal law enforcement and communities in and around the Blue Ridge Parkway to be on guard for a likely serial killer on the loose. If they were able to at least rattle the cage somewhat of the unsub, it might be enough to force him to go underground and away from potential targets. Till they could nail him. And Garrett wouldn't rest till the deed was done.

Chapter Eight

Madison sat on the U-shaped bench in the breakfast nook, looking at the autopsy report that Garrett had sent her on her laptop. It was painful to read about the nature of and verdict on Nicole Wallenberg's death. Like Olivia, she'd been murdered by stabbing. A survival knife was thought to be the weapon of choice by the unsub. By all accounts, it seemed that they were looking at a serial killer and one who was elusive and violent enough to send a chill through Madison.

We can't let this monster get away with this, she told herself. Even then, the fear was that the longer it took to find the perp, the more likely it was that he would strike again.

She closed out the report and went onto Zoom for a video conference with her brothers, Scott and Russell Lynley. Both worked for the FBI as special agents, albeit in different capacities and locations. Scott was older and separated from his wife, Paula. Madison hoped they would be able to patch things up. Russell, who was younger, was married and about to bring a new Lynley into the world.

When they appeared on the screen, Madison broke into a grin, feeling comfort in talking with her brothers. Both were incredibly handsome and gray-eyed, much like their father. Scott had a square face and thick coal-black hair in a comb-over, low-fade style, while Russell had more of an oblong face to go with black hair in a high and tight cut.

"Hey, you two."

"Hey," they spoke in unison and paused before Scott said solemnly, "Heard you lost an NPS ranger."

"Yes, we did." Madison was not surprised that the news would reach them before she could pass it along. "Nicole was stabbed to death off the Blue Ridge Parkway," she said painfully.

"Sorry about that," Russell voiced, his thick brows knitted.

She twisted her lips. "Worse is that it comes on the heels of a similar death on the parkway of a friend of mine."

"Yeah, Annette mentioned that to me the other day. I reached out to you."

Madison acknowledged this and said, "It's certainly unsettling."

"So, what, we're talking about a serial killer lurking around in the Blue Ridge Mountains?" Scott put forth.

"Seems that way," she responded. "Between the location, manner of attack, type of injuries and the kind of knife believed to have been used to murder them, yes, I'd say a serial killer is at large."

Russell scratched his nose. "Who's heading the investigation?"

"Garrett Sneed," Madison answered equably.

Scott frowned. "Not the same ISB special agent who bailed on you?"

"One and the same," she admitted, though knowing it wasn't quite as simple as that.

"I thought he went to Arizona," Russell said. "Or was it New Mexico?"

"Did Sneed come back to give you more headaches?" Scott asked.

"Enough, already." Madison realized that they were just doing what overprotective brothers did in trying to look out for her best interests in their own ways. "Garrett and I are good." *Or at least no longer bad in terms of miscommunication*, she thought. "Anyway, this isn't about my love life. Or lack thereof. It's about Garrett coming in to do his job in investigating one, now two, homicides in the Pisgah Ranger District."

"You're absolutely right about that." Russell tilted his face. "He's obviously good at his job, as are you. Whatever you need to work out on a personal level, I'm sure you will."

She grinned. "Thanks for saying that."

He nodded. "We always have your back, sis."

In trying to lighten the mood, Scott said, "Still, if you ever need us to gang up on Sneed, we will."

Madison chuckled. "I don't think that will be necessary. He's one of the good guys."

"Okay." He sat back. "What can we do to help in the investigation?"

"Right now, I just need your support and an occasional virtual shoulder to cry on."

"You've got both," he said, and it was seconded by Russell.

Madison was grateful for such, knowing it worked both ways, as well as with Annette. When the chips were down, as Lynleys, they were there for each other, something she never took for granted.

After the chat ended, Madison got ready for work and headed for the parkway. Upon arrival, she parked and got out on foot and headed to the area where she'd found Nicole's body. The crime scene tape had been removed, allowing for free access. Though it was eerie to be back there, Madison thought she might check around for anything the crime scene techs and other rangers might have missed. It also occurred to her that the unsub might morbidly return to the scene of the crime. And even come after her.

Were the latter the case, she would be ready for him. Madison instinctively placed a hand on the firearm in her magnetic leather holster. In the meantime, if there was anything she could do to move the investigation along in trying to nab her fellow ranger's killer, she was up for the challenge.

Just as Madison was studying the dirt path Nicole would have taken to reach that point and happened to notice a fallen tree branch that she imagined could have been used to cover tracks, she heard what sounded like footsteps coming up fast behind her. Sucking in a deep breath to suppress the fear that gripped her heart, Madison yanked out her pistol and flung herself around at the intruder, with no plans to ask questions first.

To her surprise, a hard question was posed to her instead, as the familiar deep voice barked, "What are you doing here?"

It took Madison only an instant to come to terms with the so-called intruder as actually Garrett. Releasing a sigh, she responded sardonically, "I work here, remember?"

"I remember." He put up his hands in mock surrender. "Don't shoot!"

Realizing she was still pointing the gun in his direction, she put it back in her holster. "Sorry about that. I thought you might be—"

"The killer?" Garrett deduced. "I gathered that much." He lowered his arms. "So you came to this spot in hopes of luring him out, or what?"

"No, I came in search of evidence," she told him matter-of-factly. "Seemed like a good place to start. After all, as you've reminded me more than once, this is my investigation too." Was she acting a bit too defensive? Was that really necessary?

"It is our investigation," he reiterated. "In fact, I made my way over here for the same reason. I was just surprised to find you here ahead of me."

Madison relaxed, feeling that she'd overreacted. "Guess great minds think alike," she quipped.

He grinned. "Did you find anything interesting?"

She took a few steps toward the tree branch, pulled a latex glove out of her pocket and put it on, then picked up the branch. Turning it over, she saw a faint discoloration on one part. She held it up to him. "That could be human blood."

Garrett studied it. "Possibly."

"If so, it could belong to Nicole or the unsub," Madison said. "Forensics can tell us. If it is the killer's DNA, then CODIS might be able to identify the unknown DNA profile."

"You're right." He ran a hand along his jawline. "We'll get this to the state crime lab in Hendersonville," he said and looked at Madison curiously. "Did you find anything else?"

"Only that the area, largely hidden from the grassy hill and parking lot, suggests that the unsub made a conscious choice to either lure Nicole here or was lying in wait for anyone who happened to come to this spot to go after." Madison looked in a direction where the cluster of trees made for the perfect getaway. "He had to have gone that way to avoid detection for as long as possible."

"I think you're right." Garrett gave her the once-over, and she found herself coloring as she imagined he was undressing her with his very eyes—something she had admittedly found herself prone to doing with him from time to time since he'd returned. "We're checking dumpsters, trails, mountains and the water for the murder weapon and any bloody clothes the unsub may have ditched."

"Good." Madison hoped something would come up that pointed toward the perpetrator. She thought about Scott and Russell ribbing her about Garrett. In spite of their relationship being thrown off course for two years, Madison felt they were back on track now, even if it was unclear what train they were taking. Or, for that matter, what their next stop was.

When his cell phone rang, Garrett removed it from the back pocket of his chinos, looked at it and said, "I'd better get this." He answered, "Sneed," before saying, "Sheriff Silva. Yes, it has been a while. What can I do for you?"

Madison knew that Jacob Silva was the sheriff of Buncombe County, which bordered the Blue Ridge Parkway. She listened as Garrett lifted a brow and continued with, "Really?" Then, after a long pause, "Okay. Right. Good. Keep me posted."

When Garrett disconnected, he eyed her and said, "There's been a development…"

"What?" Her voice rose with interest.

His mouth tightened. "A woman was stabbed to death this morning in Buncombe County. The suspect, identified as Norman Kruger, carjacked another woman's vehicle and is currently on the move in her blue Hyundai Elantra." Garrett waited a beat and said tonelessly, "Silva thinks that Kruger could be the unsub, who the local press is now referring to as the Blue Ridge Parkway Killer."

GARRETT STOOD TOE-TO-TOE with Sheriff Jacob Silva, whom he'd known since his previous stint as a Region 2 ISB special agent. They were the same height, but Silva was a little heavier. In his midforties, he had brown eyes and short brown hair with a sprinkling of gray and a horseshoe mustache.

"What can you tell me about the suspect?" Garrett asked as they stood outside an interrogation room at the sheriff's office in Asheville, where thirty-four-year-old Norman Kruger was waiting to be interviewed. An hour ago, he had been taken into custody without incident after a high-speed chase had come to an end when he'd lost control of the car. Though shaken up, the carjacking victim, seventy-three-year-old Diane Fullerton, had been unharmed.

"Kruger is a real piece of work," Silva told him. "He's been in and out of jail for most of his life for crimes ranging from larceny-theft to aggravated assault to kidnapping and drug possession. He's currently being charged with first-degree murder in the death of thirty-two-year-old Frances Reynolds, thought to be the girlfriend of the suspect. She was stabbed multiple times and left for dead in her apartment. He's also facing charges of armed carjacking, unlawful use of a weapon and resisting arrest. Other charges are pending. And, obviously, there could be more, after your interrogation of the suspect."

"What about the murder weapon?"

"We collected as evidence a survival knife that we believe was the weapon he used to stab to death Frances Reynolds. It's being processed right now."

"Good," Garrett said, thoughtful. "I'll take it from here."

Silva nodded. "He's all yours."

When he stepped inside the room, Garrett knew that Madison would be watching the interrogation on live video in a different room with interest, hoping, like him, that they had the man responsible for the cold-blooded murders of Olivia Forlani and Nicole Wallenberg. He turned his attention back to the suspect, who was seated at a square metal table and handcuffed, and told him, "I'm Special Agent Sneed of the National Park Service's Investigative Services Branch."

Norman Kruger was lean, wearing a dirty T-shirt and jeans. He had dark hair in a skin-fade cut with the top textured. Snarling at Garrett, he retorted, "So what do you want with me?"

Garrett sat in a metal chair across from him and glared at the suspect. "Why don't we start by discussing why you're here," he began coolly. "You're facing a murder rap in the stabbing death of Frances Reynolds, among other charges."

"Tell me something I don't know." He jutted his chin. "That bitch had it coming to her after two-timing on me with another dude."

"What about the elderly woman who nearly had a heart attack when you ordered her out of her vehicle at gunpoint?" Garrett peered at him. "Did she have it coming too?"

"I needed some wheels," Kruger hissed. "She was just in the way."

I'll bet, he mused cynically. "Didn't get you very far for where you're going from here. Did it?"

Kruger twisted his lips. "Whatever."

He sighed, knowing it was time to confront the smug suspect over the homicides that had occurred on the parkway. "Why don't we talk about the two women murdered recently on the Blue Ridge Parkway," he said casually, noting the suspect had not asked for an attorney.

Kruger stared at him with a furrowed brow. "Not sure what you mean?"

"I'll try to clarify," Garrett snapped. "You're being investigated as a person of interest in the murders of Olivia Forlani and Nicole Wallenberg. Both were stabbed to death in separate incidents along trails off the parkway, reminiscent of your attack on Frances Reynolds."

"Hey, I had nothing to do with those."

Garrett bristled with skepticism. "Someone

fitting your description was seen running off after murdering Park Ranger Nicole Wallenberg yesterday morning," he pointed out. In reality, Garrett knew that the description of the unsub was pretty vague at best. But Kruger didn't need to know that at the moment. Especially if this helped lead to a confession when he was backed into a proverbial corner.

"Wasn't me," Kruger maintained. He wrinkled his crooked nose. "I wasn't anywhere near the parkway yesterday."

Garrett dismissed this with a wave of his hand. "So where were you?"

"I was in Charlotte," he argued.

"Doing what?"

"Playing at a dive bar called the Parties Pad," Kruger said. "I play guitar with a band that travels around the state and elsewhere. Did three sets and played pool afterward. I have witnesses. Didn't get back here till early this morning, after hitching a ride with another member of the band—Chuck Garcia. So no, you can't pin the ranger's death on me."

Garrett looked at the camera, wondering what Madison's take was on the suspect. Was this another dead end? He regarded Kruger. "We'll check out your story." He paused and then asked for his whereabouts during the time of Olivia

Forlani's murder, not ruling out that there might still have been more than one killer at work.

Kruger again claimed he'd been on the road with his band, giving dates and places they'd performed. It would be easy enough to verify. Garrett still had his suspicions, though, and asked Kruger if he would be willing to take a lie detector test. "It'll help us rule you out for the parkway murders," he told the suspect.

"Yeah, whatever." Kruger shrugged. "But you're wasting your time. As I said, I never killed anyone on the Blue Ridge Parkway."

Garrett leaned forward. "That remains to be seen."

He left the interrogation room and arranged with Sheriff Silva to have the test administered by a polygraph examiner before going to confer with Madison in a viewing room.

"So, what do you think about Kruger?" he asked her.

"He's definitely a creep," she stated flatly. "But I'm not sure he's guilty of being the Blue Ridge Parkway Killer. He seemed too arrogant and clear in his denials."

Garrett was inclined to agree. "We'll see if he passes the lie detector test and if the knife he used to kill his girlfriend yields anything."

Madison folded her arms. "If nothing else, at least they got him for what he did to her."

"Yeah."

Sheriff Silva entered the room and said with a frown on his face, "The polygraph examiner is on her way. In the meantime, we can add attempted murder to the growing list of charges Kruger faces. Just received word that he practically beat to death a man named Peter McLachlan. Kruger's girlfriend was apparently having an affair with McLachlan. Looks like he'll pull through, but he's got a long haul ahead of him."

Madison grimaced. "Kruger was clearly a loose cannon with others paying the price."

Garrett shook his head in despair. "He definitely went off the deep end in his homicidal vengeance."

"And he's going to pay for it," Silva said with certainty. "The only question left is whether or not we can pin the parkway crimes on him."

"There is that," Garrett conceded, but he only wanted things to go in that direction if Kruger was actually guilty of the serial murders.

Two hours later, they were informed that Norman Kruger had passed the polygraph and that his alibis checked out. Forensic testing of the survival knife used to kill Frances Reynolds had found no DNA or blood evidence to tie the weapon to Olivia or Nicole. Moreover, the blade of Kruger's knife measured just four inches, compared to the eight-inch knife the killer had used against Forlani and Wallenberg. This was more than enough for Garrett to move away from Norman Kruger as a suspect, even as the book was thrown at him for the murder of his girlfriend and other offenses.

Chapter Nine

"What do you say we split a pizza?" Garrett offered that evening as he rode with Madison.

"Sure," she responded, her stomach growling after missing lunch. "Takeout?"

"Yeah. Unless you'd rather eat at the restaurant?"

"Takeout is fine."

"All right. Takeout it is."

Madison took the Blue Ridge Parkway to Beaubianna Drive, where she pulled into the Dottie's Pizza parking lot.

"So, what would you like on your half?" Garrett asked, unbuckling his seat belt.

Had he forgotten that she loved pepperoni, anchovies and cheese pizza? She grinned at him. "Surprise me."

"I can do that." He returned the smile. "Back in a few."

While she waited, Madison wondered if there could still be a future for them. Or had that ship sailed and there was no need to think in terms beyond camaraderie and working together on a case?

She was still mulling this over when Garrett returned. "All set?"

"Yeah. I think you'll be pleased with the selection of toppings for your half."

"Can't wait to taste it." The inviting aroma of the pizza made her stomach growl again.

"So, your place or mine?" he asked casually.

"Hmm…" Madison contemplated this. "Mine. There's beer and wine in the fridge to help wash down the pizza." Never mind that the place was her own comfort zone.

Garrett grinned. "Sounds fine to me."

They were mostly silent during the drive, except the occasional comment on the landscape or something new that Garrett noted along the way from when he'd lived in the area previously.

When they reached her house and went inside, he hit the lights, scanned the place and said, "Looks pretty much like I remember."

Madison batted her eyes. "Did you think it would have changed?"

"Not really. Sometimes people do like to redecorate or whatever, just for the hell of it. In this case, the house is perfect just as it is."

"Thanks." *He always had a way with words*, she thought, smiling. Madison took the pizza box from him and said, "I'll set everything out. Make yourself at home."

"I'd like to help," he insisted, following her into the kitchen.

"Okay," she relented, handing him back the pizza. "We can eat at the dining room table. Napkins are in that drawer—" she pointed "—in case you've forgotten."

"I remember." After washing and drying his hands, he grabbed a batch of napkins and headed into the dining room.

Madison washed up. "Did you want beer or red wine?" she asked, taking a couple of plates out of the rustic cabinet.

"Beer."

She'd suspected as much. After setting the plates on the mahogany square table, she got out two bottles from the refrigerator. Handing him one, she sat across from him in an upholstered gray side chair. Madison noted that the pizza box was still closed.

She gazed at Garrett, who was grinning sideways as he said to her, "I'll let you do the honors."

When she lifted the lid, Madison broke into a smile as she saw that the entire pizza was covered with pepperoni, anchovies and cheese. He'd remembered. "Cute," she uttered, blushing.

He laughed. "Hey, some memories never go away."

And others? She wondered just how much he recalled about their previous time spent as a couple. "Good to know."

They began to eat and drink while talking about the investigation. "Too bad Norman Kruger didn't pan out as our killer," Garrett bemoaned.

"I know." Madison dug into a slice of pizza. His disappointment matched her own. "At least Kruger is off the streets for his own horrific crimes."

"Yeah, you're right about that." Garrett sipped his beer. "As for the Blue Ridge Parkway Killer, as they're calling him, with the technology we have working for us, he's not about to slip through the cracks."

"Something tells me he doesn't want to," she surmised. "At least not totally. If the unsub was willing to kill two women on the parkway, there's no telling how many more he's capable of killing, if the opportunity is there. Clearly, he's able and willing."

"And we're just as able to come between him and his dastardly plans," Garrett insisted. "We're onto him now, and he knows it. Homing in on other vulnerable women just got much more difficult for him, if he hopes to remain in the shadows instead of behind bars."

"I want that to be true." She took another bite of pizza. "This can't go on for much longer. Not if we want to restore sanity to the Blue Ridge Parkway. And the rest of the Pisgah National Forest, for that matter."

"It won't." Garrett's voice deepened with conviction. He suddenly reached across the table and ran a finger down the corner of her mouth. "Some cheese had managed to get away from you. Thought I'd help out there."

Her face flushed with embarrassment. Or was it more of a turn-on to feel the touch of his finger? "A napkin would have sufficed, thank you."

He cut a grin. "Maybe. But what fun would that have been?"

"I thought we were here to eat. Not have fun."

"Why not do both?" Garrett bit into his own pizza slice and seemed to deliberately allow a web of cheese to hang down his chin. "Think I could use a little help here," he said, a catch to his voice.

"Oh, really?" Madison played along and used her own finger to wind around the cheese before removing it. "Satisfied?"

He stood up and took her hand, pulling her up. "Actually, I'm not quite satisfied, not yet."

They were close enough that she could feel the heat emanating from him. "And what else did you have in mind?"

"This…" Garrett held Madison's cheeks and planted his mouth on her lips for a solid kiss. It felt good and neither seemed in any hurry to stop kissing one another.

When she finally unlocked their mouths, Madison looked him in the eye and saw the desire, which she felt too. "Are you sure this is a good idea?" she asked, wondering if he would be the voice of reason before things went too far to pull back.

"I'm sure it's an idea that's long overdue," he indicated. "Yes, I want to kiss you some more and then make love to you, Madison."

"I think I want that too," she admitted, quivering at the thought. "Yes, I do want it," Madison felt the need to make clear.

"So, let's do this." He regarded her keenly and took her hand. "I think I remember how to get to the bedroom."

"I'm sure you do." She smiled as her heart skipped a beat. "Lead the way."

Once they stepped inside the room, Garrett stopped and said, "There's something else I've been dying to do since I laid eyes on you again…"

She held his gaze with anticipation. "Oh? What's that?"

"This," he said as he unraveled her hair from the bun it was in, allowing it to fall freely upon her shoulders. He tousled the hair. "I love your long locks."

Madison knew this, but they had not been in the right situation for her to wear it down. Till now. "Kiss me," she demanded, grabbing his shirt.

"With pleasure."

They stood there, kissing one another like old lovers, which Madison knew they were. This both frightened and excited her. More the latter, as the intensity of the kiss grew as their bodies molded together while they wrapped their arms around each other. She was all in for the ride, even if the future remained uncertain.

After they shed their clothes with lightning speed, removing any barriers between them, Madison felt just a tad self-conscious in baring all to a man for the first time since their relationship had ended.

But this quickly went away with the sheer appreciation she saw in his stare that he followed with, "You're still gorgeous."

Drinking in the sight of his hard body and six-pack, causing a stir in her, she couldn't help but say in response, "So are you, Garrett."

"I'll take that, coming from you." He stepped closer and lifted up her chin. "And give this in return." Another mouth-watering kiss was laid on her, making Madison feel as though she were floating on air. When it came time for them to take this to bed, she removed a condom packet from the nightstand that had not yet expired.

Handing it to him, she smiled and said, "From the last time you were here."

Garrett chuckled. "Glad you saved it."

"So am I." Madison gazed at him desirously. "Better not let it go to waste."

"Oh, it won't," he promised, tossing the packet onto the bed to come back to later. "First things first."

Her lashes fluttered with anticipation. "What might that be?"

Garrett kissed her forehead. "A little of this…" He kissed both cheeks. "A little of that…" He ran his hands through her hair while kissing her on the mouth. "Maybe some of that and this…" He touched one nipple, then the other, causing waves of delight to shoot through Madison. It caused her desire to be with him to kick up another fervent notch.

"I get the picture," she cooed impatiently, taking his hand and leading him to the bed. "Let's move on…please."

"Got it." His voice rang with conviction as

they got on the sateen duvet cover. He draped one leg across hers. "Before we get down to business, I'd like us to reacquaint ourselves with one another."

"Oh, would you now?" Madison kissed him, moving her hand down his body teasingly as he stiffened. "I'm sensing some familiarity here."

"So am I." Garrett had a sharp intake of breath as his nimble fingers went to work on her, finding all the right intimate spots. "And I'm liking what I'm feeling."

"Umm…me too," she voiced dulcetly, body suddenly ablaze as an orgasm roared through her. When she couldn't take the pure torture of a partial victory anymore, Madison demanded, "I'd like to feel even more of you inside me. Now!"

"As you wish," he said, kissing her mouth again before ripping open the packet and putting on the condom.

But even as she longed for further fulfillment, Garrett once again showed enormous patience for his own needs as he stimulated her more before finally moving atop and working his way between her legs. Ready as ever, Madison was definitely hot and bothered when he entered her. She absorbed his quick and powerful thrusts the way the skin did the sun's rays, meeting him halfway each time.

Their mouths were locked passionately as their bodies moved in perpetual harmony. In short order, Madison climaxed again, at the same time as Garrett. She could feel the erratic beating of his heart, matching her own as the moment came and left them catching their breaths afterward.

"Wow." Garrett laughed as he lay on his back beside her. "That—you—were amazing."

"So were you," Madison admitted, resting her head on his shoulder.

"Some things in life are worth waiting for—again."

She chuckled. "You think so?"

"I know so." He kissed her hair. "This was definitely worth a two-year wait. Every scintillating second."

Though she didn't disagree, Madison was left to wonder what came next. Did he even know? Should it be an issue?

"WHAT ARE WE DOING?" Madison asked him as she propped up on an elbow, giving Garrett a nice view of her nude body.

He pretended he didn't get her drift as he took in her perfectly sized breasts, shapely form and long lean legs, while quipping, "I should think it would be obvious. It's called jumping each other's bones."

She laughed and hit him playfully on the shoulder. "You know what I mean."

He did and, as such, turned serious when facing her, while considering how best to respond without overpromising or understating where they were. "Well, I think we're simply reconnecting in one way in which we were crazy for one another," he spoke honestly. "Seems like it worked out pretty well. Don't you think?"

"Hmm…" Madison met his eyes thoughtfully. "What happened to just being friends?"

Garrett held her gaze when he responded dubiously, "Friendship comes in many forms."

"And what form would you call this?" she asked. "Friendship with benefits?"

He laughed. "I think I'd be more comfortable with friendship and the enormous possibilities it presents for a brighter future between us, in one way or another."

Okay, I came out with where I'd like to see this go, sort of, Garrett told himself. He hoped they were on the same page.

Madison raised a brow. "That doesn't scare you?"

"It might have once," he confessed. "But not now. I'm open to whatever comes next. You?"

She waited a beat and then said evenly, "Yeah, I think I am."

"Cool." He beamed and, taking in her scent,

suddenly felt himself aroused again. Running a hand across her back, he asked, "Are there any more of those packets in the nightstand?"

"There might be one or two more. Why?"

"Oh, I was thinking it might be fun to go a second round."

Her eyes lit. "Really?"

He grinned. "Well, things did go a bit more quickly than I would have liked," he admitted.

"I see." She touched his chest. "Sure you can handle another round?"

He chuckled. "Without a doubt. Being with you gives me all the energy I need."

"Then I say let's go for it," she said enthusiastically.

This was music to Garrett's ears as he started to kiss her, slipping his tongue in Madison's mouth. He absolutely loved the taste and feel of her, making him want her even more. By the time they had worked each other up into a near frenzy, he had managed to slip out of bed just long enough to put on the protection before picking up where they'd left off. Their bodies were entangled in the heat of passion and exploration.

Madison moaned as he hit her sweet spot time and time again, then called out his name when she reached orgasm while on top. Having held back just long enough to wait for that to happen,

Garrett played with her hair and brought their faces together for a toe-curling kiss before letting go in achieving his own pinnacle of sexual gratification. Only then did they settle down and ride the rapids of contentment.

"Was it just as good the second time?" Madison asked with a giggle. "Not counting our previous lovemaking sessions."

Garrett grinned slyly beside her. "What do you think?"

"Umm… I think so, judging by how wonderful it was for me."

"Good deduction." His voice deepened. "You never fail to amaze me just how incredible you are in bed."

Her eyes narrowed. "Just in bed?"

He chuckled, realizing how what he'd said might have come across. "In and out of bed," he promised. "Breaking up had nothing to do with how great you are as a person." He hoped she knew that.

"I could say the same about you," she told him while running her fingers over his chest.

"Yeah?"

"Of course. You've always been able to capture my fancy, Special Agent Sneed, even when we were no longer together."

"I'll take capturing your fancy anytime," he said lightheartedly but meant every word.

"Oh, really?" Madison brushed her lips against his. "If you think you can handle a third go at it, I'm game."

He laughed. "You're insatiable, you know that?"

"And you're not?"

"Guilty as charged." Garrett couldn't keep a big smile off his face. He loved being able to take his time in pleasuring Madison and being pleasured by her. It was the one sure area where they clicked on all levels. The fact that it felt so natural, as if not missing a beat, didn't surprise him. Hell, he'd never felt for one instant that their lovemaking wouldn't be everything it had been before. But he'd been wrong. The sex was better than ever between them. This told him that she'd been the one thing missing in his life for two years that had left him feeling a void. Now that they had rekindled things, he wasn't about to let what they had slip through his fingers again.

The fact that they were still dealing with an unsub serial killer on the parkway was troubling for sure. But Garrett was as equally committed to having a second shot with Madison as he was to stopping the murders on the Blue Ridge Parkway. Something he had never been able to do to save his mother from falling prey to a bad man.

Chapter Ten

"Are you up for a run this morning?" Madison asked, wanting to take advantage of Garrett's presence after halting her runs temporarily while a killer was on the loose. Of course, she knew he was in her bed, naked, and hadn't brought any jogging attire after spending the night. Whereas she had been up for half an hour, made coffee and, after putting her hair into a high ponytail, had thrown on a sports bra, running shorts and sneakers.

Rubbing his eyes of sleepiness, Garrett replied, "Yeah, sure. We can pop over to my cabin, and I'll get dressed for a run. There's a great trail there. Then we can have breakfast there, back here or wherever you like."

"Sounds good." Madison smiled at him, feeling a fresh surge of desire after getting little sleep. But she kept it in check, not wanting to read too much into what had happened between them—in spite of the indication by both of them that it was a building block for a renewed relationship, rather than an exciting trip down memory lane. The last thing she wanted was to end up disappointed once more. "I'll wait for you downstairs," she said, not trusting herself in getting too cozy again.

"Okay," he said simply, sitting up. "I won't be long."

Twenty minutes later, they were running along a trail meandering between bigtooth aspen, tulip and magnolia trees. Madison managed to keep pace with Garrett, who had changed into a blue T-shirt and running shorts—with his muscular arms and legs in full display—and training sneakers. She studied him. He seemed caught up in his own world, in spite of having regained a place in hers.

"You don't talk much about your mother," Madison tossed at him for some reason. In their previous relationship, she'd only been given a general accounting of what had happened to her and him thereafter. Madison wanted more but didn't feel it was her place to ask.

Garrett gazed at her thoughtfully and said, "Kind of a hard thing to talk about, you know?"

"Yeah, I get that." She acknowledged that it wasn't so easy to think about her own parents' tragic death, much less air out her feelings about losing them too soon in life. But given the way his mother had died and his own shattered childhood as a result, it was still different. "Might help, though, to share what it is you're feeling. I know it's been a long time having to carry the memory of her death."

"You're right." He took a breath. "I want to let you in on what I've been carrying around for thirty years." Another sigh. "With no father in the picture, my mother, as a single parent, meant the world to me. She taught me everything she could to a five-year-old about the Cherokee culture but not nearly what she would have, had she lived longer."

Madison flashed him a sympathetic look. "I can only imagine how much it took out of you to have been deprived of this."

"Though she's been gone a long time, I still find myself trying to come to terms with the lost opportunity," he stated musingly. "The fact that her killer was never found only makes it worse."

"Which I know is only exacerbated by the current case we're working on," she voiced sadly.

Garrett nodded, wiping his brow with the back of his hand. "Yeah. But I can't go back and undo what was done to my mother. Hard as it is, I have to live for today. That includes my job. And getting to spend time with you again."

Madison took solace in his words and was encouraged by them. "I feel the same way."

He gave her a thin smile and said, "Better head back now."

"Okay." She took the lead and stayed just ahead of him as they navigated the trail and were silent while listening to the sounds of nature all around them.

GARRETT FELT BETTER in sharing his thoughts about his mother with Madison and having been raised by his grandparents. As someone he wanted to play an important part in his life, he understood that this included being open about his history and their own potential future beyond a serial-murder investigation. In turn, he needed just as much from her if they were to have a chance in making this work.

That morning, they met up with Leonard along the parkway. His brow creased as he said, "A couple of the maintenance rangers found a blood-soaked shirt and a survival knife buried in a dumpster."

Madison reacted with interest. "Really?"

"Yeah. They were apparently in a black plastic bag and underneath other trash, as if by design."

"And where was the dumpster located?" Garrett asked curiously.

"Not far from the Blue Ridge National Heritage Area," Leonard answered.

"Hmm..." He pondered this. "If this proves to be what we think it is, that would mean the unsub went the extra mile, so to speak, to try to hide evidence of one or more murders."

"Yeah, looks that way to me," Leonard concurred.

"Where are these items now?" Madison asked the ranger.

"Turned them over to the crime lab for processing."

"Good," Garrett told him. "We need to know, like yesterday, if this is a solid lead or not."

Leonard nodded. "I hear you."

"Makes sense that the unsub in one or both murders would try to unload the evidence of the crimes," Madison said. "Especially as the investigation heats up."

"We'll see," Garrett said, preferring to reserve judgment for now, while remaining optimistic that this was a potential breakthrough development.

Two hours later, he and Madison drove to the Western Regional Crime Laboratory in Hendersonville on Saint Pauls Road. There, they met with Jewel Yasumori, a slender, thirtysomething forensic analyst, for the results on testing of the items recovered. Earlier, she had been sent the tree branch that Madison had found near the spot where Nicole had been murdered.

Garrett was impatient as he looked at Jewel, whose short black hair was in a pixie bob with tapered sideburns. He asked point-blank, "What did you learn from analyzing the shirt and survival knife?"

Jewel blinked dark brown eyes and said, "Let's start with the shirt." She turned on her monitor that had an image of a man's casual button-down blue shirt. It was stained with blood. "We tested the blood for DNA and found that it was a match for Ranger Nicole Wallenberg's DNA."

Garrett watched Madison's jaw drop with the confirmation before she asked, "Did you find anyone else's DNA on the shirt?"

"Afraid not," Jewel said. "However, we were able to gather some fibers from the shirt as trace evidence. They were consistent with fibers found on Ranger Wallenberg's clothing, which can further be used to make a case against the unsub."

Garrett took note of that and asked her with interest, "What about the knife?"

Jewel's brow creased as she pulled up an image of a survival knife on her display. It had a rubber handle. "We found blood stains on the stainless-steel survival knife with a single-edged blade that measured eight inches. They matched the DNA profiles of Nicole Wallenberg and Olivia Forlani," she told them. "As such, this was almost certainly the weapon used to kill both of them."

Madison wrinkled her nose in disgust. "The perp was so brazen as to keep the same knife to go after Olivia, then Nicole."

"But smart enough to get rid of it rather than take a chance that the weapon might be discovered on his person or property," Garrett surmised. What concerned him was the unsub getting another survival knife to carry on his killings. "Were you able to pull any prints off the knife?"

"Actually, we do have some positive news on that front." Jewel perked up. "We were able to recover a latent palm print from a right hand off the knife," she reported enthusiastically. "It was entered into the FBI's Next Generation Identification system biometric database with its Advanced Fingerprint Identification Technology and the State Bureau of Investigation's Computerized Criminal History file." She sighed. "Unfortunately, we haven't been able to get a hit as yet on the unsub, if he's in the system."

Garrett frowned. He had to consider that the perp might somehow have been able to avoid arrest or incarceration, keeping his prints from being on file. "So, no DNA potentially belonging to the unsub?" he had to ask.

"We're still probing for this." Jewel licked her lips. "It's possible that we might be able to obtain a partial DNA profile of the unsub from the palm print or the part of the knife where it was left. This will depend on the number of cells we can gather from the latent print." She paused. "Of course, if we can retrieve an unknown DNA profile, we'll be able to upload it to CODIS and see if there's a match to an arrestee or offender or DNA profile."

"That's a lot of ifs," Madison pointed out skeptically. "But at least it gives us something to work with in going after the unsub."

"My sentiments exactly," Garrett said, believing that either way he looked at it, they were a step or two closer to identifying the Blue Ridge Parkway Killer. "For instance, we've now confirmed, more or less, that a single perpetrator was responsible for the stabbing deaths of Olivia Forlani and Nicole Wallenberg. And that he's running scared in trying to bury the evidence of his crimes."

Jewel nodded and said, "Forensics has a way of allowing us to catch up to unsubs, no matter their efforts to the contrary."

"Amen to that," Madison uttered, eyeing Garrett.

"Yeah, we're thankful for that," he concurred

before they headed back to the parkway, having made progress in their endeavors of solving two homicides.

MADISON AGREED THAT forensic evidence linking the murders of Olivia and Nicole to one assailant was a breakthrough in the case. Whether this would be enough to identify the unsub remained to be seen. But at least they seemed to be headed in the right direction, even if it was still frustrating that the serial killer remained at large for the time being.

We just need to find him before he goes after someone else, she told herself while riding back to the parkway with Garrett. Like her, he was caught up in his own thoughts. Madison imagined that these meandered back and forth between his own past family tragedy and determination to prevent the present-day killer from becoming tomorrow's cold case. As for their own evolving relationship, she was willing to take it one day at a time and see where it went, while trying her best not to presume their history would repeat itself and leave them both unsatisfied.

That cloudy afternoon, a memorial service was held for Nicole Wallenberg at Julian Price Memorial Park. Attendees included park rangers and other NPS employees and volunteers.

All had come to pay their respects for whom Madison believed had been a dedicated worker who'd given her all to the job.

Garrett and her boss approached Madison as she stood alongside Leonard and other rangers. "How are you holding up?" Tom asked her in a sympathetic tone.

"Just trying to get through this," Madison confessed, something that had never become routine to her.

"You will," he said, his voice filled with confidence. "In the meantime, we'll do all we can to bring Nicole justice."

"To that effect," Garrett said, brushing against Madison's shoulder, "my boss has approved offering a twenty-five-thousand-dollar reward for any info that leads to the arrest and conviction of Nicole's killer. Which obviously will give us justice as well for Olivia Forlani."

Madison's eyes lit. "That's good to know. Hopefully this will motivate someone to do the right thing, even if it takes a cash reward to make that happen."

"It's been a proven means of loosening lips," he told her.

"You never know how these things will go," Tom spoke realistically. "But between Carly and myself, we're committed to leaving no stone unturned in solving this case. Rewards are often a last resort, but we want to jump on the momentum we have going for us. That includes showing images of the shirt worn by the unsub in the hope that someone in the public will recognize it, along with a vague description of the man seen running into the woods."

Leonard added, "We're also interviewing people who may have seen someone hanging out by the dumpster around the time shortly after Nicole was murdered."

Madison nodded. "Looks like we have the bases covered in trying to nab the unsub. Now it only needs to happen."

"We just have to let the system play itself out," Garrett told her evenly.

"Right." She met his eyes, tempering her eagerness to give Nicole the peace in death that she deserved.

"I wouldn't be surprised if we're inundated with leads shortly," he contended. "It only takes one to blow this thing wide open."

Madison concurred, and then turned her attention to some rangers who stood at a podium to say a few words on behalf of Nicole. One was Ward Wilcox, the maintenance ranger who'd been present when Madison had gotten the black bear to run off into the woods and leave parkway visitors alone. She was surprised at his heartfelt words about Nicole, whom he described as someone who could have been his daughter. These sentiments were echoed by maintenance worker Ronnie Mantegna, who said, "Nicole struck me as someone who only wanted to make a difference. For some bastard to take that away from her is reprehensible. Whoever did it needs to be held accountable."

I couldn't agree more, a voice in Madison's head told her. They all had a responsibility to come together on behalf of Nicole and Olivia in not letting the unsub get away with cold-blooded murder. It appeared as if they were doing just that. She gazed at Garrett, who seemed to be reading her mind and gave her a look of resolve in seeing this through.

After Leonard spoke to the gathering, it was Madison's turn to step to the podium. She took a moment or two to collect her thoughts before honoring Nicole's life and what she'd stood for as a park ranger. Though they hadn't exactly been friends as far as hanging out together, with Madison being older, but she'd been on friendly terms with Nicole and had occasionally offered her career advice, and they'd shared some anecdotes about ranger life. In Madison's book, that counted for something that she would carry with her for the rest of her life. Just as she would the brief time she'd gotten to know Olivia before her life had also been cut short by a ruthless killer.

Chapter Eleven

That evening, Madison did some house cleaning, feeling the need to keep her mind preoccupied. It was her proven strategy for dealing
with the difficult parts of being a law enforcement ranger and not become overwhelmed by
it. *I can take it, but I'm still human too*, she told
herself. Something she always tried to keep in
a proper perspective when having alone time.

As for Garrett, neither of them had rushed
into a repeat performance from last night. Pas-
sionate and pleasurable as it was to make love,
she didn't want to overdo it at the expense of
having something real that went well beyond
the bedroom. She sensed that Garrett felt the
same way, respecting him for that. If they were
to make it work this time, great sex would only
be part of the equation, with a happy balance
between personal and career lives essential to
success.

When she got a call from Annette, Madison

stopped dusting and took the video chat while standing in the kitchen.

"Hey," her sister greeted her.

"Hi." Madison smiled. "Thanks for rescuing me from my chores."

Annette laughed. "Actually, I could say the same about you. I needed an excuse to take a break."

She chuckled. "I'll gladly give you that."

"So, what's happening with you and Garrett? Or shouldn't I ask?"

"You may." Madison grinned. "Let's just say that we're working on getting back together."

"Hmm…" Annette's eyes widened. "Does that mean you're putting in plenty of overtime 'reacclimating yourselves to one another'?"

She colored. "We're taking one step at a time," she told her diplomatically.

"Okay." Her sister sat back. "What's the latest on your investigation?"

Madison brought her up to speed on where things stood, then finished with, "All hands are on deck, Annette, as we try to put the squeeze on the unsub."

"You'll get him," she spoke with confidence. "Having been there, done that last year, it's not something I'd wish on my worst law enforcement enemy. Much less my big sister. But between you and Garrett, along with the support staff, I have no doubt that an arrest of the culprit is imminent."

Madison flashed her teeth. "Since when did you become so much like Mom and Dad?" she teased her, still remembering when Annette had first become part of their family when brought home from the adoption agency, and had been instantly adored, proving that she belonged.

"Look who's talking." She laughed. "I think our parents left an indelible mark on all of us."

"I agree." They talked a little about Annette's married life and their brothers before they said their goodbyes.

Madison returned to cleaning the house and then took a nice relaxing bubble bath. There, she couldn't help but recall the times when she and Garrett had played footsie and explored one another in the tub during their previous relationship and then made their way to bed for some great sex. Suddenly feeling aroused, she quickly shut off those thoughts and considered what tomorrow would bring in their investigation of a deadly unsub.

THE FOLLOWING DAY, while looking over data on the case at his log cabin, Garrett got word about a disturbing text the ISB tip line had received in relation to the Blue Ridge Parkway killings.

The National Park Service routinely received hundreds, if not thousands, of tips from the public annually on various crimes and otherwise suspicious activities that took place in national parks. Every one of these was taken seriously and, when appropriate, investigated. Normally, he would have passed this off to local park rangers. But upon being sent and reading the text, it obviously merited his own attention, in light of the investigation underway.

I'm the man you're looking for. I killed those women with my trusty survival knife, then dumped it. If you want to talk, I'm ready. — Blue Ridge Parkway Killer

Garrett felt a chill at the casualness of the text message from a purported killer. Was this truly their unsub? Had guilt eaten at him like an insidious cancer so he was ready to turn himself in and atone for his crimes through the judicial system? Identifying himself as Special Agent Sneed, he texted the person back, asking for more details. The suspect responded with another text.

All I can tell you right now is I stabbed them multiple times after catching them off guard. The park ranger put up more of a fight but still ultimately succumbed to my blade like the first victim before I ran off into the woods. I'm being straight with you.

Garrett sipped on coffee thoughtfully. *Sounds like someone who was actually involved in the homicides and needed to get this off his chest*, he mused, while still remaining skeptical. Was this simply an attention-seeker who was merely repeating public information or the real deal? If this was indeed their unsub, he was likely using a burner phone to avoid being traced back to his location. They needed to bring him in to further check out or dismiss his story. Garrett asked the man for his name.

You can call me Sean.

Garrett suspected it wasn't his real name, but it was a start in establishing a dialogue. He texted Sean for a face-to-face meeting, expecting him to reject this out of hand. Instead, Garrett was shocked at what came next.

I'm ready to turn myself in, Agent Sneed. Just tell me when and where.

Not willing to look a gift horse in the mouth, in case this was their serial killer, Garrett put him to the test by asking that he report to the Transylvania County Sheriff's Office at noon. When Sean agreed, Garrett immediately phoned Ray Pottenger and informed him that the person of interest in the case was reportedly set to arrive his way in an hour.

Pottenger made arrangements to that effect, accordingly. "We'll see if he shows."

"I'll be there, if he does," Garrett assured him.

He then called Madison. "Hey."

"Hey." He could tell that she was driving and had him on speaker phone.

"Got some news." Garrett told her about Sean using the tip line and the noon meeting at the Transylvania County Sheriff's Office.

"Hmm. You really think this guy is legit?"

"We'll find out soon enough," he responded noncommittally. "He seems to know things."

"Such as?"

"Basic info on the killings that may or may not be a firsthand account."

"I'd like to be there for the interrogation, if it happens," Madison said.

"I want that too," Garrett told her, believing she deserved that much, if they were to make an arrest.

"Good."

"I'll see you then."

"Okay," she replied and left it at that.

After disconnecting, Garrett was pensive. Part of him regretted not spending last night with her. It had been a judgment call. As much as they clicked in bed, he didn't want to overplay his hand in putting more emphasis on the mind-blowing sex than the overall strength of what they had going for them. If things went as they should, there would be plenty of times ahead for much more intimacy between them. Right now, they needed to see if the unsub in the investigation had come to them, rather than the other way around.

THE SUSPECT IDENTIFIED himself as Vincent Sean Deidrick. Madison, who sat beside Garrett, studied the man sitting across from them in the interrogation room. Wearing loose casual attire, he was in his midthirties, slender and around six feet, she guessed. His medium-length black hair was in a bro-flow cut, and he had a chin-strap beard on a long face with a jutting chin. He stared back at her so fiercely with dark eyes, it caused her to turn away briefly before meeting his gaze head-on.

Garrett, who was recording the interview, had the suspect reiterate his name and state his age of thirty-four before asking him straight-forwardly, "So, to be sure, Mr. Deidrick, you're confessing to the murders of Olivia Forlani and Nicole Wallenberg?"

"Yeah, I am." His voice did not waver as he lifted the glass of water before him with his right hand and took a sip. "I stabbed them both to death and had no problem doing it."

Garrett drew a breath. "Let's talk about that." He leaned forward. "What exactly did you use to stab the victims?"

"A survival knife," he claimed.

"Can you describe the knife?"

Deidrick shrugged. "Yeah. The blade was eight inches long. Bought it at a hardware store some time ago."

"What type of handle did it have?" Madison thought to ask.

"Just a handle," he said flippantly.

"Well, was it wooden, rubber, what?" she questioned.

He paused. "Rubber, I think."

You think? Or was that a lucky guess? Madison wondered, glancing at Garrett. "So you used the same knife to kill both women?"

"Yeah, it saved me the trouble of having to use different knives." Deidrick gave her a smug look.

Garrett peered at him. "What did you do with the knife?"

"Got rid of it," he replied, taking a drink of the water.

"Got rid of it where?"

"I tossed it in a dumpster."

"Where was that?" Garrett's voice hardened.

"On the parkway somewhere," Deidrick said tonelessly. "In trying to get away, I didn't exactly take the time to keep track of my every move."

"Maybe you should have, now that you're confessing to the murders," Madison stated, her lips pursed with doubts.

He sneered. "Guess I screwed up, huh?"

Garrett angled his face at him. "What about the clothing you were wearing during the murders? I assume you got rid of them, too, since they had to have been covered with your victims' blood."

Deidrick hedged. "Yeah, I did."

"You tossed those in the dumpster too?" Garrett asked.

Deidrick waited a beat and said, "Actually, I washed the clothes. No reason to throw away something I could still wear, right?"

Caught him in at least one lie, Madison thought. How many more lies were there in his story? "Speaking of clothes, do you happen to remember what the victims were wearing when you killed them?" she asked him.

Deidrick squirmed in the chair. "To tell you the truth, I wasn't paying much attention to their clothes." He paused. "The ranger had on a ranger uniform."

Good deduction, Madison mused sardonically. It didn't sound like the voice of direct experience to her. "Tell us again how you went about killing the women and when each killing occurred." She was intent on breaking down his confession even more.

The suspect recounted what he had already said and was able to provide the correct dates and general time frame in which the murders took place. Madison was still not convinced that he was their killer. She exchanged looks with Garrett, who asked him bluntly, "Why did you kill them?"

Deidrick sat back and responded shakily, "A voice in my head told me to do it. Can't really explain, other than to say it was just something I felt compelled to do."

"Why those women in particular?" Madison asked him straightforwardly, wondering if he'd been stalking them beforehand, were he the true culprit.

"They just happened to be in the vicinity when the desire to kill hit me." He regarded her darkly. "Wish it had been you that I came upon instead, Ranger Lynley," he said icily.

Garrett looked as if he was ready to go after him right then and there. "That wouldn't have gone well for you, Deidrick," he stated. "She would have made you work even harder to get what you wanted out of it."

Madison touched Garrett's forearm to let him know that she wasn't flustered by the suspect's attempt at intimidation. "But it wasn't me," she snapped. "I'm here right now, and if you did what you claim to have done, you'll never hurt another woman again."

Deidrick furrowed his brow. "I did it," he insisted. "Killed them both."

"So you say," Garrett muttered. "Why confess now?"

"Why not?" His voice lowered an octave. "I felt I needed to before the urge to go after someone else overcame me."

"I see." Garrett gave him a quizzical gaze.

"Are you going to arrest me, or what?" he demanded.

Garrett considered the question and said equably, "First, we'd like to collect a sample of your DNA, as well as get your fingerprints, as part of the process."

Deidrick stared at him, nonplussed, and said flatly, "That won't happen till I'm charged with the murders."

As Madison exchanged glances with Garrett

in assessing the situation, she took note of Deidrick finishing off his glass of water in practically a show of defiance. She looked up as the door opened and Deputy Pottenger popped his head in. He indicated a need to speak with them outside the room.

"Will you excuse us?" she told Deidrick politely as she stood with Garrett and left him at the table. She wondered what the deputy had for them.

In the hall, Garrett was curious as to what Ray Pottenger had learned after checking out the suspect's background. It was obvious there were some major gaps in Deidrick's account of the killings, which Madison had clearly picked up on as well. That left a lot to be desired in believing him to be the actual Blue Ridge Parkway Killer.

Pottenger scratched his pate and said sourly, "Looks like Vincent Sean Deidrick has had mental health issues most of his life. He's been in and out of institutions and is apparently prone to delusions, among other conditions." The deputy sighed. "Deidrick also happens to be a true-crime addict. Combine these with the fact that most of the accurate information he gave was readily available through the media and online and his story starts to fall apart."

"Why am I not surprised?" Madison frowned. "Deidrick acted like a wannabe serial killer, and now we know why."

"He must have been following the story as it happened," Garrett decided, "and figured this was a good time to make his move for fifteen seconds of notoriety."

Pottenger nodded. "Seems to be the size of it."

"Still, he knew just enough to keep him on the radar," Garrett said. "At least till we're certain that his palm print isn't a match for the one Forensics pulled off the survival knife used in the killings."

"We'll assign a deputy to keep an eye on Deidrick for the time being," Pottenger said.

On that note, Garrett stepped back inside the interrogation room and said disingenuously, "We appreciate you coming in with the confession, Sean. We'll take everything you said under consideration. For now, you're free to go."

Deidrick's nostrils flared. "So, that's it?" he voiced with disappointment. "You're not taking me into custody?"

"Not yet." Garrett jutted his chin. "We can't just go on a confession alone, convincing as it is. There's a process we need to go through. But we have your address and cell phone number. As soon as everything is in order, we'll bring you back in and go from there. In the meantime, a deputy will show you out."

Reluctantly, Deidrick got to his feet, and Pottenger came in and walked him from the room and to the front door of the sheriff's office. Garrett watched briefly before going back into the interrogation room, where he put on a nitrile glove and carefully lifted the glass Deidrick had drank out of. There was a clear palm print that he'd left. Garrett put the glass into an evidence bag. They would get this over to the Western Regional Crime Laboratory pronto and see if they had a match.

In Garrett's mind, he doubted that would be the case. As much as he wanted Vincent Sean Deidrick to have handed them the guilty party on a silver platter, it was looking like another red herring in the effort to bring the cagey Blue Ridge Parkway Killer to justice.

Chapter Twelve

An hour later, Madison was in her patrol car on the Blue Ridge Parkway, pondering what to make of Vincent Sean Deidrick's confession. She found it hard to imagine that anyone could be so fixated on violent behavior so as to wish to become a serial killer for the vicarious thrill of it. On the other hand, if by some miracle Deidrick did turn out to be the parkway killer, then he had done them a solid by turning himself in.

At least we'd have no trouble tracking him down and bringing him back in with a deputy shadowing his every move, Madison mused.

When her cell phone rang, she put it on speaker after seeing that the caller was Garrett. He had left the sheriff's office to go directly to the crime lab to have the glass Deidrick had drunk from tested for his palm print.

"Hey," she uttered. "What did you find out?"

"That Deidrick's right-hand palm print was not a match for the print left on the survival knife murder weapon," Garrett replied matter-of-factly. "Jewel Yasumori dismissed any notion that Deidrick might still somehow be our serial killer."

"Figures," she said acceptingly.

"That's the way it works out sometimes in this business. You're going to get people who want to involve themselves in criminal activity, whether real or not. Mix that in with mental issues and you get a Vincent Sean Deidrick."

"I suppose." Madison paused. "Someone knows something," she declared. "Maybe the tip line can still work in terms of providing solid info."

"That may be the case," Garrett said. "Especially with the reward being offered."

"We'll see about that," she told him, though not holding her breath. Cash incentive could only go so far in motivating people to do the right thing. Then there was the real possibility that the killer was hidden in plain view, completely fooling those around him into believing him to be a law-abiding citizen.

"I'm on my way back to the parkway," he told her. "Should be there in about fifteen minutes. Can you meet me at the Raven Rocks Overlook?"

"Yes. Why?" she wondered.

"You'll see…" He left her hanging with his mysterious words, while arousing her curiosity.

"I'll meet you there," Madison told him simply. She drove to the overlook that was popular for its sunsets and rock climbers. After pulling into the parking area, she got out of her car and waited for Garrett's arrival, while enjoying the amazing views of the landscape.

I never tire of this part of working in the Blue Ridge Mountains, she told herself, while knowing that someone was attempting to mar its beauty with ugly acts of criminality.

When Garrett drove up, parking alongside her, Madison headed to meet him. She wondered if he had news pertaining to the investigation. "Hey," she said.

"Hey." He flashed a quick smile, replaced by a serious look. "Thanks for coming."

She blinked and considered that this could be a romantic move on his part. Or not. "What's up?"

"I wanted to show you something." He took her hand and led her to the wooden fence at the edge of the Raven Rocks Overlook. "This is where my mother was murdered," Garrett muttered, maudlin.

Clutching his hand tighter, Madison expressed sympathy as though it had just happened. "I'm so sorry."

"It was down there, where she ventured off a hiking trail." He drew a breath. "Someone was waiting for her or followed her to that spot."

Madison was speechless, unsure what to say. Reliving the memory of his mother's death, still an unsolved mystery, had to be gut-wrenching. Even after all these years. She knew that this had been triggered by the current parkway murders.

I need to try to ease his painful memories, she thought. "Your mother must have been a remarkable woman to have raised you alone, by and large, and still found the time to do something she loved."

"Yeah, she was." Garrett was still holding Madison's hand while staring out at the scenery. Suddenly, he faced her and said, "How do you feel about making our way down there?"

She glanced down. Though it looked a bit tricky, she was sure she could do it without making a fool of herself. Especially if it could help give him some closure. "I'm game if you are." She looked at him. "You sure you want to do this?"

"I'm sure," he said resolutely. "I need to."

They climbed over the fence and headed down the slope across rocks and dirt. At one point, Madison nearly slipped. Catching her in his sturdy arms, Garrett said coolly, "Watch your step."

With a giggle, while regaining her footing, she responded lightheartedly, "Now you tell me."

He chuckled. "You're doing fine."

There were no more hiccups before they reached the lower level that had grass, a dirt path with a wooded area and a thirteen-acre family farm nearby. Madison followed Garrett into the woods and watched as he surveyed the area, as if looking for clues of a three-decades-old homicide.

"She never had a chance once ambushed," he remarked. "Just like Olivia and Nicole."

Madison gazed at him. "You don't think the murders could somehow be connected, do you?"

Garrett pursed his lips thoughtfully. "Anything's possible." He added, "Right now, my mother's murder is still a cold case. The recent murders are heating up, in spite of the setbacks in identifying the unsub."

Madison pondered the possibility that the same killer could have spanned thirty years. Her brother Scott was a cold-case investigator and had cracked some previously unsolved homicides. But in most of these, the killer had laid low through the years. Could this be different?

Garrett got her attention. "After my grandparents' deaths, I kind of turned away from my people in the Eastern Band of Cherokee Indians," he remarked, a tone of guilt in his voice. "Part of me blamed them for not doing more to protect my mother—like getting someone to hike with her in the Blue Ridge Mountains instead of her going alone."

"Do you really think that was fair?" Madison questioned. "Maybe back then it wasn't any more unusual than now for a woman to hike by herself. Especially in this area that's usually considered a safe environment. I'm sure your mom had taken the trek alone other times with no problems."

"She had," he acknowledged, "and you're right." Garrett looked down. "I need to go back to the Qualla, where I still have a few distant relatives and the overall support of the Cherokee community, and make peace with the past and present."

Madison smiled. "That's a great idea."

"How do you feel about taking a ride with me to Cherokee?" he asked.

She knew that this was the tribal capital of the Eastern Band of Cherokee Indians, federally recognized as such, and located at the southern boundary of the Blue Ridge Parkway, around an hour-and-a-half drive. This would be the first time she had accompanied Garrett to his native land, as he'd been in no hurry to do so when they'd dated previously—and now she knew why. Madison had no problem taking the afternoon off and didn't think her boss would object, with other rangers on hand.

"I'd love to go to Cherokee with you," she told Garrett.

"Great."

With a grin on his face, he pulled her up to him, and they kissed. Madison welcomed this show of affection, the nearness of him causing her heart to flutter. She hoped that visiting the Qualla would be just what they needed to bring them closer together.

GARRETT FOLLOWED MADISON back to her place, where she changed into leisure clothes and put her hair into a high ponytail and joined him for the drive. There was silence mostly as they headed down the Great Smoky Mountains Expressway toward Cherokee in Jackson County where, along with Haywood and Swain Counties, the greatest contiguous part of the Qualla Boundary existed. Purchased by the Native American tribe in the 1870s and held in trust by the federal government as a sovereign nation that included forests, rivers and mountains, with the Great Smoky Mountains National Park nearby, it was a place that would always be near and dear to Garrett's heart. Having spent his youth there and embracing the heritage handed down to him by his mother and grandparents, it had never been his intention to turn his back on the Qualla. But it had taken him this long to overcome the self-guilt and blame that had kept him away. He knew now that it had been wrong to put his mother's murder on anyone but the unsub, who had used his own free will to butcher her to death and had gotten away with it.

"So, who are these distant relatives of yours living in the Qualla?" Madison broke the silence from the passenger seat. "And have you kept in touch at all?"

Garrett loosened his grip on the steering wheel as he responded contemplatively, "I've stayed in touch with a second cousin, Noah Owl, and his wife, Breanna. And one of the elders who knew my mother and grandparents, Jeremiah Youngdeer. But that's about it."

"Well, hopefully, this will give you the opportunity to reconnect and start a new chapter in your life as a member of the EBCI," she said.

Garrett grinned. "I'm counting on that." But he was counting even more on strengthening their own reconnection, which could ultimately extend to his greater ties to the Qualla as well as her family.

When they arrived in Cherokee, Garrett drove

to a residence on Black Rock Road. A red GMC Yukon was parked outside the rustic log cabin. Before they reached the door, it opened. A yellow Labrador retriever scooted out past them, followed by a tall and firm man in his late thirties with long dark hair parted on the side and deep brown eyes.

He broke into a grin and said, "Hey, stranger."

"Noah." Garrett met his gaze warmly. "Good to see you."

"You too." They embraced, and Noah shifted his eyes. "And who did you bring with you?"

"This is Madison Lynley," Garrett introduced her. "My cousin Noah Owl, who also happens to be the interim chief of the Cherokee Indian Police Department for the EBCI."

"Nice to meet you," Madison said with a smile and extended her hand.

"You too." Noah ignored her hand and gave her a brief hug. "Handshakes are strictly forbidden in these parts."

She laughed. "I'll try to remember that."

He called to the dog, "Bo, get over here!" The yellow Lab immediately bounded over to them on command, and Noah said, "Say hello to our guests."

The dog barked, and Garrett played with him a bit and said, "Good to see you again too," before Bo moved over to Madison, warming up to her instantly.

"Hi, Bo," she said spiritedly.

"What's all the ruckus out here?" a female voice asked.

Garrett turned to see Noah's wife, Breanna, step out. In her midthirties, petite and attractive with big gray-brown eyes and long and layered brunette hair with highlights, she was noticeably pregnant with what would be the couple's first child. Garrett was envious of them and looked forward to the day when he would become a father, along with a husband. "Hey, Breanna."

"Hey, Garrett." She flashed her teeth, hugged him and went to Madison, hugging her before saying, "You must be Madison, the ranger Garrett has been raving about reconnecting with."

Madison blushed, glancing at him and back. "Yep, that would be me."

"Nice to finally meet you."

"Same here."

Garrett regretted not having brought Madison there for a visit when they'd been seeing each other two years ago. But the timing had been off and he hadn't been in much of a hurry back then to return to Cherokee. He was glad to have her there now as part of his way of mending fences.

"Come inside," Noah told them.

Half an hour later, they were all sitting in rocker chairs on a wraparound deck with an amazing view of the Blue Ridge Parkway and the mountains. They talked about the parkway killings, life on the Qualla, which had seen an increase in drug activity in recent memory, and spending more time together. Garrett was certainly amenable to getting in touch with his roots again, with Madison being an essential part of that in bridging the gap, while looking ahead.

"So, how close are you to discovering who's behind the murders on the parkway?" Breanna asked, sipping lemonade.

Garrett furrowed his brow and glanced at Bo, who was lying there lazily, taking it all in. "Not close enough to say that an arrest is imminent," he admitted. "But we're doing everything we can to track down the culprit."

Madison concurred. "It's a work in progress," she asserted positively, "frustrating as it's been."

Breanna sighed. "Just keep at it, and you'll get some justice."

"That's the plan," he said, his voice intent.

Noah drank some beer and said, "This has to hit pretty close to home, losing your mother in a similar fashion?"

"It does," Garrett acknowledged. This was one reason for his return, to try to reconcile what had happened to her with the current murders. "I kind of feel that she's pushing me to get to the bottom of the current investigation as a way to make amends for the past."

"None of what happened thirty years ago was your fault," Noah told him. "You get that, right?"

"Yeah," he said tonelessly, taking a swig of beer. "But there's still a side of me that wishes I had gone with her that day to the Blue Ridge Mountains. Maybe if I had, we would've taken a different route and she wouldn't have run into harm's way."

"Coulda, woulda, shoulda," Noah voiced in rejecting the idea. "We all go when our time's up, like it or not. That wasn't your time, Garrett, and you weren't in a position then to change fate. Don't beat yourself up in reliving a tragedy that was beyond your control."

"I feel the same way," Madison expressed gently, sipping beer. "Losing loved ones is the hardest thing. Worse would be to tarnish their memories by dwelling too much on the what-ifs."

"You're right." Garrett nodded in agreement, happy to have her in his corner. But even with that understanding, there was still something that wasn't sitting right with him between his mother's murder and the current ones attributed to the Blue Ridge Parkway Killer. Was it even possible after all these years that the killer could be one and the same?

BEFORE THEY LEFT, Garrett paid a courtesy call to Jeremiah Youngdeer, who was on the Tribal Council. At eighty, he was still rock solid in build and had short silver hair and black eyes deeply creased at the corners. As a Cherokee elder, he carried the respect afforded to him among the Eastern Band of Cherokee Indians.

"Nice to be back here," Garrett told him as they walked through the Oconaluftee Indian Village, an authentic replica of a 1760s Cherokee village, on Drama Road.

"You're always welcome, Garrett," Jeremiah told him, walking with a limp from arthritis in his knee. "This is your home too, no matter where you go in life."

Garrett smiled respectfully. "I appreciate that."

Jeremiah regarded him. "I want you to know that not a day goes by that I don't think about your mother, Jessica," he said, maudlin. "As one of our own, we all felt incredible pain over the unfortunate loss of life for her at such a young age."

Garrett waited a beat before asking in a low

voice, "Do you remember my father, Andrew Crowe?"

"I do." Jeremiah's weathered face sagged. "Andrew was a hard worker. Sadly, he also developed a predilection for the bottle. It caused him to forget a big part of his heritage and commitment to family." He took a deep breath. "Your mother wanted to stay with him, become his wife. But by then, Andrew was too far gone, and he left her—and his people—high and dry. And that was it. He never returned to the Qualla."

Garrett got a lump in his throat at the thought of being cheated out of having a real father. Especially in light of his mother's early death. But since Andrew Crowe had made his choice, it was something Garrett would have to live with, as he had all these years, while maintaining strength through his mother's memory.

He eyed Jeremiah, knowing what would come next was delicate but necessary. "Is it possible that someone from the Qualla could have followed my mother to the mountains and killed her?" Given that his father had abandoned them two years prior for parts unknown, Garrett had no reason to believe that he had perpetrated the attack as domestic violence.

The elder creased his brow. After a long moment, he responded levelly, "Anything is possible. But with my ear to the ground then and the strong sense of community, I'm all but certain that it was someone from the outside who randomly crossed paths with Jessica and decided to harm her."

Garrett nodded. This was his sense too. Which gave him peace of mind on the one hand. And on the other, a renewed sense that his mother's killer might not only still be alive and well but could have picked up where he'd left off years ago in hunting young women in the Blue Ridge Mountains.

MADISON WAS HAPPY that Garrett had invited her to accompany him to the Qualla Boundary and get to know his relatives and the richness of the environment itself. They were able to step away from the pressures of the criminal investigation by hanging out at Harrah's Cherokee Casino and going to a fun Cherokee bonfire, where they listened to amazing stories by Cherokees told to the sound of drums.

When they got back, Madison spent the night at Garrett's log cabin. Putting aside any hesitancy to fall back into enjoyable old and recent habits, they made love, enjoying each other's company while extending their passions well into the wee hours of the morning. Afterward, thoroughly exhausted, they lay cuddled together in his log bed, where Madison could have sworn that Garrett said he loved her before drifting off to sleep. She wondered if this had been a slip of the tongue in the aftermath of good sex. Or had he meant it?

Given that her own feelings for the man had risen to the "starting to fall in love" category since they had become involved again, Madison could only hope that this was indeed reciprocal as they navigated the waters of a renewed romance that came with the same risks and rewards as before. Only this time would hurt far worse should things fizzle out and they ended up going their separate ways. She fell asleep on that note, while resolved to remain positive where Garrett Sneed was concerned.

Chapter Thirteen

"I'd like to take a look at the cold-case file on my mother's unsolved murder," Garrett told his boss in a video chat the following day at the cabin.

"Really?" Carly Tafoya raised a brow in surprise. "Do you think it has something to do with the parkway murders?"

He considered the question carefully, knowing full well that this was a long shot at best and a waste of precious time at worst. Nevertheless, it was a shot that he needed to pursue. "There are some similarities that simply can't be ignored," Garrett reasoned. "For one, they occurred in the Blue Ridge Mountains, albeit thirty years apart. The female victims were all stabbed to death," he pointed out uneasily. "With none of the various suspects for the two recent murders panning out, I decided I needed to expand the range of possible unsubs to include those old enough to have murdered my mother."

Carly gave an understanding nod. "Okay, I'll send you what we have on the case."

Garrett smiled. "Thanks."

"You might also check with the Buncombe County Sheriff's Office," she suggested. "They would have been the local law enforcement agency to head the investigation in working in conjunction with us."

"I'll do that." He was sure he would get cooperation from Sheriff Jacob Silva. "Can you look up the name of the special agent who handled my mother's case?"

"Yes. Give me a sec." Carly stepped away for a moment. She said when returning, "It was Special Agent Dexter Broderick. He retired about fifteen years ago and is still alive."

That's good to know, Garrett thought. "I don't suppose you know his whereabouts?"

"As a matter of fact, he lives in Buncombe County," she told him. "At least that was his last known address."

"Send me his contact info. Hopefully I can track him down."

"Will do." Carly paused. "Honestly, Sneed, linking these cases seems like a stretch, as the culprit in your mother's murder would have to be pretty old today and likely not as able-bodied as a younger man to commit two brazen murders on the parkway and make a clean getaway in the woods in a snap. I'm just saying. Don't want to see you get too keen on the prospect of solving your mother's murder, only to be left disappointed."

This was fair to point out to Garrett, leaving him little room for push back. Especially as these were legitimate points in his own mind too, all things considered. But his gut told him that, even against the odds, he might be onto something. "I appreciate your concern," he voiced evenly. "If at any time it seems like I'm barking up the wrong tree, I won't reopen a cold case that doesn't appear to be connected to my present investigation," he promised. "I'm totally committed to solving the deaths of Nicole Wallenberg and Olivia Forlani, no matter what it takes."

"Okay," Carly said acceptingly.

After signing off, for an instant, Garrett had second thoughts about going down this road. Did he really want to dredge up old and painful memories at a time when he had just started to get back in touch with his roots? Then he realized it was for that very reason that he needed to see this through, for better or worse.

Even Madison seemed to support the possible connection. He had run it by her in the middle of the night, somewhere between the sounds of intimacy and uttering his love for her. She had responded positively on both fronts, giving him reason to believe they were on the same page in terms of the investigation and wanting to be together as a couple when this was all over.

Half an hour later, Garrett was giving the material on his mother's death a cursory glance on his laptop. Jessica Rachel Sneed, age twenty-five, had been found dead below Raven Rocks Overlook on the Blue Ridge Parkway. Fully clothed in a green T-shirt, denim shorts and tennis shoes, she'd been stabbed to death. Next to the body had been a pink lightweight backpack that had contained the victim's water bottle and a few other personal effects. Garrett winced when he read from the autopsy report that his mother had had eight stab wounds to her body. The murder weapon, a survival knife, was shown and described as having a smooth eight-inch, single-edged blade. It had been found by some kids playing in the bushes.

Garrett couldn't help but think that the knife bore a strong resemblance to the one found in a dumpster and positively linked to the murders of Olivia Forlani and Nicole Wallenberg. Was this coincidence? Or an indication that a decades-old killer had a preference for a long-bladed survival knife?

DNA had been collected at the crime scene, including an unknown DNA profile belonging to the unsub that had never been positively identified. Garrett gazed at a photograph of his mother that had been taken earlier that year she'd died. He remembered it being shot by his grandfather outside their house in the Qualla. *She looks so young*, Garrett thought, with her high cheekbones on a diamond-shaped face and bold brown eyes, surrounded by long black hair worn in braids. The resemblance to himself was unmistakable.

He had to check himself at the thought that they had never been given the chance to get to know one another as adults. Hell, his mother hadn't even been around during his teenage years. Or when he'd left the nest in becoming a man and a special agent with the National Park Service. But maybe they could bridge the gap across the spiritual divide should he be able to solve her murder at long last.

Garrett turned to the info on retired Special Agent Dexter Broderick. Now seventy-five, he was apparently residing at a nursing home in Asheville on Mountainly Lane.

Let's see what blanks he can fill in, Garrett thought, and he was out the door.

MADISON RECEIVED A report of a possible armed robbery by Milepost 374.4, close to the Rattlesnake Lodge Trailhead. She headed there to rendezvous with Law Enforcement Ranger Richard Edison.

Back to business as usual...somewhat, she thought, with the Blue Ridge Parkway Killer still on her mind.

Garrett had just called to say that he was en route to see the retired ISB special agent who'd worked on the original Jessica Sneed investigation. Seemed as though Garrett was now of the belief that his mother's death might be tied to the current serial murders on the parkway. The notion gave Madison a fright. But it was also something she could see as a possibility, remote as it seemed given the wide time frame.

If Jessica's killer is still at large today, he deserves to be apprehended and sent to prison, Madison told herself. And if the unsub and the present-day perp were one and the same, all the better to solve it in one fell swoop.

Pulling off the parkway behind Richard's vehicle, Madison got out and approached him as he spoke to a thirtysomething Asian man standing beside his car, a blue BMW Gran Coupe.

Richard turned to her. "Hey."

"What happened?" she asked, looking from one to the other.

"This is Pierre Yang," Richard said. "Why don't you tell Ranger Lynley what you told me?"

Madison gazed at the brown-eyed man, who was medium in build with short dark hair in a spiky cut, as he told her, "I pulled off to the side here to take some pics, and another car stopped. A guy got out, carrying a gun, and demanded my cell phone, camera and wallet, which had cash and credit cards in it." His voice shook. "Of course, I gave them to him. He got back in his vehicle and took off. I had a second phone in my car that I used to call you guys."

She frowned. "Sorry you had to go through that, sir."

"Me too." He scratched his pate. "Guess I shouldn't have stopped here."

"You have every right to." Madison believed that the culprit had likely followed the mark and waited for an opportunity to strike, as was the case for these types of crimes. She faced Richard. "Did you get a description of the suspect?"

"Yeah." He glanced at a notepad. "White male in his teens. Slender, blue-eyed with blondish-brown hair in a fringe cut and wearing a white T-shirt, jeans and black sneakers." Richard looked at the victim. "Is that right?"

"Yes," Pierre replied with a nod.

"What type of car was he driving?" Madison asked. She listened as he described it as a dark-colored sedan similar to a Mitsubishi Eclipse. When asked about the weapon the unsub was brandishing, Pierre believed it to be a .22 caliber pistol. "We'll do what we can to help you retrieve some of your stolen items," she told him. "I would strongly suggest you cancel the credit cards right away, to limit your liability."

"I'll do that," he assured her.

"Good." Madison turned to Richard and said, "After you finish taking Mr. Yang's statement, notify the local authorities and see if they have reports of any similar crimes of late. Could be this is part of a theft ring, seizing upon any opportunities that come their way on the parkway or greater area."

"Okay." Richard adjusted his campaign hat and looked at Pierre. "Let's go over everything that happened."

Madison left them, knowing that her fellow law enforcement ranger could take it from here. She headed back to her patrol vehicle, wondering why so many teenagers seemed to be going off the rails these days. She supposed there could be many explanations, not the least of which was a misguided belief that they were owed something for nothing. If she were so fortunate to have children of her own someday, she would certainly do her best to ensure they were well grounded with strong values. Madison couldn't help but think that if their father happened to be Garrett, he would be of the same mind.

GARRETT PULLED INTO the parking area of the Seniors at Blue Ridge Retirement Village. He got out and went inside the Victorian-style facility. At the front desk, he flashed his identification and asked to see Dexter Broderick. A moment later, a fortysomething female with a platinum bouffant approached him in the lobby and said, "I'm Wendy Schneider, the nursing home manager and health services coordinator."

"Special Agent Sneed," he told her.

"You wanted to speak with Mr. Broderick?"

"Yes. I'm looking into a cold case he investigated when he was with the National Park Service."

Wendy arched a brow. "Not sure he can be much help to you, Agent Sneed," she indicated sadly. "Mr. Broderick is currently suffering from moderate dementia as a result of Alzheimer's disease. His memory loss is pretty significant, and he's easily confused."

"Sorry to hear that." Garrett had come across people with Alzheimer's in his personal and professional life and wouldn't wish this progressive disease on anyone.

"But there are times when he's lucid," she

said. "Moreover, Mr. Broderick rarely gets any visitors these days. He's currently out in the garden getting some fresh air. You're welcome to speak with him for a few minutes, if you like."

"I would like to do that, thanks," Garrett said, believing it was worth a try.

He was led through the facility and out a door to a large area with a well-manicured lawn, a variety of plants and flowers, a wilderness path and a pond. They approached an elderly, thin man who was sitting on an Adirondack rocking chair in a shaded area.

"Mr. Broderick," Wendy got his attention. "There's someone here to see you."

"Really?" Dexter's blue eyes lit beneath thinning white hair in a Boston style with a widow's peak.

"I'm Special Agent Garrett Sneed," Garrett said and stuck out his hand. Reluctantly, Dexter shook it with his own frail hand. "You worked on a case for the National Park Service thirty years ago."

"Did I?" He scratched his pate in straining to remember.

"It was a murder investigation on the Blue Ridge Parkway." Garrett took a breath. "The victim, Jessica Sneed, was my mother."

"Jessica Sneed?" Dexter's chin sagged. "Your mother?"

"That's right. I've reopened the case in trying to solve the crime," Garrett told him. "She was stabbed to death." He glanced at Wendy, who had stepped farther away to give them a little privacy but was clearly listening to every word, based on her expression.

"I'm sorry," the older man said sincerely. "I tried to find out who did it."

"I know you did." Garrett was thankful for his service and that his memory was still there on this occasion. "Do you recall anything that might be able to help me find her killer?"

Dexter sucked in a deep breath, peered at him and said, "Who did you say you are?"

"Special Agent Sneed of the National Park Service."

Dexter's eyes narrowed suspiciously. "Do I know you?"

"We just met." Garrett could see that he was losing him. "We were talking about the murder of Jessica Sneed on the Blue Ridge Parkway."

"We were?" Dexter widened his eyes, but they looked blank. "Sorry, but my memory isn't what it used to be. What is this about? And who did you say you are?"

Guess this is about as far as I'm going to get, Garrett thought, eyeing Wendy as her cue that the interview was over. He turned back to the former special agent and said, "Just a friend who came to check on you."

Dexter looked confused, then broke into a grin. "Nice of you. Thanks."

"Anytime." Garrett forced a smile. "Take care of yourself, Dexter."

"I will."

Wendy walked up to them and said to Garrett, "Hope you don't feel this was a waste of your time."

"I don't," he stressed. "NPS special agents always have a bond, no matter what. I'll show myself out."

MAYBE I'LL HAVE better luck at the Buncombe County Sheriff's Office, Garrett told himself as he took the short drive there. That was assuming this wasn't a wild goose chase in trying to open a cold case by tying it to a current investigation.

When he arrived, Sheriff Jacob Silva greeted him and said, "I had one of my deputies pull up what we had on the Jessica Sneed case and lay it out in an evidence room for you to take a look at."

"Appreciate that," Garrett told him.

"No problem." Silva furrowed his brow. "I warn you, though, it may be difficult to look at."

"I get that." Garrett met his eyes steadily. "I'm up to the task."

"All right." Silva lifted the brim of his hat. "If we can do anything else to help solve your mother's murder, we're more than willing to do so."

"Thanks. I'll let you know."

Silva gave him a thoughtful look. "You're thinking that the same killer could now be targeting women on the parkway?"

Garrett waited a beat before responding contemplatively, "All options are on the table at this point."

"They should be." The sheriff bobbed his head. "Some of the worst serial killers started early in life and stayed at it or picked back up in their later years."

Garrett kept that thought in mind as he walked into the evidence room. On the metal rectangular table was a pair of nitrile gloves and evidence collected from the crime scene on the parkway thirty years ago. In plastic bags were his mother's clothing, shoes and backpack. Also bagged was the murder weapon. He put on the gloves and opened the bag, examining the survival knife while holding it by the wooden handle. This differentiated from the rubber handle used in the stabbing deaths of Olivia Forlani and

Nicole Wallenberg. He didn't put much stock in that, as different times, different handles.

Garrett swallowed hard as he put the knife back into the bag, pained at what it had done to his mother. Had the same unsub used another knife to resume murdering women? Or was the case unrelated, if not just as sickening? Once he had perused the evidence and gone over some witness statements and incidental notes by investigators, Garrett had seen enough to warrant continuing to investigate what could well have been a one-off in the killing of his mother.

Outside the room, he spoke with Sheriff Silva, who pledged continued cooperation and added, "By the way, the sheriff thirty years ago, Lou Buckley, is now retired and living the good life in Kiki's Ridge. You might want to speak with him. I'm sure he'd be happy to tell you what he remembers about the case."

"I'll do that," Garrett said, more than willing to follow up on this with the former sheriff in the pursuit of long overdue justice.

Chapter Fourteen

That afternoon, Madison accompanied Garrett to Price Lake at Milepost 297, where they found the man they were looking for, she believed. Retired Buncombe County Sheriff Lou Buckley was standing on the pier, trout fishing. It saddened her to learn that his former colleague in law enforcement, retired ISB Special Agent Dexter Broderick, was suffering from Alzheimer's disease. Madison recalled that her grandfather had been in the early stages of dementia before eventually dying from a heart attack.

"Since Buckley's office had jurisdiction on the homicide at that time, hopefully he can provide some insight into the case," Garrett told her as they walked down the long pier.

"We'll see," she said, still wrapping her mind around the notion that a cold case could be the key to solving a current one. She wondered if the unsub was the same or if they were connected to one another in some way.

Garrett cut into her reverie, remarking, "Glad to hear that your teenage armed robber ran out of steam quickly."

"That's what happens when you're dumb enough to try to use a stolen credit card less than an hour after stealing it." She rolled her eyes at the stupidity of the young criminal. "Duh."

He laughed. "Well, thieves aren't always the brightest bulbs in the chandelier."

"I'm just happy for the victim that his items were recovered with minimal loss," she said, while knowing Pierre Yang's story could have ended much more tragically since he was robbed at gunpoint.

"Yeah." They approached the seventysomething man, who was heavyset and wearing a fishing trucker hat with tufts of white hair beneath it. Garrett asked, "Sheriff Lou Buckley?"

He turned to face them with blue eyes behind browline glasses. "Haven't been called that in a very long time."

"Once a sheriff, always a sheriff," Garrett uttered respectfully.

Lou chuckled. "True enough."

"I'm ISB Special Agent Garrett Sneed, and this is Law Enforcement Ranger Madison Lynley."

"Nice to meet you both." He was holding a

lightweight trout rod in the water. "In fact, Sheriff Silva gave me a heads up that you wanted to talk to me about a cold case—the murder of Jessica Sneed...your mother."

Garrett nodded. "That's right. I'm reopening the investigation. Anything you can tell us about the case would be helpful."

"First of all, I'm sorry she was killed that way," Lou expressed. "I seem to recall that you were, what, about five at the time?"

"Yes," he acknowledged, tilting his face to one side.

Lou glanced out at the lake and back. "Losing your mother at such a young age...you both deserved better." He paused reflectively. "I had just been the sheriff of Buncombe County for a couple of years when the crime occurred on the Blue Ridge Parkway. It threw us all for a loop, as the parkway had been relatively peaceful in those days. Initially, our office battled it out with the National Park Service on who should take the lead in the investigation. Guess I had a stronger will and won out."

Madison asked him curiously, "What takeaways did you get from the case?"

Lou considered this before responding, "The biggest takeaway, I suppose, was that the killer had to have been someone who knew the parkway inside and out. This would have given him a way in and out quickly."

"You mean like a park employee?" Garrett wondered.

"Possibly, though we were able to eliminate as suspects everyone on duty that day. Even off duty workers, for that matter. Unfortunately, we didn't have the same access and inroads to visitors on the parkway or national forest. As such, it was likely someone among this group who killed your mother."

Garrett's jaw set. "Were there any similar murders during that time frame?" He thought about the evidence he'd reviewed in the case.

Lou sighed musingly. "As a matter of fact, a year later, a young woman was stabbed to death in a similar fashion near the Yadkin Valley Overlook on the parkway."

"Was the killer ever caught?" Madison asked.

"Yeah, an arrest was made a couple of days later. Man named Blake O'Donnell confessed to the crime, while insisting he played no part in the murder of Jessica Sneed. Seemed like we had an open-and-shut case." Lou paused, frowning. "Then O'Donnell recanted his confession, claiming it had been coerced. The jury never bought it. Neither did I. He was tried, convicted and sent to prison."

"Was he ever released?" Garrett questioned.

Lou shook his head. "He was killed behind bars, five years into his sentence. Ironically, he was stabbed to death by a fellow inmate after getting into a fight."

Could the jury have gotten it wrong and sent a man to prison for a crime he hadn't committed? Madison couldn't help but ask herself. Might the Blue Ridge Parkway Killer have more murders under his belt than met the eye?

She took a step closer and asked the former sheriff intently, "Do you think it's possible that Jessica's killer could be at it again, killing women on the parkway?" She assumed he was aware of what was happening and the similarities between the cases.

Lou looked out at the lake, where his rod remained in search of fresh trout. "The unsub would likely be in his fifties and up," he muttered. "As I'm sure you know, most serial killers are younger than that. But the comparisons are hard to ignore. Even for an old geezer like me." He took a breath. "Anything's possible. If this is the direction you're going in, you're welcome to all my files on the original case, which I have in some boxes in my basement. If you'd like, I can send them over to the sheriff's office. Or to the Pisgah Ranger District headquarters. Your call."

"We'd like that," Garrett readily agreed. "The ranger district office would be good."

"Consider it done," he said. "Again, I regret that when I was the Buncombe County Sheriff, we were unable to crack the case of your mother's death. It's one that got away."

"Don't beat yourself up, Sheriff. Not all cases go as we'd like them to." Garrett looked at him sympathetically. "I've had my fair share of investigations that dried up and there was nothing I could do about it."

"Same here," Madison pitched in, wanting to ease his burden, while knowing that law enforcement was anything but a perfect science where all the bad people were held accountable for their actions. Still, she could only hope that the unsub or unsubs who'd left Jessica Sneed, Olivia Forlani and Nicole Wallenberg dead well before their times would one day have to face justice.

"Well, we'll let you get back to your fishing," Garrett told Lou, adding, "I heard that rainbow and brook trout are out in force right now."

"Yeah, they are," he concurred, "along with brown trout and smallmouth bass. If you ever want to join me, be my guests."

Garrett grinned. "We'll keep that in mind."

They walked away from him, and Madison

looked at Garrett and said, "I didn't know you were into fishing."

"I grew up fishing in the Qualla," he told her. "Not really my thing these days. But maybe once I'm retired from federal law enforcement, I can take it up again."

"Cool." She tried to picture him in retirement mode. Or herself, for that matter. If they could grow old together, all the better. Was this something he pictured as well? Or were they living in more of a fantasy world right now in being involved romantically again, with reality setting in once the cases before them were put to rest?

AS PROMISED, Lou Buckley had his files on the Jessica Sneed cold case delivered late that afternoon to the head office of the Pisgah Ranger District. That evening, Garrett went through them with Madison at her house. They sat at the dining room table poring over the materials while sipping wine, looking for anything that stood out as relevant to the current murders. Admittedly, Garrett wondered if they were searching for a needle in a haystack, given the thirty-year spread since his mother's murder. Had her killer really resurfaced and, as such, was out there for Garrett to find and bring to justice? Or was he deluding himself on a false premise?

I can't shake the feeling that there's something to my intuition, Garrett told himself as he tasted the wine. Maybe her killer had murdered another woman the following year and had been lucky enough to have someone else take the rap, giving the unsub a free pass to kill other women in the years to follow.

He looked at the sketch of an unidentified male that had been reported by witnesses as being on the parkway around the time of his mother's murder. The man was described as being anywhere from his midtwenties to midthirties and sturdily built with dark eyes and a long nose, while possibly wearing outdoor work clothes. The authorities had never been able to locate the unsub. Garrett recalled Sheriff Buckley stating that park workers had been accounted for and eliminated as suspects. Meaning the unsub had likely worked elsewhere but could still have been a local who'd known the lay of the land. So, who was he and what had become of him? Was this the killer or a false lead?

Garrett gazed at Madison, who was still in uniform but oh so sexy. And, frankly, distracting. She was the one definite positive that had come from his returning to this region to work. Wherever they went from here, he wanted it to be as a couple and all that came with it. When she looked up at him, he considered looking away but couldn't.

She batted her lashes curiously. "What?"

"Nothing," he said, as if she believed him, while he suppressed a grin.

"Right." Madison glanced at the paperwork spread before her and back. "Since I've got your attention, in looking this over and the lists of identified suspects, it seems like the one name that keeps popping up in the notes is Neil Novak. And with good reason. Take a look."

Garrett gazed at a file she handed him and saw the name. Neil Novak, age thirty-four at the time, had been an unemployed wrangler. A partial fingerprint belonging to Novak had been found on the survival knife that'd been used to kill Jessica Sneed. When confronted with this, Novak had claimed that the knife had been stolen a week earlier. As there had been no other physical evidence connecting him to the crime and Novak had had a rock-solid alibi after finding work when the murder had occurred, authorities had had no choice but to eliminate him as a suspect.

"So, maybe Novak never really had his knife stolen and faked the alibi," Madison contended, "and was able to get away with the murder of your mother."

"Hmm..." Garrett chewed on that notion.

Alibis could certainly be falsified. It happened more often than people realized. The investigators on the case could only play the hand dealt them. Sometimes they got it wrong. Even when the evidence, or lack thereof, suggested otherwise. "You're right—maybe we do need to take another hard look at Neil Novak, assuming he's still alive."

"I think so," she agreed. "And if Novak is among the living, is he local?"

"He'd be sixty-four now," Garrett pointed out. "Old enough to be out of the killing business, based on official data for the age range of typical killers—but still young enough, per se, to be able to perpetrate murders currently as the Blue Ridge Parkway Killer," he reasoned.

Madison perked up. "It's a lead anyway." She sipped her wine.

"Yeah." He gave her an agreeable look. "I think we need to learn everything we can about Neil Novak and what he may or may not have been up to."

"We will," she said steadfastly. "Wherever the leads take us, right?"

"Right." Garrett held up the sketch of an unsub. "And there's also this person to consider."

Madison grabbed the sketch, studying it. "True. Or he could have been someone's imagination or a male suspect that was totally unrelated to the death of your mother."

"That's possible," Garrett was inclined to agree, while still having to regard him as a person of interest. He drank wine as a thought suddenly entered his head. "Doesn't your brother Scott specialize in cold cases?"

"Yeah." Madison gazed at him. "Why do you ask?"

"Well, given that we've opened one, I thought you could get him on the phone to see if he could give us some input on cold cases in general."

"Really?" She flashed a look of surprise.

He chuckled. "Why not? Might help the cause." *At the very least, it could help me make further inroads in winning points with your family,* Garrett told himself. He assumed that Scott and her other siblings knew by now that they were seeing each other again.

"Okay." Madison got to her feet and grabbed her laptop. She put it on the table and sat next to him. "Sure you want to do this?"

"Of course." He grinned. "I'm not too proud to ask for help."

"Just checking." She smiled and called her brother for a video chat. When Scott accepted it, Madison said cheerfully, "Hey."

Scott smiled. "Hey, sis."

"You remember Garrett?"

"Of course," he said. "Special Agent Sneed. How are you?"

"I'm good." Garrett could read the surprise on his face in wondering what this was all about in reacquainting themselves with one another.

"So, what's up?" Scott asked.

Madison leaned forward and said, "We're looking into the murder of Garrett's mom thirty years ago."

Scott raised a brow. "Oh…?"

"We think it could be tied to a current case we're investigating," Garrett told him equably.

"The Blue Ridge Parkway killings?"

"You've got it," he verified. "Between the similar pattern and a dangerous unsub still at large, it seemed worth exploring the possibility that my mother's killer could be back and targeting other young women on the parkway. Since you specialize in cold cases, we thought you might have some general thoughts about this…"

Before Scott could respond, Madison added, "And according to the sheriff at the time, there was a similar murder that occurred in the county a year later, in which a man confessed and recanted the confession but was still convicted of the crime. There is at least a possibility that he didn't commit the crime and the unsub who killed Jessica Sneed was the real killer, which would still make it a cold case, apart from the present serial killer on the loose."

"Wow," Scott uttered. "That's a lot to unpack."

"Take your time," she quipped.

He chuckled. "Without knowing the details of your mother's case, Garrett, I can tell you that cold cases can be tricky but still resolvable, even without the benefit of the culprit resuming his activities much later down the line."

Garrett listened attentively as Scott ran off some of the dynamics of cold cases that were typically violent and/or gained national attention, citing tunnel vision and advances in forensics as key variables that merited a second look for many such open-ended cases. Having worked on some cold cases in his career, Garrett had been privy to this but was happy to get Scott's take, if only to bridge the familial gap between them for the sake of smoothing the way toward a bright future with Madison.

"Jack the Ripper is obviously one notorious example of a very cold-case killer, who got away with murdering at least five prostitutes in Whitechapel in London's East End in 1888," Scott said. "While the infamous serial killer might never be identified conclusively, other cases and your mother's death could still be solved by identifying the unsub."

"You think?" Garrett asked in all seriousness.

"Yeah. May take some time though," he cautioned. "Not to tell you how to do your job, but you'll need to reexamine evidence, reinterview witnesses, seek out new evidence, etcetera."

"We get the picture," Madison ribbed him.

"You wanted my advice." Scott chuckled. "Anything I can do to help."

"Appreciate that," Garrett said sincerely. "I never turn down any free advice." *Especially coming from one of Madison's siblings*, he mused.

"Neither do I," Scott said and waited a beat. "So, what else is going on with you two? Anything I should know about?"

Garrett deferred to Madison on that one, not wanting to put words in her mouth in sharing his own thoughts on the matter.

Blushing, she told her brother simply, "We're good."

"Fair enough," Scott responded.

"Maybe better than good," Garrett spoke up. "But what do I know?"

Madison laughed and pushed him so he nearly fell off the chair. "Trust your instincts."

Scott laughed. "You heard my sister. Never argue with her. You'll lose every time."

He had to chuckle, though not wanting to ever

test that theory any more than he had previously. "I'll keep that in mind."

After they ended the video chat, Madison said curiously, "Still think that was a good idea?"

"Absolutely." Garrett gave her a devilish grin. "Scott helped in more ways than one."

"Really?"

"Yes. He's convinced me that being on your good side always has its benefits."

She showed her teeth tantalizingly. "What might those be?"

"This for one..." Garrett kissed her and, at least for the time being, put aside the cold case he suddenly felt obsessed with thawing.

Chapter Fifteen

The next morning, Garrett gathered all he could on Neil Novak. Turned out that Novak was very much alive and living in Transylvania County. He had also spent time in prison for drug possession early in his life. Though there was no record of him being violence-prone, as far as Garrett was concerned Novak topped the list as a person of interest in his mother's murder.

"Think he'll talk with us?" Madison asked during the drive to visit the suspect.

Garrett sat back behind the steering wheel. "We're not going to give him much of a choice," he declared firmly. "If Novak had anything to do with my mother's murder, he's going to pay for it." Tightening his fingers around the wheel, Garrett added, "Same is true if he's the unsub in the Blue Ridge Parkway homicides."

They arrived at the Novak Ranch, a sprawling property with horses grazing on rolling hills, winding trails and mountain views on Chester-dale Lane in Owen Creek.

"Looks like Novak has done well for himself over the years," Madison commented after they stepped out of the car.

"Looks can be deceiving," Garrett muttered. "Beyond that, it's hard to escape from one's past if there's something there to escape from."

"True enough."

They bypassed the large Craftsman-style home and headed straight for the stables, where they heard voices. Inside, Garrett spotted a tall and slender thirtysomething woman with flaming long and wavy red hair at a stall feeding a quarter horse. Beside her was a sixtysome-thing man who was taller and heavier, wearing a white wide-brimmed cowboy hat with curly gray hair beneath and sporting a gray ducktail beard.

Garrett overheard the woman refer to the man as "Dad," and she appeared to be con-cerned about his working too hard. When they heard footsteps approaching, the two turned and stopped talking.

"Are you Neil Novak?" Garrett addressed the man.

"Yep, that's me." He peered at him through dark eyes. "Who's asking?"

"Special Agent Sneed, from the National Park

Service's Investigative Services Branch." Garrett flashed his identification. "And this is Law Enforcement Ranger Lynley."

"Hi," Madison spoke evenly to both of them.

Novak jutted his chin. "What's this all about?"

"A cold-case homicide," Garrett responded succinctly.

The woman cocked a brow. "Dad…?"

"I've got this, Dominique." Novak tensed. "I'll see you in the house."

She looked as though she wanted to object, as green eyes darted from Garrett to Madison, before landing back on her father, after which she relented, "All right."

Garrett watched as she walked away, putting some distance between them. He gazed at Novak and said bluntly, "We've reopened the investigation into the murder of Jessica Sneed on the Blue Ridge Parkway." He drew a breath. "She was my mother."

"The parkway killing." Novak scratched his beard nervously. "Sorry that happened to your mother, but that was a long time ago. What does it have to do with me?"

"A survival knife that had your partial fingerprint on it was found to be the murder weapon, Mr. Novak," Madison told him. "I'd say it has everything to do with you."

"As I told the investigators back then, the knife was stolen from my pickup truck. I have no idea who took it and no knowledge of what it was used for by the thief." Novak breathed heavily out his nose. "In any event, I was cleared of any wrongdoing."

"About that," Garrett said. "It seems like your name continued to come up in the investigation in spite of the alibi. Why do you suppose that is?"

"You tell me." Novak's brow creased. "Maybe the cops and rangers thought I was somehow capable of being in two places at once. Well, I wasn't. On the day your mother was killed, I was working on a ranch thirty miles from the parkway and had plenty of others there who could vouch for it. Including the ranch's owner. Now I have my own ranch and have tried to put that dark time behind me for good. Obviously, that isn't so easy for you. Sorry you wasted your time coming here, but I can't help you solve the case."

"Can't?" Garrett glared at him. "Or won't?"

Novak stroked the quarter horse's neck. "Can't," he insisted, his voice steady. "Look, I'm older now and have nothing to hide. If that's all, I have a ranch to run."

Madison lifted her eyes up. "We think that

whoever murdered Jessica Sneed may be back at it again," she stated.

His head snapped back. "What are you saying?"

"Two women have been stabbed to death recently on the parkway. The similarities to Ms. Sneed's murder, type of weapon used and location have given us reason to believe that they may have been committed by the same man."

Novak leaned against the stall thoughtfully, tilting the brim of his hat. "Same person thirty years later? Is that even possible?"

"Yes, it's quite possible," Garrett told him. "We think that my mother's killer may have stabbed to death another woman a year later but another man took the rap for it. So yes, that same killer could have remained dormant for years before returning to the parkway to go after other vulnerable women."

"Wow." Novak uttered an expletive. "Hard to believe the same killer from thirty years ago would be around to target others today and think he could get away with it."

"Why wouldn't he think that?" Garrett challenged him while wondering if Novak himself could be involved somehow with the recent killings. "After all, he got away with it before. Maybe more than once."

Novak wrinkled his nose. "If that's the case,

I hope you get the bastard. But I'm afraid I still can't help you. As I said, I lost the knife, so…"

"Did you lose it, or was the knife stolen, as you claimed thirty years ago?" Madison pressed him.

"Stolen," Novak insisted. "*Lost* was just a poor choice of words."

Garrett wondered if that was the case. Or could it mean he was lying about both options and had, in fact, handed the knife off to someone?

Removing the sketch from the pocket of his khaki pants, Garrett said, "This person was seen in the vicinity of the area on the Blue Ridge Parkway where my mother was murdered. Does he look familiar?"

Novak took the sketch and studied it for a long moment before replying unevenly, "Can't say that he does…sorry."

"Take another look," Garrett insisted, sensing that he could be holding back for some reason.

Novak again stared at the drawing stoically. "Nope." He handed the sketch back to Garrett. "It's been thirty years, so my memory could be failing me. Not to mention it's just a sketch that may or may not even be an accurate portrayal of the person it's supposed to. Either way, it doesn't ring a bell. I wish I could say otherwise, but I can't."

Garrett glanced at Madison, whose expression matched his own in believing they might have reached a dead end here. If Novak did know something, he was unwilling to say so. And they were in no position to apply more pressure. "By the way," Garrett put out, "just for the record, I'll need you to account for your whereabouts when the two recent murders occurred on the parkway."

Novak gave him the dates and time frame. He claimed he'd been on his ranch those mornings in question and had ranch hands who could verify this. When they heard footsteps, Garrett turned to see Novak's daughter walking toward them in her tailored ankle booties.

"You're still here?" she questioned, eyeing them suspiciously.

"We were just leaving," Garrett told her, knowing where to find her father, should they need to interview him further. He took out his ISB business card and handed it to Novak. "If you happen to remember anything pertinent to our investigation, you can reach me on my cell phone."

Novak nodded. "I'll keep that in mind."

"Thanks for your time," Madison told him in a sociable tone of voice. She gazed at Dominique. "Have a nice day."

On that note, Garrett signaled to Madison that it was time to go. They walked away, leaving the father and daughter standing there staring, undoubtedly.

Once out of ear range, he commented, "I'm not totally convinced that Neil Novak is as oblivious as he claims to be regarding the supposedly stolen knife. Or lack of recognition of the unsub in the sketch, for that matter."

"Neither am I," she said. "But between his insistence that the knife was stolen and his alibi then and apparent one now, we can only take a wait-and-see approach while continuing the investigation."

"Yeah, I suppose," Garrett muttered.

They walked back to his vehicle as his thoughts turned to wondering if he had missed something in the overall scheme of things in pursuing one or more killers with a common theme and deadly intentions.

HOURS LATER, Madison was still weighing whether or not Neil Novak was on the level in his assertions of playing no part in the death of Jessica Sneed or, in fact, had succeeded in pulling the wool over the eyes of investigators for decades, when she was notified over the radio that another dead woman had been found on the parkway.

Madison's heart lurched against her chest as she phoned Garrett with the distressing news. "We have a new problem," she almost hated to say, with his mother's cold case having resurfaced in the investigation.

He took a moment to digest the latest death and, after giving him the location, Garrett said soberly, "I can get there in fifteen minutes or less."

"See you then." Madison hung up and headed to the scene she was closer to, fearful of what this meant in the bigger picture as her workplace was once again the center of unwanted attention.

She drove down the Blue Ridge Parkway to Milepost 364 and parked before heading on foot to the Craggy Gardens Trail that was lined with wild blueberries and numerous wildflowers and offered a stunning view of the Black Mountains.

Richard Edison approached her with a dour look on his face. "It's not good," the law enforcement ranger moaned as Madison caught sight of the body lying off the trail near gnarled sweet birch trees. "The victim has been identified as Heidi Ushijima, a twenty-five-year-old seasonal interpretive ranger for the National Park Service. She was discovered by a park visitor, Nadine Dobrev, who reported it." Richard's thick brows knitted. "Looks like she was stabbed to death."

"I was afraid of that," Madison muttered. She took a couple of steps forward for a closer look at the deceased park guide, whom she'd never had the pleasure of meeting when Heidi was still alive. Heidi had short brunette hair in a shag bob and was curled into a fetal position, while wearing a ranger's beige T-shirt, brown cargo pants and tennis shoes. Blood seeped through her clothing from multiple punctures to her torso and legs.

Madison looked away, believing that the Blue Ridge Parkway Killer had likely struck again. She wondered if this brazen attack in a well-traveled but challenging area to navigate suggested that the unsub was a different, younger perp than Jessica Sneed's killer. Or could they still be one and the same?

She eyed Richard. "Any sign of the murder weapon?"

"Not yet." His lips pursed as he scanned the trail. "I'm guessing the unsub took it with him. Either to toss elsewhere like before or hold onto to use again if an opportunity arises."

"That's what bothers me," Madison said. She had little reason to believe that the unsub wouldn't continue to attack isolated females on the parkway. Not unless they were finally able to stop him cold. She looked up and saw Dawn Dominguez arrive.

"Not another one?" she asked.

"I think so," Madison had to say sadly.

Dawn frowned, making her way to the corpse. "Let's have a look."

"Someone really went to work on her," Richard said bleakly.

"Same as the others," she concurred. Wearing nitrile gloves, she gave the body an initial examination. "At the risk of sounding like a broken record, I'd say she was stabbed seven or eight times with a long-blade knife, killing her in the process."

Madison cringed as she glanced at Richard and back. "How long ago would you estimate this happened?"

Dawn felt the skin and replied, "Still relatively warm. I say she was attacked within the past two or three hours."

This corresponded with what Madison was thinking, as it was unlikely that the victim could have been in this location all morning without being noticed. She had no reason to believe the killer had moved the body to Craggy Gardens as opposed to catching Heidi Ushijima off guard or following her in the course of her hiking there. Either way, all the signs pointed toward this being the work of the Blue Ridge Parkway Killer. But just how long had he been at this?

GARRETT ARRIVED AT the crime scene at the same time as Tom Hutchison. The strain on the face of Madison's boss was indicative of the gravity of the situation with a crazed and violent serial killer in the midst, as seemed to be the case. The fact that the same person could have been responsible for his mother's murder made it all the more unsettling for Garrett.

"Hey," he spoke lowly to Madison.

"It's him again," she stated surely.

Garrett swallowed. "Talk to me."

She brought him up to speed on the death of Heidi Ushijima in a manner that measured up to the recent murders on the parkway. It was disturbing to Garrett, to say the least, on more levels than one.

"Same old story," Madison complained. "See for yourself."

Garrett looked at the latest victim, more or less validating his greatest fears that this case had taken another deadly turn. "Seems that way."

"What is going on?" Tom's tone was boisterous with disbelief as he homed in on the body and glared at the deputy chief medical examiner.

"We're definitely looking at a homicide due to stabbing repeatedly," she declared.

Tom pressed down on his hat. "This is starting to get out of hand," he griped.

"Not just 'starting to,'" Garrett begged to differ. "Someone has taken it upon himself to use the parkway as his personal hunting ground. We can't let him get away with it."

"Seems to me he's doing just that." Tom

sighed. "Do we need more manpower to track him down?"

Without answering this, Garrett said, "What we need most is to keep from panicking and realize that, in spite of his track record, the perp is only human and, whether he knows it or not, is running out of steam."

At least I want to believe that, Garrett told himself. There were only so many ways the perp could go to commit his heinous crimes and try to hide from it in a despicable cowardly manner. Whether or not they were searching for his mother's killer, the need to restore some sense of safety on the parkway and the general area itself had never been greater.

"I agree," Richard said, furrowing his brow. "Whoever's doing this seems to be acting in desperation right now. This tells me that, apart from being a loose cannon, he's also leaving the door open for us to catch him."

"We just need to find that door, which happens to be somewhere in the vast Pisgah Ranger District," Madison pitched in, "making it that much more challenging."

"Please hurry up," Dawn said, a seriousness to her tone as she removed her gloves. "Believe it or not, I do have other dead bodies that need tending to."

"We get it," Garrett said, recognizing that

they were all on the same page in the search for justice. He turned to Madison and Richard. "Find out all you can on the movements today of Heidi Ushijima, leading up to her death. Where she went. Where she lived. Why she chose to go to the Craggy Gardens. If she came here alone. You know the score."

Madison nodded. "Understood."

"Shouldn't be too difficult," Richard said. "Most of the seasonal workers hang out together and probably know one another's secrets, if there are any."

Garrett hoped that provided some answers. He said, "In the meantime, let's get the crime scene investigators out here and see what they can come up with in forensic evidence that might lead to a killer."

"On their way," Madison informed him, not too surprisingly.

"Good." They would coordinate their efforts with the local law enforcement in securing the perimeter, closing some roads leading to this part of the parkway and seeing if there were witnesses to track down and surveillance video to access. Garrett had to wonder if the unsub had left behind enough clues that hadn't been compromised by the terrain in which the corpse had been left, that could line up with other evidence gathered along the way with the clock ticking.

Chapter Sixteen

Once the body had been carted off to the morgue and the reality sank in of another murder on the Blue Ridge Parkway, Madison and Richard set out separately to see what clues they could find in the lead-up to Heidi Ushijima's death. By all accounts, the Japanese American Duke University graduate student had been well liked and had embraced her job as a seasonal interpretive ranger for the National Park Service. Madison was told by other park workers that Heidi had been in her element in teaching visitors about the parkway and Pisgah National Forest's history and cultural significance.

It was in this context of information gathering that she had apparently hiked to the Craggy Gardens, along with fellow seasonal interpretive ranger Quentin Enriques, whom Heidi had been said to be dating. But only he'd emerged alive. When Richard radioed her to say that he had located Quentin on the Cumberland Knob Trail at Milepost 217.5, Madison responded, "I'm just a few minutes away."

"He's not going anywhere," the ranger assured her.

As she drove to the location, Madison's immediate thought was could Quentin Enriques have been callous and confident enough to stab Heidi to death and then go about his business as though nothing had happened? If so, she imagined he would have needed to dispose of his bloody clothing somewhere along the way. Along with the murder weapon. Was this feasible? Or had Heidi encountered someone else at Craggy Gardens?

I have to keep all options on the table, Madison reminded herself. Just as Garrett was doing, in spite of his being drawn to the specter of his mother's murder in relation to the current happenings.

Madison reached the Cumberland Knob in Alleghany County, near the North Carolina-Virginia border, and parked. The site, which combined woodlands with open spaces, was popular for viewing different birds and wildlife. She spotted Richard talking with a tall and stocky twentysomething male with brown hair in a half-bun ponytail. He had separated the suspect from a group of tourists.

"This is Ranger Lynley," Richard told him

and said to her, "I've just informed Quentin about the murder of Heidi Ushijima. He claims she was alive and well when they split up."

"This is crazy." Quentin's lower lip quivered. "Heidi's dead?"

Madison saw the distress in his face and brown eyes that seemed genuine enough. She still had to ask, "When did you last see Heidi?"

"About three hours ago, when we were together at Craggy Gardens."

"Why did you leave?"

"I needed to move on to my next assignment," he pointed out, "exploring the Cumberland Knob area with visitors."

Sounds plausible, Madison thought. She glanced at the tourists, who were taking pictures of the surroundings and seemed only mildly curious. "Did you see anyone else on the Craggy Gardens Trail?"

Quentin shrugged. "I passed by some people here or there, but no one who was traveling alone," he claimed. "Or otherwise seemed suspicious at the time."

Richard peered at him. "I understand that you and Heidi were dating?"

"Yeah, we hung out," Quentin admitted. "It wasn't anything serious. We were both just here for the summer."

"So, you didn't have a fight or anything at Craggy Gardens?" Richard questioned.

"No," he insisted. "We were cool."

"Did Heidi ever indicate to you that she wasn't cool with someone else?" Madison posed to him. "Either within the NPS or outside of it?"

Quentin shook his head. "If she was having a problem with anyone, Heidi never shared it with me."

Madison gazed at him while thinking that, given his age, at the very least he didn't square with a person old enough to have murdered Jessica Sneed. But might there have been some other connection between the killer then and now?

"Sorry we had to put you through this," she voiced sympathetically, giving him the benefit of the doubt that he was another innocent secondary victim of murder.

"You're just doing your job," he muttered.

"We may need to talk to you again," Richard cautioned him. "But for now, you're free to rejoin your group, if you like."

"Or take some time off to grieve," Madison told Quentin.

They had no reason to hold him further, she realized. It wouldn't make dealing with Heidi's death any easier for him or them. When Quentin walked away with his head down, Madison surmised, "He didn't kill her. No signs of being cut himself. Or being able to dispose of the evidence and return to his duties without missing a beat."

"I was thinking the same thing," Richard said, frowning. "We'll keep at it."

Madison nodded. Once back in her car, she phoned Garrett with an update. "So far, we've hit a brick wall among Heidi's colleagues and the guy she was dating. He's only in his twenties, by the way," she threw out, conflicting with the cold to new cases homicide theory.

"Heidi was likely killed by someone outside her workplace or social circles," Garrett argued. "As to the age disparity in connecting the serial killer to my mother's murder, there's always the possibility of a copycat killer."

She agreed. "There is that."

"If this proves to be true or the Blue Ridge Parkway Killer of today is unconnected to a thirty-year-old homicide that stays a cold case, I'll have to accept that."

So would she. But for now, Madison still trusted his instincts and had to believe the link was there in some way, shape or fashion. "As long as the co-investigations persist, we'll just have to see where they take us."

"All right."

When they disconnected, Madison found herself looking ahead and knowing that they made a great team. Love did that to people who connected on a deep level. It was something that she hoped would blossom into an even greater appreciation of one another.

"IN LIGHT OF the latest homicide on the Blue Ridge Parkway, I've gotten the go-ahead from my boss, Wilma Seatriz, in Washington, DC, to raise the reward to fifty thousand dollars for any meaningful information that leads to the arrest and prosecution of the unsub," Carly told Garrett an hour after he had updated her on the murder of Heidi Ushijima.

He was at his temporary cabin, video chatting on his laptop with the South Atlantic-Gulf regional director. Carly had managed to convince Seatriz, the NPS associate director for visitor and resource protection, who oversaw the Division of Law Enforcement, Security, and Emergency Services that Garrett worked for, of the importance in upping the ante to catch a killer. Though Garrett hated the thought of paying money for a solid lead, he hated even more the reality that the unsub had managed to elude them thus far. As such, with three women recently stabbed to death on the parkway and at least one murdered decades ago by perhaps the same killer, it was imperative that they use every means at their disposal to get justice. Whether or not doubling the reward would do the trick was anyone's guess.

I'm definitely on board with giving this a shot, Garrett told himself. "That's good," he said. "The public can still play an important role in solving this case."

"Maybe it won't need to come to that," Carly argued, wrinkling her nose. "I mean, we have the finest federal investigators in the business, starting with yourself. If anyone can crack this case the good old-fashioned way, it's you, Sneed."

Garrett resisted a grin, flattered by the suggestion while feeling the pressure of being put on a sneaky pedestal. He also read between the lines. She would rather they keep the cash in the federal coffers, if at all possible, to have handy for another day. "I'll see what I can do" was the best he could promise, while knowing she fully expected that and then some.

Carly waited a beat, then asked, "Are you still angling the parkway serial killer as being connected with the death of your mother?"

Garrett sat back, thoughtful. "I have no proof of that," he admitted, "but looking at it squarely, I believe it to be a real possibility that the unsub has crossed decades in taking lives and has either simply gotten lucky or maybe was incarcerated for committing other crimes, only to resume targeting women in the Blue Ridge Mountains once freed."

"Well, I trust your instincts," she said assuredly. "On that note, I've asked a criminologist that the NPS has worked with in the past to speak with you about the investigation."

"Oh...?"

"Her name is Katrina Sherwood. She specializes in serial killer cases, has written three books and may be able to give you some added perspective in trying to track down the Blue Ridge Parkway Killer."

As if he could refuse what amounted to a directive from his superior, not that he would turn down assistance from an expert on serial killers, Garrett responded, "I'd be happy to speak with Ms. Sherwood."

Carly smiled. "I'll text you her number, and you can give her a call."

"I'll do that," he promised.

"Keep me posted on the investigation."

Garrett nodded. "I will."

After ending the conversation, he left his makeshift office and grabbed a beer from the refrigerator. He thought about Madison and how much they had managed to recapture since starting over. He relished being able to take this and run with it, no matter the distance, in wanting to find that dream of a life together at the end of the rainbow.

Walking back into the living room, Garrett lifted up his cell phone and saw the number Carly had texted for Katrina Sherwood.

No time like the present, he thought, in giving her a call.

She answered after two rings with, "Katrina."

"Hi. I'm Special Agent Garrett Sneed," he told her. "Carly Tafoya asked me to contact you regarding a case I'm working on."

"Right. The Blue Ridge Parkway murder investigation," she acknowledged. "Carly brought me up to speed on where things stand and the possible cold-case connection."

"Okay." Garrett felt this was a step in right direction.

"Why don't we switch to video," Katrina requested. "It's better for a real dialogue. Don't you think?"

"Absolutely." He sat down on a wingback accent chair and tapped the Video icon on the phone. Katrina Sherwood appeared. African American and attractive, she was in her forties with bold brown eyes and curly blond hair in a Deva cut.

She flashed her teeth. "Nice to meet you, Agent Sneed."

"You too," he said evenly.

"Why don't we get down to business," she told him. "You're dealing with a serial killer in your midst who's stabbing to death women on the parkway, right?"

"Yes. He's apparently picking his victims at random but may also have been stalking them before things took a deadly turn."

"Typical," Katrina asserted matter-of-factly. "That is to say, it's typical that many serial killers seek out victims randomly, but just as many others may have stalked their victims for a while and then killed them when the best opportunity presented itself to do so. There are no absolutes when it comes to serial homicide and the heterogeneous nature and characteristics of the offenders," she stressed, "apart from the fact that a serial killer by definition kills two or more people in separate incidents, which I'm sure you understand."

"I do," Garrett conceded, "all too well. I am curious, though, as to your take on why stab the victims instead of, say, shooting or strangling them, given the messiness of a stabbing attack."

"Frankly, most stabbing serial killers give little thought to the messy nature of such assaults. Think Jack the Ripper, John Eichinger or Kenneth Granviel, to name a few." She twisted her lips musingly. "Some serial killers simply choose stabbing over other ways to kill because they get some kind of perverse thrill in the violence and suffering that goes along with it. Other serial killers may choose a knife as a more accessible weapon or easier to use to kill than say, trying to strangle the victim. Yet other serial killers may view inflicting pain upon another as a power grab."

Garrett grimaced as he pictured his mother being victimized this way. Though he had some idea, he asked, "Why start killing, only to stop for years or even decades before starting back up again?"

Katrina narrowed her eyes. "You're thinking about the murder of your mother, thirty years ago?"

"Yeah," Garrett confirmed and took a sip of his beer. "And the possibility that her killer may have killed another woman a year later, then laid low for decades, only to rediscover stabbing to death vulnerable females."

"I see." She took a breath. "Well, killers stop killing for all types of reasons," she explained. "These include fear of being caught, illness, romance, imprisonment for another crime or just deciding enough was enough. In the case of The Ripper, for example, the unsub apparently ended his killing ways abruptly after 1888, by some accounts, and never resuming. On the other hand, Lonnie David Franklin Jr., a serial killer also known as the Grim Sleeper, took a fourteen-year hiatus between killings. Similarly, serial killer Dennis Rader, aka the BTK Strangler, went over a decade since his last kill before being captured.

"My point is that if the man who killed your mother has resurfaced after all these years to target other women, assuming he hadn't kept it going elsewhere in the country, it could be for any number of reasons. These include boredom, death in the family, an impulsive desire to get back in the game, opportunistic circumstances or an aura of invincibility, having been successful the first time around without getting caught."

Garrett gave an understanding nod. "I get where you're coming from," he told her bleakly. It also gave him food for uneasy thoughts to gnaw on. Had his mother's killer come back to terrorize the Blue Ridge Mountains and Pisgah Ranger District once again? Or had another staked his claim in following suit as the Blue Ridge Parkway Killer?

THE KILLER HIKED in the mountainous forest and meadows. He enjoyed the solitude on the Blue Ridge Parkway, though at times encountering elk, peregrine falcons, white-tailed deer, wild turkeys and even a black bear every now and then. It was nature at its finest, and he was part of it. The fact that he had killed more than once and planned to do so again was who he was at his core. As was the case for any animal predator he ran into.

He continued to make his way through hollows and coves, mountain ash and yellow birch trees, and black huckleberry shrubs en route to his destination. Whistling, he broke the silence, save for the sporadic sounds of indigo buntings and red-winged blackbirds meandering through the trees. His thoughts moved to Heidi Ushijima, his latest victim. A flicker of guilt ripped through him that he'd taken her life. It disappeared in an instant, realizing that it was something that'd had to be done.

He had known beforehand that Heidi had had to die. The only question had been when. She'd provided him the answer when he'd overheard her talking about heading to the Craggy Gardens Trail. Accompanying her had been another seasonal interpretive ranger, Quentin Enriques. He had watched the two kissing from time to time, making it clear that they'd been sweet on one another.

Given that the desire to kill Heidi had nearly overcome all reason, he might have had to take out Quentin too. Only after a while, he'd left Craggy Gardens alone to go elsewhere. Then some others had come along, and Heidi exchanged pleasantries with them before they, too, had moved on. That was when it had been time to make his move. While Heidi had been preoccupied with wildflowers, he'd taken her totally by surprise. At first, recognizing him, she'd actually believed he'd simply been out and about.

Only when she'd seen the new eight-inch serrated knife he'd produced, after ditching the last one, had the small talk come to a screeching halt. When she'd tried to make a run for it, he'd anticipated her move and surprised her by being quicker. He'd caught up to her and gone to work with the knife. Ignoring her cries, he'd finished the job in short order. He'd thought he'd heard someone coming and made his planned escape, using his knowledge of the parkway to hide from sight. When the coast had been clear, he'd continued to put distance between himself and his latest victim.

He reached his tent and felt as though it offered him the sanctuary he needed—till it was time to move on to greener pastures, where he could start fresh in appeasing his deadly appetite. But not before he could turn his attention to the pretty law enforcement ranger, Madison Lynley, who in time would soon come to feel her life being drained away when he struck time and time again with his blade.

Chapter Seventeen

"Agent Sneed," the raspy voice said. "This is Neil Novak."

Garrett was driving that morning when the call came. "How can I help you, Mr. Novak?" he asked coolly, though more than curious in hearing from the rancher.

"We need to talk," Novak said tersely.

So talk, Garrett thought, wondering if this would be a confession. "I'm listening."

"In person," he insisted.

"All right," Garrett told him. "I can be at your ranch in twenty minutes."

"Actually, I'd like to speak at my attorney's office."

With that, Garrett assumed what he had to say might constitute legal jeopardy and piqued his own interest all the more. "Not a problem."

"Her name's Pauline Vasquez," Novak said. "She's with the Eugenio, Debicki and Vasquez law firm in the Kiki Place Office Building on Twelfth Street and Bentmoore."

"I know where it is," Garrett said. He remembered Madison interviewing Pauline Vasquez about murder victim Olivia Forlani when they visited the law firm a few days ago. Was Vasquez's representation of Novak coincidental? Or something more unsettling in the scheme of things? "I'll be there," Garrett told him, agreeing to meet in half an hour.

"By the way," Novak said, a catch to his voice, "bring that sketch with you."

"Uh, okay." Garrett tried to read into that. Was he actually ready to come clean about the unsub in the composite drawing?

After disconnecting, Garrett glanced at the cowhide leather messenger bag on the passenger seat. It contained the sketch of the unsub and other case materials.

He phoned Madison on the parkway and said, "You won't believe who I just got a call from."

"Who?" she asked.

"Neil Novak."

"Really?"

"He has something to say," Garrett told her. "But will only do so in the presence of his lawyer, who happens to be Pauline Vasquez."

"No kidding?"

"I kid you not." He paused. "Novak has asked to take another look at the sketch of the unsub."

"Interesting," Madison hummed. "When is this meeting taking place?"

He told her and said keenly, "You should be there."

"Wouldn't miss it," she assured him. "If Neil Novak has something to get off his chest with legal representation, it must be something huge."

"Yeah, that's what I was thinking." Garrett gazed at the road ahead. "Let me know where you are, and we can drive there together." She gave him her location, and he went for her, knowing that Madison's curiosity was piqued as much as his in what this was all about. He longed for the day when they could spend even more time together on their own terms.

MADISON SAT IN an accent chair beside Garrett on one side of a white rectangular meeting table in a conference room with a wide floor-to-ceiling window. On the other side was Neil Novak; his daughter, Dominique Novak; and their attorney, Pauline Vasquez. One could hear a pin drop, making Madison wonder just where this was going in relation to their criminal investigation.

After a tense moment or two, Pauline pasted a thin smile on her lips and said, "Thanks for coming, Special Agent Sneed and Ranger Lynley."

Garrett leaned forward. "So, exactly why are we here?" he cut to the chase. For her part, Madison couldn't help but think that it could have been her friend Olivia representing the firm in this matter, had the partnership not been handed to Pauline prior to Olivia's death, without her ever being the wiser.

"My client, Mr. Novak, has information he believes to be relevant to your investigation into a cold case," the attorney responded. "But to be clear, the info is strictly voluntarily given and implies no guilt or knowledge beforehand."

"Got it," Garrett told her laconically and gazed at Novak. "What would you like to say to us?"

Novak scratched his beard. "Did you bring the sketch?"

"Yeah." Garrett produced it and slid it across the table.

Novak picked it up and studied it for a beat before setting the sketch back down. He sucked in a deep breath and uttered, "I've seen him before."

"Where?" Madison asked. "When?"

"Asheville," he asserted. "Thirty years ago."

"Did you know him?" Garrett asked straight-forwardly.

"Yeah, I knew who he was, but we weren't friends or anything."

"Do you recall his name?" Madison asked, peering at him.

"Deschanel, I believe…" Novak said after a moment or two. "Yeah, it was Bryan Deschanel."

Taking his word on this for now, Madison watched Garrett make a note to that effect; then he asked him bluntly, "Did you give Bryan Deschanel the knife that was used to kill Jessica Sneed?"

"No, definitely not!" Novak insisted. "I can't even say if he was the one who took my knife. I do remember seeing him hanging around my truck but never made the connection between that and the stolen knife." He drew a breath. "Not till you showed me the sketch yesterday."

Garrett frowned. "So, you lied to a federal law enforcement officer when questioned about the sketch? Not a smart move."

"I didn't want to get involved," he claimed. "Apart from that, I couldn't be sure at the time without seeing the sketch again that it was the same guy I thought it might be."

"Are you saying you never saw the sketch before we showed it to you?" Madison asked, knowing that it had been part of the official investigation back in the day. How could he, as a person of interest and suspect, not have been shown the sketch?

"Never!" Novak asserted. "Don't ask me why, but the police never showed up at my door with this and I never saw it in the newspaper. Otherwise, I would've said something."

"My dad's telling you the truth," Dominique spoke up, tucking hair behind her ear. "It was me who talked him into coming forward and saying what he knew. Or thought he did. He would never have tried to impede a murder investigation. Or cover up for a killer."

"That should be obvious, just by us being here right now," Pauline argued. "My client is doing his civic duty by telling you what he knows. What you do with it is up to you, but as Mr. Novak was cleared of any involvement three decades ago, this is where his obligation as a citizen ends."

Garrett relaxed his rigid jawline. "We have no desire to go after your client, Ms. Vasquez," he told her.

She smiled. "Good."

"But we do have a few more questions for him," Garrett said.

Novak met his gaze. "Go ahead."

"Have you seen Bryan Deschanel lately?"

"Haven't seen him in thirty years," Novak alleged. "If I saw him on the street, I doubt I'd even recognize him today. Beyond that, as I recall him being a troublemaker who others thought was messed up in the head, he's not someone I'd want in my life or my daughter's."

"What kind of trouble?" Garrett asked him.

"He had anger issues and was prone to violence and vandalism."

Madison couldn't help but think about the viciousness of the attack on Jessica Sneed as well as the three recent victims of fatal stabbings. Could Bryan Deschanel have been responsible for all of these?

She eyed Novak and said, "It's possible that Deschanel is still around and is now targeting women on the Blue Ridge Parkway. Including a third woman stabbed to death since we last spoke to you."

"Yeah, heard about that." Novak lowered his chin. "Made me wonder if there could be a connection of some sort with what happened thirty years ago."

"I wondered too," Dominique said. "When my father told me about the possibility that the same person who murdered your mother, Agent Sneed, could be doing it again, I managed to convince him that he needed to do the right thing and speak up. And we are."

Garrett nodded. "I appreciate your coming forward," he told them.

"If it can help you solve your case, it will have been well worth my trouble," Novak said.

Pauline rested her arm on her leather briefcase and said, "I understand that there's a fifty-thousand-dollar reward on the table for information leading to the arrest and conviction of the so-called Blue Ridge Parkway Killer?"

Madison frowned. "So, this is all about money?" *Blood money*, she thought.

"It's not what you think," she responded quickly and turned to the Novaks.

Dominique sat up straight. "We don't care about the money," she stressed. "But if for whatever reason we qualify for receiving it, we intend to donate every cent to organizations that focus on violence against women." She sucked in a deep breath. "Five years ago, I lost my mother to such a senseless act."

As Dominique's words sank in, Madison stood corrected on her initial assumptions and said sincerely, "I'm sorry to hear about your mother."

She nodded, and Novak said, "So, as you see, Agent Sneed, we have more in common than you thought."

"Guess we do," Garrett conceded.

"Anyway, any such reward would all be facilitated through Ms. Vasquez," Dominique stated.

"We would certainly see to it that their wishes were carried out to the letter," Pauline assured them.

Garrett responded, "Whether or not the information given to us results in anything is still up in the air. Right now, our goal in representing the National Park Service is to try to locate Bryan Deschanel and see what he's been up to. Or may have been running from for the past three decades."

Pauline smoothed a brow. "I understand."

"We'll be in touch," Madison said as the meeting adjourned and she left with Garrett, equipped with intel on a person of interest in both a cold case and one that seemed to be getting hotter with each passing day.

"YOU THINK BRYAN DESCHANEL is alive and well, lurking around the Blue Ridge Parkway, killing women?" Madison asked point-blank as Garrett drove down Hayten Road.

It was a good question, he knew, and one they both needed an answer to, one way or the other. "My gut tells me that Deschanel is still among the living," Garrett said flatly. "And that he may be closer than we think."

"And your mother's killer?"

"Yes." There was no sugarcoating this. Garrett cringed at the thought. "When you put the pieces together, beginning with the unsub's sketch ID'd by Neil Novak—I think that Deschanel stole the knife from Novak's pickup, used it on my mother and likely attacked another woman the following year. I believe he's been lying low ever since. At least till recently, when deciding to resurface on the parkway and use his guiles to murder more women, while operating with impunity in plain sight. I'm betting that the latent palm print Jewel pulled from the survival knife used to kill Olivia Forlani and Nicole Wallenberg belongs to Deschanel and no other."

"I think you may be spot on," Madison stated. "We need to find Deschanel, wherever he's hiding, and hold him accountable for his crimes."

"Right." Garrett turned onto Overlook Road and approached the Blue Ridge Parkway. "I'll run a criminal background check on Bryan Deschanel and see what else I can learn about the man and his whereabouts. In the meantime, be extra careful on the parkway while he's still on the loose and dangerous as ever."

"I will," she promised, placing a hand on his shoulder. "You too. I have a feeling that Deschanel, evidently used to having his way, is a threat to anyone who comes into contact with him."

"I agree." Garrett grinned at her. "I can take whatever he dishes out and give back thrice as hard."

Madison smiled warmly. "I'm sure you can."

He knew she was capable of handling herself too and was armed, while having backup among other rangers. But till they had the dangerous suspect in custody, Garrett doubted he'd be able to relax and feel confident that she was out of harm's way. That was something he couldn't afford to take for granted.

Chapter Eighteen

Garrett went back to his cabin and, on the laptop, dug into Bryan Deschanel's criminal background and any other information that was accessible. Running his name through local law enforcement databases, the National Crime Information Center, the North Carolina DMV, the FBI's Next Generation Identification system, and various social media sites, Garrett found that Deschanel had no criminal record, per se, or outstanding warrants. Nor did his name show up in a Google search, on Facebook, Instagram or Twitter.

But Bryan Deschanel had been a person of interest in the death of his mother, Garrett noted, when digging deeper into police reports, and newspaper accounts in a search on Google. Helena Deschanel had died in a mysterious house fire when Deschanel had been in his late teens. Though suspected of causing the fire, police had lacked the evidence to prove it, and he'd been let off the hook. In his twenties, Deschanel had had other skirmishes with the law but had never been charged with a crime. He'd once been accused of domestic violence, but the victim had inexplicably withdrawn her complaint.

Garrett cocked a brow when he discovered that Bryan Deschanel had been an early suspect in the stabbing death of twenty-nine-year-old Vicki Flanagan, who'd been killed on the Blue Ridge Parkway by the Yadkin Valley Overlook a year after the murder of Garrett's mother. Blake O'Donnell, who'd confessed to the crime and then recanted, had been ultimately convicted for it. *What if Deschanel was the true culprit and O'Donnell innocent after all?* Garrett wondered.

He went through the files again that ex-Sheriff Lou Buckley had lent them in the investigation, looking for any mention of Bryan Deschanel. Garrett found it. Deschanel had been questioned briefly as a potential witness by a deputy, but somehow no connection had been made between him and the sketch of the unsub. It made Garrett wonder if he was off base in suspecting Bryan Deschanel of being a three-decades-long serial killer.

Not when I look at this squarely, he told himself. The circumstantial evidence was there. Some physical evidence too, that might link the suspect to at least two of the murders. Along with too many facts that, when put together, had to be more than merely coincidental. Still, Garrett was troubled that Deschanel was not showing up on the radar. And hadn't apparently in years. Could he be dead, with someone else stepping into his shoes as a serial killer?

Garrett went even further in searching for evidence that Bryan Deschanel was no longer alive. Nothing came up in a Google search or other data. It was almost as though the man had dropped off the face of the earth. *I'm not buying it*, Garrett thought. He cross-checked Deschanel's name for any possible aliases that might be known to authorities. Nothing registered, frustrating him.

Still, the idea that Bryan Deschanel had either engaged in identity theft or simply created from scratch or know-how a moniker he was going by to more easily operate without his past catching up to him was gaining steam with Garrett. He was all but certain that the murder suspect was not only alive and well but living or working within the vicinity of the Blue Ridge Parkway.

Garrett grabbed the sketch and studied it. But that was from thirty years ago. If Deschanel was still alive, what did he look like today? With that thought in mind and no known actual photograph of the suspect, Garrett believed that an age-progression sketch of Deschanel would give him a more accurate image to work with and circulate to other law enforcement.

He got on his cell phone and requested a video chat with Caitlin Rundle, a forensic artist at the North Carolina State Bureau of Investigation that the National Park Service had used in other criminal investigations. Thirty-something, she was following in the footsteps of her father, Karl Rundle, a retired renowned crime-scene sketch artist. Caitlin accepted the call after three rings.

"Agent Sneed," she said, gazing back at him through blue eyes, with short blond hair framing her face.

"Hey, Caitlin." Garrett straightened his shoulders. "I need a big favor."

"Sure. How can I help?"

"I'm investigating a thirty-year-old cold-case homicide," he explained. "All I have right now on my chief suspect is a hand-drawn sketch that was done of him at the time. I need a better representation of what he might look like today."

Caitlin smiled. "I think I can assist you with that," she said with confidence. "Just send me what you have, and I'll do my best to give you a digitally enhanced image that is age appropriate for the unsub today."

"Wonderful." Garrett's eyes crinkled at the corners.

"How soon do you need it?"

"Would yesterday be soon enough?" he responded dryly.

She gave a little chuckle. "I'll get on it right away."

"Great." He gave her the relevant information he had on the serial killer suspect, including a digital picture of the composite drawing of him.

While Garrett waited to hear back from Caitlin, he again studied the clues that led him to believe that Bryan Deschanel was still alive, responsible for at least four murders by stabbing and posed a serious threat to even more women on the Blue Ridge Parkway.

MADISON WAS SITTING in her car, reading the chilling autopsy report on the latest female to die on the parkway. According to the deputy chief medical examiner, Heidi had been the victim of numerous stabbings—had been attacked with a knife seven times—to her back, buttocks and legs, resulting in death by homicide. The murder weapon was described as a sharp serrated-edge knife with an eight-inch blade.

What a monster, Madison told herself, hating that another fellow ranger had been brutally murdered in an unprovoked, callous assault. The fact that such a picturesque and usually hospitable setting as the Blue Ridge Mountains and

Pisgah National Forest had been turned into a killing field made it all the harder to digest. Worse was that there was a good chance the perpetrator had also murdered Garrett's mother and managed to get away with it.

Till now. With Bryan Deschanel being fingered as the man in the thirty-year-old sketch, at the very least, this told them that he was likely Jessica's killer. And had quite possibly murdered another woman the following year. Though much older now, the stars lined up to the notion that he might have come back to carry on his homicidal tendencies today. If so, now that they had drawn a bead on him, it was just a matter of time before his reign of terror was over. Until then, Madison hoped that no other woman would see her life cut short by a madman.

When she got a call over the radio, Madison heard Leonard say with a sense of urgency, "We just got a report of a woman injured below the Raven Rocks Overlook."

The spot immediately struck a chord with Madison. It was the very area where Jessica Sneed had been killed. Had her killer done a repeat performance thirty years later?

"I'm on my way," Madison told Leonard.

Afterward, she relayed this to Richard and

Tom, calling for backup while hoping they could quickly seal off any escape routes.

Madison drove to the parking area for the Raven Rocks Overlook. She spotted a gray metallic Land Rover parked there. Getting out of her car, Madison approached the vehicle cautiously. It was unoccupied but had tourist brochures spread out on the front passenger seat. Did this car belong to the injured woman?

Peeking below the overlook, Madison saw nothing unusual. She wondered if this could be someone's idea of a practical joke. It had been known to happen sometimes on the parkway. Usually the work of mischievous teenagers. But given the recent happenings on the parkway, Madison had to believe that a woman might truly be in distress and needed her help.

She made her way down the incline and headed toward the woods, where she thought she heard a sound. Was it an animal? Or human? Removing her pistol from the duty holster, Madison saw Ward Wilcox, the maintenance ranger, approaching her.

"Stop," she ordered instinctively, knowing this was outside his normal work area.

He obeyed, standing rigidly. "Ranger Lynley."

"What are you doing here, Ward?" Madison eyed him suspiciously aiming the pistol at him.

"I was told I was needed," he said simply. "What are you doing here? And why are you pointing your gun at me?"

"We received a report of an injured woman below the Raven Rocks Overlook," she told him. "Then I run into you... In light of the recent murders on the parkway, maybe I have good reason for holding you at gunpoint." Peering at the maintenance ranger, Madison wondered if she was looking at the Blue Ridge Parkway Killer. And Jessica Sneed's killer?

"Hey, I'm just as confused as you are," Ward insisted. "And I swear to you, I didn't hurt anyone. I certainly had nothing to do with the parkway deaths of those women." He took a step toward her.

"Don't come any closer!" Madison aimed the gun at Ward's chest as he stopped. "Put your hands up where I can see them, Ward. I mean it."

He complied, while saying tonelessly, "You're making a mistake. I'm innocent."

"We'll see about that." She took a couple of steps backward to put a little more distance between them and, while keeping the gun on him with one hand, removed her radio with the other to report the mysterious situation and that she was holding Ward Wilcox as a possible suspect in one or more crimes. She knew that erring on the side of caution was her smartest bet. No sooner had she gotten off the radio with help on the way that Madison heard what sounded like heavy shoes hitting the dirt behind her.

Before she could turn, Ward shrieked, "What the hell do you think you're doing?"

Suddenly, Madison felt a fist slam into the side of her head. Blurry-eyed, she caught sight of a familiar man and thought he said something wicked to her before she went down like a rock and everything went dark.

WHEN GARRETT HEARD back from Caitlin, she said coolly, "Agent Sneed, I've finished an age-progression digital sketch of Bryan Deschanel and what he might look like today, taking into consideration some standard characteristics that typically accompany aging into one's fifties and sixties."

"Let's see what you've got," Garrett responded eagerly on the speakerphone while in his car and heading toward the Blue Ridge Parkway, where he had been trying to reach Madison, to no avail.

"I'm sending it to your cell phone right now," Caitlin told him. "Keep in mind that I did this on short notice and not from an old actual photograph. But it should give you some perspective on your person of interest."

Garrett pulled over, grabbed the phone and gazed at the age-progression composite drawing of Bryan Deschanel, causing his heart to skip a beat in shock. It was a dead ringer for someone he had met before. Ronnie Mantegna, an NPS maintenance worker. And someone who had easy access in and out of the Blue Ridge Parkway without drawing undue suspicion, while being familiar with the landscape accordingly.

"What do you think?" Caitlin asked anxiously.

"I think you did a great job," Garrett told her. "Thanks for the quick work."

"Anytime." She paused. "If you need me to further enhance the sketch for greater clarity, let me know."

"I will." He disconnected and tried to contact Madison again. Still no pickup, concerning him. Getting back on the road, he called her boss, Tom. When he answered, Garrett said, "I can't seem to reach Madison."

"She went out on a call after a woman was reported injured," he said.

"What woman?"

"We're still trying to sort it out."

Garrett tensed. "What can you tell me about Maintenance Ranger Ronnie Mantegna?"

"He's been working for us for the last six months," Tom replied. "Let me take a quick look at his file... He's fifty-six, never married, has wilderness experience and been good at his job. Why do you ask?"

"I think that Ronnie Mantegna is an alias for Bryan Deschanel," Garrett said without prelude. "The man I believe to be responsible for my mother's murder thirty years ago and the Blue Ridge Parkway killings today."

Tom grunted and said, "Tell me more..."

Garrett gave a rundown of his solid case against Mantegna and sent Tom the age-progression digital image. "He's been right before our eyes the entire time I've been back here," Garrett stated knowingly. "And may be the one targeting another woman on the parkway now."

Tom mouthed an expletive. "We need to warn Ranger Lynley." He sighed exasperatedly. "Except I haven't been able to reach her either."

"Where did she go to respond to the injured female?"

"Raven Rocks Overlook." Tom made a sound, as if to himself. "According to the GPS tracker on her vehicle, that's where Madison still is, at Milepost 289.5."

"I'm almost there," Garrett told him, ending the conversation as he put on some speed, hoping to reach the destination in time.

Bryan Deschanel must have lured Madison to Raven Rocks Overlook, he figured, where Deschanel had stabbed to death his mother so long ago. Now in some sort of warped homicidal impulse, under the cover of his moniker Ronnie Mantegna or not, Deschanel planned to let history repeat itself by taking Madison's life in the same manner, Garrett couldn't help but sense.

I have to stop that bastard from killing the true love of my life—destroying any chance at a long-term future together. The thought that Mantegna could succeed in taking away another person so near and dear to him, decades apart, was unbearable to Garrett. He reached Milepost 289.5 and raced to the Raven Rocks Overlook.

MADISON OPENED HER eyes to a splitting headache, feeling as though she had been someone's punching bag. It took a long moment of trying to regain her equilibrium before she remembered what had happened. She'd been facing Ward Wilcox, believing he might have harmed a woman near the Raven Rocks Overlook and done even worse things, when someone had clocked Madison from behind. Her first thought was that maybe Ward had been partnered in crime with another person. But then she recalled right before being sucker punched that Ward had seemed just as unprepared for the moment and to be trying to warn her of impending danger. Before it had been too late.

"I see you're awake," she heard the familiar voice.

Realizing she was on the ground in a wooded area, Madison ignored the pounding in her head and turned her face slightly to the right. Hovering above her was Ronnie Mantegna, a maintenance ranger.

"Ronnie..." she managed as the wheels began to churn in the perilous moment she faced. Especially while taking note of the long-bladed serrated knife he was holding.

"Actually, my real name's Bryan Deschanel," he said smugly. "I'm guessing you've already come to the realization that I'm the one who knocked you out."

Madison knew she needed to play dumb while trying to figure out how she could still get out of this alive. "Why did you hit me?" she asked innocently. "And where's Ward?"

"You're entitled to know those answers. First question. I hit you because I needed to relieve you of your firearm without the risk of getting shot in the process. Plus, it was easier for my other plans for you." Deschanel glanced at the gun stuck inside his pants at the waist. "I'm the one you and Special Agent Sneed have been looking for."

"The Blue Ridge Parkway Killer?" Her mouth hung open as though in total shock. In reality, the pieces of the puzzle had already begun to fall into place the moment she'd gotten a grip on the circumstances she'd found herself in.

"You got it!" His eyes lit with triumph. "I killed them, and you're next, Ranger Lynley. For the record, though, I've been at this for a long time. My first kill was my own mother. She pissed me off one too many times, and I'd had enough. Made it so the fire seemed like an accident due to faulty electrical wiring, which I knew a thing or two about. Got what she deserved." He laughed, thoughtful. "Next was Agent Sneed's mother, believe it or not, who was hiking in this very spot before we ran into each other, catching her completely by surprise, and I did what I needed to do."

Madison's head had cleared enough that she was able to sit up without feeling dizzy. But he was still brandishing the knife and had her gun. Again, she sought to be genuinely taken aback by his revelation. "You really killed Jessica Sneed?"

"Is it that hard to believe?" He laughed. "I'm only halfway into my fifties. Meaning I was just in my midtwenties back then. Same was true the following year, when I stabbed to death another unsuspecting woman on the parkway. Got away with it too, thanks partly to some other idiot volunteering to take the fall before he tried to backpedal. But it was too late."

So, he admits to killing his mother, Jessica and a third female from three decades ago and earlier, Madison told herself. But why the long pause between then and now? "If you got away with it, why would you risk everything by starting to kill women again?"

"Yeah, about that... It's something inside me that I can't seem to control," he argued, rubbing his jawline. "Well, in trying to fit in as a law-abiding citizen, guess I was able to control my dark impulses for a while through drugs, therapy and whatnot." Deschanel pursed his lips. "But I grew tired of playing Mr. Nice Guy and ditched the drugs and therapy. I was happy to be myself again."

So that explains the long gap between serial killings, Madison thought. Too bad his inner demons had taken over again. It did little, though, to get her out of a predicament that placed her entire future in jeopardy. One she hoped to have with Garrett. Or had that page been turned forever?

"Anyway, I lured you here by falsely reporting that a woman was in distress," the killer explained calmly. "I was counting on them sending you in particular, as this is your neck of the woods, so to speak, to patrol."

Madison sought to buy more time as she studied the woods for escape routes. "Just let me go, Ronnie or Bryan," she said. "I'll give you a head start, and you can go anywhere you'd like."

"Yeah, right." His head snapped back as he chortled. "Since you've been cozying up with Agent Sneed, something tells me you wouldn't hesitate to blab to him about what I did to his mother the moment I allowed you to live. Sorry, no can do."

"You never said what happened to Ward Wilcox," Madison questioned. She scanned the area for any signs of him but saw none. "Did you kill him too?"

"Actually, Ranger Lynley, you did," Deschanel responded with a wry chuckle. He glanced at her pistol. "After roping him into showing up here to remove debris, I forced Ward to run into the woods, then fatally shot him with your gun. That was what you managed to do just before he cut you up with his knife that I intend to place in his hands once I'm through stabbing you to death. Then I'm outta here to look for a new place to settle down and cause trouble, while getting away scot-free with the parkway murders—again."

Madison scrambled to her feet, realizing that the serial slayer had her at a disadvantage. She considered going for the gun. Perhaps the element of surprise would cause him to let down his guard long enough to take it and shoot him before he could react. But with him holding the sharp knife firmly and having shown prowess as an attacker, she wasn't comfortable with those odds.

Deschanel bristled while moving toward her. "Sorry it's come to this, but it is what it is."

Or not, Madison thought. Her first instinct was to run. Though he was obviously in good enough shape to kill and evade detection and capture, she was sure she could outrun him as a jogger. But what if she were wrong? What if he proved to be just as quick on his feet, if not quicker, and caught her from behind? Wasn't that what had likely occurred with some of his other victims who'd had the same miscalculation?

Madison had never had any formal martial arts training. But she had learned some hand-to-hand combat and defensive tactics during basic training. Moreover, her law enforcement family members had taught her a thing or two about survival skills. If she didn't make use of them now, when would she ever?

"Since you're going to kill me anyway," Madison said to the Blue Ridge Parkway Killer as he got closer, "can you at least find a way to pass along to my family that I loved them with all my heart?"

Deschanel seemed taken aback by the odd request but replied, "Yeah, sure, I'll do that for you, Ranger Lynley."

In the split second of time she was afforded, Madison noted that he had lowered the knife just enough to give her a window of opportunity to strike him before he could cut her. Balling her fist, she drew her arm back as far as she could before thrusting it forward with all her might. The fist landed squarely in the middle of his nose. The sound of bone cracking was quickly drowned out by the howl of pain that erupted from his mouth like an injured wolf.

During this distraction from his deadly intentions, Madison tried to grab her pistol from Deschanel's waist. But he was somehow able to recover enough to slice the knife across her wrist and throw her hard to the ground in one swift motion.

"You'll pay for breaking my nose," he spat, wiping away blood streaming down his face and neck. "You're going to die a horrific death, Ranger!"

Madison bit back the discomfort from her cut wrist and sucked in a deep breath as she wondered if his frightening forecast of her impending death was about to come true as he raised the knife threateningly with every intention of adding her to his three-decades-long list of victims.

Chapter Nineteen

When he'd spotted Madison's Tahoe in the parking lot of the Raven Rocks Overlook, alongside a Land Rover, Garrett didn't wait for the results of the run on the license plate of the Land Rover. By the time he had reached the area beneath the overlook and gathered with rangers and sheriff's deputies, Garrett had verified over his cell phone that the vehicle was registered to Ronnie Mantegna, the alias for serial killer Bryan Deschanel. It was clear to Garrett that Deschanel was intent on repeating history, dating back three decades, with Madison to be his latest victim.

I can't let that happen, Garrett had told himself with determination, as he removed the service pistol from his shoulder holster. He'd ordered everyone to spread out in search of Madison and the murder suspect in the woods. When Maintenance Ranger Ward Wilcox was found barely conscious but alive, having been shot in the chest, he fingered Ronnie Mantegna as his shooter and confirmed that he had taken Madison.

At least she was still alive, Garrett felt, as he'd zeroed in on the area he suspected Deschanel planned to make his move. It was the spot where the murderer had taken the life of Garrett's mother so many years ago. When rangers and law enforcement converged on the wooded location, Garrett gulped as he saw Deschanel holding a knife to Madison.

Just as it seemed like the perp would stab her before they could stop him, Madison delivered a head-snapping fist to Deschanel's nose. She attempted to reach for her gun that he had taken, but Deschanel appeared to slice her wrist and throw Madison down to the ground. As Garrett approached the culprit, who was holding the serrated knife in an offensive posture, he literally shot the weapon right out of Deschanel's hand, taking away a finger at the same time.

When Deschanel went for Madison's gun, Garrett tackled him, and the firearm fell harmlessly to the ground. Atop the criminal, he slugged him once in the jaw and another hard shot to his bloodied nose, causing the man to whine like a baby.

"You're under arrest, Bryan Deschanel," Garrett voiced sternly, "for the murder of Jessica

Sneed, the attempted murder of Law Enforcement Ranger Madison Lynley, and a number of other crimes you'll have to answer to."

Resisting the strong urge to pummel his mother's murderer as payback, Garrett instead remembered that he was an NPS ISB special agent, bound by the law above all else, and climbed off. He turned him over to the Buncombe County Sheriff for processing, and Deschanel was promptly placed under arrest.

Garrett immediately raced to Madison, who was on her feet, her wrist bleeding. "Paramedics are on their way," he told her, having taken preemptive steps in requesting medical assistance during the drive to the parkway, in case needed.

"It's not that bad, really," she insisted.

"Bad enough to need stitches."

She grinned and glanced at Deschanel as he was being escorted away. "You should see the other guy."

"I already did." Garrett laughed. "Glad you were able to soften him up a bit for me to finish the job."

She chuckled, masking her discomfort. "Hey, that's what teamwork is all about, right?"

"Right." He hugged her, careful not to press against her wrist, while feeling grateful that she hadn't been killed. "Other than the cut, did he hurt you?"

Madison touched the side of her head. "Come to think of it, Ronnie Mantegna—er, Bryan Deschanel—did knock me unconscious when I wasn't looking to bring me to this spot."

Garrett shuddered. "All the more reason to get you to the hospital to be checked out."

"I suppose."

He was handed a piece of cloth by a park ranger to tie around her wrist to stop the bleeding. "That should do the trick," he said, knowing it couldn't take the place of stitches. Or painkillers.

"Thanks." She looked at Garrett sadly. "Deschanel confessed to killing your mother in this area."

Garrett's brow creased, feeling maudlin. "I guessed that was why he brought you here. Some sick kind of history repeating itself."

"Speaking of which, Deschanel also confessed to killing his own mother and getting away with it," Madison told him as they headed out of the woods, "along with stabbing to death Vicki Flanagan the following year, near the Yadkin Valley Overlook. He was practically giddy at the idea that Blake O'Donnell had taken the rap for the murder."

"Not surprised by any of that," Garrett muttered, having already come to the conclusion that Deschanel had been responsible for both murders. "His depravity apparently knows no bounds."

"I agree." Madison made a face. "He also took full credit as the Blue Ridge Parkway Killer. Plus one, with the murder of Ward Wilcox." Her mouth twisted mournfully.

"We can subtract one." Garrett watched her carefully for any signs of a concussion from the blow to Madison's head. Or loss of blood. "Wilcox is still alive. He was shot in the chest but is expected to pull through."

"Thank goodness." She sighed. "Ward was an innocent pawn in Deschanel's scheming and tried to warn me, but it was too late."

"Actually, Wilcox was right on time," Garrett told her. "Before losing consciousness, he confirmed that you were still alive when he last saw you and that you were with Deschanel."

She nodded appreciatively.

They reached the Raven Rocks Overlook just as the paramedics arrived. "You were right to believe that one unsub was responsible for serial murders over three decades," Madison pointed out.

"Yeah, bittersweet." Garrett frowned. He took no great joy in making the right call of solving a cold and current case at once. It still wouldn't bring back his mother. Or the other four women to die by Bryan Deschanel's hand, for that matter. But it would allow all the surviving family and friends of the victims some closure. Himself included.

Right now, he was just happy to know that Madison had lived to see another day. Hopefully many days. Days they could spend together. But first was for Madison to be given a clean bill of health as she got in the ambulance after her ordeal with a ruthless serial killer.

THAT EVENING, Madison was at her mountain chalet resting, her wrist sewn and wrapped, headache barely noticeable, and relieved that she was alive and the nightmare over. Once he recovered from a broken nose, jaw and one less finger, serial killer Bryan Deschanel would be headed to jail. But as much as she wanted to focus on the satisfaction of knowing that the death of Jessica Sneed had at long last been solved and her son could put this cold case to rest on a personal and professional level, Madison's current thoughts centered on what their own future held. Garrett, as attentive as he had been all day, catering to her every need to make sure she was comfortable, had been strangely silent as to where his head was. Was he deliberately trying to drive her mad? Make her question that she was reading what they had correctly? Or was he still indecisive as to what he wanted and with whom? Only to decide that it might be time to put in for another transfer, rather than deal with tender matters of the heart?

As they sat on her midcentury sofa watching television, Madison decided it was time to lay her cards—or heart—on the proverbial table. She grabbed the remote from the glass top of the coffee table, cut off the television, and turned to Garrett before asking, "So, did you mean it?"

He faced her. "Mean it?"

"That you loved me?" She held his gaze. "You said that when…"

"I know when I said it." Garrett flashed a thoughtful grin, pausing. "I meant it, every word."

Her heart fluttered. "You never followed up on those deep words of affection."

"That's because I was waiting for the right time to do so," he claimed.

She batted her lashes. "You mean when I had to pry it out of you?"

He chuckled. "Not exactly."

Madison was confused. "Care to explain?"

"Okay." Garrett turned his body to face hers. "After our last attempt at a relationship went south, I was determined to make sure that this time around we wouldn't find a way to pull away from each other. That included allowing the relationship to grow at its own pace. Without the pressures that came with premature declarations of love. The last thing I wanted was to scare you off."

"That would never have happened," she insisted.

"Never say never," he stated wisely. "Except when it comes to knowing that I don't want to spend the rest of my life with anyone but you, Madison."

Her eyes lit. "You mean that?"

"With all my heart." He took her uninjured hand, which happened to be the one with the wedding-ring finger. "The truth is it scared the hell of out me when I thought for even an instant that Bryan Deschanel might have taken you away from me. I knew then that I never wanted to let you get away again. This evening was about giving you some time to heal and reflect, without having you believe that my asking for your hand in marriage was borne out of some sense of duty because of what Deschanel nearly got away with. Or as a doing right by my mother homage of some sort as the type of woman I imagine she would have loved for me to marry and be a mother-in-law to. While that last part is true, I want you as my bride strictly because I'm madly in love with you and want us to make the most of the years ahead, as husband and wife." He sucked in a calming breath. "So, with all that being said, Madison Lynley, will you marry me and make this special agent the happiest man on this planet?"

"Hmm…" She hesitated. "And where would we live as a married couple?"

"Wherever you'd like," he answered smoothly. "The great thing about working for the National Park Service and having the experience to back it up, with over four hundred individual national park units spread across the country and US territories, we can pretty much live anywhere we choose to."

"Good point," she had to admit.

"As for a ring, it's been on the back of my mind, but I hadn't really homed in on it," Garrett said and leaned his face to one side. "Been a bit preoccupied of late, you know?"

Madison laughed. "Excuses, excuses."

He gave her a serious look. "So, is that a yes?"

She pretended to think about it for a moment or two, then answered unequivocally, "Of course it's a yes! Yes, I'll marry you, Garrett Sneed."

He beamed. "Yeah?"

"Yes, with pleasure." She flashed her teeth. "Oh, and just for the record, I would have gladly married you wherever we lived and even without a ring, if that's what it took to get you down the aisle." Madison regarded him in earnest. "I love you, Garrett, and want to get to know more about your culture, and you can learn whatever you don't already know about my family."

"We'll have a lifetime to accomplish that and much more, Madison," he promised. "Why don't we seal the deal with a kiss?"

"Say no more," she answered him, lifting her chin up and moving toward his lips for a long, deal-sealing kiss to warm the heart and soul.

Epilogue

A week later, Garrett happily placed a three-stone 18-karat rose-gold engagement ring on Madison's finger, thrilled to see her light up with this reflection of his love and commitment to her. He looked forward to a repeat performance when it was time to place the wedding band on her finger next year.

The following spring, they went jogging on the Boone Fork Trail off the Blue Ridge Parkway on a warm day. The five-and-a-half-mile loop trek was a habit Garrett had gotten used to during their off time from their National Park Service duties, after deciding to make their home together in the Blue Ridge Mountains. They meandered their way through the woods, abundant with rhododendrons and lush meadows, and spied Carolina ducks swimming in Boone Fork Creek.

"Bryan Deschanel was transferred to Central Prison," Garrett mentioned of the close-custody male prison in Raleigh.

Madison looked at him. "Really?"

"Yeah. Guess he got into some kind of skirmish at Piedmont Correctional Institution and was moved elsewhere from Salisbury for his own safety."

"Hmm..." She drew a breath. "As long as they keep him locked up for good."

"You can be sure of that," Garrett told her. He thought about the evidence that had helped bring Bryan Deschanel down. In retesting the survival knife that had killed Jessica Sneed, a forensic unknown DNA profile had been discovered that had proved to be a match for Bryan Deschanel's DNA. He'd been linked as well to the murders of Olivia Forlani and Nicole Wallenberg through his right-hand palm print that had matched the latent palm print from the survival knife used to stab to death the women. Lastly, DNA from murder victim Heidi Ushijima had been found on the same serrated knife that Deschanel had used to cut Madison, tying him to at least four murders and one attempted murder. He'd separately tried to kill Ward Wilcox with Madison's Sig Sauer pistol.

With the solid case against him, Deschanel had pled guilty to avoid the death penalty and had been given a life sentence without the possibility of parole. The $50,000 reward that had led to the serial killer's arrest and conviction had been awarded to

Neil Novak. He and his daughter, Dominique, had been true to their word in donating the entire sum to female victims of violent crime groups.

Madison grabbed Garrett's hand and brought them to a stop. "Your mother would be proud of you."

"You're probably right." He was thoughtful, wishing she had been around to see him now. "That would have to begin with being smart enough to fall in love with the right person."

"Is that so?" She blushed, lashes fluttering wildly. "Just how smart are you?"

Garrett took her shoulders and said sweetly to Madison, "Sometimes, actions speak louder than words." With that, he gave her a searing kiss and knew their love was pure genius.

* * * * *

INTRIGUE

Seek thrills. Solve crimes. Justice served.

Available Next Month

Big Sky Deception B.J. Daniels
Whispering Winds Widows Debra Webb

....

K-9 Shield Nichole Severn
The Red River Slayer Katie Mettner

....

Crash Landing Janice Kay Johnson
Cold Murder In Kolton Lake R. Barri Flowers

Larger Print

Keep reading for an excerpt of a new title
from the Romantic Suspense series,
HUNTED HOTSHOT HERO by Lisa Childs

Prologue

The hotshot holiday party ended without the bang everyone had been expecting and dreading, no one more so than
Rory VanDam. Ever since that reporter dredged up the
plane crash that had happened five years ago.

No. Ever since the plane crash.

No. Even before that.

Rory had been waiting for the big bang or the next crash.
While he'd been waiting the longest, the other hotshots
had begun to expect bad things to happen, too, and not
just because of their jobs. Being a hotshot firefighter was
more dangerous than being a regular firefighter because
they battled the worst blazes—the wildfires that consumed
acres and acres of land and everything in their paths. But it
wasn't the job that put them in danger lately, it was all the
bad things that had been happening to the hotshots. Explo-
sions. Murder attempts. Sabotage.

But tonight, the holiday party ended with an arrest but no
gunshots, no fight, not even a fire. The party was over now
and the hotshots, who had traveled to their headquarters
in Northern Lakes, Michigan, to attend it, were tucked up
in the bunks at the firehouse unless they had other places
to stay. And, since falling in love and getting into relationships, many of them had other places now. So maybe
it wasn't just bad things that happened to hotshots. But for

Rory, to fall in love or have someone fall in love with him would be a very bad thing. He couldn't risk a relationship with anyone ever again.

So, with nowhere else to stay, he was lying on his back on one of the bunks, staring up at the ceiling. Despite that arrest tonight, Rory was still uneasy, waiting for the next bad thing to happen.

The immediate danger was only over for Trent Miles tonight. The person who had been threatening Trent in Detroit, where Trent worked out of a local firehouse when not on assignment with the hotshots, followed him up to Northern Lakes. While the young man had run Trent and his girlfriend off the road the day before, he hadn't harmed anyone tonight. Trent's girlfriend, a Detroit detective, quietly arrested her and Trent's would-be killer. Except for that whole running them off the road thing, Rory was relieved that the killer was the only one who'd followed Trent up to Northern Lakes and not the man's sister again.

Trent's sister, Brittney, was beautiful, with her long curly dark hair and big topaz-colored eyes. But Brittney Townsend was also an ambitious young reporter who would sell out her own soul for a story. Or at least her own brother.

Not that Rory could judge anyone for selling out their soul, not when he'd already done it himself. But it still affected him, leaving him feeling hollow and empty inside and alone even in a bar full of other people like he'd been earlier tonight for the party. His coworkers. His friends. At least he hoped they considered him a friend and not the saboteur.

Who the hell was behind all the damn dangerous "accidents" the hotshots had been having? Broken equipment. Like the lift bucket coming loose with Trick McRooney in it and all of the cut brake lines on trucks that had sent or nearly sent hotshots to the hospital. And the loose gas line on the stove in the firehouse kitchen that had caused the explosion that had taken out Ethan's beard and revealed his real identity as the Canterbury heir.

Rory touched his jaw where stubble was starting to come in again. And his uneasiness grew. His disguise was being clean-shaven and short-haired; something he hadn't been for a while until his hotshot training and his new identity.

His new life. But this new life was proving to be every bit as dangerous as his last one. And he couldn't help but think that this life was going to end, too.

As he lay there, he heard the rumble of an engine and then another and another. The firehouse was on Main Street, but there was never much traffic in Northern Lakes at this hour and especially during the winter. And these engines weren't just passing by, they were running inside the building.

The fire trucks.

Who started up the truck engines?

They hadn't been called out to a fire because the alarm hadn't gone off. It would have woken up everyone in the bunk room if it had. And as far as he knew, he was the only one awake because all around him, other hotshots snored.

Trent Miles stayed behind in Northern Lakes after his girlfriend left. A couple of the younger guys, Bruce Abbott and Howie Lane, stayed because they'd been drinking at the party. And a couple of the older guys, Donovan Cunningham and Carl Kozak, stayed, probably for the same reason.

Michaela was here, too. The female hotshot worked as a firefighter in St. Paul, which wasn't far away, but while she hadn't been drinking, the party ended too late for her to want to make the drive home.

Not everybody staying was a hotshot. Stanley, the kid who

kept the firehouse clean, was sleeping here tonight with the firehouse dog, Annie. Stanley's foster brother, Cody Mallehan, and his fiancée, Serena Beaumont, had recently gotten licensed as a foster home and had taken in a kid who was allergic to Annie. And Stanley didn't like to be separated from the big sheepdog/mastiff mix that had saved his life.

His life wasn't the only one she'd saved, though. She'd rescued many other hotshots and their significant others over the past year since Stanley had adopted her to be the firehouse dog. Maybe she was about to make another rescue because she whined and crawled off the bunk below Rory where she'd been sleeping with Stanley. Then she jumped up, put her paws on the side of Rory's bed, and she whined again, obviously as confused and concerned as he was about those running trucks.

"You hear 'em, too," Rory said, and he jumped down from his bunk. While the diesel trucks didn't emit as much carbon monoxide as gas engines, if all of them were running, like he suspected they were from the sound, the level could get high enough to kill.

The air was already getting thick. He coughed and sputtered, trying to find his voice to wake the others. "Hey…" he rasped out the words. "Hey…"

Annie barked, but it wasn't as loudly as she usually barked. Rory needed her to bark as loud as she had the first time she'd seen Ethan without his beard. He needed her to wake the others, or they might not be able to wake up ever again if the carbon monoxide level rose any more.

And he needed to get the hell downstairs and shut off those trucks. He would pull the alarm in the hall, too, before going downstairs. That would certainly wake up everyone easier than he and Annie could.

But once he stepped through the door to the hall, something struck him hard across the back of the head and neck, knocking him down to his knees before he fell flat on his face. His last thought as consciousness slipped away was: Would he be able to wake up again or was his most recent life ending right now?

NEW RELEASE!

Rancher's Snowed-In Reunion

The Carsons Of Lone Rock
Book 4

**She turned their break-up into her breakout song.
And now they're snowed in…**

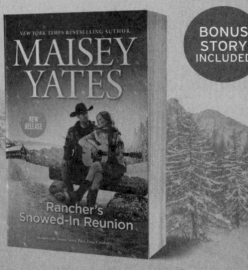

Don't miss this snowed-in second-chance romance between closed-off bull rider Flint Carson and Tansey Sands, the rodeo queen turned country music darling.

In-store and online March 2024.

MILLS & BOON

millsandboon.com.au